SWORD OF ARELION

SWORD OF THE GODS
Book 1

I0536697

Amanda S. Green

Hunter's Moon Press

2015

OTHER TITLES

Nocturnal Origins
Nocturnal Serenade
Nocturnal Interlude

Written as Ellie Ferguson

Hunted
Hunter's Duty
Hunter's Home

Written as Sam Schall

Vengeance from Ashes
Duty from Ashes
Honor from Ashes *(coming Fall 2015)*

SWORD OF ARELION

Sword of the Gods
Book 1

Amanda S. Green

ISBN-10: 0692467246
ISBN-13: 978-0692467244

Hunter's Moon Press

Cover art: Portrait of mystic elf woman by Vladimirs Poplavskis
Cover design by Sarah A. Hoyt

If you enjoyed this novel, please check out http://nocturnal-lives.com for more titles.

Thank you for your support.

DEDICATION

To the Twisted Writers: AJ, CJ, Jess, Joe and David. Thanks
for all the support.

SWORD OF ARELION

Sword of the Gods
Book 1

CHAPTER ONE

THE OLD MAN SAT BEFORE THE FIRE, HEAD BENT, EYES CLOSED. HIS chin rested on one upraised fist. The other hand, gnarled fingers loosely curled, rested on the table top. At first glance, he appeared to be dozing, oblivious to everything going on around him.

The fire crackled loudly and sparks flew as the logs collapsed onto the grate. At the same time, the old man started and his head jerked up. Rheumy blue eyes, too alert for him to have been sleeping just a moment before, scanned the room. For a moment, his gaze seemed to rest on the one unfamiliar face in the tavern before moving on. Then, as if he knew he had nothing to worry about, he pushed a lock of long, gray hair from his weather-worn face. With a heavy sigh, he once more lowered his head onto his fist and closed his eyes.

Intrigued, Fallon studied the old man from across the room. When Fallon first arrived at the tavern almost an hour earlier, the common room had been crowded with men, and a few women, in search of a mid-day meal or drink. They had gathered around the long, cluttered tables, voices loud and raucous, especially when they called for service. But not once had they complained about the old man sitting by himself at one of the few small tables near the fire. Instead, they greeted him respectfully, beaming proudly if he returned their greetings – which he almost always did.

Tipping back his chair, Fallon stretched his long legs before him with a weary sigh. He should get back on the trail.

Kirris would be more than a little displeased if anything delayed his mission, not that Fallon could blame him. The information he carried could save the lives of many by preventing a civil war from breaking out and tearing Cartesia asunder. All he had to do was get it to the Order. Its leadership would make sure the right people were warned.

Yet there he sat, torn between the need to follow orders and something else, something he had yet to identify. Something had drawn him here and he knew he needed to find out what. But did he dare tarry much longer, knowing what depended on him completing his current mission? He had seen nothing untoward so far. Could he be wrong? Or worse, could this be some sort of trap designed to delay him?

Gods above and below, he wished he had the answer.

Two hours earlier, he had been on the trail. He had not planned on stopping, at least not until his mount needed to rest. He most certain had not planned on leaving the trail and going into town. The key to successfully completing his mission was anonymity and the best way to accomplish that was to not be around others. Prying eyes and probing questions were the enemy of any courier. That was one of the first lessons he learned after joining the Order. After all, there was always someone willing to pay the right price for information and that, Fallon knew, could lead to death – or worse – not only for the courier but also for those his information could protect.

Still he sat in the dark, smoky tavern, unsure of what brought him there. All he knew for sure was that the closer he had come to town, the stronger the call to leave the trail. There had been no denying the pull, the need to follow his instincts. Someone or something needed the sort of help only a Knight of Arelion could give. He just didn't know who – or why – yet.

So he sat and waited, the sense of urgency just as strong

and just as unexplained as it had been on the trail.

He had no doubt Kirris would have his head, figuratively at least, for leaving the trail. Of all the towns Fallon could have ridden into, it had to be this one. Luck, good or ill, had brought him to New Grange. Not only was it the largest town for miles around, sitting at the intersection of several major trade routes, it was also the capital city of the duchy of Lineaus. That alone increased the chances someone would realize what, if not who, he was and that almost insured they would ask questions he would not, could not answer.

Frowning, Fallon tugged at the sleeves of his rough woolen coat. Because his mission required secrecy, he wore a homespun tunic and thick wool trousers under his coat. His sword hung in a well-worn leather scabbard from an equally worn leather belt. He had taken great care to make sure nothing about his outward appearance betrayed his association with the Order. He prayed that did not come back to haunt him.

Time was not on his side. If he didn't soon learn why he had felt compelled to come here, he would have to leave. He didn't like it, but he had no other choice. His mission was too important to delay on the off-chance something might happen here. Not that he liked it, not when the feeling that this was where he was needed was so strong.

Movement to his left caught his eye and he turned his head toward it. The serving wench he had seen earlier shoved the kitchen door closed with her foot as soon as she entered the common room. One hand carefully balanced a small tray holding a plate of food and a battered tankard. She reached out with the other hand to snag a rag from the end of the bar. As before, she did not look up, did not appear to make eye contact with anyone.

Nothing about her looked out of the ordinary, at least not

for a place like this. When she served Fallon earlier, she had almost faded into the background. The furniture had been more in the present than had she. Frowning, Fallon watched as she moved across the room. No one seemed to pay her any mind. It was as if they didn't realize she was there.

Fallon swallowed hard and continued to watch. His heart beat a little faster. This wench was why he had felt compelled to come here. He knew it just as surely as he knew she was no ordinary serving wench, not when she all but shimmered with a power so strong and untamed every instinct called for him to take her in hand before someone got hurt.

Dear Gods, was she one of them or had she been put there to be his downfall?

Forcing himself not to react, Fallon quickly reinforced his mental shields. Then he once again turned his attention to the source of such surprising power. Like so many serving wenches in all too many taverns, she looked unremarkable to the naked eye. She shuffled around the common room, head bent. Hair, dark as night either from natural color or filth, hung in oily hanks, obscuring her features. Her clothes were little more than filthy rags, something he had not realized earlier. To the casual observer there was nothing, absolutely nothing remarkable to her.

But to the inner eye. . . .

He couldn't call attention to himself, Fallon reminded himself. He didn't know who the girl was or how she had come to possess such a strong yet untrained power in this of all places. So he rested his elbows on the table and schooled his features into what he hoped the others would see as nothing more than bored curiosity as he watched the scene unfold. He had a feeling if he failed in that simple task, the girl would be on her guard once again and any chance he had of finding out what was going on would be gone.

That was the very last thing he wanted. Every fiber warned of trouble, a trouble that centered on the girl. Her aura screamed of fear and pain. But without attempting a reading – something he wouldn't do unless he became convinced she was in immediate danger – he could not tell what the trouble was or how deeply it ran.

That left him only one choice. He had to remain in New Grange until he got to the bottom of whatever was going on. He would have to find another way to get the information he carried to the Citadel.

"Master Longbow." The girl spoke softly and dropped to one knee at the old man's side. "Sir." This time she placed a light hand on his where it rested on the tabletop.

The old man lifted his head and turned his rheumy blue eyes on her. "Eh, child? What is it?"

"Sir, I brought you something to eat and drink." She placed the plate and small tankard on the table before him.

"No, lass, though I thank you for your kindness. But I will not let you get into trouble because of me." The old man tried to push plate and tankard back to her. "I know Giaros has sworn to punish you should you try to help me again." Longbow's expression hardened, revealing a strength that surprised Fallon. "He might not be able to prevent me from coming here without bringing down the wrath of our liege lord but he can punish you as I know he has in the past."

Fallon listened, his sense of unease increasing. With each moment that passed, the more convinced he became that something was very wrong. Most tavernmasters would not care if their servers gave away food of their own. They most definitely would not punish the server for doing so. If that had been happening, it might explain why the girl's mental shields had been so tightly in place. But it did not explain why she had lowered them now.

5

But that wasn't the only difference. Before, she had said nothing more than necessary to do her duties. Not once had Fallon seen her make eye contact with anyone. Now, with Longbow, she suddenly, unexpectedly seemed more sure of herself. There was no doubt that she was more determined. The steely glint in her hazel eyes as she tried to convince the old man to eat belied a strength of character that surprised Fallon.

By all we hold holy, who is this child and why has she gone untrained?

Fallon shook his head. That was a question to be asked and answered later. A much more important question had to be answered first.

How had she come to be in Lineaus, a realm where those who possessed any sort of special talents were sent away – or worse?

"Please, Master Longbow. There will be no trouble for me. My master is away from the tavern. Besides, there is naught he can complain of. This is mine by rights, given by Cook for my mid-day meal," she assured the old man.

Even so, Fallon caught the way she glanced nervously over her shoulder in the direction of the tavern entrance, as if making sure the master she spoke of was nowhere to be seen.

Fallon watched the exchange in growing concern. While none of the few who still lounged over the remnants of their mid-day meal made any attempt to insert themselves into the conversation, he saw several nod, whether in agreement or approval, he didn't know. That was another indication that they held this Longbow in high regard despite his well-worn clothing. Could the old man have been a loyal member of either the royal household or the Duke's Company in his younger days? As such, he could not be harmed or slighted without bringing the wrath of the duchy's current ruler down on the head of the offender. That would explain Longbow's comment at least.

But that didn't explain the girl. Now that he'd had the chance to study her, Fallon realized she was younger than he first thought. Certainly, she had yet to see her eighteenth winter. Even so, she was taller and thinner than most from this realm. Her voice was light and held a musical lilt that also seemed to confirm that she was not originally from this part of the Imperium. There most definitely was more to the girl than met the eye.

"Child, please. This is your meal. Do not give it away," Longbow said.

"Master Longbow." She pushed the plate back toward him. "I have heard the tales of how you saved the royal family when the raiders of the Black Web invaded. That alone is enough to give you the respect the duke has ordered. My master is wrong to treat you as he does. So please, take this. A few missed meals will harm me none and will do you a great deal of good."

Before anything more could be said, the tavern door flew open with a resounding bang. Instantly, the girl spun in the direction of the sound. Fear flickered across her expression before disappearing behind an impassive mask. Then she bent her head, her dark hair falling so it hid her expression. As she hunched her shoulders, Fallon frowned. Gone was the girl who had tried to help Longbow. More telling was the sudden dampening of the power Fallon had felt emanating from her. Had she thrown her shields up on purpose or had it been instinct?

Forcing himself not to react, Fallon shifted slightly on his chair. Now he could watch not only the girl and Longbow but the newcomer as well.

A short, burly man with thinning blond hair and scraggly beard stalked across the room. His bare arms were heavily muscled. There was a cruel, angry glint in his light blue eyes as he closed the distance between himself and the girl and Longbow. Watching him, all but tasting the bitter darkness of his aura, Fallon had no doubt he presented a grave danger to both the girl and Longbow. But how could he respond without interfering in what, to this point, was simply a matter for the local authorities?

"I thought I told you not to serve this old fool unless you saw the glint of his coppers!" The man swept plate and tankard from the table with an angry snarl that had the girl stepping back, fear radiating off of her. "It is not my duty to feed useless old men who should long be dead. He eats only when he gives value for the meal."

"Master."

She lifted her head and looked the tavernmaster in the eye. At the same time, she stepped to her left, putting herself between the man and Longbow. She swallowed once, almost audibly, and stood her ground. Instead of groveling before the man as many others in her position would, she held her ground. Whatever he had done to her, the tavernmaster had yet to break her spirit. That meant she had not been under the man's cruel hand for too very long.

At least Fallon hoped not.

But he still did not know enough to determine the best course of action.

He closed his eyes and concentrated on the girl. Emanating from her was an aura of fear and anger so strong it battered relentlessly against him. Instinctively, he reinforced his mental shields before probing gently, carefully below the outer layer of her emotions. As he did, his own anger reared its head like an enraged bull and he fought it down, surprised by the depth of his reaction.

Suddenly and without warning, Fallon suddenly found

himself linked with the girl. Her emotions whirled dizzily, black and red, around him. Nausea churned in the pit of his stomach and he clamped down on it. For those few fleeting moments, he was part of the girl and experiencing all she did. Knowing the danger of remaining linked with her without having laid the proper foundation, he quickly broke free.

Breathing deeply, more than a little shaken, Fallon leaned back. Never before had he been pulled so quickly and unexpectedly into a link. There was very definitely much about the girl that needed exploring. But that had to wait until he figured out what his first move should be. He knew one thing for certain. After sharing the link with her, it was clear the situation was far worse than he had feared. Now he had to act on her behalf. Failure to do so would be a violation of the sacred oaths he had sworn to the Lord and Lady.

"Master, I gave him only my own mid-day meal. He asked for nothing," she said defiantly as Fallon's awareness returned to the common room.

"Dante Giaros, do not be so foolish as to punish the girl for being charitable to an old man." Longbow climbed stiffly to his feet. As he did, there was a hard, lean look to him that did as much to convince Fallon he had been a dedicated soldier in his younger days as did the way Longbow unconsciously reached for the sword he no longer wore.

"Hold your tongue, old man," Giaros reached out and grabbed the girl, jerking her to him. "She is mine and I will do with her as I please. There is nothing you or anyone else can do to stop me."

As if to prove his point, the tavernmaster's hand caught the girl with a vicious backhand. Her head snapped back. Her lips disappeared in a smear of blood. Before she could fall, he grabbed the front of her tunic and shook her like a rag doll. Then he tossed her negligently to one side. Off-balanced, she stumbled two steps and fell, striking her head against the stone hearth.

Moaning softly, she struggled to her knees. As she did, Giaros pulled his wide leather belt from the loops of his dirty trousers. With a sadistic grin, he sent the belt, buckle first, flying in her direction. She cried out in pain as the heavy metal buckle connected with her ribs. Before the next blow could land, she curled in on herself, her arms covering her head. Not that it stopped the tavernmaster from landing three more savage blows across her back and shoulders.

With surprising speed, Longbow closed the distance between himself and the tavernmaster. As Giaros prepared to strike the girl yet again, the old man grabbed his arm. Surprised, the burly younger man spun to face him. At the same time, the girl, whimpering in fear and pain, dragged herself a few feet away.

"Old man, never interfere with how I deal with my property," Giaros roared and threw Longbow off as if he weighed nothing more than a feather, laughing as the old man fell to the floor. "The next time will mean your death."

To emphasize his point, Giaros pulled his booted foot back and savagely kicked Longbow in the ribs. When two of the nearby patrons moved to intercede, Giaros turned to them, glaring. They raised their hands and quickly backed out of the tavern. The few other patrons present suddenly became very interested in the remnants of their meals.

For a moment, Fallon simply stared at the scene before him. Anger quickly replaced disbelief and he surged to his feet. In one fluid movement, he slid out of his coat. His right hand rested on the hilt of his sword. He might be required by his oaths to give the tavernmaster the chance to step back but he dearly hoped Giaros refused. Part of him wanted very much to treat the man in much the same way he had the girl and

Longbow.

Then a glint of metal near the girl's right ankle caught Fallon's eye. Gorge rose in his throat as the implications of that simple band of metal hit him. No! It couldn't be. Not even in this godsforsaken land. His fury turned cold and hard as the need for vengeance all but sang through him.

"Hold!" he ordered as he moved to stand between Giaros and the man's victims.

"Who do you think you are to interfere in the affairs of my household?" the tavernmaster demanded.

It was a valid question, especially since Fallon was not wearing the armor and other accoutrements that marked him as a member of the Order of Arelion. Since it was, he reached under the collar of his tunic. His fingers closed over the heavy chain and a moment later he produced the intricate medallion marking him as a Knight of the Order. As he did, he heard several of those gather gasp softly. Then there was the scraping of chair legs against the floor followed almost instantly by the sounds of someone rushing outside.

"Someone who cannot and will not stand by and allow you to continue this travesty. I warn you not to try my patience any further," Fallon said coldly.

Standing there, ready to pull his sword and skewer the tavernmaster if he so much as moved wrong, Fallon heard the sounds of people beginning to gather in the doorway behind him. Angry murmurs, discussions about helping Giaros against the armed stranger were shouted down by others saying Giaros was only getting what he deserved. Hopefully, the standoff would continue outside. The last thing he needed just then was to have his attention divided. That would give the tavernmaster the chance to escape, or worse.

Not that he didn't expect Giaros to try something foolish. Fallon recognized the look in the man's eyes. Cornered animals had that same look just before charging their opponents. After all, if there was nothing to lose, why not try for the unexpected?

Fingers tightening around the hilt of his sword, Fallon rocked up onto his toes and then back. He would not be taken unawares.

Suddenly, the murmuring behind him silenced and the sounds of booted feet racing in the direction of the tavern replaced it. Shifting slightly, ready to react should Giaros decide to try something, Fallon cut his eyes to his right. As he did, the crowd parted and half a dozen members of the local militia entered.

"What seems to be the problem here?" the commander demanded as he motioned for several of his troopers to see to the injured.

Even as the troopers hurried to carry out their commander's instructions, Fallon stepped forward. Longbow lay almost motionless near the hearth while the girl, still curled in a tight ball, sobbed softly. Frowning, the commander moved toward her, a concerned look darkening his expression.

Fallon waited, giving the commander time to take stock of the situation. As he did, he relaxed slightly. Almost ten years had passed since he had last seen the commander. At that time, he had been impressed with the man's sense of duty. He hoped that impression hadn't been wrong. More importantly, he hoped the man had not changed in the intervening years.

"Commander, it's Master Longbow!" one of the troopers said as he knelt at the old man's side.

"Is he seriously injured?" Commander Darrias asked.

"He doesn't appear to be, sir, but the physician should see to him."

"And the girl?" Darrias nodded to where she lay.

"She has been brutalized by this man, Commander," Fallon

reported. "They both have."

"Sir Fallon!" Darrias snapped to attention and crisply saluted. "You say the girl's been brutalized?"

"Aye. This man—" He pointed to Giaros with a look of distaste. "This man has broken the laws of this duchy and the laws of the Imperium. From what I gathered, she has been beaten and brutalized by the tavernmaster on more than one occasion. Giaros himself called her his *property*." He all but spat out the last word.

"He lies!" Giaros lunged forward, hands outstretched as if to grab Fallon, only to be pulled back and held firm by one of the troopers.

"Quiet!" Darrias bellowed. "Sir Fallon?"

"He held her as his slave, Commander."

Darrias paled and then straightened his shoulders as if bracing himself for what he had to do. "Did she tell you this?"

"She didn't have to." Fallon heard the bite in his voice and didn't care. The time for tact had passed. "The truth is there for anyone who cares to look."

There was no sense telling Darrias how he *saw* it. The commander would only fall back into fear and superstition like all who came from this godsforsaken realm did. That was the problem with this part of the Imperium. The inhabitants were suspicious of the gifts of the Lord and Lady. So he had to be careful about how he explained the situation to Darrias.

"Take a good look at her, Commander. My guess is that she is not of this realm. Besides, who treats a servant or member of their family as she has been treated? Look at her neck. Her wrists. Her ankles. If those aren't Sarussian slave bands, I will lay down my sword for good."

Without a word, the commander knelt at the girl's side, his expression drawn. Gently, he eased her slightly forward so he could examine her back. The cloth of her tunic was torn and bloody where Giaros' belt had landed. Angry looking welts were visible when Darrias lifted her tunic for a closer examination. From where he stood, Fallon saw older injures as well and it was all he could do to keep from cursing long and hard. Bad as the injuries were, he knew they were far from the worst.

Darrias reached out with a hand that shook slightly to touch the thin metal band that had been hidden beneath the collar of the girl's tunic. Softly, he assured her everything would be all right even as he checked her ankles and wrists. Then his voice turned hard and Fallon relaxed slightly. Darrias now knew he spoke true. Hopefully that meant the tavernmaster would soon be dealt with.

"Sergeant, hold this scum in close custody. Then send word to the keep that the duke's presence is required at once. Sir Fallon's accusations appear to be well-founded."

Giaros flinched under the cold anger reflected in the commander's eyes.

"If the duke questions why I've sent for him, explain that there has been an incident involving Master Longbow that requires his immediate attention."

The sergeant nodded once before dispatching a trooper to the keep.

"Corporal Bemis, go to the clothier and secure something for the girl to wear besides these rags. Have him charge it to the Company," Darrias continued.

"Aye, sir." The young man saluted and then hurried off.

"Now, lass, everything is going to be all right," Darrias said gently as he helped her sit up. "Can you stand?"

"I-I think so."

Fallon watched as the commander helped her to her feet. He frowned as she hissed in pain, her right hand flashing to left side of her ribcage. Then, as the commander looked at her in concern, she shook her head, denying the pain Fallon knew she had experienced too many times before. She seemed as unaware of the pain as she was of the blood streaking the left side of her face or of that eye rapidly swelling shut.

Very gently, Commander Darrias led the girl to the table where Longbow had been sitting earlier. Fallon smiled in gentle reassurance as she slid onto one of the chairs. If she saw it, he didn't know. Instead of responding to him, she looked around almost frantically until she saw the old man being helped to his feet. She drew a long, shuddering breath before visibly relaxing.

"Sir, are you all right?" she asked once Longbow sat next to her.

Very interesting. She no longer calls him Master Longbow. In fact, to hear her now, I would guess she is from one of the northern or western realms.

So how had she managed to fall into Giaros' hands? That was but one of many questions Fallon knew he had to answer.

"Aye, lass," the old man assured her with a weak smile. "It will take more than the likes of Dante Giaros to kill this old warrior."

Fallon saw the doubts that lingered in her eyes.

"Sir Knight, my appreciation for your help. I fear age and time have combined to slow me to near uselessness." Despite the fact he was obviously in a great deal of pain, Longbow sat straight and proud before sketching a slight bow in Fallon's direction.

"Never that, Master Longbow," Fallon assured him. "You served this young lady well today, just as she tried to serve you. It is I who should apologize for not reacting sooner to what was clearly a dangerous situation."

"Master Longbow, you and the girl should drink this." Commander Darrias placed a pitcher of mulled wine on the table before them. One of the troopers followed with two tankards. "When the duke arrives, he will need to hear what happened. Will you be up to it?" He looked at the girl, concern still reflected in his expression.

"I will, Commander," she responded as Fallon poured out for her. "Sir, will I have to remain here?" Fear roughened her voice and Fallon cursed silently. He had no doubt the prospect of spending another night at the tavern terrified her.

"No, child," he assured her before the commander could respond. "You now have my sworn protection. I promise you won't be forced to spend one more night in this place unless you want to. Further, unless I'm convinced you wish to remain in the duchy and will be safe here, you will accompany me when I leave."

"Is truth?" She looked to Longbow for confirmation.

"It is, lass. Sir Fallon is a Knight of Arelion. He and all those like him will care for you now," the old man replied with a reassuring smile.

Watching the girl out of the corner of his eye, Fallon saw first the relief and then the doubt that flashed across her expression. For a moment, her reaction puzzled him. Then understanding dawned. She had no guarantee any of them spoke true and she certainly had to wonder if she was, by trusting him, merely trading one form of slavery for another. He knew he would feel that way if their situations were reversed.

Somehow, he had to reassure her. But how? How to win her trust and how to find out who and what she was? All he could do was trust in the gods. They had brought him here. They would give him the insight and the knowledge needed to deal with this very special and very frightened girl.

He hoped.

CHAPTER TWO

FALLON DIDN'T KNOW WHETHER TO NOD IN APPROVAL OR SIGH IN frustration as one of the troopers calmly explained to yet another townsman that the tavern was not open for business. No, he did not know when it would reopen. No, Giaros could not come out and explain. He was currently "unavailable". No, he really could not say more than that.

At least that much was the truth. Giaros sat in the far corner of the room, a burly trooper standing on either side of him. Each rested heavy hands on the tavernmaster's shoulders, making sure he did not try to get to his feet. Looking at him, Fallon had no doubt the only thing keeping him quiet was Commander Darrias' threat to gag him. The threat had been enough to finally silence Giaros' threats and invectives and it had happened none too soon. Fallon had been ready to silence the man in a much more permanent manner.

Part of him still wanted to.

Frowning, Fallon turned away from the tavern's entrance and looked to where Darrias stood talking with his sergeant. As he did, Fallon's fought the urge to move to the captain's side and demand an explanation for the delay. Almost an hour had passed since word had been sent to the keep requesting the duke's presence. There had been no response and the duke had yet to appear. That worried Fallon more than he wanted to admit, even to himself. Either the duke did not understand the urgency of the situation or he simply did not care. Either option meant trouble, not only for those involved but also for the duchy and, very possibly, for the entire Ardean Imperium.

If the duke was so naïve that he did not understand how serious the situation happened to be, the duchy could very easily find itself at the mercy of raiders – or worse. A ruler who didn't recognize the presence of Sarussian slave bands in his lands opened the door for an evil so deep and dark it would be next to impossible to displace. It was likely the followers of Balaar already had a foothold in this land and the duke had, very possibly, condemned his subjects to a life of fear and suffering. That was bad enough.

Worse, far worse, was the possibility that the new duke simply did not care about what had happened. Such a monarch opened his lands to suffering willingly, gladly. Often, he was the cause of it, even if not directly. By encouraging raiders and slavers, by not taking steps to protect his people, a ruler violated the trust put in him. If that were the case, the Order would have to consider stepping in.

Fallon prayed that wasn't the situation here.

Of even greater concern to Fallon just then was the girl. The troopers had done what they could to treat her injuries but it wasn't enough. There was a sallowness to her skin and a glazed look to her eyes that worried him. He wanted a physician to examine her, to make sure she had suffered no serious or lasting injury at the tavernmaster's hands. Then he needed a detailed report of all her injuries, old and new. That report would be the best proof of the crimes the tavernmaster had committed against her.

It might also help answer other questions he had about the girl, questions like where had she come from and how had she come to find herself in Giaros' hands?

But that was only part of what Fallon wanted done. The girl needed to leave the tavern as soon as possible. Every time Giaros uttered a sound, she started nervously, hunching her shoulders as if expecting a blow. Her eyes flickered between the man and the troopers guarding him. Clearly, she knew Giaros would strike out against her at the first opportunity. Unfortunately, Fallon knew she was right to be afraid. One look was all it took to recognize the madness in the man who had hurt and enslaved her.

No, she needed to get away from the tavern as quickly as possible.

His patience finally coming to an end, Fallon moved almost silently to the girl's side. They had waited long enough. No matter what Darrias or anyone else said, Fallon was determined to take her some place that would not be a constant reminder of all she had suffered. Once he had, he would secure the services of a physician. Unfortunately, this realm's fear of gods-given *talents* meant there would be no Healer around and that was who the girl really needed. A Healer would be able to deal with her emotional and mental wounds as well as the physical. But, since one was not available, a physician would have to do.

That presented him with his next challenge. He had already spent more time here than he could afford. Every hour delayed put more people in jeopardy. But he knew he needed to make sure the girl was safe. So he had to find a way to get the information he had collected to Kirris without much more delay. Once he had done that, he could focus fully on the situation here.

One thing he was certain of, as soon as the girl was able, they would leave New Grange and the duchy. She would not stay there one day longer than necessary to insure the tavernmaster paid for what he had done.

Finally, the outer door swung open. Fallon turned in time to see a young man, not much older than a boy really, step inside. To the Knight's surprise, the troopers snapped to attention and crisply saluted.

"Commander," the newcomer began in a surprisingly deep voice. "What is so important that I had to leave a council session?"

"My lord Duke." Darrias bowed slightly. "My apologies for calling you away from your duties, but the situation is such that you must decide what action should be taken. Left to me or my men, it would mean the tavernmaster's life."

For a moment, the young duke looked at Darrias, concern written on his expression. At the same time, Fallon studied him. What he saw did little to reassure him.

Duke Tomas Althanas was not much older than the girl. His straw colored hair was thick and unruly. His light blue eyes reflected displeasure, whether at the interruption of his regular routine or at Commander Darrias' words, Fallon couldn't tell. In fact, had it not been for the royal colors of his tunic and trousers, as well as the intricately braided knot at his right shoulder, Fallon would have mistaken him for a messenger from the duke. Now he hoped the duke's youth did not interfere with what had to be done.

"Very well. Commander. Tell me what has happened."

As he spoke, the duke looked around the common room. Fallon watched as his mouth grew tight at the sight of the small pool of blood at the base of the hearth where the girl had fallen. Then the young man continued his examination of the room until his gaze fell on Longbow. There could be no mistaking his concern as he watched one of the troopers finish tending to the old man's wounds.

"Master Longbow! Are you all right?"

"I am, my lord." Longbow tried to stand but the trooper stopped him. "Due to the quick action and intervention of Sir Fallon." Now he nodded in Fallon's direction.

"My lord, allow me to introduce myself. I am Sir Fallon

Mevarel, knight of the Order of Arelion." He stepped forward. "I stopped at this tavern to partake of some refreshment before continuing on my journey. This lass served me well and I have no complaint about her. However, I have seen much since my arrival that not only concerns me but alarms me as well."

"And what, pray tell, might that be, Sir Knight?"

Doing his best not to omit a single detail, Fallon quickly told of his time at the tavern. The young duke listened closely, occasionally interrupting to ask a question. When Fallon told how the girl tried to help Longbow only to find herself on the receiving end of what was clearly the latest in a long line of beatings by Giaros, the duke turned to face the tavernmaster. Cold fury danced in the young man's eyes and his hands fisted at his sides. Seeing it, Fallon relaxed slight, hoping it meant the duke was not as inexperienced and callow as he had feared.

"Master Longbow?" the duke prompted.

Frustration filled Fallon at those two simple words. He was not used to having his word questioned. Nowhere else in the Imperium would such a thing happen. The members of the Order were respected and recognized as the enforcers of not only the High King's laws but, more importantly, the laws of the Lord and Lady.

But then, he reminded himself, *Lineaus is like nowhere else in the Imperium.*

Fortunately.

"It is as Sir Fallon says, milord. Dante Giaros has refused me food and drink, even when I have offered to pay. He begrudges me a seat by the fire, saying I am bad for business. It is no secret he has given the girl a clout whenever she has tried to help me."

From where he stood by the girl's side, Fallon nodded slightly. The young duke might not have been overly impressed by what he said but he appeared to accept everything Longbow told him as truth. Even so, Fallon still worried. No one seemed to want to discuss the fact the girl had been enslaved and that had to be dealt with and dealt with quickly.

Frowning, Fallon glanced down at the girl. She sat silently, head bent. Her hair covered her face and he wondered if that was a mask of protection she had learned to use. Hide her face, hide her emotions. Then, as Longbow continued to answer the duke's questions, describing earlier times he had seen Giaros lay hands on her, she hunched her shoulders defensively, as if to ward off any further blows. Such a reaction served as further confirmation of Fallon's suspicions and he hoped the duke saw it and understood.

Gods above and below, what terrors had she been forced to endure at the tavernmaster's hands?

"Is there more?" The duke's voice was tight with anger.

"There is." Fallon did nothing to hide the condemnation he felt. "It was my understanding that this realm, as a member of the Imperium, had long ago outlawed slavery."

"Of course it had!"

"Then would you care to explain why she wears not only a Sarussian slave collar but matching slave bands at wrists and ankles? As a member of the Imperium, you are bound by imperial law. I find myself wondering if you willingly flaunt that prohibition or if you simply turn a blind eye to what goes on."

For several moments the duke stared at Fallon, anger suffusing his face. Fallon knew he had very likely gone too far but he did not care. Slavery was a capital crime in the Imperium. Every realm upon joining the Imperium had to agree to follow all imperial laws. Otherwise, it faced the prospect of imperial forces marching into the capital and deposing the local leadership. Was that what it would take to bring Lineaus into compliance?

Then, to Fallon's surprise, the duke moved to kneel in front of the girl. The anger reflected in his face just moments before was gone. Concern replaced it. Good. Maybe he finally understood just how serious the situation happened to be.

"What is your name, child?" the duke asked gently, much more gently than Fallon expected.

She stared at her hands where they rested in her lap, fingers clasped so tightly together it hurt. But that was nothing compared to the pain lancing her ribs with every breath she took or that where the tavernmaster's belt had broken the skin of her back. Not that pain was anything new to her. It had been her almost constant companion for so long she now expected it.

What she wasn't used to was being the center of attention. Her master had told her to never bring attention to herself. Having so many eyes watching her, so many people discussing her as if she wasn't even there unsettled her. If she could, she would flee the room but something told her that would not be allowed.

So she sat as still as she could, praying they would soon leave her be. Her master would be so angry when they did. She hurt now but it would be nothing compared to what he would do to her once they were alone. Blessed Elanna, why hadn't she tried to give Master Longbow her mid-day meal sooner? If she had, her master would have been none the wiser.

"What is your name, child?"

She lifted her head slightly and studied the young man kneeling in front of her. With his blond hair and blue eyes, he looked like so many who frequented the tavern. But he wasn't one of those she had served. She would have remembered his fancy clothes. Then she remembered the others had called him *duke*. What did he want with her?

Unsure, afraid of what Giaros might do should she answer, she glanced to her left. Longbow sat at her side, his expression concerned and yet oddly reassuring. He placed a gentle hand on her shoulder and nodded. He wanted her to answer the young man. *The duke*, she reminded herself. She had trusted Longbow before but could she now?

"H-he calls me Sparrow." She spoke softly, so softly the words were barely audible. Still, they sounded almost like a shout in the silence of the common room.

"And your age?"

"H-he told me eighteen winters." Without taking her eyes from the duke's face, she nodded to where the troopers held Giaros in place.

"Child, don't you know how old you are?"

She heard Longbow's concern and tears pricked at her eyes as she shook her head. There was so much she didn't know, but how could she tell them that?

"No." If possible, she spoke even softer than before. Why couldn't they leave her alone?

"Child, look at me."

Something about the voice made her comply. She looked up from her hands as someone knelt next to the duke. The stranger, the one who had tried to protect her from her master, knelt there, his expression troubled. He reached out and she started nervously. He paused and then gently brushed a lock of hair back, revealing more of her face than she had let anyone see in so very long.

"Child, my name is Fallon Mevarel. I am a knight of the Order of Arelion. I swear you have nothing more to fear. I will make sure nothing else happens to you." He spoke softly, almost as softly as she had, yet there was such confidence in his words and the way he looked at her that she wanted to believe him. But how could she? She had learned the hard way how foolish it was to trust anyone but herself. "Will you answer a question for me?"

She nodded almost reluctantly.

"You said the tavernmaster calls you Sparrow. Is that your name? Is it what you call yourself?"

She closed her eyes as a single tear tracked down her cheek. Why couldn't he leave her alone? She didn't want to think about what he asked and what she knew he would ask after that.

"N-no." She licked her lips, struggling to find the courage to continue.

"What is it then?" The knight's hand cupped her cheek so lightly she could barely feel it. Never could she remember anyone treating with such care.

"I don't know." Once again, she ducked her head and stared at her hands.

"Child, are you telling us that you don't know your name or how old you are?" the duke asked.

She nodded, too ashamed to look at him or at anyone else. She was a nobody, not worthy of having a name. That was what her master had told her. She was property to be used and discarded at his whim. Would these people feel the same?

"How did you come to be called Sparrow?" the knight wanted to know.

"My master named me. Said I was his caged bird with no more sense or beauty than a common sparrow."

She glanced up and, through the mask of her hair, saw Fallon's expression harden as he glanced at Giaros. A spark of hope, faint but real, seemed to come alive at the very core of her being. Maybe she could trust him, this stranger who saw more in the span of a few hours than others had in so very long.

"What do you call yourself?"

Call herself?

A slight, bitter smile touched her lips. She could tell him, just as she could tell him how much she had hated being called Sparrow, hated all it had stood for. But that would reveal much, perhaps too much, about what she thought and felt. After so long of hiding that part of her from everyone, and most especially from her master, did she dare trust this stranger?

But what did she have to lose?

"Please, child. We need to know what to call you and it would be best if it was a name you prefer." Longbow's hand closed over hers and gave it a reassuring squeeze.

She drew a deep breath, wincing as her ribs screamed in pain. She could do this. She had to do this if she was to ever break away from her master.

"Call me Cait."

Fallon thought his heart would break at that one soft word. Her voice – Cait's voice – was so filled with despair it hurt. If he had had any doubts before, he no longer did. Not when he looked at the way she stared at her hands, rough and reddened from hard work, not when he recognized the word and its slightly foreign sound. She had chosen a name for herself that was the opposite of that given to her by the tavernmaster. He had wanted to cage the bird. She wanted to kill it, or at least to kill what it represented. Cait, which she pronounced as *kawch*, was the word for *cat* in the northern parts of the Imperium. Had she heard someone use the word or was it a clue about where she came from?

He couldn't worry about that – yet. First, he needed to do everything possible to make sure the duke understood the extent of the trouble in his realm. But he also had to make sure Cait never spent another moment at the mercy of Giaros, or anyone like him. Once that was done, he could worry about how she had come to be there.

"Cait. I like it." He smiled and once more reached out. This time he tilted up her head so she looked him in the eye. He needed her to see that he spoke true. "I have a feeling it fits you much more than Sparrow ever did."

She gave him a small, shaky smile, but it was enough to give him hope she had not yet been broken by Giaros.

"Will you answer a few more questions for us?"

She nodded once.

"How long have you been here?"

She closed her eyes as if trying to remember. "This will be my second winter here."

Longbow nodded when Fallon looked to him for confirmation. As he did, anger flared. How could so many people have seen what was happening around them and yet not do anything? Fallon wanted to climb to his feet and pace – or mete out instant justice to Giaros and all like him. Instead, he stayed where he was, focusing on Cait and making sure he did everything he could to reassure her so she felt safe enough to tell him what he needed to know.

"And before you came here?"

She shook her head, tears once more leaving tracks down her dirty cheeks. Fallon closed his eyes, putting a tight rein on his emotions. Thank the Lord and Lady he listened when instinct pulled him in the direction of New Grange. If he had ridden past, he had no doubt the girl would not have survived much longer. From what he could tell, it was a miracle she had lasted this long.

"Cait, don't you remember anything from before you came here?"

Another shake of her head.

"I know I am asking much and I am sorry. But it is important that I know everything you can tell me." Using his fingertips, he gently brushed away her tears. He waited, praying she understood. Then she nodded again. This time, however, she looked directly at him instead of at her hands. He hoped that was good. "What is the first thing you remember?"

"Waking in a small tent. It was cold. No, I was cold, so cold. I tried to sit up but I couldn't. Everything seemed to hurt. Then I realized I was bound, hands behind my back, ankles crossed. It was dark and I was alone." She paused and then softly thanked Fallon as he pressed a mug of mulled wine into her hands. He waited as she sipped, knowing better than to rush her. She needed to tell this in her way and in her time. Not that it made waiting any easier.

"I think I passed out. Maybe I slept. I don't know. But suddenly he was there." She glanced once again at the tavernmaster. This time, anger lit her eyes and Fallon nodded in approval. "Another came in after him and they dragged me outside. Neither said anything as they put those bands on me. Once they had, the second man freed my ankles and said it was time to sample the *merchandise*. He—" Another nod at Giaros—"raped me." Tears rolled freely down her cheeks and she reached up with one grimy hand to wipe them away. Fallon waited, knowing there was more. "When he finished, they told me I belonged to him. Coin was exchanged and a chain was locked to my neck band. That is when he led me out of the camp."

"What else did the tavernmaster say about your relationship?" the duke asked.

"That I was his property. If I did as I was told, I would be rewarded. If I failed to please him, I would be punished."

This time she glared at Giaros. Seeing it, Fallon smiled in

approval. Her spirit might have been battered but it had not been broken. That would help her recover both mentally and physically – if he could get her away from there before anything else happened.

"Cait, you said there was pain when you woke. Can you describe it?" Fallon asked, hoping that might help determine why she could remember nothing before that terrible day.

"Aye, sir. I seemed to hurt all over. I later realized I had a number of injuries, some almost healed."

"Your head? Did it hurt?"

She nodded. "It did. It was hard to focus and the light hurt my eyes. It was bad for several days after I woke."

A head injury then as well as everything else. But how had she been injured and by whom?

"What about the other man? What can you tell us about him?" Fallon knew her answers could tell him a great deal, at least about who held her before Giaros. That would at least give him a place to start.

"Big. Skin was wind burned but still pale. He spoke strangely, as if his native tongue was not this one." She shivered as she recalled him and Fallon wished he didn't have to ask her to relive that time. "His hair was dark, darker than mine, and there was a band of white in it."

Wasteland raider then. But what was a nomad from that godless land doing this far north? More importantly, when and how had he gotten his hands on Cait and what in the name of all that was holy had he done to her before handing her over to Giaros?

Fallon frowned thoughtfully. Learning that Giaros had been doing business with the raider boded ill for not only the tavernmaster but for Lineaus and the rest of the Imperium as well. For years, the raiders had believed it their right to enslave and kill anyone who was unfortunate enough to wander into their lands. For generations, they had pressed the borders, trying to gain inroads into the Imperium. If they were getting bold enough to look for, and find, those within the Imperium willing to do their bidding, then Lord and Lady help them all. Trouble was most definitely on the horizon.

"All right, Cait." The duke held up a hand to forestall any other questions. "What about your life here? How did Giaros treat you?"

She swallowed hard. The last thing she wanted to think about were those first days after waking. To give herself time, she once again lifted the mug to her lips and sipped. As she did, she knew she should have no more. With no food in her stomach, it would not take much for the wine to affect her and one lesson she had learned early on was never to lose control. It was a hard-learned lesson and one she wasn't about to forget just because it appeared her situation was changing.

"I was nothing to him, less than an animal," she began only to be cut off by an angry denial from the tavernmaster.

Instinctively, she hunched her shoulders and looked for someplace to hide. She knew that tone of voice, just as she knew what would happen should he get his hands on her any time soon. She would be lucky to survive the beating. He had been so angry before the knight had interfered. Now his rage was deadly and she would be the one to pay the price if he managed to get free.

"Quiet!" Commander Darrias ordered.

Cait flinched as the commander followed up his order with a savage blow to the tavernmaster's midsection. Even as Giaros gasped for breath, a sense of satisfaction filled Cait. Too many times had she been on the receiving end of such blows. Now, to see the man treated in much the same manner, she could feel that faint glimmer of hope in the pit of her stomach building. Maybe this was real and her nightmare was about to end.

Not that she would let her guard down. There were still too many unknowns and too much that could go wrong. So she focused on the commander, watching as Darrias extended his right hand. A moment later, one of his troopers handed him a leather thong. Without a word, the commander nodded and stepped forward. Cait swallowed hard as memories threatened to overwhelm her as Darrias quickly bound Giaros' hands behind his back. Much as she had suffered at the tavernmaster's hands, this was too close to what he had done to her.

"My apologies, Cait. I promise he won't interrupt again." The soft statement drew her attention back to the duke. "I only have a few more questions. Did you ever try to leave Giaros or tell someone what had happened? Also, did he force you to lie with him after that day in the camp?"

Cait once again looked down at her hands. They were wrapped around the mug where it rested on the table before her. She hated remembering. It brought back all the pain and fear and threatened to overwhelm her. Why couldn't they just leave her alone? Then a gentle hand closed over her shoulder. Looking up, she found Fallon watching her, compassion and understanding reflected in his eyes. Seeing it, she smiled slightly. She could do this. She had to. Otherwise, they might make her return to the tavernmaster and she would not survive that. If he didn't kill her, she would kill herself. She would not give him power over her ever again.

"I did try to escape, milord, several times. The first was on the trail. The next was not long after our arrival." She closed her eyes and the memories came flooding back. "Two days after we left the camp, I managed to slip my bonds before we broke camp. It was early, not quite dawn, and he didn't seem to be paying that much attention. I ran but I wasn't fast enough. He caught me and then he beat me until I lost consciousness. When I woke, he gave me my first lesson about how the slave bands could be used." She shivered violently at the memory. "He chained me like an animal so I could only move on hands and knees. For the rest of the day, I had to follow the mules like a stray dog. Then he beat and raped me again. From then until we arrived here, when we would make camp at night, he would chain me to a tree. He promised I would never get away from him again."

She paused, her mouth working as she swallowed against the bile the rose in her throat. She could feel his hands on her, rough and painful. His breath was fetid. Madness – or something worse – filled his eyes and she knew he would take a great deal of pleasure in dealing out as much pain as he could before he finally killed her.

No! It was just a memory. That was all. He couldn't hurt her any more. He was the one now tied and helpless. She could do this. She had to do this.

"The second time I tried to escape, he caught me before I could leave the tavern. It was late, after the last customer had left. I thought he would kill me, he was so angry. Instead, he dragged me down to the cellar where he beat me again. Then he chained me so I couldn't move, much less leave. He kept me down there for two days without food or water. Except when he came to me at night, he kept me gagged. He promised he would kill me if I did anything to bring attention to myself. From that day on, he made sure the opportunity to escape never came."

"Why didn't you say something to me at least, child?" Longbow asked.

"He threatened to kill anyone I told, sir. He said if he even thought I'd said anything untoward to someone, he would kill them and make me watch. I couldn't risk him hurting anyone else." Tears burned her eyes and she angrily dashed them away.

"She lies!" Fear laced Giaros' voice so heavily Cait prayed the others realized it meant she spoke true.

"I said to be quiet!" Darrias turned and backhanded the tavernmaster, almost knocking him from his chair.

"What about my other question, Cait?" the duke asked.

"Milord, he did force himself on me. I know not how many times. I quit counting long ago."

"When was the last time?" Fallon asked.

"A few months ago." At least she thought it had been that long. She couldn't be sure.

"Do you know why he stopped?"

"I asked what he would do if he got me with child."

She could almost smile at the memory. She had known the moment Giaros dragged her upstairs to his rooms what he had in mind. Something inside of her seemed to snap. She no longer cared what happened. If he beat her into unconsciousness, at least she wouldn't know if he raped her. Death would be a welcome release.

She had asked the question before she knew what she was doing. The response was something she had never thought to see. Giaros stopped, his breeches around his ankles, his shirt dangling from one hand. His expression looked like he had just been hit by a tree and then he paled. Without a word, he pulled up his breeches. Then he grabbed her by the arm and hauled her down to the cellar where he chained her and, just before locking the door behind him, he warned her to be quiet or face his wrath. Then the door closed and she listened as the bolt slid into place. That had been the last time he'd forced himself on her.

As she remembered that night, Cait sensed Fallon

stiffening at her side. When she looked up at him, she was very glad not to be in Giaros' shoes just then. The knight looked as if he would like nothing more than to pull his sword and use it to make short work of the tavernmaster. That did more to reassure Cait than anything short of Giaros' death and her departure from the duchy could have and she clung to that for all she was worth.

Despite what the duke said, there were more questions. How often had he hit her? Had he treated her injuries? Had she ever been seen by a healer? She answered as best she could, all the while wishing they would just stop. Hadn't she said enough already to convince them she was telling the truth.

"Cait, we're almost done," Fallon said softly. She nodded, not quite believing him. "But now we need to see where you stayed. Can you show us?"

Swallowing hard, she nodded. Fear knotted her stomach at the thought of returning to the cellar. Could this be a ruse to get her down there so they could do with her as they wanted? No, she couldn't – she wouldn't – believe that. Not when Fallon looked at her, so worried and caring, and not when she could see the fury reflected in Commander Darrias' eyes whenever he looked at Giaros. She needed to trust these men not to betray her. But it was so very hard . . . .

She slid her hand into Fallon's and let him draw her to her feet. Without a word, she led them through the tavern to the cellar entrance at the back of the kitchen. The heavy wooden door was closed, the bolt slid into place. Darrias stepped around her and slid the bolt back and opened the door. At his signal, one of the troopers appeared with a lantern. He led the way down the steep, uneven steps, Darrias just behind him. With Fallon following closely, Cait descended into the setting of so many of her nightmares.

She said nothing as the men looked around. She didn't

have to, not when the cellar itself told the tale. Resting on the stone floor in the far corner of the dark, dank room were the thin mattress and threadbare blanket that had been her bedding. Cait shuddered at the sight of the heavy metal rings set into the stone floor along the sides of the mattress and the short chains attached to them. Most nights, those chains had been secured to her slave bands, leaving her a helpless victim to whatever depravity Giaros wanted to visit upon her.

Her other nights had been spent chained to the man's bed. It might have been more comfortable but there had been no pleasure in it. Those nights she had been raped and abused, often by others besides Giaros. She had learned to fear those times even more than those lonely nights in the cellar. At least on those nights, unless Giaros came to her, no one hurt her and she could escape in her dreams for a little while at least.

"Cait, did you ever see any others like you?" Fallon asked as they once more made their way to the common room.

She shook her head and then smiled slightly as he once more seated her at the table and handed her the mug of mulled wine. Gods above and below, she wanted to trust him.

"You have my deepest apologies, Cait. Until now, I did not want to believe you. I did not want to think such evil could exist in my lands without me knowing about it. For that, I am truly sorry." The duke inclined his head, his expression as serious as she had seen since his arrival. "There is little I can do to make up for what you have suffered, but I hope you will let me begin by accepting my offer for you and Sir Fallon to take up residence at the keep until the council has met and determined the appropriate punishment for the tavernmaster."

"It would be our honor, my lord," Fallon answered for them both. Then he looked down at Cait and she realized he wanted to make sure she agreed. She nodded. Just then, she would agree to almost anything if it meant she could leave the tavern and never return. "With your permission, milord, I think it best we leave this place. It holds nothing but pain and fear for Cait. More importantly, her injuries need to be seen to. Then I want those cursed bands removed. She has been forced to endure them all too long already."

"Of course, Sir Fallon."

"Once that is done, milord, I think the two of us must discuss how such an abomination could exist in your duchy for so long without someone discovering it." Fallon's voice was so cold that Cait looked at him in surprise. "Steps must be taken to insure there are no others suffering as Cait has."

"I assure you, Sir Knight, that I share your concern and want those same questions answered." If possible, the duke's voice was even colder than Fallon's had been. "Come morning, the council shall convene to hear this matter. But for today, Commander Darrias and his people will question the tavernmaster about Cait and what has happened."

"Very well." Fallon inclined his head and once again rested a reassuring hand on Cait's shoulder. "I insist upon one other thing, milord. Giaros must be confined. He cannot be given the opportunity, no matter how small, to cause Cait more harm or to escape justice."

"Agreed." The duke quickly issued the necessary orders and Commander Darrias assured him he understood. "Shall we go?" he asked, pointedly turning his back on the tavernmaster as Giaros once more began pleading his cause.

Fallon nodded and helped Cait to her feet.

"Sir Fallon," she said softly as they followed Longbow and the duke into the golden warmth of the afternoon sun, the first she had felt in more than a year.

"Just Fallon, lass."

She paused and glanced skyward, one hand lifting to shield her eyes. Everything seemed so bright, so clear and clean.

Despite the pain from her injured ribs and back, she breathed deeply, filling her lungs with fresh air for the first time in much too long. Then she smiled slightly, praying this wasn't all a dream. Even if it was, it was worth it. She had forgotten how beautiful a day could be. Now if it would just last.

"There is no way to thank you for what you've done." She fell silent, wondering what those looking through open doors and windows thought of the strange procession moving through the streets in the direction of the keep. How many of them had come to the tavern over the many months she had been there? How many had seen her, had seen the bands she wore and ignored them. Anger flared and she pushed it down. There would be time for that later. But now she had to focus on what was happening and do everything she could to make sure she was never returned to Giaros. She would rather die first. "What happens now?"

"After we've been shown to our rooms, your injuries will be treated and those accursed bands removed. Then you can bathe, eat and get some much deserved and needed rest."

"And after the council meets?" Damn that note of fear in her voice. It was never good to show weakness. It would be used against her. That was another lesson she had learned at Giaros' hands.

"I promise to see you settled and safe well away from here, Cait."

She glanced up at him, surprised by the fierce determination that shone from his expression. As she did, she knew intuitively that she could trust him. Even so, until the bands were removed, she would not be able to accept it was all real. Maybe then she could finally begin to believe things were going to get better.

CHAPTER THREE

FALLON STOOD JUST INSIDE THE SLEEPING CHAMBER AND WATCHED as Cait looked around in undisguised awe. It was not difficult to guess what she was thinking. Standing there, surrounded by luxuries she probably had not guessed existed before then, she had to wonder if it was all a dream, one she would awaken from all too soon and then find herself once again at the tavernmaster's mercy.

Mercy!

Fallon doubted there was an ounce of mercy in Giaros. He certainly hadn't shown any to Cait. No one who knew the meaning of the word could have treated her the way he had. Now it was Fallon's mission to make sure he paid, and paid dearly, for all he had done – but only after he answered each of Fallon's questions not only about Cait but about those who had sold her to him.

Shaking his head, Fallon turned his attention back to his young charge. The last thing he wanted was for her to realize how angry and worried he happened to be. So he schooled his expression to hide his emotions and then smiled as she continued her examination of the room.

Floor to ceiling windows lined the far wall. Thick, rich draperies the color of the finest red wine covered them. In the center of the room, just to Cait's right, stood a large bed. Its brightly stitched canopy matched the coverlet. Heavy wooden furniture, artistically carved and oiled with something smelling faintly citrus, and several paintings added to the beauty of the room.

Cait finished her tour of the room and shook her head. Disbelief washed over her expression as she reached out to run a hand over one of the bedposts. How hard it must be to accept that this was all real. From what he had seen, he doubted she had known any real kindness, much less comfort, while with Giaros. Somehow, he had to convince her that life was behind her now and she was safe. More than that, he would see her safely settled at the Citadel, the only place he could be sure she would never again face the hardships she had known here. But that had to wait until he knew Giaros had been punished. The tavernmaster could not be allowed to be in a position to harm anyone else ever again.

Then, seeing how Cait's disbelief turned to fear, Fallon hurried to her. As he neared, she turned and buried her head against his chest. Deep, heart-wrenching sobs wracked her thin body. Not quite sure what to do, he carefully wrapped his arms about her. For one brief moment, she stiffened at his touch. Anger once again filled him as he realized that even a touch could plunge her into her own personal hell. Damn Giaros and whoever else had harmed the girl!

"Easy, Cait," he soothed, praying she understood on some level that he wanted nothing but to comfort her. "You're safe. I promise." She released a shuddering breath and he felt her nod against his chest even as a new spate of tears came. "It's all right, Cait. Just cry. You'll feel better for it."

His right hand stroked her dark, matted hair. As he held her, he wondered how long it had been since she had allowed herself to cry. It wouldn't surprise him that she hadn't since arriving in New Grange. Giaros would have viewed her tears as weakness and would have used them against her. Gods above and below, what had that bastard done to her?

Perhaps the better question would be what hadn't he done

to her?

"Cait, listen to me." He kept his voice soft and reassuring. At least he hoped he did. "You are safe now. I know you have no reason to believe me, but it is true. Nothing else is going to happen to you.

"Soon the physician will be here to treat your injuries. Then we will get those bands removed. Once we have, you can rest."

"Is truth? I won't have to return to the tavern?" She looked up at him and wiped away her tears with a hand too dirty and rough for one so young.

"It is." For the first time since their arrival at the keep, he let her see his anger. She needed to know he did not approve of what had been done to her. "You will never have to return, not even as a patron, unless you wish to. You have my word on that, just as you have my word that I will do everything in my power to see Giaros punished for what he did to you." He waited as she took a step back and tilted her head up so she could see him better. "Cait, I swear as a knight of the Order to see you settled and cared for well away from here."

He waited, watching as she carefully considered what he said. A moment later, she cocked her head to one side, her expression thoughtful. He said nothing, hoping it meant she was considering what he said. Then one corner of her mouth quirked up in an almost smile and some of the fear that had been reflected in her eyes cleared. A moment later, she reached up and shoved the hair out of her face. He recognized it as the symbolic move it was. By brushing her hair back, she was removing the mask she had worn for so long. It was a small thing, and he knew she would have times when she would fall back to the habit of hiding from those around her, but it was enough. She had taken the first step toward trusting him.

Before anything more could be said, a soft knock sounded

at the outer door. Fallon motioned for Cait to stay where she was. She nodded, the fear once more returning to her expression, not that it surprised him. Her entire world, bad as it was, had been upturned in the matter of little more than an hour. She had nothing to tell her how to react or what to expect. All Fallon could do was be there and do his best to reassure her – and make sure nothing else happened to her.

Damn Giaros! How easy it was to send the girl back to the hell he had made for her. It would be a long time before she truly trusted anyone, if she ever did. For that alone, the tavernmaster deserved to die.

"Cait, it's all right," he said from the outer room as he closed the door behind the newcomers. "It is the physician and a lady's maid from the duke's household. May we come in?"

If she wasn't ready to see them, he would not force her. He would do nothing to damage the tentative trust she was starting to show in him.

He waited, the others just behind him. Then Cait appeared in the doorway to the sleeping chamber. She looked scared but she had not hidden. Nor had she tried to run. Fallon nodded slightly, marveling at the courage it had to take for her to agree to let them come to her.

"Child, my name is Jacov Artil. I am the duke's personal physician and by his order I am to examine you and treat your injuries," the tall, thin man said gently as he paused a few feet in front of Cait. "This is Dyara Malias." He nodded to the small, almost dainty, woman who had entered with him. "She shall prepare a bath for you, child, and help you once we are done. If that is all right?"

Seeing Cait nod a bit hesitantly, Fallon didn't know whether to smile or cry. She was trying so hard and yet it was easy to see that she was completely baffled by what was happening. It wasn't difficult to guess that she had had no one

42

really help her once she fell under Giaros' hand. The closest thing she'd had to anyone caring about her had been Longbow and that had not been enough, not nearly enough.

"Sir Fallon, if you would leave us now, I will begin my examination."

"No!"

Fear, so strong it almost strangled her, filled her at the thought of being alone with the newcomer. He was one of them, one of those who had seen her but overlooked what was happening. She had served him more than once but he had done nothing – NOTHING – to help her. Now he wanted to be alone with her? Didn't Fallon understand? He had promised to be there for her, to protect her. Didn't he know she needed him now?

She shook her head and backed up, one step, two, until she felt the bed behind her. Then, before her panic took full root, she looked at Fallon. The knight's eyes flashed in anger. Without a word, he stepped past the physician and hurried to her side. Fallon's arm went around her shoulders and he softly reassured her that he was going nowhere.

"My apologies, young lady. I should have thought before speaking. Sir Fallon may stay if it makes you feel better." Artil inclined his head. There was nothing but concern and understanding in his voice. Maybe he had been as unaware about what was going on as had Master Longbow. "I will need you to undress so I can treat your injuries."

For a moment, Cait studied him. Her earlier fear receded a little. Perhaps it was because he agreed to let Fallon remain. Or perhaps the strange, intricate tattoo of blue and red in the center of his forehead that marked him as a graduate of the Healers' College, as well as his slightly foreign accent, reassured her. Then, with a start of surprise, her eyes went wide. How did she know what the tattoo meant? She'd never heard of the Healers' College before. At least she didn't think she had. Nor had she seen him, or any other physician for that matter, during those long, dark months with Giaros except to serve him a mug of mulled wine on occasion. Not once had the man really looked at her, much less talked with her. She knew he had never introduced himself or said what he was. Yet she knew what the tattoo meant. Could this be a memory, her first since waking in the tent so long ago?

If so, why weren't there others? Why couldn't she remember what happened or who she was?

By all that is holy, why did this have to happen to me?

"Cait, it's all right. I'll be right here. But he does need you to undress so he can see to your injuries." Fallon spoke softly, as if he understood her hesitance as well as how the request to disrobe threatened to plunge her back into the nightmare of her time with Giaros.

She nodded slightly, not trusting her voice. Then, forcing down the last of her hesitation, she stripped out of the filthy rags that had been her only set of clothing for the last several months. As she stepped out of them, Artil bent and, wrinkling his nose in distaste, lifted them between thumb and forefinger before tossing them to the far corner of the room. Before she could protest, Fallon softly assured her she would never have to wear them again.

Soon Cait stood before the physician, her only adornments the Sarullian slave bands. His jaw clinched so tightly she could see the muscles bunch, Artil asked her to remain still. Then he slowly circled her several times, his gaze intent. He moved close but not once did he touch her. Finally, he returned to stand before her and looked deep into her eyes. As he did, Cait felt as if he was peering into her very soul. Then, after what

44

seemed like an eternity, he asked her to be seated.

For more than an hour the physician worked. He cleansed and probed injuries both old and new. After treating the welts crisscrossing her back and shoulders, Artil placed several careful stitches in the cut on her forehead and secured a clean patch in place over the wound. His voice softly assured her that he would do all he could to ease her pain so she could rest. Then he straightened and the lady's maid stepped forward to drape a soft woolen robe about Cait's shoulders before moving to the outer door.

Cait looked up at Fallon, unsure what she should do now. She saw the worry, even anger, in his eyes. Reaction built by too many months of fear and pain had her shrinking back. Then she shook her head and forced herself to stop and think. He wasn't mad at her. Nor had he even threatened to raise a hand to her. He wasn't Giaros. She had to remember that.

Breathing deeply, she counted to five and then exhaled. Then she looked once more at the knight. She knew the source of his anger. All she had to do was think. She had seen his expression grow darker and darker as Artil examined her. It was as though Fallon felt every wound, old and new, that marked her body. Then, as if feeling her watching him, he gave her a reassuring smile that didn't quite reach his eyes.

Surprisingly, that reassured her more than any words would have. It was enough to tell her that he would do all he could to avenge what had been done to her. But, more importantly, he would make sure it never happened again. That was important. The thought of another suffering as she had was worse in some ways that all the pain she had suffered at the tavernmaster's hands.

Cait chewed her lower lip for a moment, desperately searching for the words to express her appreciation not only to Fallon but to Artil as well. Her eyes burned as tears filled them.

Then, before she could speak, a soft knock sounded at the sleeping chamber door. Instantly, Fallon stepped between Cait and the doorway, his hand resting on the hilt of the sword he still wore at his side. Heart pounding, fear returning, Cait huddled behind him, barely daring to breathe as the door swung open to reveal Commander Darrias and another man. An almost hysterical laugh bubbled up inside of Cait and she fought it down when the commander sketched a respectful bow in her direction. Then she turned her attention to the other man.

This man was a stranger but she had a good idea what, if not who, he was. From his leather apron, scarred from use, and his heavily muscled arms, Cait guessed he was the duke's smith. Her guess was quickly confirmed when he moved to her side and began to closely examine the collar about her neck.

"Cait." Fallon's soft voice once more focused her attention on him. "This is Jerrys. He is going to remove the bands. It will take time and it may hurt some. But he will be as gentle as possible. Just remember that this will soon be over."

"Perhaps she should sit and have a glass of wine to help her relax?" the lady's maid suggested, looking from Artil to Fallon.

Fallon nodded and the small blonde hurried out of the room. As she did, the smith, his fingers playing with the edges of the collar, muttered softly to himself. Cait forced herself to remain as still as possible but it was difficult to resist the urge to jerk away from the touch of his rough hands. He was here to help her. She kept repeating it, willing herself to believe it. Then she started in surprise as the small woman placed a tankard in her right hand. Lifting it, Cait sniffed and then sipped. Wine. She took a deep gulp and closed her eyes. All she could do was wait.

Using finely edged chisels and probes, the smith worked.

From time to time, he would hold out a hand and bark out an order for someone to pass him this tool or that. Sweat poured off Cait's face as he began manipulating the small lock forged into the collar. When he cursed angrily because Giaros had fouled the mechanism, she almost cried out in frustration. Would she never be rid of the collar? Then he laid a heavy hand on her shoulder and promised it would not be long before he rid her of the accursed thing. He just had to try something else.

Taking another long draw from the mug of wine, Cait prayed he soon finished. The sound of the file rasping on the collar tore through her, irritating and frustrating. Heat from the friction caused by the file began to burn her neck. Not wanting to do anything to cause him to stop, she bit her lip and forced her whimpers to remain trapped in her chest. Not that it slowed her breathing or stopped the sweat streaming off her face as he worked. Finally, with an exclamation of triumph, the smith announced that he was through the metal. Soon the band would be off.

Never before had any words sounded so sweet. The thought of taking her first breath without the weight of that accursed collar bearing down on her was almost as intoxicating as the heady wine she had sipped. From the moment she had first been fitted with the collar, there had not been a single breath she had taken that had not reminded her of the collar and all it stood for. Now, knowing she would soon be free of it, she could finally believe the horror of life as she had known it was about to come to an end.

Suddenly, a loud *snick* filled the air and the collar popped open. Before Cait could react, Fallon reached out and gently removed the band from her neck. As he handed it to Commander Darrias, the smith went to work on the band about Cait's right wrist. The lady's maid refilled Cait's glass and gave her a small smile of reassurance.

"Sit still just a little longer, child. This should not take as long," the smith said, his voice as rough as his hands and just as gentle. "The locks aren't fouled here."

By the time the smith removed the last band, the one fastened around her left ankle, Cait was ready to collapse. Drenched in sweat and more than half drunk, she wanted nothing more than to be left alone with Fallon. It had all been too much and it had happened too quickly. She needed time to accept that she was now free of the bands. It would take longer to truly believe she was free.

As the last band snapped open, Jerrys sat back on his heels and carefully removed it from her wrist. As soon as he had, Darrias reached for it. As he put it and the other bands into a dark cloth bag, Cait hoped she never saw them again. They were part of a life she never wanted to think about, much less return to. Then, before she could ask about what would happen next, the commander motioned to the smith. Without a word, the men bowed slightly first to Cait and then to Fallon. Then they left the sleeping chamber.

As the door closed behind them, Cait sagged against the back of her chair. It felt like days, maybe even years, had passed instead of only an hour or so. Her time with Giaros had taught her what it meant to be physically exhausted. What she felt now went beyond that. She was spent, physically, mentally and emotionally. All she wanted was to be able to sleep but did she dare? What if all this was a dream and, when she woke, she would once again be at the tavernmaster's mercy?

"Easy, Cait, it is almost over. I promise," Fallon soothed as Artil once more moved to her side.

"Sir Fallon is correct, Cait." The physician's touch was gentle, almost featherlike as he applied a cool, sweet-smelling salve to her neck where the collar had been. Before she could reach up to touch the area, he shook his head. "No, child. Let me finish." The hand he placed on her shoulder gave a quick, reassuring squeeze. "I won't lie to either of you. There has been more damage done than I can heal. The salve will help keep the scarring to a minimum, but that is the best I can do."

Cait nodded and let him gently bandage her neck.

One look at her wrists was all she needed to understand why the physician was concerned. The slave bands had rubbed the skin beneath them raw. Old wounds had never properly healed. Dirty scabbing, thick and crusty, mixed with barely dried blood from newer wounds. Mouth tight, Cait refused to show how badly not only the wounds themselves but the knowledge she would always bear the scars hurt. She had hoped being free of the bands would help her forget all she had been forced to endure. But no. The scars would forever remind her of her time with Giaros and the way everyone who had come into the tavern had failed her.

"Sir Fallon, the salve needs to be applied three times daily and the bandages changed. Dyara will be able to see to that as well as to her other dressings," Artil said as he finished bandaging Cait's left ankle. "I shall let Commander Darrias know my findings before making my report to the duke. I have no doubts that young Cait here was abused many times by the tavernmaster, both physically and mentally." The physician's voice was so hard, Cait shuddered. Then, as if realizing he might be scaring her, he placed a gentling hand over hers where it rested in her lap. "Child – Cait, I beg for your forgiveness. I remember seeing you those few times I went to the tavern but I never *saw* you. Had I, I would have made sure the duke acted to free you. Nothing I say will ever be enough to make up for that but I pledge I will do everything I can to ease your hurts and help you heal. I will also make sure the duke understands just what was done to you. All I ask is if you think of anything else I can do, you will but ask."

She nodded, unable to speak. A cloud of doubt began to eat at her. Had she been to blame for no one realizing what had been going on? It was possible. She had tried so hard to avoid calling attention to herself so Giaros would have no reason to hurt her. Could she have simply asked for help and it would have come?

"Thank you," Fallon said. "I am sure you understand how difficult this is for Cait right now."

"I do." He waited until Cait looked up. There was pain in his expression and that helped. Knowing he hurt for her, that he felt guilty for not realizing what had been happening, helped push aside some of the doubt. "Now, young Cait, you need to eat and then rest. But a hot bath first to clean away the dirt and ease your hurts."

She nodded, not knowing what to say. A bath? She could not remember the last time she had been allowed to have more than a bucket of cold water to use to wash with. To enjoy the luxury of a bath was something she had never hoped for.

"Come, child. Artil was right. You will feel better after a bath. Then we can eat and talk about your future," Fallon said gently and helped her to her feet.

Half an hour later, Cait lay mostly submerged in a deep tub of steaming water. Eyes closed, she relaxed as the heat eased her hurts even more than the physician's salves had. Dyara's hands gently massaged her legs, easing the knots in them Cait had long ago gotten used to. It was enough to have her drifting slowly but inexorably toward sleep.

A slight change in the pressure of the room alerted her something had changed. Heart racing, memories flooding her, Cait forced herself not to react. Slowly, carefully, she turned her head. Through barely slitted eyes, she watched as the door opened just enough for someone to slip inside. A moment later, Fallon appeared. He carried a stack of what looked to be folded clothes and a pair of boots. Seeing him, Dyara lifted a finger to her lips, motioning for him to be quiet. He nodded, placed everything on the rack by the door and then backed out. As he closed the door behind him, Dyara returned to the task of massaging Cait's legs.

A few minutes later, Cait stood and carefully climbed out of the tub. As she did, the lady's maid wrapped a thick, soft robe, a different one from earlier, around her. For a moment, Cait simply stood there, relishing the feel of the material against her bare skin. How different it felt from the roughly woven tunic and trousers she had worn. Hugging it close, she sighed softly. Then the small blonde escorted her to the dressing table in the sleeping chamber.

"What now?" Cait asked a few minutes later as her companion plaited her freshly washed and trimmed hair into an intricate braid that fell just past her shoulders.

"Once we finish here, you shall share a meal with Sir Fallon. Afterward, you are to get some rest," the blonde replied. "Are you feeling better now?"

"Much better. Thank you," Cait answered honestly. Despite the pain from the beating at Giaros' hands, she felt better than she had in a very long time. Amazing what a bath, some salve and the absence of fear could do. "What should I wear?" After all, they had disposed of the only clothes she had. Not that she ever wanted to see, much less wear, those filthy rags again.

"Sir Fallon brought some clothes for you earlier. Most will do for later. There is a sleeping shift you can wear under your robe." Dyara motioned to the stack of clothing now resting on the foot of the bed.

"May I ask one more question?"

"Of course."

A look of relief lit Cait's expression for a moment. "Exactly who is Sir Fallon and why did everyone believe him?"

"He is a knight of the Order of Arelion. We listened because the knights are sworn to protect all peoples and to enforce the Codes. They help patrol our lands, keeping the followers of Balaar from invading and enslaving those they encounter. If a knight gives his word, he never breaks it. Because you are now under Sir Fallon's protection, you will be safe. He would willingly die to ensure it."

As Dyara spoke, Cait could almost hear another voice, this one soft and lilting, telling her much the same thing. For a moment, she sat very still, trying to capture that elusive voice. But, as with that earlier flash of memory, it was gone as quickly as it came. Sighing heavily, Cait wondered if she would ever know who she really was or where she came from. Then, with a start, she realized that, for the first time since waking in that strange tent a lifetime ago, she was beginning to remember. The thought comforted her some.

A few minutes later, Cait held out her arms and watched in bemusement as Dyara helped her into the sleeping shift. In the last hour, she had been cosseted and coddled more than she had ever dared hoped. Part of her feared it was merely an attempt to get her to drop her guard. Another welcomed it as a sign that the hell she had endured for so long was finally over. Still, it felt so strange to have someone else dress her, especially since she was perfectly capable of dressing herself.

Once dressed, Cait followed Dyara into the outer room. As they appeared in the doorway, Fallon climbed to his feet. He quickly looked Cait over and nodded, obviously pleased with what he saw. Then he motioned for her to join him.

"Longbow?" she asked as she took a seat at the table. She could not bring herself to say "master". Not now. Maybe not ever. "Is he all right?"

"He is," Fallon assured her as he sat across the table from

her. "Commander Darrias said he has been seen by a physician and suffered no lasting injuries. Come morning, he shall join us here for breakfast."

Cait nodded, relieved to know the old man had not been seriously injured standing up for her.

"Sir Knight, I am in your debt for the aid you've given me this day." As she spoke, the fingers of her right hand touched first her forehead and then her chest before she bowed slightly, palm upraised.

At the motion, Fallon's face lit with speculation. Cait saw and wondered at it. Then, realizing what had brought the expression to the knight's face, she paused. The movement had seemed natural, something she had done many times before. Except she had not. She could remember no other time she had done so. What did it mean – the motion, the fact she had made it and the fact Fallon had reacted to it?

More importantly, did she really want to know?

Deciding that she did not, at least not just yet, she pushed aside the questions. There would be time enough later, after she had eaten and rested, to ask those questions and any others she might have. At least she hoped there would be.

"Cait, you owe me nothing. I did only what was necessary," Fallon assured her as he motioned for her to eat. "I promise to ask no questions tonight save one. How did you come to be called Cait?"

"From our first day together, the tavernmaster called me Sparrow. I hated it. I knew it was not my name. It didn't matter that I knew no other. All I knew was I wanted to call myself something, anything but what *he* named me," she answered between bites. "Cait came to me and it felt right."

"All right. I have one more question and then I promise to leave you in peace." He waited until she looked up from the meat she had been cutting and nodded for him to proceed. "Do you remember anything from before the day you woke in the tent?"

"No, sir." She wasn't ready to speak of those brief flashes of memory, if that was what they were. "What will happen at the council session tomorrow?" she asked to change the subject.

"I'm not sure. I assume the council will ask to hear the evidence against Giaros. Then they will deliberate his fate. I assure you, as a knight of Arelion, he will be made to pay for what he did to you."

"Thank you."

"Just remember that you have nothing to worry about, Cait. You have my sworn protection. I will not let any further harm befall you," he continued, as if understanding that she needed the reassurance just then. "Now eat. You need some food in your belly and then you need to get some rest."

With a smile, Cait did as he instructed. Even as she did, she wished she could simply leave the duchy without having to recount once again what she had been through during her time with the tavernmaster. After all, how many people had she seen during that time, people who had witnessed the way Giaros treated her? Yet they had done nothing to help. It took the arrival of a stranger to free her. Did she dare count on those same people to mete out justice to the man who had caused her so much pain and fear?

CHAPTER FOUR

FALLON STOOD IN THE DOORWAY TO THE SLEEPING CHAMBER, ONE hand resting on the hilt of the sword buckled at his waist. In the faint light coming from the fireplace across the room, he watched Cait sleep. Her features were relaxed and she looked younger than the tavernmaster had said.

"Stay with her," he said softly as he turned back to the sitting room. "If she wakes, send for me."

The lady's maid nodded and slipped into the sleeping chamber. As the door closed behind her, Fallon turned his attention to Darrias. The commander stood near the outer door, his expression serious. Fallon knew he didn't approve of what he planned but he didn't care. He had a duty to uphold the Codes and he would do whatever it took to do so.

But there was one thing he needed to find out first.

"I dispatched a squad with your message to the Order's nearest compound," Darrias said, as if reading Fallon's mind. "They should arrive in three days, four at the most."

"Thank you." That eased one concern and let him concentrate on the problem at hand. The knight-commander at the compound would make sure his report, not only about his mission but also about what he had found here, reached the Citadel without further delay.

"The duke has instructed me to do whatever is necessary to assist you." Darrias paused as Fallon sensed his uncertainty. "Fallon, the duke is a good man. He will be a better one as he matures. This--" A nod in the direction of the sleeping chamber—"has shaken him. Gods above and below, it has shaken all of us. To know such evil could exist here and none of us know it." He frowned and shook his head. Fallon guessed it would be a long time before the man forgave himself for not realizing what had been happening.

"He has issued orders to do whatever we must to insure there are no others like Giaros within our borders. He only requires that the tavernmaster be in good enough shape to attend the council session come morning."

Fallon nodded. At least the duke was being reasonable. "Of course. However, Giaros doesn't need to know that."

Darrias gave a short laugh. "Shall we get this over with?"

Fallon nodded and, after one last look at the sleeping chamber door, he left the suite.

Time to get to work and possibly get his hands dirty.

That bitch!

That lying, ungrateful bitch!

When he got his hands on her –

Dante Giaros drew a long, shuddering breath and clenched his teeth as the ugly reality of his situation sank in. He would never get his hands on the bitch. He would be lucky to live through the next few days. Even if the Duke's Council somehow decided he was innocent of the charges against him, he would still have to deal with the knight and he had no illusions that would end well.

How could it when he sat on the cold stone floor of a cell not as large as the larder of the tavern? It seemed an eternity since he had been unceremoniously tossed in there. The only light came from a small window, little more than a slit really, and had long since dimmed to almost nothing. Only the occasional snatches of conversation from the guards as they patrolled outside broke the silence. The stench of the cell caused his stomach to roil and he swallowed against the gorge that rose in his throat.

The sound of metal rasping against metal filled the cell and he shrank back against the wall. Could it be morning already? Surely not. He didn't remember sleeping and they had not fed him. Not that it mattered. He was at their mercy, at least for the moment.

The door slowly opened and light flooded the cell. Gasping, Giaros blinked and raised his right hand to shield his eyes. Was this it? Were they here to lead him to his death – or worse?

"On your feet!"

Instead of obeying, he did his best to become one with the stone wall at his back. With the light coming from outside the cell, he could not identify the four men who stood in front of him. They were faceless, dark nightmares he wanted nothing to do with.

When he failed to obey, one of them snapped his fingers and pointed. The two to his right stepped forward. Sweat pricked out on his forehead and he moaned softly as they bent. Hands, strong as iron, closed over his upper arms and hauled him to his feet. Before he could react, his arms were extended in front of him. His wrists were bound tightly. Then the man who had spoken jerked his head and Giaros had no choice but to let them drag him out of the cell.

His knees turned to jelly and his bowels to water at the sight that greeted him. This was his worst nightmare come true. The smith stood in the center of the room, a brazier before him. Heat from the coals radiated up and out. Nearby were a number of the smith's tools. But it was the sight of the five metal bands, bands he knew all too well that had the tavernmaster struggling to breathe. He knew what they were, how they could be used. Gods above and below, he couldn't, he wouldn't let these bastards put them on him.

"Secure him." Darrias' voice was so cold, Giaros shuddered.

Without a word, the two guards forced the tavernmaster forward. His heels scrabbled against the stone floor, seeking and failing to find a purchase. His eyes went wide as they moved him closer and closer to where the smith stood. The smith watched, his expression cold and hard. Then he turned and reached for his heavy leather gloves, gloves that would protect him as he heated and manipulated the metal of the slave bands.

"No," he wailed, dropping to his knees.

Not that it stopped the guards. They simply shifted their grip on his arms and pulled him until he knelt in front of the smith. A moment later, one of them attached a hook to the rope binding his wrists. The guard gave a nod and someone out of Giaros' field of vision pulled and the tavernmaster found himself being forced to his feet. Slowly, oh so slowly, he was lifted until his toes barely touched the stone floor. Then the rope was tied off and he was left hanging.

"Feet!" Darrias snapped.

Stretched so tightly that every muscle screamed in pain, Giaros fought for calm. He knew how helpless he was. He ought to. How many times had he secured the girl this way? He had taken so much pleasure in teaching all he could do to her. Were his captors about to treat him to the same lesson?

"W-what do you want?"

Gods, how did it all go so wrong?

Fallon watched as Darrias instructed his troopers. None of them addressed the prisoner. They barely even looked at him.

Only the smith did, his harsh gaze leaving no doubt what he thought about the man. With each moment that passed, the tavernmaster's fear and desperation grew. Fallon had seen the moment Giaros recognized how he was secured. Good. His fear would work against him.

He caught Darrias' eye and nodded. The commander nodded in response and moved to stand in front of the prisoner. Without a word, he reached out. His hands fisted at the collar of the tavern-keeper's tunic, which was almost as filthy as the clothes Cait had worn. The sound of cloth tearing filled the room. Giaros tugged against his bonds, trying futilely to put some distance between him and his captors.

"The prisoner is yours, Sir Knight."

Darrias stepped back and Fallon took his place. As he did, he closely studied the man secured before him. Sweat streamed down his face. His chest rose and fell in rapid, shallow breaths. His fear filled the room. Even as part of him relished the reaction, Fallon knew it was wrong. As much as he wanted the man to pay for what he had done to Cait --- and who knew how many others – he would not stoop to the tavernmaster's level. He just didn't have to let Giaros know it.

"You have one chance to clear your conscience and make your peace with the Lord and Lady." He spoke softly, almost casually as he reached out and lifted the man's face so Giaros looked him in the eye.

"Y-you can't! The duke said I was to appear before the council."

"But I can." A slight smile lifted the corners of his mouth. "I am a member of the Order of Arelion. Our mission, by divine decree as well as by the decree of the High King, takes precedence over any local matter." He paused and let that sink in. "Look around you. These are the duke's men. Would they be here, assisting me, if the duke did not recognize my authority?"

"I-I did nothing wrong," he sobbed.

"Smith, are you ready?" Fallon glanced at the smith and fought his grin as the burly man reached out and ran a finger across the band that had been secured around Cait's neck not that long ago.

"Aye, Sir Knight."

"And did you bring the other items I requisitioned?"

"I did." He reached for the rough cloth covering something next to the bands.

"No," Giaros wailed as he stared at the featureless metal mask. It had openings for his nose and mouth and nothing more. Once put into place, he would be blind and effectively deaf.

"Yes. The Codes demand that all those suspected of slavery be secured in such a way they cannot see the grace of the gods nor listen to the glory of Their creation. No one is to look upon the accused's face until judgment has been passed. Then and only then can the mask be removed because the prisoner must be allowed to meet his fate with all his faculties intact." Fallon reached for the mask and picked it up. He made sure the tavernmaster could see how the second piece would fit over the back of his head and lock around his neck.

"A slaver is lower than an animal and is to be treated as such. I offer you one and only one chance to be shown mercy. You will answer my questions or I will instruct the smith to secure the mask in place. Then he will place the same slave bands on you that you placed on the girl. Except when you are being fed or being given drink, you shall be gagged because the Codes demand that all precautions be made to prevent the righteous from being tainted by your words. You will then be caged and removed to Aucheng where the Imperial Council will hear the evidence against you and render judgment."

"Darrias, please. You can't let him do this."

"I not only can, I will assist him." Disdain filled the commander's voice. "So I recommend you answer his questions."

"But he hasn't asked me anything!" Giaros' voice went up almost a full octave.

Fallon nodded slightly. So far, the tavernmaster was reacting exactly how he expected. Bullies like him almost always crumpled when faced with the consequences of their actions. Still, it had almost been too easy. Something warned him that there was more going on than he knew and he had a feeling he would not get the answers to all his questions. Well, it wouldn't be the first time. All he could hope for was that Giaros gave him enough information to start the hunt.

And to make sure there were no others like Cait in the duchy.

"Then here is your first question. Who did you purchase the girl from?"

The man walked casually down the street in the direction of the tavern. As he did, he looked around, a slight frown creasing his brow. A month had passed since he had last been in New Grange. In the year and more that he had made his monthly trips to the capital, nothing ever seemed to change. But it was different today. There was an air about the town, a sense of both concern and anticipation that worried him.

His concern deepened as he neared the tavern. By this time of day, the tavern should be starting its evening rush. But instead of finding the doors open and the lamps burning, the tavern was dark. A few people milled around near the entrance but none moved to go in.

Something was wrong, very wrong. He could feel it in his

bones. One part of him screamed to leave, to get away as quickly as possible before anyone started asking questions he would not answer. But another part told him to stay. He needed to find out what was going on. His master would demand it if he know of this development.

Steeling himself, he moved closer to the tavern. His frustration grew as one explanation dawned on him. That fool of a tavernmaster had finally been caught. Caught at what was something he would have to find out. He knew first-hand that Giaros extorted his customers with information they let spill when too much drink had been partaken. He also ran whores for some of them. But none of that would necessarily mean closing the tavern. Only one thing would. Someone had realized what the girl was. If that was the case, both he and Giaros were as good as dead. His master would see to it.

Damn his luck. He should have dealt with both Giaros and the girl months ago. He had warned the tavernmaster of the danger he was courting. But the man had been so sure no one would realize what was happening under their noses. Things had gone well for so long that he had almost begun to believe the man. Now it looked as if he may have finally made that one mistake his master would not forgive.

But maybe all was not lost. He needed to find out exactly what had happened. Maybe the tavernmaster had saved them all a bunch of grief and had killed the girl in a fit of temper. If that were the case, the duke would try him for murder. Giaros knew better than to betray the secrets he held. Nothing the authorities could do to him would compare to what his master would do. Balaar did not accept failure nor did he allow betrayals to go unpunished.

"Has something happened?" he asked one of the men he recognized from his previous visits to the tavern. Because they had both enjoyed the girl's services, he had no fear the man might betray him. The fool would not dare risk his manhood should the duke find out what he had done.

"Aye. Giaros has been arrested and will stand before the Duke's Council come morning to answer charges of slavery." The man spoke softly, his eyes darting about as if trying to see if anyone was close enough to overhear. "A knight of the Order exposed him."

The man who called himself Wolf struggled not to react to the news. Of all the townsman could have said, that was probably the worst. If the Order decided to look into what had been going on, so many plans, plans within plans, could come crumbling down and Balaar would blame only one person – him.

"And the girl?"

"She has been removed to the keep where she and the knight are guests of the duke."

Gods below, it kept getting worse.

"Friend, I would recommend you make yourself scarce until after they have dealt with Giaros. The man is a coward and will offer up anyone, no matter how false the charges, to save his own skin."

With that, he turned and disappeared into the shadows. Hopefully, his words had been enough to get the townsman to thinking about ways to deal with the tavernmaster before he had a chance to betray them all. In case he hadn't, he needed to put time and distance between them. Then he could figure out how to present what happened to Balaar without bringing down his master's wrath.

Or so he hoped.

CHAPTER FIVE

CAIT WOKE EARLY THE NEXT MORNING TO THE SOUNDS OF BIRD song and vendors hawking their wares in the streets beyond the keep. She lay still for several long moments, savoring how the soft mattress embraced her body and the kiss of the silkiness of the sheet covering her. What a wonderful way to begin the day. Comfortable, warm and safe. No need to fear the day would bring another assault or worse.

Before she could gather the energy to toss back the sheet and climb to her feet, the door to the outer room all but silently opened. Fear sparked and she clutched at the sheet as instinct built from necessity took over. She closed her eyes and slowed her breathing. She willed herself to relax, to do nothing to let the newcomer know she was awake, much less that she knew they were there. Maybe it had all been a ruse and someone else was about to take Giaros' place in her life. Mouth suddenly desert dry, Cait waited, fighting the urge to call out to Fallon for help.

Then the unexpected happened. Soft footsteps crossed the floor in her direction. Gentle hands pulled the sheet about her shoulders, tucking it around her so she would not be chilled by the morning air. A moment later, she heard a soft swoosh as the draperies were pulled back and then fastened open. Bright morning sun filled the room and Cait slowly, carefully opened her eyes, her body tensed for flight. She instantly relaxed at the sight that greeted her. The lady's maid from the day before stood in front of the window, smiling in greeting.

"Good morning, m'lady. I hope you slept well last night," Dyara said as she hurried to help Cait sit up.

"Very well. Thank you." Cait shook her head ruefully. This morning was so different from all the other mornings in her short memory that she did not know what to do.

As if sensing the young woman's uncertainty, the blonde smiled in reassurance. "First a bath. Perhaps even a massage. You will feel better for it. By then, your breakfast should be ready."

"Please." Cait reached out and tentatively touched her companion's arm. "Who are you?"

Another question almost as important to Cait was "what was she?" The blonde was an enigma. Cait had seen no slave bands and she remembered the others, Fallon in particular, telling her that slavery had been outlawed in the duchy. Yet there was no doubt in her mind that the blonde's role was to serve her much as she had served Giaros. So what was the difference between her position with Giaros and this woman's in the keep?

"I am Dyara Malias, m'lady," the blonde replied as she produced a soft robe from the wardrobe across from the bed. "Commander Darrias, my good uncle, told me how Giaros treated you and asked me to do whatever I can to assist you for as long as you are the duke's guest."

"If not slave, what are you?" Cait still saw little difference in their roles and it fanned the flicker of doubt still making a knot of her stomach.

"I am a lady's maid for the duke's household. I hope to one day become the headwoman."

"Then you are free? You could leave this position if you wished?"

"Aye, m'lady. It is the law. We are all free in Lineaus."

All but me. And why? Why did it take a stranger to realize what was happening?

"M'lady, I cannot explain why Giaros treated you as he did. All I can do is try to atone for his crimes."

Could she read minds?

"Now, let us get you into the bath."

Without a word, Cait followed Dyara into the bathing room. As she did, she tried to push aside the anger once more growing deep inside her. Dyara was no more to blame for what happened than was Longbow. Cait kept reminding herself of that. But it changed nothing. No one had acted to help her before Fallon came to her aid. Would anyone have ever helped her if he hadn't come into the tavern?

After her bath, Dyara instructed Cait to stretch out on a long wooden table with its fur covering that rested across the bathing room from the marble tub. Cait dropped the towel Dyara had wrapped around her and complied. Once she settled into a comfortable position, Dyara's hands expertly massaged the tight muscles of her back and shoulders, being careful not to aggravate Cait's injuries.

Relaxing under the woman's careful ministrations, Cait sighed softly. Her eyelids grew heavy. The rhythmic movements, so strong and familiar, eased away much of the tension caused by not knowing what to expect next.

Cait's eyes flew open as she came suddenly wide awake. *Familiar!* Her body remembered being treated thusly. It had to be from before waking in the slaver's tent. Giaros had never treated her so gently. Why couldn't her mind remember? What was it about this massage that seemed to touch something deep inside of her? Something that remained so elusive.

Gods above and below, why could she not remember?

And why, as she soaked in the tub of hot water a few minutes later, had the choices of soaps and oils seemed so familiar? She certainly had never been offered such luxuries by

Giaros. In fact, she had been lucky to get a bucket of cold water once every fortnight. None of it made any sense.

Later, Dyara helped Cait to her feet. Cait felt foolish as the woman settled a robe across her shoulders. This was so different from the life she had known and all this cosseting was so foolish. She was perfectly capable of taking care of herself. But what could she do without insulting not only Dyara but the duke as well?

"Your injuries are healing nicely, m'lady," Dyara said as she carefully rebandaged Cait's neck after applying the salve left by the physician.

Cait nodded, relieved. When Dyara picked up the brush, she leaned back and relaxed. The rhythmic strokes, the deft play of Dyara's fingers as she braided her hair stirred something deep inside. Closing her eyes, Cait breathed deeply and sought for the elusive memory she knew was there. It stayed just out of reach, teasing and frustrating.

A few minutes later, Cait stared at her reflection, not sure she could believe her eyes. Gone was the soft robe. Now she wore a pair of soft leather trousers the color of a starless night, a white silken tunic and wide leather belt. After helping her into a beautifully stitched vest, Dyara circled her slowly, nodding in satisfaction. Bathed, rested and dressed in clean clothes, Cait was a far cry from the filthy, frightened creature Fallon had rescued just the day before.

"Dyara, where did these clothes come from?"

"From Sir Fallon and my uncle's troop. They wanted to be sure you have all you might need. I also know the duke is having some things prepared for you as well."

Why would they care so?

Not knowing the answer, Cait stood and carefully wiggled her toes and then her ankles to settle the soft leather boots in place. Then she watched as Dyara turned to the chest and produced a beautifully tooled dagger. With bowed head, the lady's maid presented the blade to her.

With fingers that shook ever so slightly, Cait reached for the blade. She held the dagger in her left hand, relishing the feel of it. Something – instinct or forgotten memory – told her it was a fine forging, perfectly balanced. That knowledge was yet one more thing she could not understand. All she knew for certain was it felt very good, almost natural, to have such a fine weapon in her possession. With a nod of thanks, she slipped it into the sheath on her belt, smiling slightly as she did.

"Dyara, thank you for your assistance yesterday and again this morning. It has helped me begin to understand that not everyone is like Giaros." That much was true. Still, part of her held them responsible for turning a blind eye to something they had not wanted to see.

"It has been my pleasure, m'lady," the blonde assured her. "I shall return to assist you after the council meets. Should you need me before then, please send word."

"I will," Cait promised.

In the doorway to the sitting room, Cait paused and quickly looked around. How long would it be before she could move from one room to another without that quickening of fear and suspicion, before her eyes quit searching the darkest corners in search of anyone or anything that might be a danger? Then, seeing Fallon and Longbow seated at the table, waiting for her, she shook herself. There was no danger. At least not at the moment.

As if sensing her concern, the men looked up and smiled in greeting. She smiled in return before hurrying to Longbow's side. Her concern for him overrode her need to know what the day would hold for her. During it all, he had been the only one to show her the slightest care. He had stood up for her and he had tried to protect her from the tavernmaster and had been hurt doing so. She would never forgive herself if he had been seriously injured.

"Are you all right, sir?" Her stomach clinched at the sight of his bruised and swollen face.

"I am, child." Even as he spoke, she sensed a sadness and something else in him. "Child – Cait, I cannot tell you how sorry I am. I should have realized what was happening and I did not. I won't ask for forgiveness, but I swear I will see Giaros pay for what he did to you."

"Sir, no." She shook her head. He was not responsible. It would do none of them good if he continued to blame himself.

"Cait is right," Fallon said.

She smiled slightly in appreciation. She owed him so very much. There were not enough words to thank him. Never would she be able to repay him for what he had done by freeing her from the tavernmaster's evil grip. But she had to try – somehow.

"Sir Fallon, how can I begin to discharge my debt to you?" she asked as she took the chair to his right. "I owe you so much."

"You owe me nothing, Cait," he assured her. When she tried to protest, he shook his head. "Cait, it was my duty and my pleasure as a knight of the Order to come to you aid. If any repayment were necessary, you have already given it. Seeing the change in you, seeing you come to life after nothing more than some food, sleep and a change of clothing is enough. It was my pleasure to have been able to help. If you must thank anyone, thank the Lord and Lady for guiding me here."

"I already have. But I still wish to repay you." Knowing he did not agree, she decided this was not the time to press the issue. But she would not forget and she would find a way to repay him, no matter how long it took.

"Eat, child," Longbow said. "And we shall tell you what to

expect of this day while you do."

She nodded and then served herself from the various dishes on the table before her. As she did, one corner of her mouth quirked up in a rueful smile. There was more food on the table than she had seen in a week or more with Giaros. Suddenly hungry, she speared a piece of meat with her fork and dropped it onto her plate.

"The council?" she asked between bites.

"Commander Darrias will escort us to the council chamber when the time comes," Fallon began. "When he does, you are to stay close to my side. I don't anticipate trouble but I am a cautious man. Besides, it will not hurt to remind everyone that you are now under my sworn protection. There shall be justice delivered by the council or the Order will step in."

"Thank you and I shall do as you say." Even as she took her next bite, she wondered about the Order and how it could help her if the council failed to act.

"Now, when you are called before the council, tell them everything about your life with Giaros. I know it will be difficult but it is necessary. For the council to deal with the tavernmaster as he deserves, they must know the entire tale. Remember, they will not hurt you. They just want to know the truth."

"I understand, Sir Fallon."

"Just Fallon," he corrected with a smile. "Now, do you have any questions for us?"

"A few," she admitted and paused to wipe her mouth. "How long will the council session take?"

"That depends on how much testimony the council wishes to hear, child," Longbow said.

She nodded, her expression grim. The thought of having to appear before the Duke's Council terrified her. She knew nothing of how it worked or what it would do after hearing her testimony. Still, it made sense for it not to want to rush the process. Not that it made her feel any better. How could she trust a group of strangers to see justice done?

"Please, what will happen to me now? I know of no home save for the tavern and I don't ever want to return there." The fear in her voice was real as were the tears that burned her eyes.

"Then you shall not return there, Cait," Fallon assured her, covering her hand with his and giving it a quick squeeze.

"Sir Fallon speaks true, child. Duke Tomas will see you well cared for," Longbow put in.

"And, as I said last night, if staying in Lineaus isn't what you want, you will accompany me when I leave. I will see you well and safely settled elsewhere," Fallon added.

A sharp knock at the door sounded. Cait started nervously, her first instinct to flee to the relative safety of her sleeping chamber where she could bolt the door behind her. The only thing that kept her in her chair was Fallon. While not relaxed, he did not appear overly concerned by the interruption. Still, as he called out for the newcomer to enter, Cait saw his hand crept toward the dagger at his belt. Only then did she realize that her left hand rested on her own dagger. Swallowing hard, she waited.

A moment later, the door swung open and Commander Darrias stepped inside. Cait felt her jaw drop in surprise as the man marched forward, stopping a few feet from the table before bracing to attention and snapping a salute in her direction.

"Commander," Fallon said as he got to his feet and stood protectively at Cait's side.

"Sir Fallon, Master Longbow, Mistress Cait, the duke and his council request your presence in the council chamber," he announced formally.

That simple statement sent Cait's heart racing. A lump of fear threatened to choke her and she swallowed hard against it. All the doubts returned in a rush. The time had come for her to learn if she had truly been rescued or if it was all some sort of cruel, sadistic joke.

"Very well." Fallon looked down at Cait, his expression concerned. "Are you ready?"

Of course she wasn't ready! There were too many doubts, too many unanswered questions. They were all asking her to trust them but none of them save Fallon had given her reason to. Not even Longbow. He had been there, day in and day out, and yet he had not seen what was happening. But what choice did she have?

Not trusting her voice, she nodded.

Soon they were following the commander through the corridors of the keep. As they did, Cait looked around in amazement. How different the keep was from the smoky tavern. Here, the wooden floors had been cleaned and polished until they shone like marble. Rich tapestries covered the walls. Ornately carved doors dotted the corridors. Beyond those doors, Cait assumed the daily life of the keep continued as though nothing out of the ordinary was about to happen.

At least for the moment she felt safe. Fallon walked to her right and Longbow to her left. Still, when members of the commander's troop fell into step behind them, a shroud of uneasiness fell upon her and she could not shake it. Did Commander Darrias expect trouble or was this a none-too-veiled attempt to remind her that she had nowhere to go? Then, before she could voice her concern, Longbow softly assured her that the guards were there for appearances only. It was simply the Duke's way of letting everyone know that they were honored guests and should be treated accordingly.

Honored guests? Then why did she feel more like the

condemned being escorted to the gallows with the six armed troopers bringing up the rear?

Fallon watched Cait as they walked through the corridors of the keep, his expression thoughtful. The more time he spent with her, the more convinced he became that there was more to her than he first thought. The selection of Cait as the name she called herself, a word not well-known in this part of the Imperium, was but one indication he was right. Then there had been the way she had touched forehead and chest before extending her hand, palm up the day before. That simple gesture was yet another indication she might have been raised in the north. The evidence continued over breakfast. When Cait had carefully wiped her mouth with her napkin instead of using her sleeve, he had known she was no mere serving wench. Her familiarity with the various eating utensils seemed to suggest she came from a family that either served in a lord's keep or that might be middle class itself. So who was she and why had the Order not been alerted to the fact she was missing?

When they finally arrived at the council chamber, the small group paused. Commander Darrias softly instructed their escort to rejoin the rest of the squad. Their right fists snapped to their chests and then they turned and quickly marched off. As they did, Darrias pushed open the heavy double doors and bowed slightly as he motioned his companions to enter.

Without a word, Fallon lightly grasped Cait's elbow and escorted her inside. As he led her toward the front of the gallery, Cait breathed deeply. He understood. She must be filled with doubts and questions and concerns. The fact she had not tried to run and hide spoke volumes about her personal courage. She had no guarantees that the council would believe her. Part of her had to wonder if they might not try to force her to return to Giaros.

A few moments later, they settled onto padded chairs. As they did, a bell pealed loudly from somewhere beyond the room. Cait started nervously and looked around. Then other bells tolled in the distance. Before she could ask, Longbow leaned over and explained that the bells signaled that the Duke's Council was about to convene. The first sounding warned all interested parties that they had ten minutes to gather. The second sounding would call the council to order.

"What will happen when they arrive?" she asked softly as others began filing into the room.

"Once the duke calls the council to order, the judicar will read the charges against Giaros. Then the duke will charge the judicar to present the evidence," Longbow said.

"Is that when I will have to give my testimony?"

She sounded scared, not that Fallon could blame her. After all, she had spent the last year as the tavernmaster's slave. Who knew what had been done to her before then. Now she had nothing but their word that she would not be returned to that life. Fallon knew it would take time for her to truly learn to trust anyone again.

"Cait," Fallon began. He knew he had to do his best to reassure her before her fear grew any stronger. "I give you my word as a knight sworn to the service of the Lord and Lady that you will never have to return to Giaros or to the kind of life you knew with him. I mean it. You are free to chart your own life from now on. If that means leaving with me, I will welcome your company and will make no demands upon you beyond your friendship. Please believe in me and have faith in the protection of the gods."

"Sir Fallon speaks truthfully, Cait," Longbow took up. "The

Order of Arelion is sworn to fight such evil as you have experienced. He will see you well and truly settled elsewhere if you choose not to remain in Lineaus."

Cait nodded, a thoughtful expression on her face. Then a spark of hope filled her eyes. Fallon saw it and breathed a sigh of relief. Good. The prospect of being able to leave this place called to her. It did not matter that she remembered no other home. In another place she would have the opportunity to build her life into anything she wanted. She might even find that her memory would return if she left the duchy. Hopefully that would be enough to convince her to give serious thought to his offer.

Before anything more could be said, a second bell sounded. Almost instantly, a door at the far end of the room opened. Eyes wide with wonder, Cait watched as eight men and women dressed in the finest clothes she had ever seen filed into the room. They moved purposefully to the long table in the center of the raised dais and took their places behind ornately carved chairs.

The next person to enter the room was a tall, extremely thin man nearing his later years. Dressed in black robes, he looked slightly sinister. As he moved to stand near the end of the table, Cait turned a questioning look to Longbow. The old man softly explained that this was the judicar, the Duke's legal advisor and interpreter of the Codes.

Then, with the sounding of a single clear trumpet call, the door once more opened and Duke Tomas entered. Dressed in dark trousers and a white tunic decorated with intricate needlework, the duke did not appear nearly as young as he had the day before. There was a grimness to him that should have warned everyone present just how serious the proceedings were to be.

"Commander Darrias, have the prisoner brought in," the

duke ordered before being seated in what Fallon guessed was a miniature replica of his throne.

While Giaros was brought in, the judicar quickly announced to those gathered that the only ones to speak that day would be those called upon by the council. No one else would be allowed to address the gathering and the focus of the session was this one matter only. Then the door in the west wall swung open and the commander's troop entered. In the center of the troop was Giaros.

Fallon heard Cait gasp softly and reached over to lightly touch her arm in reassurance. He understood seeing the man plunged her back into the deep morass of fear and pain she had experienced at the tavernmaster's hands. He knew the moment she saw the chains about his wrists and ankles as well as the bruising and swelling to his face. Some of the tension that held her seemed to ease. Good. She needed to understand that Giaros was no longer a threat. More importantly, he was getting a small taste of what he had put her through. Now he knew what it felt like to be chained like an animal. Hopefully he hated it as much -- no, more -- than she had. It was past time for him to truly know what it felt like to be helpless and scared, to be a victim.

"Lord Judicar, you may begin," the duke said as Commander Darrias softly instructed two troopers to remain with the prisoner in the make-shift dock to the left of the dais.

"My lord Duke, honorable Councilors, we are here this day to determine the fate of Dante Giaros, tavernmaster and owner of the Black Duck Tavern. He stands accused of committing the following acts against the peace and laws of Lineaus and the Ardeun Imperium," the judicar began.

He went on to list the various charges against the man, ignoring the angry murmur of the crowd as he announced the charges of rape and slavery. At the sound of the crowd's discontent, Commander Darrias discretely signaled for the troopers to be ready to react to anything that might occur.

"Are your witnesses present and ready to give testimony, Lord Judicar?" the tall woman councilor sitting at the duke's right asked. Her eyes were hard as she looked at Giaros.

"They are, Councilor Margarite."

"Then, Dante Giaros, what say you to the charges against you?" the duke wanted to know.

For a moment, the tavernmaster said nothing. Fallon leaned forward. As he did, Giaros started, fear crossing his expression. Sweat pricked out on his forehead. Good, let him remember their *conversation*. Let him think about what would happen if he failed to tell the truth.

"M'lord, she was no slave. But what was I to do? I took her in out of the goodness of my heart. All I asked in return was that she give good service to my customers and to me. She could have left any time she desired. All she had to do was speak."

Fallon frowned, not believing what he heard. Somehow, someone or something had gotten to Giaros since last night. Someone or something he feared more than the Order and the Codes. So be it. He had brought his fate upon himself.

"And Master Longbow?" the judicar asked.

"All I have ever asked is that he not take away from my paying customers."

"Pray proceed, Lord Judicar."

"Aye, milord." He bowed first to his young duke and then to the council as a whole. "I will forego with an introductory statements as I am confident the honored Councilors know by now the basis for the charges against Dante Giaros. For my first witness, I call Mistress Cera."

At the sound of her name, a small, overweight woman sitting down the aisle from Cait and her champions got to her feet. Hesitantly, she stepped forward. Her gray, scraggly hair was stuffed under a white kerchief. Her pale blue eyes reflected her nervousness as did the way her hands clutched at the white apron fastened over her homespun skirt. After bobbing a quick curtsy before the dignitaries, she turned to stand so she could not see Giaros staring at her in undisguised hatred.

"Mistress Cera, you are sworn to answer the judicar's questions truly. Do you understand?" Councilor Margarite asked gently.

"Aye, my lady." Her hands once again knotted the material of her stiff white apron and she swallowed nervously.

"Then proceed, Lord Judicar."

"Your name is Cera Iopola and you are the cook at the Black Duck Tavern?"

"Aye, sir."

For the next few minutes, Cera answered question after question about what she had seen and heard at the tavern. Fallon felt Cait's disbelief and anger growing with each answer. When Cera described for the duke and his council how she often found Cait beaten so badly she could barely move and yet could not convince Giaros to allow the girl to see a physician, Fallon fought the urge to stand and demand answers to questions he knew he shared with Cait. Why hadn't the woman told someone what she had seen? Why hadn't she tried to help Cait escape? If she had done either, Cait's pain and fear might have ended sooner.

It was the same with the other witnesses the judicar paraded before the Duke's Council. Regular customers, both tradesmen as well as soldiers, testified how Cait would serve them well, often receiving both verbal and physical abuse from the tavernmaster in return. So many had seen and yet none had acted -- none but Fallon. No matter what the duke said, when this was over Fallon would take Cait far from here. She deserved much better than she had received from these people.

"Call your next witness, Lord Judicar," the duke ordered.

"Master Janus Longbow, please come forward."

Fallon nodded slightly as the old man stood. Hopefully this meant they were finally getting close to wrapping up the proceedings against the tavernmaster.

Cait tore her thoughts away from the anger that had been growing inside of her when she heard the chair next to her slide back. Turning her head, she breathed deeply to see old Longbow getting to his feet. Standing tall and proud, looking much as he must have as that young soldier who had saved the duke's family so long ago, he marched forward. A moment later, he sketched a formal bow to the duke and council before turning his attention to the judicar.

As they waited for the judicar to begin, Cait took time to study the old man. The bruise along his jaw where Giaros had hit him was a myriad of blues, purples and greens. He wore a pair of brown trousers and a white tunic. What surprised her the most was the leather sword belt and blade he wore around his waist. Never before had she seen him armed with anything more than a belt knife. He was once again that proud soldier of his youth.

"Master Longbow, you have heard the testimony of the witnesses. Will you kindly tell the duke and his council your story now?" the judicar asked respectfully.

After another slight bow, the old man began. As he spoke, he told of how Giaros had, for several years past, done his best to prevent him from coming to the tavern. Then, when Cait appeared on the scene, things got worse. Not so much in how Giaros treated him but in how it broke the old man's heart to learn how Cait would be punished, often severely, for simply trying to perform a kind act for him. Yes, he had seen Giaros raise a hand to the girl on more than one occasion. No, he had not seen a single act of kindness from the tavernmaster where Cait was concerned. Yes, he felt sure Cait would have been seriously injured, if not killed, had Sir Fallon not intervened when he had.

"Our appreciation, Master Longbow, for your testimony. You have served Lineaus well once again. I assure you the slights against you shall be redressed," the duke said as he got to his feet and moved to stand before the old man. "I have just one question before you return to your companions. Did you ever see anything about Mistress Cait to convince you she was anything more than a mere chattel to Giaros?" He spoke gently, as though he knew the old man blamed himself for not realizing what was going on right under his nose.

"Never, my lord. She was treated as though she was nothing more than a piece of property to be used and abused as the tavernmaster pleased."

"Lies!" Giaros roared in denial. He tried to step forward only to be held firm by his guards.

"Gag him!" the duke ordered. "I will not put up with his interruptions again."

Nodding slightly, a smile on his lips, Commander Darrias moved to stand behind the tavern master. Placing his hands on the man's shoulders, he forced Giaros to his knees. The crowd looked on as a piece of rough cloth was forced into the man's mouth and secured in place by a wide leather thong. When the duke nodded in satisfaction, the commander stepped back, leaving the tavernmaster on his knees, two troopers holding him where he knelt.

"Pray continue, Lord Judicar," the duke instructed the man.

"I call Sir Fallon."

"Soon this will be over, Cait," the knight said softly before moving forward.

As Fallon began his testimony, Cait allowed herself to relax just a little. This time anger did not fill her as she listened to someone tell of how they had seen Giaros mistreat her. After all, Fallon had been the one to realize what was going on and to act. She could not be angry with him. She owed him her life. Somehow, she would one day find a way to repay him, no matter how long it took.

For the next half hour, Fallon spoke. He described in detail how he watched Cait busily serving those who came for their mid-day meals. There had been something about her, a composure or attitude that had intrigued him. Because of that, he had lingered over his own meal instead of getting back on the trail as quickly as he had planned.

"Duke Tomas, Honored Councilors, there is one thing you must understand," Fallon said, his expression hard as he looked each of them in the eye. "I have no doubt that Cait was held as a slave. The evidence is clear. Giaros had her secured through the use of Sarullian slave bands. Her nights were spent chained in the basement or to the tavernmaster's bed, helpless to keep that *man* from beating and raping her. While I cannot say why no on in this realm realized what was going on, I can say this. The Codes are clear. The evidence is as well. Giaros is guilty of enslaving this young woman and of raping her. If you do not act upon the evidence and punish him accordingly, I must and I assure you the Order will investigate. That means the matter will come to the attention of the High King and the Imperial Council."

"We understand your position, Sir Fallon. Rest assured that the Codes shall be upheld," the duke said a bit stiffly. "Now, I believe we have all the evidence we need but, as Sir Fallon pointed out, the Codes must be satisfied. Commander

Darrias, hold the accused firm while Mistress Cait gives her testimony. Once she is done, he will have his chance to speak. Then remove him to the stockade."

"As you wish, milord."

"Very well. Mistress Cait, if you will step forward."

Swallowing hard, Cait climbed to her feet. As she did, Fallon smiled in reassurance. Seeing it, she smiled slightly in return. This was necessary. She knew it. Just as she knew that, after all she had lived through this past year, she could live through the simple retelling of it all.

CHAPTER SIX

WITHOUT A WORD, CAIT MOVED TO STAND BEFORE THE DUKE AND his council. Her stomach churned until she thought she might vomit. Swallowing hard, she fought for control. No matter how badly she wanted to, she would not turn and run as far and fast as she could away from there. She needed to remember what Fallon had said. There was nothing to be afraid of. Giaros would never again hurt her. He was the criminal and had finally been recognized as such. All she had to do was tell the truth. That was all. Nothing more.

Even so, she could not help feeling scared. After all, what did she really know about any of these people, Longbow and Fallon included? In the back of her mind, doubt nagged at her, eating away at her precarious hold on calm. What if she was simply trading one cruel master for another? What assurance did she have that Fallon would do as he promised? Despite all her doubts, she knew she had no choice. To refuse to testify would mean her return to Giaros and certain death. That left only one path open to her. She had to testify and pray she was not making a mistake that would lead to a life as bad, if not worse, than the one she had.

"What is your name, m'lady?" the judicar asked, his voice soft and gentle. That surprised her. She had not expected him to treat her with such care.

"He—" She nodded to where Giaros knelt between the two guardsmen.—"called me Sparrow. I prefer Cait, sir. That name feels right."

"Where are you from, Mistress Cait?"

"I know not, sir." Her voice turned soft with remembered pain. Then seeing how Giaros stared daggers at her, she drew a deep breath. A moment later, she blew it out and made up her mind. For the first time in memory, she was the one in control and she would not let him get away with what he had done.

"Please explain," the duke said.

For the next few minutes, Cait described once more how she woke in the slaver's camp. She answered each of the judicar's questions about her physical condition as well as what she could about the man who had been with Giaros. Then, wanting to be sure those gathered believed her, she reached up and brushed back her dark hair, revealing the thin line of a scar at her left temple.

"Sir Fallon," the judicar began, motioning Fallon forward once more. "You have heard Lady Cait's description of the man who was with the accused the day she woke. Would you have a guess about who he might be?"

"I do," Fallon said as he moved to stand next to Cait. As he did, Cait looked up at him, glad to know he stood with her. "It sounds as if he was from the Wastelands, Lord Judicar. It is very possible he was a slaver in the real sense of the word, as are many from that godforsaken land."

"Pray continue, Cait," the duke said, frowning at Fallon's answer.

She closed her eyes and gathered her strength around her. Fallon's nearness, the support she could feel coming from him, helped. She could do this. She *would* do this.

Determined, she once again began speaking. From time to time, one of the Councilors would interrupt her tale of how she had been brought to the duchy and forced to work in the tavern during the day and *service* Giaros at night. Tears burned in her eyes, blurring her vision but she refused to shed them. She had not allowed herself to cry in front of Giaros for all those months he held her. She was damned if she would do so now. But it was hard and it hurt so very much.

"M'lady, I wish we could spare you this pain but we have to know," Councilor Margarite said gently when Cait paused to collect her thoughts. "You have told us how Giaros raped and beat you for his own pleasure. Can you tell us how often he did so?"

"I cannot. Since he brought me here, it occurred many times, sometimes several times a day. But he did stop several weeks ago."

"Why?" The duke leaned forward in interest.

"I asked him what he would do if he got me with child." Voice flat, eyes hard, the very thought that she might have carried the man's child sickened her.

"And his reaction?" Councilor Margarite wanted to know.

"Was to beat me into unconsciousness."

"And afterwards?" the judicar inquired.

"Each night, after the tavern closed and I finished the cleaning, he would secure me as he had before. He would lie with me and force me to do *things* to him." She shuddered violently, desperately praying they would not ask for details. "Then he would beat me until I at least acted as if I had lost consciousness."

He might not have been raping her any more but the alternative was just as bad. Never would she be able to forget what he had forced her to do, to herself and to him. Nor would she forget his taunts as he lay beside her, his hands pawing her as if she was nothing more than a whore, not even as good as a whore.

Damn him!

"Cait, I promise this will not take much longer," the duke said gently as she reached up to wipe away the single tear that had escaped from the corner of one eye. "Do you need a recess?"

"Thank you, milord, but no." The sooner her story was told, the sooner she would learn what the future held for her.

"Very well. Did the tavernmaster let others use you the way he did?"

"Aye," she answered faintly, dropping her head and studying the tips of her boots. That had been the worst of it. The strangers he had forced her to lie with often been even crueler than he.

"What?" Councilor Margarite exploded. "M'lady, please tell us who these people were and what happened."

"I know not who they were, Lady Councilor. They were strangers. They would come to the tavern after hours and I never saw them more than the times when I was forced to lie with them."

"And what happened?" the judicar prompted.

"Giaros would chain me to a bed upstairs and make sure I was gagged so I couldn't scream or call for help. Then the men would have their way with me. Sometimes it would be several of them at a time."

"Was rape the extent of it?"

"No," she whispered, wishing it would all just end. Had they not heard enough? Then she felt Fallon's arm slide across her shoulders and he pulled her protectively against him. Strange, but she didn't flinch away from him as she would have any other man. He was her anchor just then, that oak she had imagined earlier. "There were beatings and worse."

"That's enough, milord. Don't make her relive any more of the horror," Fallon said firmly.

"Agreed, Sir Knight," the young man replied, his voice tight with barely controlled anger. "Sir Fallon, you have pledged your support of Mistress Cait. I charge you to keep her safe and well. Anything either of you need shall be yours. You merely has to ask."

"Thank you, my lord. May Cait return to our suite now?"

"In a few moments, Sir Fallon. She must hear how Giaros responds to the charges against him," the judicar answered and Fallon nodded grimly.

"It's all right," she softly assured him when he looked down at her in question. Maybe if she kept telling herself that, she would believe it. "All right, Dante Giaros, you have heard the evidence against you. Have you anything to say in your defense?" Duke Tomas demanded once the man's gag had been removed.

"It is all lies, milord. I was a good master to the girl, taking her in when she had nowhere to go," he swore fervently. Even though he sounded sincere, the sweat pouring off his face and the dark flash of his eyes said otherwise. "I never mistreated her. Sure, I cuffed her one occasionally but it was just to keep her in line. As for lying with her, that was my right and little enough to demand in exchange for all I did for her."

"Physician?" Margarite asked, looking to where Artil stood at the rear of the room.

"He lies, Lady Councilor," the physician commented coldly. "I examined Cait yesterday at our duke's request. My findings confirm everything she said and more."

"And the slave bands?"

"I have them, my lord Duke," Commander Darrias replied, stepping forward. "I was present when the smith removed them and took them into my possession at that time. They have not been unguarded since then."

"Very well. I think the evidence is clear but I wish to meet with the council in private to determine this *man's* fate," the duke continued grimly.

"But I did nothing wrong!" Giaros screamed, struggling to

break free from the grasp of the two troopers holding him.

"Remove him!" Duke Tomas ordered. "Word shall be sent out to the entire duchy as to when this council will reconvene to levy his punishment. In the meantime, guard him well, Commander. I want nothing to happen to him before his punishment is meted out."

"Aye, my lord," Commander Darrias replied and motioned for the troopers to return Giaros to the stockade.

"Mistress Cait, you should rest some now. This evening, I would be honored if you would join me for dinner. Master Longbow, Sir Fallon, your presence is also requested," the duke continued, ignoring the tavern master's screams and curses as he was forced from the room.

"We would be honored to join you, milord," Fallon said as he helped Cait to her feet.

"Excellent. I shall send for you later."

Fallon nodded once and then escorted Cait from the council chamber.

Late that night, Fallon stood before the floor to ceiling window in the sitting room, one hand holding back the heavy draperies as he stared blindly into the night. One part of him registered that the streets below the window were empty of all but the nightly security patrols and the few people who had closed down the local taverns and inns. Inside the keep, as far as he could tell, he was the only soul still awake.

And that suited him. He needed the solitude to think and to plan. The last two days had been more than a little unsettling for him. The events had caused him, for the first time since taking his oath as a Knight, to abandon his assigned duty - at least temporarily. That did not sit well. But neither did the alternative. If he continued with his assignment, he would have to leave Cait behind and he would not, could not do that. Not after everything he had seen and heard. Perhaps in another day or two they could both leave. By then, the duke and his council would surely have made a decision about the tavernmaster's fate.

Hopefully, they did the right thing. Gods help them if they failed to because Fallon had been truthful when he said he would take action. The first would be to see Giaros appropriately punished for all he had done to Cait. Then he would see to it that the duke and council were taken to task by not only the Order but also by the High King for failing to enforce the Codes.

Breathing deeply, striving for calm, Fallon let the draperies drop back into place. Then he turned and moved almost silently across the room to a chair in front of the fireplace. The only light in the room came from the banked coals. For a moment, he considered lighting one of the lamps but quickly decided against it. If for any reason Cait woke, he did not want to disturb her. That was the last thing he wanted. The girl needed, and deserved, all the uninterrupted rest she could get. He only hoped she had finally managed to fall asleep.

The thought of the girl, the young woman really, who slept in the next room brought a slight smile to his lips. With each moment he spent in her company, Fallon became more and more convinced there was something special about her. Her build and coloring served to confirm his guess that she was not native to this realm. Her manner of speech and her accent, and those had changed subtly since he first saw her, all but screamed that she had not been in the duchy any longer than she remembered. Beyond all that, the ease with which she comported herself at the dinner table belied a training in social skills she did not remember.

And all that told Fallon she was more than a wench who

had the bad fortune of falling in with a slaver. No, if they ever discovered Cait's background Fallon felt sure they would learn she came from a prosperous family, either a family of scholars or perhaps an adjunct branch of one of the royal houses. But not a major branch. Surely if that was the case, the cry and alarm that would have gone up when she disappeared would have reached every section of the Imperium. Even if it had not, the Order would know and its members would have been on alert.

Not that any of it mattered just then. He did not have the luxury of worrying about what might have been. No, Fallon's main concern just then was how to get Cait out of Lineaus and to the Citadel. Her *talent* cried out for training and, from personal knowledge, he knew she had to feel it as well, even if she did not understand what that feeling was. Her mental healing was even more important. She had to learn to accept that she was not to blame for what happened as well as learn that Giaros was the exception and not the rule. Until she did, she would never be able to truly trust anyone else.

Shaking his head as a physical means to change his train of thought, Fallon reached for the mug resting on the table to his right. The tea had long since gone cold but it was something to do. Sipping, frowning at the slightly bitter taste, he rested his head against the back of the chair and closed his eyes. Instantly, the image of Cait as she had appeared after dinner that evening sprang to mind. He smiled slightly, still unusually pleased by her request as she appeared from her sleeping chamber.

They had returned from their meal with the duke and his mother half an hour earlier. Cait had instantly retired to her sleeping chamber. While he prepared a new report to be couriered to the Citadel, Fallon heard the sounds of the lady's maid helping Cait undress and bathe. As he listened with half an ear, he knew how important that simple service was for Cait. By pampering her, the duke showed her that the life she had known was an aberration. It also helped instill in Cait a little sense of self-worth. Besides, the realities of the situation being what they were, Fallon did not dare perform the duties Dyara did. To do so would be to plant the seed in Cait's mind that he was simply another version of Giaros, his only goal that of putting her at her ease before he started making demands.

When the door to the sleeping chamber opened, Fallon looked up in surprise. Dyara had bade him good night a few minutes earlier, assuring him that Cait had retired for the night. The sight of Cait, dark hair hanging loosely, a rich green robe wrapped tightly around her, brought Fallon to his feet. He recognized the uncertainty in her eyes, the touch of fear. Worried she had had a nightmare, he moved to stand close, but not too close, to her.

Without a word, Cait took one hesitant step toward him. Not quite knowing what to do, he reached for her hand and gently led her to the chairs in front of the fire. He watched closely as she sat and carefully tucked her robe around her legs. For several long moments, she said nothing. Instead, she simply stared at her hands where they lay in her lap, clasped so tightly her knuckles shone white.

"What's wrong, Cait?" he asked, unable to bear the silence any longer.

"Fallon, what's going to happen to me?"

The look she turned to him broke his heart. So much despair and fear in someone so young. Worse, he could understand it and that fed the anger he had held under such tight control since first seeing the slave bands the day before. He breathed deeply and then exhaled before answering. The last thing she needed was his anger. No, he needed to give careful thought to his answer, just as he had to take careful note of her reaction to it.

"Cait, I can't even begin to imagine all you must be feeling right now," he began, leaning forward, elbows on knees. "And I know you have absolutely no reason to trust me. By the gods, after all you have been through, you have more than just cause to distrust everyone!"

His anger broke through and he clinched his jaw, cutting off the rest of the tirade he knew would follow. But, surprisingly, the girl did not flinch away from it. Instead, she seemed to relax just a little. The stiffness of her shoulders eased and she leaned back in her chair. As she did, Fallon suddenly understood. She needed to see that he was furious about what had happened to her. He had not helped by refusing to let her see the depths of his anger. But it was that anger that told her he was not like the others in this duchy. He would not turn a blind eye to what had happened and he would not abandon her to those same blind eyes after the tavern master's punishment was announced.

"Cait." He let the ripple of anger run through his voice but controlled it so it did not control his tongue. "I meant every word I said to you. If you want, you will accompany me when I leave here. Truth be told, I want you to. I don't want to think about leaving you here where you have known so much pain. I want to show you that most people aren't like the ones here.

"But understand this. These people aren't intrinsically bad. They are, however, so deeply private that they will not act or interfere unless forced to. They convinced themselves that they weren't seeing what was right before their eyes. For that, I will never be able to forgive them. But I can't condemn them either, no matter how much I want to. That said, I can and will make sure the Order's leadership knows what has happened so we can have a larger presence here to make sure it never happens again."

As he spoke, he reached for her hand and gently, lightly gave it one quick squeeze. Then he released it, not wanting her to draw any impression from that simple action except the one it was meant to be, an expression of reassurance. Even as he did, he wished one of the women of the Order had accompanied him. If one had, the situation would be easier for both of them.

"If I had my way, we would leave tomorrow," he continued. "But we have to remain until Giaros' punishment is announced. To be honest, we will have to stay until that punishment is administered. I want to make sure he gets what he deserves. Also, Kirris will want to know what the duke did so he can report to the High King."

"If I go with you, what will I do?"

There. The fear was back in full force. Cursing himself for not dealing with it first, Fallon rubbed a hand over his face. He was not used to dealing with scared young women. Give him a sword or bow and he was perfectly at home. Right now he felt out of his depth. But he had no choice. He was the only knight in residence so he had to muddle along the best he could.

"Whatever you wish," he answered simply. "Cait, if you choose to go with me to the Citadel, you will have a whole new world open to you. You can petition for admission to the Citadel to train as a member of the Order. You can also petition for admission to any of the collegiums nearby. If that does not suit you, you can go into a trade or travel. It is entirely up to you.

"You are free. No one has the right to tell you how to live your life. The only rules you must obey are those laid out in the Codes."

Fallon fell silent and sat back, waiting. Cait's eyes had closed but there was an expression of concentration on her face. He hoped she was thinking about what he said. Not just thinking about it but doing her best to accept it. Most of all, he hoped she understood that he wanted nothing from her except for her to choose not to remain in Lineaus.

"All right," she said finally, voice soft but firm. "I don't think I could stay here. I know I don't want to."

"Of course not." He smiled in approval. "Now, you've had a very eventful couple of days. Why don't you try to get some sleep?"

"I can't." Her frustration rang clear. "Every time I close my eyes, I'm back at the tavern with *him*."

"Will you let me show you something that might help?"

Even as he made the offer, he all but held his breath. If she agreed, he would attempt to teach her how to center and then clear her mind so nothing could intrude to disturb her. He doubted she would be able to master the technique without a great deal of practice. After all, it was not as easy as it sounded. Besides, she had so much battering at her mentally, it would be very difficult for her to let down her defenses as she would need to in order to center. But it would be a start.

"What?" Suspicion tinged her voice.

"One of the first things we are taught when we go to the Citadel is how to clear our minds and center ourselves. It helps keep the negative thoughts and emotions from intruding. That is what you need tonight. If I don't miss my guess, telling the council what Giaros and the others did to you made it all real again."

She nodded in response.

"Then will you let me help you?"

After the briefest of pauses, she nodded. Relief flooded through him because this was her first real act of trust. It was an important hurdle she just cleared. Not daring to waste a moment for fear she would change her mind Fallon pushed himself to his feet and reached down. He waited patiently until she placed her hand in his. With a smile of encouragement, he helped her to her feet. Then he led her back into her sleeping chamber.

"If at any point, you start to feel uncomfortable, I want you to tell me. I will never force you to do anything you don't want to do," he continued, stopping just inside the room.

"All right. What do you want me to do?"

"You need to get comfortable. You can sit or stretch out. I'd recommend sitting."

She nodded and padded across the room. Fallon watched as she settled onto the floor in front of the open window, her legs folded beneath her. Her hands rested on her knees, palms up, fingers relaxed. Fallon felt his eyes widen as she did. Of course, it could simply be coincidence that she had settled into the position most members of the Order preferred when meditating. It was just one more bit of information to store away for future consideration.

For the next half hour, Fallon took her through the beginning exercises of ground and center. Sitting across from her, he extended his senses so he could *feel* how she did. Once she settled some, not yet finding her center but definitely closer to it than she had been, he started her on the mind clearing exercises. Almost instantly, the tension fled from her expression and she sighed softly. Satisfied, not wanting to push her too much that night, he gently touched her right hand.

"Enough. To bed now," he said softly and she nodded slightly.

With an ease that had him wishing he was her age once again, she fluidly got to her feet. Fallon followed, watching closely as she slipped out of her robe, revealing a thin sleeping shift. A moment later, she slid between the sheets. Almost instantly, even before she could thank him or say good night, sleep descended upon her. More than a little pleased, Fallon blew out the single candle on the table beside her bed and left the room, closing the door behind him.

That had been little more than an hour earlier. Now he needed to perform the same exercises he had shown Cait so he could sleep. Otherwise, all the questions, all the concerns he had about her would keep him awake the rest of the night.

CHAPTER SEVEN

"HE'S HERE."

Cait looked up at the sound of Fallon's voice and her heart beat a little faster. She did not need to ask who *he* was. For two days they had waited for Commander Darrias or one of his men to come with word that the Duke's Council had finally come to a decision about the tavernmaster. For two days there had been nothing. In an attempt to fill the time, Fallon had escorted her about New Grange. He had made sure she was outfitted with what she would need when they were finally able to leave this accursed town. Travel clothes, heavy boots, supplies and even a mount were found. Throughout it all, Cait had been all too aware of the way people looked at her, about the whispers they thought she would not hear. Too many blamed her for what happened, for bringing shame on their city and on the duke.

Anger bubbled at the memory and she fought it down. Part of her understood their reactions. It was much easier to blame her, the outsider, for what happened than it was to admit they had refused to see what was happening under their own noses. Knowing it did not make it hurt any less, however. So she longed for the moment when she could finally leave this godsforsaken place.

After that first day, she had asked Fallon if they could stay in their rooms. She had seen the concern in his eyes but he asked no questions. Instead, he asked if she would like to continue the studies they had started that first night. She had accepted quickly, glad to have something to keep her occupied. Her time with Giaros had taught her the need to keep busy. Bad things happened when she wasn't. Even though she knew it would not be that way with Fallon, it would take time to unlearn the habits she had used to save herself at least a little pain.

It helped but not enough. Not when, with each passing day, her doubt and fear grew. Surely the duke and his council had seen and heard more than enough to convince them of the tavernmaster's guilt. Or were they like the townspeople? Would they blame her for what happened and, if they did, would they try to force her to remain? The very thought of possibly having to return to the tavern and the nightmares it held had her thinking of death. That long sleep would be far preferable to being under Giaros' hand once again.

Now, finally, they had word. She only hoped it was word she could live with.

Cait nodded and carefully climbed to her feet. Fallon waited as she crossed the room to join her. Then, as she stepped into the sitting room, he closed the door behind her before leading her to one of the chairs in front of the fire. Then he moved to admit Darrias, at least that is who she assumed had come, into the suite.

Commander Darrias thanked Fallon and then stepped smartly into the room. When he braced to attention and inclined his head respectfully in her direction, Cait nodded in return. She felt foolish doing so. Who was she to be treated so grandly by the commander of the guard? She had even asked Fallon that the night before. He had smiled and said not to worry about it. Darrias was doing only what he should, nothing more.

"Sir Fallon, Mistress Cait, it is my duty to inform you that the duke and his council have come to a decision regarding the tavernmaster, Dante Giaros." He paused and his eyes shone with satisfaction. That had to be a good sign, didn't it?

"And?" Fallon prompted as he moved to stand next to Cait's chair. His hand closed over her shoulder and she reached up to grasp it. She needed that connection, and the reassurance it offered, as they waited to hear what the commander had to say.

"He has been adjudged guilty of all charges levied against him."

Relief washed over Cait. Tears ran down her cheeks unchecked. Finally. They duke and his council had heard what happened and had believed her. That was all that mattered. All the rest of it could be put behind her. It would take time but at least she would not be returned to the tavernmaster. For that, she could be thankful.

"His punishment?" She barely dared ask the question that meant almost as much to her as had Fallon's earlier inquiry.

"Will be announced formally by the duke and his council come morning. Your presence is requested." The commander paused again and this time uncertainty flashed across his expression before he had himself under control once again. "Our laws require you to witness his punishment. I wish it weren't so. You have suffered more than enough because of that *man*—" He spat out the word.—"but it is our way."

Cait swallowed hard and nodded. Much as she hated to admit it, she knew she needed to see it as well. That would be the only way she truly believed Giaros had been made to pay for what he had done to her.

"With your permission, I will send escorts half an hour after sunrise."

"Thank you, Commander."

Cait watched as Fallon escorted him to the door. So many emotions filled her: anger, expectation, relief, fear. She clung to the knowledge that it would all soon be over. But would it? Giaros might be punished but would she ever be able to get past all he had done to her?

She did not know who she was or where she was from. She had no family, no connections and no friends. No, that was not quite right. She had Fallon. He might not be a friend – yet – and he certainly was not family but he was the closest she had. He had done what no other had for her and she could trust him. She knew that as surely as she knew she could not, would not ever return to Giaros, no matter what the circumstances.

"Thank you." She reached up and wiped away the tears running down her cheeks. She hoped he understood all she wanted to say but could not, not yet at any rate. Her emotions were still too raw and there were still too many things that could go wrong.

"For what?"

"For everything. For making sure I never have to return to the tavern again."

"Cait, you did it," he assured her as he led her back to her chair. "Your strength in standing up and telling what Giaros did to you is what convinced the duke and his council of the man's guilt."

"But it started with you, Fallon. You saw what was happening and you refused to let it continue. You helped me when no one else had. For that, I thank you. It is something I will never forget."

"You should thank the gods for bringing me here." *As should I.* "Now, it is late and we will need to be up early come morning. You should try to sleep."

With a nod, she climbed to her feet. Before disappearing inside her sleeping chamber, she turned and thanked him once more. Then the door shut behind her, leaving him to his thoughts.

Cait woke early the next morning, well before the dawn sun crested the horizon. She lay still, assessing how she felt. It was still difficult to believe she lay on a real bed with a clean sheet and woolen blanket covering her. Better yet, the pain she had lived with most days was less than the day before. It was amazing how quickly the body could heal when it wasn't being subjected to almost constant beatings – or worse. It was almost enough to let her finally accept that she would never have to return to the tavern cellar with its thin pad and threadbare blanket.

Pushing aside such thoughts, she tossed back the covers and climbed to her feet. She padded almost silently to the bathing room. When she returned a few minutes later, she wore a pair of loosely woven trousers and a loose shirt. Clearing her mind as Fallon had taught her, she turned her attention to her body. With several days of enforced rest, most of her injuries had healed to the point where she could do some light exercising. That brought a smile to her lips and she began a routine Fallon had showed her, one designed to warm up her muscles so she could then begin stretching.

That was how Dyara found her half an hour later as she all but silently entered the room. Seeing the petite blonde, Cait limberly climbed to her feet, pushing her sweaty hair back from her face. Almost instantly, Dyara was at her side, extending a small hand towel so Cait could mop her face.

"You must be feeling better, m'lady," the blonde commented in approval.

"I am, thanks to your care for me, Dyara."

"It has been my pleasure to be of assistance. Now, if you have finished, let me draw your bath. While it heats, I shall give you a massage."

"Dyara, you really don't have to. I can certainly take care of my own bath." Didn't Dyara realize how uncomfortable it made her to be waited on?

"M'lady, I have heard of the evidence against Giaros, of what he did to you," the lady's maid began hesitantly as she escorted Cait into the bathing room. "I pray that you know what was done to you violates all we hold dear."

"I realize that, Dyara. But that doesn't mean you have to wait on me. After all, I am no lady, far from it in fact."

"I know not of your background, Mistress Cait, but your manner is not that of a commoner." As she spoke, she helped Cait undress, dropping the sweaty clothes into the woven basket by the door. "Beyond that, the duke has instructed us to treat you as we would any member of his household. It is but one way to attempt to make amends for all the tavern master did to you. Even without my lord Duke's order, I would treat you as such and it is my honor to do whatever you wish of me."

Realizing she had no say in the matter, Cait merely nodded and once more turned herself over to the blonde's care. As she did, she tried to relax, to put out of her mind for at least the next few minutes what the day would bring. The rhythmic pressure of Dyara's hands as they worked the knots from her back and shoulders only served to underscore her own nervousness. No matter how hard she tried, she simply could not forget that in a very short time she would once more have to stand before Giaros as she waited to hear the council's decision.

Later, dressed in a pair of soft leather trousers tanned a blue so deep they were almost black, soft white blouse and matching leather vest that tied up the side, Cait left the sleeping chamber. In her left hand, she carried her belt and dagger. Her hair was once more pulled back in an intricate braid, the end tied with a leather thong. A twist of leather thongs dyed the same color as her trousers and vest had been tied across her brow to hold back any hair that might escape the braid. Breathing deeply, she stepped into the outer room and nodded in greeting to Fallon and Longbow.

"How do you feel, child?" Longbow asked as she took her seat at the table.

"Much better, sir," she answered honestly, smiling at Fallon in appreciation as he handed her a mug of hot tea.

"Did you sleep all right?" Fallon wanted to know, watching closely as he waited for her response.

"I did," she assured him. The last thing she wanted was for him to worry. "I do have some questions though."

"Of course. What are they?"

"What will happen today? I understand that the duke and his council have reached their decision and will be announcing it. But what else?"

"If all goes as it has in the past, the punishment will be carried out immediately after it is announced. The duke, as his father before him, does not believe in delaying such things," Longbow said. "I assume it will be the same today and that is why we are to gather in the courtyard instead of the council chambers."

With a nod, Cait turned her attention to the food before her. She quickly chose a selection of fresh fruit, bread and meat. For the next few minutes, she savored every bite and helped herself to more. No longer did she feel hungry all the time. Better, she knew she did not have to leave the table unsatisfied. But she did not gorge, understanding that would simply make her ill.

How different her life had become in a matter of just a few days. It still seemed more like a dream than anything else. If her ribs did not grab at her painfully from time to time or her cheek ache where Giaros had struck her, she might be tempted to believe it was a dream from which she would soon wake. But it wasn't. She kept telling herself that, as if it were a mantra.

This was her new life, her new reality.

But for how long?

Half an hour later, the three left the suite. The moment they stepped into the corridor four members of Commander Darrias' troop fell into place around them. Wordlessly, they made their way through the corridors of the keep in the direction of the courtyard. Suddenly nervous, Cait could not focus on the beauty of the keep and its furnishings. Her entire being focused on what was about to happen, knowing her future very well might depend upon it.

As she stepped outside, Cait blinked in surprise. The sun shone brightly, not a cloud in the sky to diffuse the light. But that was not what brought her up short. It was the sight of the large crowd already gathered to hear the council's pronouncement. An almost hysterical urge to laugh bubbled up inside her at the sound of the vendors moving through the crowd, hawking food and drink just as if this was a gather day instead of a day of judgment.

Tearing her eyes away from the crowd, Cait scanned the courtyard. At the far end was a large raised platform. A series of wooden steps climbed to the platform. In the center stood a wooden frame at least six feet tall. Nearby was a large tub of hot coals and a number of tools, the use of which Cait did not want to consider. The possible explanations turned her stomach.

Before she could turn to Fallon, could say she wanted to go back inside, be anywhere but there, their escort led them to the front of the crowd. Then, as if knowing how she felt, Fallon slipped an arm about her shoulders and bent his head. His soft reassurances braced her. She had nothing to worry about. No one in the crowd could hurt her.

Suddenly, a single trumpet call sounded and the crowd fell silent. A few moments later, the duke and his council appeared from the keep. As they made their way toward the platform, Duke Tomas signaled for the prisoner to be brought out. The time had finally come to pronounce sentence and see it carried out.

A short time later, six burly, heavily muscled troopers escorted Giaros toward the platform. The tavern master's hands and feet were chained. The defiance he had shown during his trial had been replaced by a fear so strong Cait could almost smell it. Now he knew how she had felt for so long and part of her relished the knowledge of it.

As they neared the platform, Giaros's struggles increased. His boots dug into the ground and he tried to break free from the troopers holding him. The six all but carried him up the steps, ignoring his curses and pleas for mercy. Then, as they held him on his feet, Cait felt a tinge of pity for the man as his eyes all but rolled in terror.

"Dante Giaros," Duke Tomas began as he climbed the steps leading up the platform. As he did, he nodded once and the troopers forced the tavernmaster to his knees. "You have been charged with assault on Master Longbow and Mistress Cait, failure to provide common courtesy to Master Longbow as decreed by my royal father before me and then by myself, and, most heinous of all, of multiple charges of rape and slavery. The Duke's Council has heard the evidence in this matter and has decided in a unanimous verdict as required by the Codes that you are guilty of all charges."

"NO!" the tavern master screamed, struggling desperately to gain his feet. Commander Darrias quickly crossed to him and roughly cuffed him across the head, silencing him.

"Commander Darrias, if he speaks again, gag him," the duke ordered and a ripple of approval ran through the crowd.

"With pleasure, m'lord."

"It is also the decision of the council and one with which I completely agree that the tavern master's punishment will be handed down immediately," the duke continued. "The Codes require that we give you one last chance to give evidence that might mitigate your punishment. So, Dante Giaros, will you name the slaver who furnished you with your victim?"

"I cannot," the man whispered, head bowed.

"Then I have no choice but to pronounce sentence." The duke paused, as if to give the man one last chance to reconsider. When Giaros said nothing, he shook his head, a look of infinite weariness touching his eyes.

"Let it be known from this day forward that the name Dante Giaros has been stricken from our rolls. This man has no name and no place within our society. Never again is his name to be spoken. He is shunned, removed from all but judicial records and all his possessions and holdings made forfeit. This is the first judgment against him.

"For his refusal to grant common courtesy to Master Longbow in accordance with ducal decree the unnamed one shall receive ten lashes.

"For the assaults, he shall receive twenty lashes each.

"For committing one of the most heinous crimes one can commit against another, the prisoner shall be the same as it would be for anyone to so abuse a woman within the borders of this realm. He shall be castrated just as a farmer castrates a randy bull.

"The most serious of his crimes, that of slavery, has but one punishment and it shall be the last to be carried out. The prisoner shall be executed by my hand. Let this be a reminder that such actions shall never be tolerated in this realm or any other realm of the Imperium. May the gods have mercy on his soul."

Listening as the duke detailed the tavern master's punishment, Cait breathed deeply, not sure she really believed it. The sentence was harsh, much more so than she had expected. Even though she had known Giaros faced death, she had not truly thought to see it handed down. But what surprised her the most was the pity she felt for him. Bad as he had treated her, she did not want to see him suffer nor did she want to be responsible for his death.

"Are you all right?" Fallon asked softly as he bent so his head was even with hers.

"Aye. It's just hard."

"It is but it is necessary. None of what happens next is your fault. He brought it all on himself, even his death. He could have avoided it had he simply named the one who sold you to him."

The next hour was one of the longest Cait has ever known. The moment the duke stepped off the platform, Darrias motioned to his men. They forced Giaros to his feet and dragged him to the wooden frame. His chains were released and he was secured to the wooden framework, legs spread, arms extended their full length over his head. Before he could protest, Darrias grabbed a handful of hair and forced the tavernmaster's head back. Giaros opened his mouth in a gasp of pain and a thick leather pad was forced between his teeth. A wide leather thong was then wrapped about his head twice before being tightly tied behind the man's head, trapping the pad in his mouth. Now his cries and curses were muffled and he was prevented from choking on his own tongue.

With that done, Darrias pulled his dagger and quickly cut away the prisoner's clothing. Once Giaros stood naked before the crowd, Darrias stepped back and nodded to a dark clad man. The master of the whip stepped forward and unfurled a nasty looking whip. The tavern master's cry of pain as the first lash landed was greeted by a cheer from many of those gathered. The cheer repeated with each successive lash, turning to the count.

Once the fifty lashes had been delivered, the master of the lash turned and carefully rolled up the whip. Then he bowed to the duke and his council before stepping back. His part was done.

Commander Darrias stepped forward then. He stopped in front of the prisoner. One gloved hand reached out and grabbed the tavernmaster by the hair. Cait's stomach roiled dangerously as Darrias stared at the sweat streaked face, his other hand lightly slapping the man's cheek to bring him back to consciousness. Finally, after what seemed like an eternity, Giaros moaned softly and blinked up at the commander with eyes Cait doubted really saw anyone or anything.

"It's almost over, Cait," Fallon soothed, his arm holding her close. "Can you make it?"

"I have to."

She moved slightly so she could see what was happening without moving away from Fallon. She needed his support just then. This was so much worse than she expected. So much worse than anything she had ever wanted. There had to be a justice to it but just then she did not see it. All she saw was torture, a torture that did nothing to make up to her for all she had endured.

As Artil climbed to the platform, the crowd erupted with calls for him to do more than just castrate the prisoner. Even so, most of them did turn away when Giaros screamed through his gag as the physician castrated him. Then it was over and Giaros hung limply. From where she stood, Cait could not tell if the man had lost consciousness or if he had died. Either would have been a blessing as far as she was concerned.

"Cut him down and prepare him," Duke Tomas ordered grimly as he once more climbed onto the platform.

Cait watched, unable to turn away, as Commander Darrias

moved to where the duke stood. Darrias dropped to one knee in front of the duke, a sword extended before him. The duke's gloved hand wrapped around the hilt of the sword and a moment later he held it aloft. Unlike the blades Cait had seen Fallon and others carry, this one had no point. Runes had been etched into the blade and they all but danced in the morning sun. As the duke lowered the blade, a cleric stepped forward and began softly chanting.

Heart pounding, breaths shallow and fast, Cait waited. The duke moved to where the tavernmaster knelt in front of the block. His hands had been bound behind him. His eyes were wild as he looked around. Was he hoping someone would come to his aid?

Gods above and below, why couldn't they get on with it? This was nothing but torture for all concerned.

"You have one chance to save yourself," the duke said. "Will you name the one you bought Mistress Cait from?"

Pale from fear and the loss of blood, Giaros shook his head. Cait swallowed hard. Who or what could scare him so badly that he would not grab at this chance to save himself?

Did she really want to know?

At the duke's signal, two guardsmen forced Giaros down. While one held him, another quickly bound him to the block. As they did, the cleric's recitations grew louder. A hush fell over the crowd as the duke took his stance. As he lifted the blade, Cait looked away. She would not watch as the man's life was ended.

"The laws of this duchy and of the Imperium shall be obeyed," the duke said as he turned back to the crowd a moment later.

Cait swallowed against the bile in her throat at the sight of the blood pooling around the block. As she did, she prayed she could soon return to their rooms. She wasn't sure how much more she could take.

"Commander Darrias, remove this carrion. His head is to be displayed on the main trade road with a copy of his crimes and sentence. Let all know what awaits them should they try to follow in this piece of filth's footsteps."

"Aye, m'lord Duke."

Darrias instantly motioned for two of his troopers to step forward. They grabbed Giaros' body by the ankles and dragged it to the edge of the platform. An ox-drawn cart waited there. Without a word, they rolled the body into the back of the cart. One of them jumped to the ground and tossed a tarp over the body. A moment later, Darrias handed down a bloodstained bag. Cait didn't need anyone to tell her it contained the tavernmaster's head.

"The council came to several other decisions after hearing the evidence against the unnamed one," the duke continued as the troopers carried out his orders. Cait struggled to focus on what he said. "Master Longbow, to make amends for all you suffered at the hands of the nameless one, the Black Duck Tavern is now yours as are all the possessions and holdings associated with it.

"As for you, Mistress Cait, we can never adequately make up to you for all your suffering. However, to make an attempt, you shall receive all other monies held by the unnamed one that are not associated with the tavern. You shall also receive all clothing and other items you need. They are my household's payment to you for failing you. You are free to remain here or to go with Sir Fallon. The choice is yours."

"Thank you, my lord," she replied softly.

"Sir Fallon, has the council fulfilled its duties to your satisfaction?"

"It has, my lord," he replied. "Now, with your permission, I would like to escort Mistress Cait back to her rooms to rest.

This has been very difficult for her."

"Of course, Sir Knight."

"Come, let's get you away from here", he urged.

More than willing to do just that, Cait turned and started back toward the keep. She wanted, -- no, she needed – time to think about all she had seen and how she felt about it.

CHAPTER EIGHT

CAIT SLOWLY WALKED DOWN THE CORRIDOR TOWARD THE SUITE she shared with Fallon. As she did, she sighed heavily. Almost a week had passed since they had witnessed Giaros' execution. Despite the fact both she and Fallon had wanted to leave the next morning, they had been unable to. The duke, shaken by the discovery of what Giaros had done to Cait and wanting to make sure there were no others like the tavernmaster in the capital, had asked them to stay. Fallon had agreed even though Cait knew he hadn't wanted to. When she had asked about it, he explained that Lineaus had long spurned the help of the Order. If he could use what happened to give his people a foothold here, he had to try. If he were successful, it would not only benefit the Order but the Imperium as well.

Not that it made the waiting any easier on her. She had learned those two days while they waited for the duke and his council to hand down their verdict on Giaros that spending time in town was not something she felt comfortable doing. She did not want to think about the whispers she might hear now, after the man had been put to death. It didn't matter that his crimes had more than merited such a harsh penalty. He had been one of them, someone they had known for years. It was only natural there would be some who would resent what happened.

So, while Fallon met with the duke and his advisors, she wandered the keep and its grounds. One thing she learned, and something that had brought her some pleasure, was that she could read. It was difficult at first, almost as if she had to retrain her mind to do something it knew but had forgotten. Now if she could only do the same where her memory was concerned . . . .

Stop it!

She knew better than to wish for something that might never happen. She and Fallon had talked about it quite a bit over the last few days. It was possible her memory might one day return but there were no guarantees. So, to keep from obsessing on *what ifs*, she had decided to look forward. There was a whole world out there she knew nothing about. It was time to see some of it and decide what she wanted to do now that she was free.

Free!

She smiled slightly at the thought. Even now, knowing Giaros could no longer hurt her, it was hard to accept that she could do what she wanted when she wanted. Fallon had stopped her on more than one occasion when she fell back into the habits Giaros had engrained in her. The first time she tried to wait to eat until after Fallon had, the knight had prepared a plate for her himself. Then, when she would have cleared away their dishes later, he stopped her and reminded her that was no longer her duty. Seeing how it had upset him when she reverted to old behaviors, she did her best not to do so again.

Maybe by the time she returned to their suite, Fallon could tell her when they would finally be able to leave this place.

As she neared the suite, Cait heard voices. She slowed her pace and focused on the sounds of at least two men speaking. A slight smile touched her lips to recognize Fallon's voice. A moment later, she realized the second speaker was Duke Tomas. The fact they were using the suite to discuss their business surprised her. Always before, they had met in the duke's office. It must have been something they did not want others overhearing that caused them to move this particular meeting. Not wanting to interrupt, she looked around, gnawing her lower lip uncertainly. Then, remembering the small alcove just down the corridor, she smiled and made her way there.

Fluidly, gracefully, she folded her legs under her and sank to the floor. Once settled, she closed her eyes and cleared her mind in the first step toward finding her center. Fallon had been working with her daily on the exercises and she finally felt like she had almost accomplished the task. Perhaps this time she would.

Once her mind was cleared of all concerns, she turned her consciousness inward. The first step was to relax, to let the tension flow from her body like water. She visualized it doing just that, even *seeing* it as it flowed from her body into the air around her. With that done, she continued her inward trek, letting her consciousness flow on its own toward her center.

With an almost audible *crack* Cait felt her energies suddenly come together, to center. In her mind's eye, she saw that energy center flowing from her into the earth. As it did, she felt as if she had been moving at a tilt that was suddenly corrected. She felt grounded, whole for the first time. Wrapping the strength of that feeling around her, she turned her thoughts to the questions Fallon had put to her just that morning, questions she had been asking herself.

No longer did she dwell on the past. Instead, she turned her thoughts to the future, a future she had some control over. She simply had to decide what she wanted. Where did she want to go and what did she want to do? To the best of her knowledge, she had no special skills. There was no way to tell what kind of training, if any, she had received prior to losing her memory. All she knew was that she had the desire to learn all she could, to see as much as she could to help fill the void left by the loss of her memory.

So deep was her meditation that she was unaware of Fallon's presence until he dropped to his knees in front of her and cleared his throat. Slowly, she drew her consciousness back from center and opened her eyes. Seeing the man, she smiled slightly. Her smile broadened as she recognized his look of approval. He might not realize she had finally found her center but he did know she had been meditating. Then she took his hand and let him draw her to her feet.

"You could have come inside," he commented as he poured her a mug of watered wine a few moments later.

"I heard you speaking with the duke and didn't want to interrupt," she explained.

"I do appreciate it," he admitted. "We were concluding an agreement to bring more of the Order's members here. The duke has agreed to let us build a compound outside the capital so we can train those who wish to join our number as well as to allow our clerics to lead the religious ceremonies. Young as he is, the duke recognizes the growing unrest spreading throughout the land and the need to be prepared for trouble."

"I don't understand." She folded her legs under her as she settled on one of the chairs, her mug in one hand.

"Evil is always present, Cait, always looking for a way to rear its ugly head and cause trouble. There are times when it is more prevalent than others. For a number of years, the worst trouble the Imperium has faced has been the bands of raiders and brigands coming out of the Wastelands. Now the evil of those following Balaar is growing and it is the task of my Order and the other orders bound to the service of the Lord and Lady to see to it that they don't win.

"What happened to you is an example of how bad things are becoming. For generations, since joining the Imperium, slavery has been outlawed here. It has been outlawed even longer in the rest of the Imperium. That one of our people could so easily throw off that injunction and enslave you proves that the evil one is at work.

"Something else that worries me is the length of time Giaros was allowed to get away with all he did to you. Those living here have grown complacent. They feel that they are perfectly safe and no real harm, the sort of harm the followers of Balaar bring, can reach them. Because of this, their obedience to many of the Codes has lapsed. It isn't through anything the young duke has done. Unfortunately, the trouble began with his father and his father before him. At least Duke Tomas recognizes the problem and knows the duchy needs to return to the ways of the Lord and Lady."

As she listened, Cait nodded thoughtfully. What he said made sense. People who thought they were invulnerable don't feel the need to follow the old ways. So, when things did happen, they tended to turn a blind eye, convincing themselves that there was no problem. That explained why they had seen how Giaros treated her, had seen the results of all those beatings but did not recognize what it meant. They hadn't wanted to because that would mean admitting something terrible was happening right in front of them and they would have to act.

But there was more. When Fallon mentioned the Lord and Lady, a spark seemed to warm her. A sense of familiarity filled her. It went beyond the fact that he had spoken of the gods before. No, this time it felt real, personal. Without conscious thought, her right hand reached up and she touched forehead, lips and chest with her thumb, that fist closed.

"Cait, why did you do that?" Fallon asked and she thought she heard surprise, maybe even hope in his voice. Cait swallowed hard doing her best not to react to the question, not to let her own hope grow. After all, it had been a simple movement, nothing to get excited about.

119

"I don't know." Voice soft, she closed her eyes. She let her mind flow but no answer came. Again. And Fallon still waited for an answer. "When you mentioned the Lord and Lady, it seemed right. I *felt* something. I'm not sure what. Then, before I knew what I was doing, I made the sign. Does it mean something?"

"It does." He leaned forward and poured himself another mug of tea before continuing. "It's a sign of devotion made by the members of the Order. I'm beginning to think you received instruction from one of our members at some point and that you looked to the Lord and Lady for protection."

"It feels right." Even if it had done little good. "Does that mean I'm like you?"

"Not that you are a sworn member of the Order. You're too young and we would know if one of our own had gone missing. What it could mean is that you trained with one of us in preparation to taking your vows. But that still doesn't explain why we weren't aware that you were missing. There are other explanations. It is possible you took your religious training at one of our compounds." He sipped and she guessed he needed a moment to think. She certainly did. So many possible explanations and still no answers. "I just don't know," he said finally.

That was the problem. No one seemed to know. Only Giaros had any answers and he had refused to give them. Why? After all he had done to her, caused to be done to her, hadn't he owed her at least something of an explanation?

Frustration burning a hole in her stomach, Cait climbed to her feet. She could feel Fallon's eyes on her as she moved to stare out one of the windows. For all she owed him, for all she was beginning to trust him, she simply could not tell him how she felt. She was unsure she actually understand her emotions yet. All she knew was that she could not remain in Lineaus.

She had to leave and something, some sense, told her she had to do so soon.

"Fallon, how much longer until we can leave here?" she asked, her back to the man. She looked out the window, hoping he would not guess how much she still feared the possibility he might leave her there. It was a foolish fear but that did not make it any less real.

"Just another few days. I'll have finished with the duke by then and our supplies will be ready."

There was a pause and she heard him climb to his feet. A soft tread warned her that he neared. The old fear rose up for a moment only to be forced down. Fallon would not hurt her. She knew that. So there was no need to tense every time he approached.

"Where will we go?"

"I have to finish my mission, Cait. That means we will be on the road for a while before I can take you to the Citadel." He paused, one hand resting reassuringly on her shoulder. She reached up and gave it a light pat before letting her arm drop. "And, I will keep the promise I made to you earlier. If we come across some place where you want to stay, as long as I am convinced they will care for you, I will see you well settled. However, I'll be honest, I want you at the Citadel."

There was a note in his voice, an earnestness that caused her to turn. Seeing the determination in his eyes, she nodded slightly. She did not understand why it was so important to him that she go to the home of the Order. Perhaps this was the time to ask.

"What would I do there?"

Damn but the fear was back. She heard it in her voice and knew, from the way Fallon tried to hold back a flinch, he did as well. She hadn't meant it to sound as if she expected them to put her in *service*. She didn't. But that was how it sounded.

Would she ever get past the feelings of betrayal and suspicion that filled her?

Stop it! Give yourself time. Time to adjust and time to learn.

"Cait." His voice turned gentle once again. His eyes filled with compassion. "You won't be forced to do anything you don't want to do. If you want to study our ways and join the Order, you will be allowed to stand as a Candidate. If that doesn't suit you, you can find a place to apprentice, to learn a trade. Or you can study at one of the other collegiums. The only requirement you will find placed upon you is that you do something to earn your way, whether in the trades or as a Candidate.

"There's another reason I want you to come with me. We have some of the best Healers in the Imperium. I want them to see you because I'm hoping they can help you recover your memory. Then we can find out exactly what happened to you, perhaps even reunite you with your family."

As appealing as that sounded, as often as she had dreamed of just that, she shook her head. If she had a family out there somewhere, would they not be searching for her? What if they were the ones who had sold her to the slaver? No. She couldn't accept that. She wouldn't. So that left only one other explanation. Her family was dead.

She breathed deeply and blew it out in a gust. Best not to dwell on that. No. Think instead about the future. That was the important thing now.

"Cait, I know you're scared and more than a little suspicious. You should be." She looked at him in surprise. She should be? "Anyone would be after going through all you have. All I can say is that I will die before I let anything else happen to you."

He spoke so earnestly that a new fear filled her. He really

would die to protect her. Why? She was nothing, meant nothing. Why would he be willing to give his life to protect her?

"Child, I want you to sit down and listen to me," he said as he once more led her to her chair before the hearth. He took a moment to stir the embers before tossing another log onto the fire. Then he knelt on one knee and took one of her work hardened hands in his equally callused hands. "Cait, as a knight of Arelion, I am sworn to protect the peoples of the Imperium. That is one reason why I will do everything I can to help you.

"But it goes beyond that. I haven't told you the entire story behind why I happened to have been in the Black Duck the other day."

The entire story? A flash of alarm filled her. Mouth tight, she fought it down. She owed it to Fallon to listen to him without letting emotion cloud her mind. She owed him that and so much more.

"You know I am on a mission for Kirris, Knight-Commandant of the Order." Even though it really wasn't a question, she nodded in affirmation. "Nothing in my mission parameters had me coming to the capital, much less to the tavern. In fact, I had been doing all I could to keep my presence, if not a secret, at least not well known. Then, as I neared the area where the trade road splits, I *knew* I had to follow the fork coming here. Something was wrong and I had to forego my mission until I discovered what it was and did all I could to correct the situation.

"That same feeling that brought me to the capital led me to the tavern and you." Now he smiled slightly, giving her hand a quick pat. "Cait, I'm convinced the gods brought me here because of you. The moment you were no longer held by Giaros, that driving feeling eased. But it hasn't left, not completely. Clearly, the Lord and Lady have a plan for you and part of that involves getting you to the Citadel."

"But how can you be sure?"

"I believe we've both seen glimpses of it this last week. A perfect example is what just happened. The way you made the sign of devotion. I haven't taught it to you and I know you didn't see it from anyone in this duchy. Besides, you said it *felt* right."

"But what does it mean?"

And why does it scare me so?

"I don't know. All I can say is that it appears that They have plans for you. Also, I think it means we had best continue your lessons. Something tells me we don't have any time to waste."

"When do we begin?"

Excitement replaced the residual fear and resentment. To be able to learn something, anything new had been her dream for as long as she remembered. So much had been denied her. Now Fallon offered her the world. Besides, by working with him she might just remember something. Even if she did not, she would at least be doing something to help her make her way in the world so she would never have to use her body to survive.

"As soon as you've eaten." He smiled in approval and she felt herself all but beam in response.

Pushing out of the chair, she all but danced to the table. Fallon chuckled lowly as she reached for a plate and began spearing fresh fruit. Feeling freer, lighter than ever before, she laughed and tossed him an apple. If she had to eat, so did he.

Three days later, Cait sat astride a magnificent black gelding, waiting with barely contained excitement for Fallon to finish checking their packs. The gelding and the beautifully crafted tack had been provided by the duke from his personal stables. The monies awarded her were carefully tucked away in her saddlebags with the exception of the little she carried in her belt pouch. Then Fallon mounted and she laughed gaily, excited they were finally about to be on their way.

"Ready, Cait?" he asked with an understanding smile.

"Aye." Her voice rang with anticipation.

"Then let's ride."

Laughing gaily, she put heels to the gelding and cantered after the Knight down the street toward the town gates. She breathed deeply, glad this chapter of her life had finally come to an end. No matter what the future held for her, it could only be better than what she had known.

More important, she was free.

FREE!

CHAPTER NINE

CAIT WOKE SUDDENLY, COMING FULLY AWAKE IN IN AN INSTANT. Every nerve seemed to be alive, on fire. Something was wrong. She knew it just as surely as she knew she lay on the hard ground, her head pillowed against her saddle as it had been each of the last four nights on the trail. But something was different this time. She simply did not know what.

Swallowing hard, she forced herself to lie still. All those months with Giaros had taught her how to hide the fact she had awakened. Alarm, persistent and nagging, slowly coalesced into caution. Eyes closed, she listened, ears straining as she searched for some clue as to what had awakened her.

She heard nothing, not a cricket singing nor the muffled scrabbling of the small animals inhabiting the forest. Silence was not, in this situation, their friend. It meant something had upset the normal nocturnal routine. But what? More importantly, what should she do?

Slowly, carefully, she opened her eyes just a crack. Darkness, relieved only by the light from the fire, cloaked the area where they camped. At the edge of the clearing, their horses were picketed. Slowly, carefully, Cait continued her study of the area, not daring to open her eyes more than she had. Nor did she dare lift her head.

Only shadows dancing at the edge of the firelight greeted her. Not reassured, she turned her attention to Fallon. He slept barely more than an arm's reach away. Whatever had awakened her had not yet disturbed him. That bothered her. It bothered her almost as much as the fact she *knew* something was wrong.

Slowly, oh so slowly, she eased her left hand toward her saddle. She had no intention of facing what had awakened her unarmed. Giaros had taught her that as well. She would no longer be a victim, not if she had a choice. Her fingers closed about the hilt of her dagger and she instantly felt better, not so helpless. Now, to wake Fallon without being too obvious about it.

Just as slowly as before, she reached across the dirt to where the man lay. Her touch was gentle, the pressure of her fingers just enough to rouse the knight and warn him not to make any sudden moves. Because he lay facing her, she saw his eyes flicker open. They quickly surveyed the immediate area before fastening on hers. Relieved she was no longer the only one awake, she silently mouthed one word – *trouble*. He nodded slightly, his right hand creeping to where his sword rested between them.

Suddenly, a blood-curdling shout shattered the silence. Fallon's hand closed about the hilt of his sword and he surged to his feet. As he did, other cries of anger and of challenge sounded from the trees to their right. Fear choked Cait, almost paralyzing her, and she desperately wanted to be anywhere but there.

The shadows darkened and then coalesced into the forms of three men, their faces gaunt masks of hatred. Cait watched as they moved closer. Fallon, sword at the ready, stood between her and their attackers. But he was only one against three. What chance did he have with those odds?

She couldn't lay there, cowering under her blanket as Fallon fought. She couldn't.

She wouldn't.

Not daring to consider what she was about to do, Cait

tossed the blanket aside and climbed to her feet. She held her dagger in her left hand, ready to meet any challenge that came her way. Her heart pounded and she struggled to fill her lungs as she watched and waited.

Lord and Lady, protect us!

For several moments, or maybe even a lifetime, Cait stared at their attackers in fear. Could they be the spirits of men long dead? Then, as they neared, she almost laughed in relief. No spirits these. They were men, just men. Men who looked as if it had been a long time since their last decent meal. Their clothes were of tattered homespun material. Only one held a sword and it, like them, looked as if it had seen better days. As for the other two, one carried a pike while the other wielded a heavy axe. Hatred, cold and hard, made masks of their faces and Cait knew in that moment they meant to see both she and Fallon dead.

"Get out of here, Cait!" Fallon yelled, his sword swinging up to meet the first of the attackers to reach him.

At the sound of his voice, she instantly turned. Her feet, bare save for the heavy woolen socks she wore, raced almost silently across the grass. A moment later, she slid to a halt a few feet from where their horses were tethered. Her gelding strained against the tether holding him firmly to the picket line Fallon had set up when they made camp a lifetime ago. Eyes reeled and he reared, kicking out at imaginary enemies. Fallon's chestnut mare stood still, huffing slightly but doing nothing to try to break away.

What should she do? She couldn't leave Fallon to face the three. She wouldn't, not after all he had done for her. But what could she do to help? She didn't know how to fight. Even if she did, her dagger offered little help. She needed a sword.

A sword!

Before they had left New Grange, Fallon had taken great

pains to go over all their supplies with her. When she had asked why, he explained that he wanted her to know everything they had on hand. He did not anticipate trouble but, should it come, he wanted her to be prepared. So he made sure she knew what foodstuffs, medicines and even weapons would be close to hand. She had thought him overly cautious but now she thanked his foresight, especially since it meant she knew about the extra blade he kept wrapped in a blanket secured to the back of his saddle. Determination warring with fear, Cait turned back to the clearing. There, just a few yards away, lay the blanket and saddle. Inside would be the blade. If she could just reach it.

With Fallon doing his best not to become boxed in by his three opponents, Cait once more raced across the clearing. This time, as she neared the fighting, she dropped to her knees and slid to a halt next to Fallon's saddle. Her hands frantically clawed at the blanket roll, struggling to undo the leather straps holding it tight. Nearly sobbing in frustration, she fought the buckles. Then, as one of the men turned and saw her, she unfurled the blanket. She grabbed the leather wrapped hilt of the sword and pulled it free from the worn scabbard protecting it.

Something – instinct, long forgotten training or instruction from the gods – took over. Cait pivoted to her right. Her left arm raised, lifting the sword into a defensive position over that shoulder. Just in time. The attacker's axe met the sword and traveled down the length of the blade. As it did, Cait slid further to the right, doing her best to ignore not only the jarring pain from the impact but also the knowledge of the damage the axe could do should it make contact with any part of her body.

As the sounds of fighting filled the clearing, something seemed to awaken deep within Cait. A feeling of knowledge, of familiarity settled upon her. She *knew* what to do with the sword, how to use it. She didn't take time to think about it. She didn't dare. Instead, she opened her mind, trusting the gods not to betray her, and concentrated on the man before her. She knew her life depended on not letting any doubt creep in to distract her.

The silence of the night was torn by the sounds of the battle. Cries of pain mixed with curses and threats. Metal striking metal rang sweet and sure. The smells of blood and sweat filled the air. Cait did not dare think about the predators it would call to. Instead, she held the slim, slightly curved blade in her left hand, the dagger in her right as she prayed for the strength to finish the fight.

Then, suddenly, she saw the opening she had been looking for. Her opponent raised his axe high. From the angle of his body, she had no doubt he meant to bring it down across her exposed right shoulder. Good. Very good. That left his mid-section vulnerable. All she had to do was keep her calm and stay focused. That was all.

Praying for the strength to do what was necessary, Cait shifted slightly to her right. As she did, she dipped the tip of her blade toward the ground. Her eyes stayed locked on his. She knew, somehow she *knew*, they would betray his next move. So she focused on the madness in them, ignoring the *squish* of blood and more through her socks. It was best not to think about that. She had to focus on her opponent. Nothing else mattered.

There! That slight tightening around his eyes. *Move!*

Twisting her hands skyward, leading with the hilt of the sword, Cait swung upward. The tearing of cloth preceded the tearing of flesh as the blade traveled from hip to opposite shoulder. Stunned, the man dropped his axe and stumbled back two steps. His hands clutched at his abdomen as if by doing so he could hold back the blood and more.

Pressing her advantage, Cait followed as he took another step back. Anger, stronger than any she had felt before, filled her as this man and his companions merged in her mind with Giaros. Her lips pulled back and she bared her teeth. He looked at her, fear in his eyes. She twisted her hands again and swung the sword down. It caught him between chin and shoulder. His cry of pain turned into a whimper as blood poured from the wound, a fountain of dark red in the firelight. Eyes wide, he dropped to his knees. She spared him one last look as the life fled from him and he pitched face first onto the dirt.

Wiping the blood from her eyes, Cait turned to where Fallon still battled the remaining two bandits. Her feet flew across the clearing, sword trailing from her left hand. Then, with a war cry to rival any ever uttered, she ducked her right shoulder and barreled into the sword-wielding attacker, catching him mid-body.

With a muffled curse, the man went down, Cait on top of him. As they grappled in the dirt, Cait dropped her sword. It offered little help in a wrestling match where there was no room to swing or block. But her dagger was something else. Just as she had known how to use the sword, she knew the dagger would be a much more effective weapon in a close-quarter fight.

As they scrabbled on the ground, Cait felt the heavy blows of attacker's sword hilt landing against shoulder and side. Sharp pain radiated from her left thigh, tearing a gasp from her lips. Then, somehow, she managed to bring one knee up between them. With a grunt of effort, she shoved the man off. Instantly, she scrambled after him, dagger poised to strike.

Cursing, the man tried to climb to his knees but Cait was too fast. She struck out with her left hand, catching him across the jaw with the hilt of her dagger. Stunned, he fell back. Before he could recover, she was on him. Without a second thought, she drove the blade deep into his chest. Muscles straining, she fell on top of him, shoving, until the blade would go no further.

Blood welled around the blade, spilling over her hands. She didn't care. She couldn't. Not yet. Not as long as danger still existed for her or for Fallon.

Leaving the dagger buried deep in the man's chest, she climbed to her feed and looked wildly around for her discarded sword. As she did, she saw Fallon duck under the pike. The knight's sword glinted in the firelight as it swung up, blocking the pike before he twisted and pulled his blade across the man's abdomen. Before the bandit could even register he had been injured, Fallon drove his own dagger into the man's chest, killing him.

It was over.

Finally.

Cait dropped to her knees, gasping for breath. Then she shook her head in disbelief. She had thought she'd be safe once they left New Grange. Everything Fallon had told her led her to believe it. Then this happened. Why? Why had the men attacked them and why had she been forced to kill?

The memory of what she had done, the smell of the blood – and worse – spilling onto the dirt and grass returned. As it did, her stomach rolled. Bile filled her mouth and she crawled away to be ill. Nothing she had done, nothing she had experienced had prepared her for the events of the last few minutes.

As she retched, tears burned her eyes and streamed down her face. Later, Cait realized someone was gently wiping her face with a damp piece of cloth. Not that she cared. All she wanted was to forget what she had done, to get the stench of death off of her.

"Cait?" Fallon sounded worried. "Are you all right? Did they hurt you?"

All right? She would never again be all right. But then, had she ever been? The irony of it all brought an almost hysterical laugh burbling up from deep inside her. She clamped her jaw on it, nodding instead, not trusting herself to speak for fear she might vomit again.

"W-who were they?" she asked finally, running the back of her hand across her mouth, grateful she could not see what covered it.

"I don't know – yet." With gentle hands he helped her to her feet. Then, as he looked at her, he frowned. Worried, she looked down. For the first time since the end of the fight, aches and pains seemed to radiate from almost every inch of her body. The worst were at her shoulder and thigh. Maybe the blood staining her clothes didn't all belong to her opponents.

Not wanting to think about it, knowing if she did she might once again lose control, Cait limped across the clearing to where the discarded sword lay in the grass. She bent and retrieved it. As if of their own accord, her hands wiped the blood and dirt from it using a corner of her tunic. Once done, she turned to look for her dagger, quickly averting her eyes away from the sight of it sticking out of the man's chest. Nice as the blade was, she could not bring herself to remove it.

Before she could say anything, Fallon stepped past her. With his body between her and the fallen bandit, she waited. When he straightened a moment later, he presented her with the dagger, thankfully free of blood and gore. She took it without a word and slid it into the sheath on her belt. Then she extended the sword to him.

"Keep it, child. You earned it this night." He crossed to his saddle and bent. When he returned a moment later, he handed her the scabbard that had protected the blade and guided her hands as she sheathed the blade.

"Fallon, why? Why did they attack us?" She hated the quiver of fear in her voice. She hated it because she knew he heard it and she did not want him thinking any less of her.

As important as that question happened to be, another bothered her more. Even so, she refused to voice it. How could she when she feared what the answer might be? So it weighed on her, forcing her to admit its existence, at least to herself.

How had she known to fight like that?

It went beyond simply picking up the sword and getting lucky. Before they left New Grange, she had watched Fallon sparring with Commander Darrias. She had watched closely as Fallon and Commander Darrias worked against one another using practice blades. There had been a grace, deadly though it was, as they sparred.

Thinking back on the fight, she knew she had not matched them when it came to skill but she had wielded the blade as if she knew how to use it. The feel of the sword in her hand had been familiar, almost natural. Had she been trained to fight before waking in the slaver's tent or had it been a gift from the Lord and Lady? Not that it mattered. All that did was that she and Fallon still lived.

Could that have been another flash of memory, so quick she couldn't fully grasp it? If so, could it help shed light on who and what she was?

Not that it helped her cope with what she had done. The taking of a life, even the life of someone determined to take her own, rocked her to her very soul. She desperately wished it had not been necessary. But it had been and now she had to find a way to live with it.

The only question was how?

"Cait, you did what you needed to do to save yourself and

to save me," Fallon said gently, as if reading her thoughts. "You can't blame yourself for actions those fools brought on themselves."

"I'll try." She didn't know how, not when the bodies rested a few feet away and the smell of death hung heavy in the air. "What now?"

"We dress our wounds, check the bodies to see if they carry anything to explain who and what they were. Then we ride. I have no desire to wait around to see if they have friends in the area."

Cait sighed in relief. The last thing she wanted was to stay there. Then, before she could do anything else, he slid an arm about her waist and carefully helped her to a soft spot of grass well away from the bodies. As she settled onto the turf, tears sprang to her eyes and she momentarily returned to the hell she had known with Giaros. Then Fallon softly assured her he would be right back. The concern, the care in his voice forced the nightmare down once more.

A few minutes later, she sat silently as Fallon treated her injuries. Relief filled her to know most of the blood that covered her clothes had not been hers. Even so, her arms were marked with already forming bruises and numerous small cuts. But those were nothing compared to the long, deep gash running down her left thigh.

"As soon as I have bound this up, change into clean clothes. I'll take care of the bodies while you do," he said, sprinkling some sort of powder onto the gash. She flinched in pain, hissing as the powder burned for a moment. Then the wound seemed to grow cold and the pain subsided.

"What about you?" She grabbed his hand, preventing him from getting to his feet. "I need to see to your wounds."

"And you shall. But let me do this first."

She nodded and lay back. The soft grass cushioned her.

The night breeze felt cool on her bare skin. Trying to clear her mind so she would not think about the events of the last half hour, she listened as Fallon worked, his voice lulling her into, if not sleep, at least rest.

For the moment at least, she could let him care for her, confident he would let nothing else happen.

Fury coursed through him, overriding the fear. Those fools! He should have known better than to have enlisted their kind for this mission. But what choice had he had? That thrice-damned knight had upset all his carefully laid plans in New Grange, no thanks to that fool Giaros. His master had warned him about using the tavernmaster. He should have listened.

Just as he should have listened to his own concerns about *this*.

Teeth bared in an animalistic snarl, he watched as the knight knelt next to one of the fallen before carefully searching him. As the man put something to one side, he thought hard. Had he given the three anything that could lead back to him or, more importantly, to his master? No. There had been nothing but the passing of a few coin with the promise of more to come.

The only good thing to come from this was the fact that none of the three had survived the attack. But that was little solace when he thought of what his master would do once he learned of this latest failure. Perhaps it was time to go to ground himself, at least until his master's anger had time to cool.

If he should live that long. Those who failed the master tended to have very short lifespans.

No, he needed a plan, a new plan, one that would satisfy both his master's need for a victim and would keep him alive. Then, watching as the knight moved to the next body, an idea formed. Perhaps there was a way to not only placate the master but to also keep his own skin intact.

He stepped back into the deepest shadows and reached for the pouch on his belt, His fingers found the soft fur and the familiar tingling filled him. Then the pain came, muscles twisting, bones contorting. It would be easier to keep watch on the knight and the girl as a wolf than as a man. Once they were well away, he would return and set the stage to save his own skin.

Or so he hoped.

As the sun crept over the distant horizon, limestone walls of a fortified compound came into view. Fog swirled in the morning breeze, distorting the compound's immediate surroundings and cloaking them in an eerie mist. Fallon held up one clenched fist and Cait reined to a halt at his side. She waited silently as he studied the area. After the attack two days earlier, she knew he looked for any sign of trouble. After all, the last thing either of them needed or wanted was to run blindly into something they might not be able to handle, injured and exhausted as they were.

Astride the gelding, her injured leg throbbing painfully, Cait studied the compound. Limestone walls showed signs of age but looked strong enough to withstand almost any attack. Watch towers were situated at set intervals around the walls, allowing the compound's inhabitants to see anyone or anything nearing, no matter from what direction. In the center of the near wall stood a wide gate, the road leading directly to it. Was this their destination?

Please let that be their destination.

Apparently satisfied with what he saw, Fallon softly told Cait they could proceed. He nudged his mare forward and she matched the pace. It was a slow, easy pace that could not be taken as anything untoward. Even so, when a horn blew in the distance, Cait swallowed hard. She'd had more than enough surprises to last the next few years. She did not want any more.

As they neared the gate, several people appeared. They were dressed in light blue leather trousers and matching tunics. On their right shoulders were white and yellow knots. Before she could ask, Fallon softly explained the young men were journeymen for the Order, on duty to challenge anyone seeking entrance to the compound.

"You travel early, Sir Knight," one of the journeymen, the elder of the two, commented as the riders halted before them.

"Our business requires it," Fallon replied simply. "Is your Knight-Commander in residence?"

"He is. Shall I send word of your arrival?"

"Please. Tell him we need a few minutes of his time as soon as possible."

"I'll notify him at once," the second journeyman said before hurrying off in the direction of the largest of the four buildings Cait could see.

"If you will come with me, I'll escort you to the Knight-Commander's office. The yeomen at the stables will care for your mounts," the first journeyman continued as he motioned to several nearby youth. Almost instantly, two of them broke off from their companions and hurried to take the newcomers' mounts.

Fallon dismounted and then turned to help Cait from the saddle. She softly thanked him, carefully putting weight on her injured leg. Her breath hissed but she waved off his assistance. It was not that bad. She'd just been in the saddle too long, or so she told herself. So, limping heavily beside Fallon, she followed the journeyman across the courtyard toward what she guessed was the administration building. As they did, the youngsters led their mounts in the direction of the stables.

"Sir Knight, I am Aarom, first year journeyman. Welcome to Deneram Grove, third dedicated compound of the Order of Arelion," the young man said as they walked. "Once I have escorted you to the Knight-Commander's office, I will see to food for you and your companion."

"We appreciate it, Journeyman Aarom." He motioned for Cait to stay close. "If you have a Healer or physician assigned here, their services would be appreciated at well. We had an encounter with some bandits during the night and need to have our injuries seen to."

"Of course, Sir Knight. I will see to it as soon as I've delivered you to the Knight-Commander's office."

As they walked, Cait wondered what to expect. So far, nothing about the compound struck a familiar cord. She had no idea who or what this Knight-Commander was or what he would be like. She dearly hoped he was like Fallon. She wasn't sure she could deal with any more surprises, good or bad.

Tension knotted her stomach as they entered the building. So much had happened over such a short period of time. All she knew for certain was that she desperately wanted to sleep for a week so her body could heal and, hopefully, her mind could make some sense out of what had happened.

A few moments later, the journeyman opened a door at the far end of the first floor, revealing a large office beyond. He motioned them inside and then moved to stoke the coals in the fireplace across the room. Once done, he excused himself and left the office, closing the door behind him.

Cait slowly limped across the room to stand before the fire. As she warmed her hands, she looked around. This was a working office, from the battered desk covered with books and stacks of paper to the weapons on the wall and the armor stand in the far corner. Then she caught sight of herself in the mirror over the fireplace. Pain and exhaustion etched deep lines from the bridge of her nose to the corners of her mouth. Pain also dulled her eyes. How either of them had managed to keep going without rest was almost more than she could fathom.

"Cait, sit. You need to get off that injured leg of yours." Fallon pushed a chair toward her, nodding for her to do as he said.

"I am tired." She hated admitting it, especially when she could see his exhaustion in the droop of his shoulders and the shadows under his eyes.

"Of course you are. These last few weeks have been anything but restful."

"To say the least." She managed a soft laugh as she carefully lowered herself onto the chair and stretched her legs out before her. It felt good to be off her horse.

"I promise you'll be able to get some rest just as soon as we've seen the Knight-Commander."

She hoped so but she couldn't keep her doubts at bay. Everything about her life was different from what she had known. She wanted to trust Fallon, to believe him when he said the other members of the Order were like him, but it was hard when all she had known were the likes of Giaros and those in New Grange who had turned a blind eye to her suffering.

Stop it!

She did her best to push aside the doubts before Fallon realized what she was thinking. As she did, she reminded herself that most anything would be better than the life she had known. If she discovered he had lied, she would leave. It was as simple as that.

Or so she hoped.

At the sound of the door opening, Fallon turned. A smile

touched his lips to see the tall, slender man who entered. More than five years had passed since he had last seen the man who had once been his tacticsmaster. There was a bit more gray in Bentallo Asvalor's dark hair than before but the spark in his grey eyes was still clear and the feeling of power strong. Seeing Cait's head jerk up, her eyes wide in surprise, Fallon nodded slightly. Her reaction surprised him but not all that much. He already knew Cait was sensitive to such things. That had been one of the main reasons she had been able to trust him as quickly as she had. She might not realize it yet, but she recognized the *touch* of the gods and responded to it. That was just one more bit of information to file away for future reference.

"This is an unexpected surprise, Fallon. What brings you here?" the Knight-Commander asked as he pulled up a chair to join them. "And do you need a Healer? You both look as if you've seen some trouble." Concern now colored his voice and his expression darkened.

"We have seen trouble, Bentallo. Around midnight, three bandits tried to overrun our camp," Fallon confirmed. "But, before we tell you about it, let me introduce you to my companion. This is Cait. I'm escorting her to the Citadel.

"Cait, this is Knight-Commander Bentallo Asvalor. He's an old and dear friend as well as one of my favorite instructors when I was still a journeyman."

"I'm honored to meet you, Knight-Commander," she replied and struggled to her feet. A gasp of pain was torn from her as she placed weight on her injured leg and she fought to keep her balance.

"Sit, child. Sit." The Knight-Commander moved quickly to help her back onto her chair. "And call me Bentallo. I'm not much for ceremony as Fallon can tell you."

"Thank you." She smiled slightly, not sure what else to say.

"Now, tell me what I can do for the two of you, Fallon."

"First, you can do just as you offered. Let us avail ourselves of your Healer. Thanks to the Lord and Lady, Cait woke and realized there was trouble before the bandits attacked. She killed two of them in the fight."

"Where did this occur?" The Knight-Commander's voice was sharp with concern.

"In the glen near the river southwest of Jiharna. We were overnighting there before continuing on our way here."

"Do you believe the attack had anything to do with why you delayed completing your current assignment?"

"I don't know."

Not that he didn't have his suspicions. It wasn't unheard of for bandits to attack travelers but those three had been anything but normal bandits. He knew it. He could not prove it, however. Nor did he want to go into it in front of Cait. She had been through enough already. There was no need to add to her worry.

"We can discuss it later," Bentallo said as a light knock sounded at the office door. "Enter."

The door swung open and two women stepped inside. The first was a tall blonde with piercing blue eyes the color of the noon sky. Like the Knight-Commander, she wore sky blue trousers and tunic. The waist of her tunic had been rubbed to a sheen where a wide belt usually rested. Her right hand stayed close to her side, ready to draw her sword even though she did not currently wear one.

The second woman looked to be well into her middle years. Her gray slacks were slightly faded and her white tunic wrinkled. Graying hair was pulled back and tied with a leather thong. Exhaustion clouded her green eyes as she looked at Bentallo in open question.

"You sent for us?" the blonde asked as she stepped further

into the room.

"I did, Sharra," Bentallo replied. "I believe you know Fallon. His companion is Cait. They were set upon during the night by three bandits. I want you to lead a troop out to the clearing near the river southwest of Jiharna. See what you find. Report back to me as soon as possible."

"Understood. If we find signs of other such scum in the area?" She arched one delicate eyebrow in question.

"Deal with them. They can't be allowed to continue terrorizing the countryside."

"I'll leave right away," she said and quickly left the room. As she closed the door behind her, they could hear her calling out to someone.

"Sharra is my aide and will see to it that the area is secured from the likes of those who attacked you," Bentallo assured his guests. "Now, this is Meron. She's our resident Healer. Meron, Cait needs your attention right away. She was injured in the fight and then they rode straight through to reach the safety of the compound."

"I understand, Knight-Commander. What rooms have you assigned them?" Even as she spoke, she dropped to one knee before Cait and quickly studied her, a frown playing at the corners of her mouth.

"The guest quarters near my rooms. I've already instructed Aarom to see to their outfitting."

"Very good." She stood and extended a hand to Cait. "Come along, Cait."

For a moment, Cait hesitated. Fallon smiled in reassurance. She studied him for a moment and then nodded. Without a word, she followed the Healer out of the office.

"Now, old friend, tell me what is so important about that youngster that you are willing to risk the rather fierce anger of our commander by not completing your mission," Bentallo said seriously once they were alone.

"It's a long and complicated tale." He sighed wearily and accepted a mug of hot tea from his companion.

"I have the time, Fallon."

"You've read my reports?"

Bentallo nodded.

"Then you already know most of it." Fallon sipped his tea, wondering what to say next. "Bento, I can't explain it in any other way than to say the Lord and Lady led me to her. I have no doubt she would not have survived much longer, just as I have no doubt there are forces at work I don't understand, at least not yet."

He knew the Lord and Lady had plans for Cait. Any doubts he might have had disappeared when Bentallo entered the office. Fallon had seen the man's reaction when he first felt Cait's power, a power that almost always existed only in those already sworn to the service of the gods. More importantly, it was rare to find it in someone so young.

"I have several suggestions for you, my friend," Bentallo said as he got to his feet and began to pace restlessly. "Stay here while Cait recovers from her injuries. In the meantime, I will send word to Kirris confirming my support for the decision you have made so far. I will also say that I've ordered the two of you, after conferring with our Healer, to remain at the compound until your injuries are healed."

"Thank you."

"All I ask in return is that you look into what has been going on here. Although you already have a very good idea of what we've been dealing with after what happened to you at that clearing.

"For my part, I will see to it that Cait receives as much training with both weapons and hand-to-hand combat as we can give her. I'll also make sure she is outfitted with a decent sword and some armor. The armory should have something it can fit to her without delaying your departure any longer than necessary."

"I appreciate it, Bento. I knew we could count on you."

"It's my pleasure, old friend." He paused as Fallon yawned broadly. "Now, let me show you to your room. As soon as she finishes with Cait, Meron will see to your injuries. Then I want you to sleep yourself out. When you wake, you can give me a formal report I can forward to Kirris."

Fallon nodded. Bed suddenly sounded very good.

CHAPTER TEN

THE NEXT MONTH WAS ONE OF THE BUSIEST AND MOST FULFILLING Cait had ever known. She found herself working as hard, if not harder, than she ever had when she had been with Giaros. But it was different, so wonderfully different. Unlike when she had been forced to submit to the man's every depraved wish, she now worked for something she wanted and she reveled in it. For the first time in the only life she had known, she was doing something for herself.

"I thought I might find you here, Cait."

Hearing the healer's voice, Cait turned and smiled. The first day she had been allowed to leave her rooms, Meron had brought her to the meditation garden. The healer had suggested the peace and beauty of the garden might help settle her mind. Then she had taken time to reinforce Fallon's lessons. Now it was almost a ritual for Meron to join her there before the morning meal. They would talk and meditate and Cait found herself looking forward to those times.

"How do you feel?" Meron looked at her closely and Cait had a feeling she saw more than just the physical when she did.

"A little sore from yesterday's workout." The memory of sparring with Lady Sharra returned and, along with it, the aches and pains from finding herself thrown on her backside more than once.

"From what the good Sharra said when I saw her, you more than held your own."

"I don't know about that." Cait shrugged even as a spark of

pride filled her.

"Come, let's walk."

Meron linked arms with Cait and they slowly walked off. This, too, was part of their morning routine. Unless Meron surprised her this day, the healer would lead her deeper into the garden, to parts where few ever came. Cait liked that part of the garden the best. The plantings there had been allowed to grow wild, no careful pruning to keep them in check. The isolation, combined with the naturalness of the area, had been a balm to Cait's soul and she often found herself there when she was not scheduled for lessons or time with either Meron or the Knight-Commander.

"Something bothers you this morning, Cait," Meron commented a few minutes later. "What?"

"Nothing, really."

How could she tell the healer she was worried she had done something to anger or upset Fallon? More than a week had passed since she last saw the knight. In that time, no one had said anything to explain his continued absence. His only message to her had been a note left after their last meeting. He had business to perform for the Knight-Commander that would keep him busy for a while. If she needed anything, she was to let either Bentallo or Meron know.

"Cait?" There was no censure in Meron's voice, only concern.

"Have I done something to upset Fallon?"

The question was out before she knew it and she silently cursed. Then, to her surprise, Meron reached out and pulled her close. For a moment, she stiffened, memories of Giaros rushing over her. Breathing deeply, she forced herself to relax. Meron wasn't Giaros. She was far from it. Her embrace was meant to comfort, not cause pain. She had to remember that.

"Dear heart, you have done nothing wrong. I swear to

you." Meron stepped back, a reassuring expression on her face. "Fallon is out with some of Sharra's troop. They are looking for where the bandits who attacked you came from. They are also making sure there are no others like them in the area."

Relief filled Cait. She should have known. Fallon had told her he would be carrying out different assignments while they stayed at the compound. It was his duty as a member of the Order to offer whatever support and service he could to the Knight-Commander. She had to remember that, just as she had to remember that the man could not spend every day looking after her. He couldn't nor did she want him to, not if it meant ignoring his duty.

But that brought another concern to mind. Meron and the others had done so much for her. They had healed her wounds and had taught her so much in such a short period of time. They did their best to prove that life did not have to be like she had known with Giaros. For that and for so much more, she owed them more than just her thanks.

"Meron, how can I ever repay you and the others here?"

"Cait, you owe us nothing and we ask no service of you," Meron assured her as they turned to leave the garden. "In fact, unless I have misjudged the time, you are due for another lesson with Lady Sharra. I don't think you want to be late for that, do you?"

"Not at all." Excitement coursed through her at the thought of another lesson with the knight.

"Then you had best get changed. That good lady doesn't like to be kept waiting."

Grinning, Cait hurried across the compound. The sooner she changed, the sooner she could see what new – and more than likely painful – lesson Lady Sharra had in store for her.

Fallon carefully considered how best to make his latest report to Bentallo, knowing the Knight-Commander would forward it to the Citadel. There was trouble in the area. He had known that even before the bandits attacked him and Cait. But now, after weeks of scouting the area, finding not only more bandits but, all too often, the results of their work, he knew the trouble ran deeper than he thought.

Sitting there, he thought back to the bandit his squad had captured earlier that week. Like the three who had attacked him and Cait, the man had seen better days. It hadn't taken long to discover he was one of those Bentallo referred to as the disenfranchised, those who had come to the area looking for an easy life. Often they came from the south, fleeing the raids coming out of the Wastelands. Most of those coming north were willing to work to build a new life. But there were always a few who would rather take from those willing to work than to do the work themselves.

There had been something different about this bandit. Fallon had yet to put his finger on it but his actions went beyond looking for easy coin. Bandit yes, but more.

Fallon stood and moved to stare out the window. Below him, members of the Order hurried about their business. He saw them but paid them little attention. Instead, he thought about what he had found at a campsite not long before they captured the bandit.

The fire had gone cold not too many hours before Fallon and the others came upon the camp. Three bodies, two male and one female, lay nearby. They had been slaughtered. There was no other way to describe it. From the packed dirt nearby, Fallon guessed a wagon and at least one ox had been driven off. But what bothered him was the lack of footprints by any but the three who had been killed.

Jaw tight, anger and worry rising, he returned to the desk

and his report. There were several explanations, at least a few of them reasonable. But he knew why there were no other prints. Not that it made him feel any better. If he were right, there could be no doubt Balaar's followers had a stronger foothold in the area than he feared.

A knock at the door sounded and he looked up. Frustrated because he had let the time get away from him, he slipped his report into the single drawer in the desk and locked it. Best not to leave it out where prying eyes might see. He trusted Bentallo and the Knight-Commander's staff but there were others in the compound he did not know. He didn't think any of Balaar's followers would be able to infiltrate the compound without someone realizing it but he was not going to run any risks.

A moment later, he opened the door and smiled to see Cait standing before him. He could not deny the change in her the last month had wrought. Eating not only well but regularly had put some much needed weight on her. Working with the knights had toned her muscles. But it was the confidence reflected in her expression that reassured him the most.

Then, to his surprise, she reached out and hugged him. It was a bit hesitant, at least until he returned it, but it was more than he had dared hope for. After all she had been through at Giaros' hands, the fact she could initiate physical contact with another person, especially a male, spoke volumes about her emotional strength.

"I missed you," she said shyly as he stepped into the hallway, closing the door behind him.

"And I missed you," he assured her. "But it looks as if you have put your time to good use."

She grinned and quickly told him what she had been doing during his absence. But the time they reached Bentallo's rooms, she was asking how his latest scouting mission had gone.

"I'll be telling all of you soon enough, Cait," he said as Bentallo motioned them inside. Then he watched as Cait hurried to where Meron sat. A moment later, the young woman slid to sit on the floor at the healer's feet. Interesting and something he needed to ask about – when Cait was not around.

Also present was Sharra. The blonde looked as tired as he felt. Not surprising since she had been riding patrol as often as had he, as well as performing her other duties and training with Cait. At least with her there, they could compare notes and maybe start forming a plan of action that would let him leave with Cait for the Citadel sooner rather than later.

"Did you find anything of interest, Sharra?" Fallon asked as a yeoman poured wine for them before leaving the room, closing the door behind her.

"Nothing good, I'm afraid." She sounded grim as she reached for her wineglass. "Too many unsuspecting travelers have fallen victim to bandits like those who attacked the two of you. My squad came across one of their camps the other day. It's obvious from what we found that the bandits have been operating out of the hills for some time." She paused and took a long sip of her wine.

"But what really concerns me was the feeling of evil around the camp. It was so strong I could almost taste it. Our horses refused to go close to the main encampment. Believe me when I say there was no way we were going to spend the night there." Now she lifted her glass and drained the rest of her wine in a single gulp.

"When we returned the next morning, we searched the area and our worst fears were confirmed. We found a small altar dedicated to Balaar. We destroyed it and cleansed the area. Now we have to face the fact that the thrice-damned fools who attacked you and others like them have sworn their lives to evil. You're lucky to have survived."

Fallon nodded grimly, not liking what he heard. Unfortunately, Sharra said nothing he had not already suspected. Such evil as had been attacking this land had to come from Balaar or his minions. At least it did not appear to have taken deep root yet. That meant they might be able to turn it aside before much more damage occurred, assuming they acted quickly. But, to do so effectively, they had to find the root. Someone had to be behind the sudden influx of bandits. Their raids were too well-timed, usually hitting the merchant caravans loaded with the best goods and wealthiest passengers. The key was to discover the bandits' contact and deal with him, or her, once and for all.

From where she sat near the fireplace, her long legs stretched before her, Cait listened closely as Sharra and Fallon compared notes. As she did, she could feel the Knights' concern, even anger. This trouble with the bandits clearly worried them a great deal. She understood that. What she did not understand was how such trouble could have started in the first place. Surely the closeness of one of the Order's compounds would frighten the followers of Balaar. Or, if not frighten them, at least give them pause so they would not set up an operation so close. But they had. Why? And why were the people who lived in the area not supporting the Order and the compound better? Could they have lost their faith? That was the only explanation she could come up with and it bothered her as much as the news of the bandits seemed to bother the others.

"Unfortunately, we have our work cut out for us," Bentallo commented as if he had been reading Cait's thoughts. "Even though I have done my best to keep our teachings and ways alive in this region, as did my predecessor, the people became too confident over the years that they were safe and no longer had to depend upon the good will of the gods to protect them. Only a handful have remained true to the way of the Lord and Lady."

"Aye," Fallon said. "That is much the same as I saw in Lineaus."

"I don't understand," Cait said and then clamped her jaw shut. She couldn't believe she had said anything. Hopefully, Bentallo would understand she had not meant anything by interrupting him.

"Cait, never be afraid of asking a question." Bentallo smiled at her in reassurance. "And, to answer the question you didn't ask, greed and laziness are all the opening Balaar needs. He finds our baser desires and instincts and turns them into something that rots our very souls. If we don't remain ever vigilant, he worms his way in and then turns us into his servants and his slaves. I fear that is exactly what has happened here."

"Bento, it's not your fault that those outside the Order have lapsed," Sharra said firmly. Cait watched as she reached for the man's hand and pressed it to her lips. Obviously, the two shared more than just a professional relationship. For some reason, that comforted Cait. "You've done more than anyone could expect, Kirris included. When you first came here, there was but a mere handful of yeomen and journeymen. Now we sport a full complement. That is thanks to you and you alone."

"And to you, my dear," he commented with a smile. "But Sharra's right. When I first came, the Order's presence was minimal at best. At least I've managed to get the youngsters involved again."

"So much the better. It gives us a foothold," Fallon said. "Perhaps they can be our first line of attack by confronting their own families about what has been happening."

"But should that be risked before more is known about what's been happening and why?" Cait nervously chewed her lower lip, more than a little surprised she had dared voice an opinion. "From what I understand, those in the early stages of their training are especially susceptible to corruption by Balaar because they are still learning exactly what their special *talents* are and how to use them. They can be tricked into opening up to Balaar by false *talents*. Dare you risk them until you know where the danger really comes from?"

Bentallo looked at her in surprise before smiling ruefully. "Cait, you speak with more wisdom than the rest of us and you are right. We don't dare risk them until we know more."

"Fallon explained at least part of the mission he had been on when he found me and I know he has been sending reports here to be forwarded to the Citadel." She climbed to her feet and moved to the window across the room. As she stared outside, a sudden restlessness had fallen over her and she could not identify its source. All she knew was that she had something she was supposed to do. She just did not know what. "I also know he wants to leave soon to take me to the Citadel. Listening to what Lady Sharra had to say, I can't let him do that. He needs to stay here and do what he has to in order to help you."

"Cait," Fallon protested.

"No, my friend." Bentallo held up his right hand to keep Fallon from saying more. "Cait, under most circumstances I would agree with you. But not now. It is clear there are other forces at work here, forces focusing on you. I agree with Fallon that you must begin your studies immediately. That means getting you to the Citadel as soon as possible."

"But-" She couldn't let them do anything that would put the compound or the surrounding area in danger.

"Cait, I appreciate what you are trying to do. We all do," Bentallo said and the others nodded in agreement. "But we are agreed on this. As soon as Fallon and I feel he has gathered enough information to give Kirris a good idea about what is happening here and why, the two of you will be on your way. Until then, we will do what we can to help begin your education and answer your questions."

"Enough," Sharra said as a light knock sounded at the door, announcing the arrival of their dinner. "We can finish this later."

"Your thoughts?" Fallon asked as the door closed behind Cait.

They had finished dinner half an hour earlier. After spending time discussing what Cait had been doing during Fallon's absence, the young woman excused herself. It had been a long day and she was tired, not that she had fooled Fallon. He knew she needed time to think about all she had heard. Truth be told, so did he.

"If I hadn't seen it with my own eyes, I wouldn't have believed it," Sharra said with a shake of her head. "I had the drill master push her harder than before. She stayed up with him, even using some counter moves I can't master unless I'm fresh and she had been working out for hours."

"Your recommendation?" Bentallo wanted to know.

"As I said, I couldn't believe what I saw. So I took to the drill field and stood against her. We used steel instead of practice blades. I'm the best swordsman here save yourself, Bento, and she drew first blood in an accurate and extremely well controlled strike. If she hadn't been on the field for several hours while I was still fresh, I truly believe she might have bested me. As it was, we fought to a draw."

"What about her training?"

"The Citadel is the only place for her," she answered with a conviction that reassured Fallon. "Instinct tells her how to fight and pray. I have to believe someone in the Order, most likely someone from the knightly discipline judging by the way she fights, trained her. From what I've seen, they trained her so she would be prepared to join our ranks. I have no solid proof but I *know* it."

"I have to agree with you. I could *feel* her even before I entered my office the day you arrived, Fallon. She has a very definite aura of good and she has a power that could have come only from the gods. The Lord and Lady have plans for her and we are merely Their tools along the way."

"So we are all agreed?" Fallon waited until they nodded. "Just as soon as I can, I take Cait to the Citadel despite my instructions from Kirris."

"You have no other choice, my friend." Bentallo stood and moved to the window where Cait stood not too long before. "I'll send a message with you for our Knight-Commandant explaining that I am in full agreement with each action you have taken in this matter. That should be enough to keep him from landing on you with both boots for returning early."

"I appreciate it, Bento. But will Cait be ready by the end of the next fortnight?" He wanted to leave before the weather began turning.

"She's ready now," Sharra told him. "But the extra time will allow her more time to train and to become more familiar with our ways. Hopefully, it will awaken in her subconscious some more of our teachings. All of that will be for the better."

"Then so be it," Bentallo said before he refilled their wine glasses. "May the blessings of the Lady and the protection of the Lord be with us all."

Silently repeating the man's prayer, Fallon hoped the

upcoming journey was as uneventful as the one here had not been.

Standing before the window, Bentallo looked down at the main training arena. At his side stood Fallon. For almost ten minutes, they had closely watched the senior journeymen's afternoon workout. They were not the ones holding the men's attention, however. Their attention was focused on Cait.

Squaring off against her was Sharra. The knight appeared to be having a hard time holding off Cait's attack. The girl's blade moved surely, rapidly through the air as they fought. If one did not know better, it would be easy to assume Cait was a knight of long standing because of her prowess with her blade.

Bentallo shook his head in disbelief as Cait reached out and deftly flicked Sharra's blade from her hand with a single quick movement. Then he turned away from the window. Even though Fallon and Sharra had warned him, he had not truly taken their words to heart. But now, seeing Cait easily defeat one of the best knights he knew, he found his agreement with Fallon's course of action growing even stronger.

"So?" Fallon asked with a hint of a smile as he, too, moved away from the window.

"If I had any doubts before, I no longer do," the Knight-Commander said finally. "You must get her to the Citadel as soon as possible. In fact, if I did not need all my people here, I would send an escort with you. Nothing else can be allowed to happen to her until the will of the gods has been revealed."

"I'll make sure she gets there safely," Fallon assured him. "And the sooner we leave, the better to my way of thinking."

"Agreed. I'll see to it that everything is ready for you by first light. Make your best speed home, Fallon. Then send back word that you arrived safely. I shan't rest easily until I hear from you."

"I will," he promised. "If you will have your message for Kirris ready this evening, I won't have to disturb you when we're ready to ride out come morning."

"I'll will but I shall also be there to see you off."

Nodding, understanding Bentallo was as worried about Cait as was he, Fallon sighed softly. He would not feel safe until they were at the Citadel where no harm could befall the girl.

Only then could he allow himself to relax.

CHAPTER ELEVEN

AS THEY CRESTED THE HILL, CAIT ROSE TO HER FEET, LETTING HER legs take on her weight. With her thighs protesting the sudden change, she slowed the gelding to a walk. Then, as she lowered back into the saddle, she sighed softly, wearily. They had been riding since just after dawn, pausing only long enough to let their mounts rest and she was heartily tired of the saddle. Hopefully, Fallon would soon call a halt to their day's journey and she could stretch her legs.

Then, as if reading her mind - or at least hearing her sigh - Fallon signaled for her to stop. Relieved, she let the gelding slowly pace forward until it stood shoulder to shoulder with the man's mount. Then a gentle pull on the reins brought the horse to a halt. Hoping this meant they had reached the end of the day's journey, Cait turned in the saddle to face her companion, her friend

Friend.

She smiled slightly at the thought. That much was true. Over the last several months Fallon had become her friend just as he had been her mentor and protector. Every night on the trail, he had done his best to answer any and all questions she had. Then he would continue the lessons from the previous night. They talked about everything from etiquette to philosophy, history to politics. And now, as they neared the end of their journey, Cait was heartily glad for those nights. The knowledge, and the confidence it brought with it, helped keep her fear of failure at bay.

A light touch on her arm brought her attention back to the present. As she looked up at Fallon, he smiled. Then, without a word, he pointed toward the valley below. She followed his hand, her eyes going wide in excitement.

Below, in a vast expanse of greens and golds, stretched a number of broad fields. From the looks of them, most of the crops were well into their growing cycle. Neatly planted rows of grains were interspersed with cotton. Moving among the rows were farmers, at least she assumed they were farmers, busily tending their crops.

Beyond the fields lay two areas marked by large, packed dirt surfaces and three bar fences enclosing them. In the larger of the areas, several people worked out on horseback. As Cait watched, intrigued by the expert way they controlled their mounts while sparring with blades or staves, Fallon explained that they were some of the knight-trainees.

Eyes fixed on the horsemen, Cait nodded. She knew trainees spent time mastering the techniques needed to fight from horseback. Then, as one of them took a fall, she winced in sympathy. Fallon's chuckle assured her the rider would be all right, that such falls were to be expected. Her sigh of relief echoed his chuckle as the rider quickly climbed to his - her? - feet and stood before the offending horse as if giving it a very vocal and imaginative piece of his mind for letting him fall.

Tearing her attention away from the trainees, Cait looked to the second enclosure. Empty, she saw it had been set up for something different from the equitation arena. Tall racks lined one side of the arena. Bales of what looked to be hay stood at the far end, something propped against them. For several long moments, she could not guess their purpose. Then, with that sudden clarity or insight that had come to her on occasion recently, she understood. This was where some of the weaponry classes were taught. The bales prevented stray arrows from becoming dangers to any passersby. The racks were weapons racks.

Hopefully, she would one day be able to use that arena as a trainee.

Cait turned her attention to the massive complex of buildings beyond the fields. Situated on the cliffs overlooking the wide river she and Fallon had crossed earlier that day, the complex made an impressive sight. Ramparts rose from the green of the cliff top, ending in defensive parapets. The stone walls, weathered but still obviously well tended, were high enough to prevent easy breaching. The ragged cliffs and the rapids of the river below prevented access by water. Stone watchtowers were visible beyond the double walls, ensuring that any approach would be seen. Only by the use of sorcery could an attack take place without those inside the walls having ample time to prepare a defense.

"This is my home, Cait. Your home now," Fallon commented as he tossed back the hood of his cloak and lifted his face to the late afternoon sun. As he did, she saw his relief and understood. They had finally reached the one place he felt sure could keep her safe.

A knot of nerves twisted her stomach and she swallowed hard. She should have guessed but had denied it. Now, with the Citadel rising up before her, she felt all the fear of failure, of the future crashing over her. So much depended on what happened next and she prayed she did not do something to let Fallon down. He had risked so much by bringing her there -- his life as well as his place in the Order. She knew, even though he had denied it, that he could get into a great deal of trouble for leaving Deneram Grove before his mission had been completed. But he had taken that risk for her. Now she had to do everything possible to live up to his expectations.

But could she? And what would she do if she failed?

"Do you have any instructions for me?" she asked softly, hoping he did not hear her fear.

"Easy, Cait. Relax. We're home now and there's nothing to worry about." He gave her a brilliant smile and she forced herself to smile in return.

Even as she did, she realized he was right, at least as far as it went. The Citadel represented the closest thing she had ever known as a home. She certainly could not call Lineaus home. Not after all Giaros had done to her and the way the people had refused to see it until Fallon forced them to. Deneram Grove had felt comfortable but still there had been no sense of belonging. Maybe that would change here.

Sitting astride her gelding, Cait knew Fallon watched her. She could feel his eyes on her and guessed why. During their time together he had become almost too good at reading her moods. So he would know how nervous she was. Cursing herself for letting her fears surface and ruin his homecoming, she shook herself and forced those negative feelings down as deeply as she could. After all, there was no reason to be scared. Fallon would do nothing to hurt her. If he said they were home, she had to trust him and accept it as truth.

Home. Once they arrived, their time would not be their own, at least not for a while. There would be meetings with both the Knight-Commandant and the Adept. Both needed to know what had happened in Lineaus and on the way to Deneram Grove. Then there was the question of whether or not they would accept Cait's petition to stand as a Candidate for the Order.

Expelling her breath in a noisy gust, Cait turned once more to Fallon. "What do I call the Knight-Commandant?"

"Either Knight-Commandant or sir unless he tells you differently," he answered. "Let's ride now. We should be there within the hour."

With a nod, Cait once more touched her heels to the gelding's flanks and followed Fallon as he trotted off. A hint of excitement touched her, pushing back her fear. If everything went as Fallon had promised, she would soon be within the safe confines of the Citadel. There she would be allowed to study and, if lucky, join the Order. That was all that mattered. Her silly fears were just that. Silly self-doubts that she would not allow to dampen Fallon's joy at coming home or hers at the prospect of beginning her life.

As they neared the main gate, two heavy wooden doors large enough for several large wagons to move through simultaneously, the riders slowed their mounts to a walk. At the same time, a young man and young woman slightly older than Cait appeared from the guardhouse to one side of the gate. They wore the dark blue trousers and tunics of the senior journeymen. Swords hung at their sides. Then, as they recognized Fallon, they smiled before snapping to attention and smartly saluting.

"Welcome home, Sir Fallon. You're back sooner than expected," the fair haired young woman said. As she spoke, a broad grin creased her attractive face.

"Thank you, Kala. It's good to be back," he replied with a matching smile. "Is the Knight-Commandant about this afternoon?"

"He's in his office, Sir Fallon," the young man responded before Kala could. "Shall I send word of your return?"

"Please. And tell him I need to see him as soon as possible." With that, he turned his attention to Cait and she gave him a nervous little smile. "The stables are to the right. Why don't you take our horses on? I'll join you there in a few minutes. I need to check us in on the books."

Cait nodded slightly even though the last thing she wanted was to be separated from him. Fear licked at her and she forced it down. After all, he would not tell her to leave him if he felt there was any danger. So, steeling herself, she waited as he dismounted and handed her the reins to his mare. She gave him a smile, wanting him to know she was all right, before she rode off in the direction he indicated.

Following the directions given her, Cait soon made her way to the stables. As she neared the large stone buildings, several youngsters appeared. From the looks of them, she guessed they were new recruits, assigned to the stables until they learned how important a horse and its care were to the members of the Order.

"Ah, Fallon's back," a young man said gaily as he appeared from around the side of one of the buildings.

Dismounting, Cait looked over her shoulder to see who had spoken. The fact he knew Fallon's horse impressed her. Further, his tone of voice left no doubt he looked forward to seeing the knight once more. Wondering who he was and how well he knew Fallon, Cait turned to face him.

Standing a few feet away was a tall, muscular young man not much older than herself. His thick black hair fell across his brow. His skin was tanned from hours in the sun. In one hand he held a training blade. A quick glance at the glove he wore on that hand showed the scars proving he had wielded a real blade and knew how to use it.

"M'lady, that is Sir Fallon's mount, is it not?" he asked uncertainly as she turned to him. Obviously her appearance made him unsure of his initial assumption.

"It is." How should she react to his form of address? She was no lady. "He is at the main gate and should be here shortly."

"The lads will see to your mount, m'lady," he assured her as the boys waited patiently to take the reins from her. "Is there anything I can do for you while you wait for Sir Fallon?"

"Thanks but no. It's good to just stretch." Even as she answered, she found herself smiling. There was something compelling about the young man. She felt drawn to him, much as she felt drawn to Fallon. Could it have something to do with being a member of the Order?

"Forgive me, m'lady, but have you been gone from the Citadel long?" He placed the wooden practice blade on top of the short stone fence to his right. As he did, Cait nodded slightly, approving of his economy of movement. However, before she allowed herself to concentrate on that, she had to clear up something.

"You call me lady. Why?" She took the two steps needed to reach the fence and turned to face him, the sun no longer in her eyes.

"Because you are a knight. It would be most rude of me not to address you properly. I must apologize for not knowing your name. And I am negligent yet again. I am Stefan Dantir, second year journeyman in the knightly discipline."

"My name's Cait, Stefan, and I'm no knight."

She would not let his misconception continue. Yet, even as she spoke, she saw his disbelief. For a moment, she wondered at it. Then she understood. She looked the part of a knight, dressed as she was. Bentallo and Sharra had made sure she wore the dark tunic and trousers most knights of the Order wore when traveling. Beneath them, cushioned by soft underclothing, was her mail. The sword she carried as well as the shield draped across her back completed the picture.

"Not yet, at any rate," Fallon corrected as he joined them. "It's good to see you, Stefan," he added as he clasped the young man's arm in greeting.

"And you, sir," Stefan replied with a wide grin.

"Now, I want you two youngsters to get to know one another. But that has to wait for a while. The Knight-

Commandant needs to hear my report and meet Cait," the Knight continued, leading them away from the stables. "But you shall take a tankard or two with us this evening, Stefan. I want to hear how your training has gone in my absence."

"My pleasure, Sir Fallon."

"Then, accompany us to the administration building. I'm sure Kirris will have some instructions for you."

As they slowly walked across the courtyard, Cait followed closely. While Fallon and Stefan spoke softly, obviously pleased to be reunited, she took the opportunity to look around. So much activity. It was as though the Citadel was a busy city. Everywhere she looked, someone appeared to be hurrying toward some unknown destination. The sounds of students drilling could be heard even though she could no longer see the drilling fields. The clang, clang, clang of blacksmiths working punctuated the air. This was clearly a vibrant community, much more than she had ever imagined and she prayed she found a way to fit in.

Five minutes later, yet another journeyman escorted them into the Knight-Commandant's office. Cait paused just inside the room and looked around. Most of the surfaces were cluttered with scrolls, books and maps. The floor also held a number of stacks of papers and books. At the far end of the office, before the fireplace, was a large desk. No a single inch of its surface was visible. Behind the desk sat the Knight-Commandant himself.

"Stefan, see to it that a room is prepared for young Cait. Then tell the kitchen to send up food and drink. We will be here for a while. Once you've seen to all that, wait outside. When I'm done with Cait, you may escort her to her room and help her get settled," he instructed the journeyman.

"Right away, sir," the young man replied before quickly leaving the office.

"Now, Fallon, I've read the reports you forwarded for me as well as those from Bentallo and Sharra. I agree you took the only course you could, given the circumstances," the man continued as the door closed behind Stefan. "However, before we get to that, I want to hear what you can tell me about the state of affairs at the Deneram Grove compound."

As Fallon made his report, Cait took the opportunity to study the man who now controlled her destiny. Seated, she could tell he was tall but not as tall as Fallon. However, where Fallon gave the impression of grace and agility, there could be no mistaking the Knight-Commandant's powerful build. His arms were thick, like young oaks. Cait did not doubt for a moment that he could easily kill most men with his bare hands if he was of a mind to.

But his build was not what captured Cait's attention. His face was. His expression was so serene, so peaceful it almost unnerved her. Only his eyes, a piercing blue that seemed to bore into her very soul, broke that illusion. Seeing how he watched Fallon, Cait knew he missed very little. That worried her because she did not want him to see just how very nervous she was.

"Very well, Fallon," he said once the man finished his report. "I want you to return to Deneram Grove as soon as possible. In the meantime, I shall send several others to get started. You'll take command, answering only to Bentallo, when you return to the compound."

"I understand," Fallon assured him.

"Now, I wish to speak with you for a few minutes, Cait," Kirris continued and smiled slightly in reassurance.

"Yes, sir." She sat on the edge of her chair, back straight.

"I understand from the reports sent to me by Bentallo and Sharra that you have no memory of your life before waking in the slaver's camp. Is that correct?"

"I have no real memories, sir."

He frowned slightly at her choice of words. "Please explain."

"There have been several times when I have felt something was familiar, usually an action of some sort. But I can never remember why."

"Will you give me some examples of what you mean?" His voice modulated into reassuring tones.

She quickly told him about that first evening at the keep when she felt as though she had been bathed and massaged much as Dyara had done. When he asked if there were other incidents, she related them, noting when she spoke of the warding sign and of how she felt as she took up Fallon's spare blade when the bandits attacked, the Knight-Commandant's eyes lit with renewed interest. Finally, when there was nothing more to say, she leaned back and wondered what he would make of it all.

"I feel certain that these are precursors to your memory returning, Cait," he commented thoughtfully a few moments later. "Did you have the Healer at Deneram Grove see if they could do anything to help her, Fallon?"

"I did and Meron thought it best for us to wait until we reached here. She said her herbs and *talent* weren't enough for the task."

"All right. I'll speak with the healers and the Adept about it." Kirris paused for a moment, rubbing his chin in thought. "Stefan!" he called suddenly, startling Cait.

"Yes, sir?" the young man asked as he stepped inside the office. Obviously, he had been waiting just beyond the door for the man's summons.

"Cait, Stefan here will escort you to your room and help you settle in. Food and drink will be sent up shortly. I recommend you bathe and rest some after you eat. Morning will come all too soon and it will be a busy day for you."

"Run along, Cait," Fallon told her when she looked at him in question. "I'll be in to check on you as soon as I can."

With a smile she really did not feel, she stood and moved to where Stefan waited. A moment later, she was gone, the door closing behind her.

Leaning back, fingers steepled before him, Kirris blew out a long breath and shook his head. No matter what he had been prepared for, the reality of it had been so for beyond it. He had been sure Bentallo and Sharra had exaggerated in their messages in an attempt to keep Fallon from trouble. That belief had not lasted long, however. The moment his office door opened to reveal the Knight and his companion, a *power* seemed to fill the office. Never before had Kirris felt such energy associated with Fallon. Then, seeing Stefan and the dark haired young woman with the knight, he realized with shock that Fallon was not the source of the energy. What Bentallo had written was true. This young stranger possessed a *power* unlike any he would have expected from someone not a confirmed member of the Order and that knowledge had rocked him.

"All right, Fallon, tell me what you did not earlier."

"There really isn't much more to tell, Kirris," he replied as he comfortably slouched across his chair. "Cait shows all the signs of having trained extensively with someone from the Order. I'm convinced she has no memory of her life before waking as a slave and, as you experienced when she entered the office, there is a *power* to her that cannot be denied."

"Too true. There for a moment, I thought you had taken the next step in the discipline."

"Kirris, that *power* has been there since I first laid eyes on her," Fallon said and went on to describe exactly what he had seen and felt that day in the tavern.

"Very well, Fallon. If she passes the Adept's examination, she will be allowed to stand as a Candidate. Provided the Adept finds no hidden imperatives or anything else that would make Cait unsuitable to join our ranks, it will be left to the will of the gods."

"I ask for nothing more, Kirris."

"Good. You and Cait shall dine with me tonight. We will tell her my decision then."

Fallon got to his feet and left the office, closing the door behind him. As he did, Kirris rang for his aide. The sooner he spoke with the Adept, the better. Until Cait had been cleared of any hidden imperatives, he would not rest easy. He had learned long ago that what you least expected often rose up to bite you.

CHAPTER TWELVE

EARLY THE NEXT MORNING, CAIT WOKE. FOR SEVERAL LONG minutes she lay still, simply enjoying the feel of the soft sheets and comfortable mattress. After so long on the trail, it felt good to be in a real bed again. Then, even as the thought formed, she chuckled softly. How quickly she had become accustomed to the simple comforts of life, comforts she had never known with Giaros.

At the thought of the tavernmaster and all he had done to her, she shuddered violently. Hugging the sheet around her, she cursed softly. For the first time in weeks, she had dreamt of that horrible time. It did not take much to know why. Kirris. The Knight-Commandant was the reason the past had intruded on her dreams for the first time since leaving the Deneram Grove Compound.

The night before, over dinner, Kirris asked her to tell her story once more. While she understood why he asked, in the light of day she wished he had not wanted to hear it so soon. The pain and fear had stayed close to her heart, even in sleep. Now, instead of being well rested, she felt worn and wished she dared go back to sleep. But that simply was not an option that morning.

As she lay there, Cait's thoughts returned to the previous day. When she first left the Knight-Commandant's office, Stefan had escorted her to this room. After assuring her that her gear had already been delivered and showing her where she could bathe, he left her to rest. It had not taken her long to clean up and then drop onto the narrow bed. She had fallen asleep almost instantly, the food that had been brought for her left untouched.

She woke in time to join Fallon and Kirris for dinner. Stefan once again appeared at her door, this time to escort her back to the Knight-Commandant's office. He waited patiently as she changed clothes and quickly rebraided her hair. When she joined him in the corridor, he nodded in approval and then started off, trusting her to keep up with him.

Over dinner and a tankard of ale, Kirris and Fallon told her all they had discussed during the course of the afternoon. She listened closely, all but holding her breath, until the Knight-Commandant promised she could stand as a Candidate, providing she passed the Adept's examination.

When she asked what he meant, Kirris assured her it was nothing to worry about. Still uncertain, she turned to Fallon. He simply told her that the Citadel's resident soothsayer, and Adept of the religious side of the Order, would test her to make sure she carried no hidden imperatives that would make her unsuitable to stand as a Candidate.

Now, in the light of a new day, Cait's concern returned. If an imperative had been planted in her mind, she did not know it. It frightened her to think that after all she had been through to get the Citadel she might be refused the opportunity to join the Order.

Lord and Lady, please give me the courage to see this through so I may serve You as You see best.

Then, realizing she was only putting off the inevitable, she tossed back the sheet and climbed to her feet. It did not take long to dress, her long hair braided and tied back. Because she had been instructed not to eat before her session with the Adept, she moved to the table and single chair that rested below the room's only window. Climbing on top of the table so she could look outside, she sat. Once comfortable, she assumed a meditation pose and cleared her mind. Hopefully, she would find the calm she so desperately craved just then.

Half an hour later, Cait gradually eased out of her meditative state. As she climbed off the table, a light knock sounded at the door. She swallowed against the sudden lump of fear in her throat. It was time to begin.

When she opened the door, she was greeted by Fallon and Kirris. With them was a small, slender woman. Her brunette hair was lightly streaked with grey. Her face was slightly weatherworn. Cait assumed she was the soothsayer, the Adept who was to determine if she was suitable to stand as a candidate.

Cait stepped to one side and motioned for the three to enter her room. Kirris was the first to enter. He was followed by the woman and then Fallon. The Knight smiled at Cait in encouragement as he moved past her. As he did, she wished there was something he could do to help. But, until the test was over, she was on her own.

"Cait, please have a seat on your bed," Kirris instructed as he sat on the chair before the window. "Now, you have slept the night and, I assume, meditated. Do you still wish to stand as a Candidate to the Order?" he asked once she did as he said.

"I do, sir. There is nothing I want more than to dedicate my life to the service of the Lord and Lady."

"Then, let me introduce you to Adept Berral Solveig. She is the Order's senior Soothsayer and head of the religious discipline. It is her duty to make sure you aren't carrying any hidden imperatives that would prevent you from joining the Order."

As he spoke, the woman moved forward. Cait watched closely as she took a seat on the edge of the bed at her side. The air between them turned electric and the woman's green eyes widened slightly in surprise. As they did, Kirris smiled slightly, knowingly.

"Cait, I want you to undress now," Berral said and Cait looked at her in undisguised surprise. "Child, I need to see the scars you bear from the time before you woke in the slaver's camp. As you learn our ways, if that is the road the Lord and Lady have chosen for you, you will find that much can be learned from how a scar has formed. You can tell if it was magicked or if there is still foreign matter in it. I wouldn't ask you to do this if it wasn't necessary. If it will make you feel better, the men will leave the room."

Despite the fear, and shame, she felt, Cait shook her head. "That won't be necessary."

Without another word, she stood and undressed. A few moments later, she stood in the center of the room. Her arms hung limply at her sides and she stared straight ahead, forcing herself to remain calm as she remembered all those other times she had been on display before Giaros or one of his cronies raped her.

But this time was different. She knew it. She held tightly to that knowledge like a lifeline. These men would not harm her. They could not without violating the oaths they held so dear. Biting her lower lip, she breathed deeply and struggled for a calm that seemed almost impossible to recapture.

Berral stood and moved behind Cait. With gentle hands and a feather-like touch, she traced several of the scars that marred the otherwise smooth skin of the girl's back before moving on. While she frowned in anger at the number of scars, the Adept also nodded in satisfaction.

"Cait, I want you to lie back now and try to relax," she said as she led the girl back to the bed.

"All right." Cait did as she was told, reminding herself yet again that there was nothing to worry about. "Now what?"

"Close your eyes and clear your mind. You'll feel my hands on either side of your face. Just relax and let me do the work."

Cait breathed deeply and did her best to do as instructed. The moment her eyes closed, she felt the Adept's fingers rest lightly against her temples. Almost instantly, a veil of sleep fell over her. Her last thought was that she would not even know what happened to determine her fate with the Order.

"Well?" Kirris demanded as Berral stiffly climbed to her feet. Curiosity burned brightly within him as did the need to know exactly what the Adept had learned.

Frustration licked around the edges of his control when the woman did not immediately answer. Instead, she bent and carefully covered Cait so the now sleeping young woman would not get chilled. Then, seeing the look of compassion on Berral's face as well as the way her hand lingered gently on Cait's shoulder, he relaxed slightly. That had to be a good sign. He knew it. Berral would not worry about the youngster if she had been tainted by Balaar's touch. In fact, he knew the Adept would have simply sent the girl into the sleep of death had that been the case.

But he still needed to hear her say it.

"Berral?" he prompted once more.

"I found nothing to indicate she's a danger to the Order or to prevent her from standing as a Candidate," she replied and flashed Fallon a grateful but all too weary smile as he handed her a mug of cool water.

Thank you. Kirris lifted his eyes heavenward. That helped but there was still more he needed to know.

"What of her memory loss? Were you able to do anything about it?"

"No." She shook her head regretfully. "That I was unable to

Heal."

"But?" He had heard a note of something in her voice he could not immediately identify.

"I managed to travel down her memories to that terrible day when she woke in the slaver's camp. There was nothing beyond it for me to follow. All her previous memories have been blocked."

"Blocked? Does that mean she will never regain her memory?" Fallon demanded, deep disappointment shadowing his expression.

"Not necessarily. What it does mean is that she won't recover her memory until something happens to trigger the block's removal."

"Who put the block in place? Could you tell that much?" Kirris drummed his fingers on his thigh, not sure he wanted to know the answer. If some person had put the block in place, they were more powerful than Berral and that worried him. But if the block had been put in place by the gods that, frankly, scared him.

"All I can say with any certainty is that there's a very strong feeling of good to the block. My guess is that either the Lord, perhaps even the Lady Herself, put it in place to protect Cait. That's the only way to insure that she doesn't remember what happened to her before she's strong enough to deal with those memories."

"What do you mean?" Concern roughened his voice and he looked sharply at the Adept. He was unsure if he liked this turn of events or not.

"It's all very simple, really. Even though the block has a definite feeling of good to it, there is no mistaking the pain and fear it hides. I know that despite the fact that I could get no clear picture of the memories behind the block. It's my guess that before Cait woke in the slaver's camp, she had been tortured most cruelly, very likely by a follower of Balaar."

"That would explain how she came to be in the slaver's hands," Fallon commented thoughtfully.

"True. It would also explain the scars she bears. They speak of her being subjected to more cruelty than the brute you rescued her from could have dealt her. She wasn't with him that long and, from the testimony at the trial, he never hurt her that severely. She might have been bruised and battered but she was always able to work." For a moment, Kirris chewed the inside of his mouth in thought. "So it's up to us to help her build a new life and to learn who she is." That much he knew.

"Your decision then, Kirris?" Fallon all but demanded.

"She shall have two days in which to rest and prepare, Fallon. I trust you will see to it that she does what's necessary. Because of all you, Bentallo and Sharra have reported, I won't require her to go through the yeoman phase of training if she manages to pass the Tests." He smiled slightly as relief lit Fallon's face. Then he saw Berral's nod of approval. "So, with the blessing of the Lord and Lady, Cait will soon pledge her service to Them as a journeywoman. It will then be up to the Gods to decide where she can best serve Them."

"A wise decision, Kirris, and one with which I agree completely," the Adept commented with a slight smile. "And, if you have no further need of my services at the moment, I shall go get some rest before seeing to my other duties. This has taken more out of me than I anticipated."

"Of course, Berral. My thanks for your assistance." Now that she said something, he could see how tired she appeared. Her face seemed drawn, her color pale. As she left the room, he made a mental note to be sure to check on her as soon as he could. "Now, Fallon," he continued. "I assume you wish to be Cait's sponsor."

"I do."

"Very well. You will remain here until after the ceremony and her installation. Then I want you to conclude your mission."

"Understood. Shall I stay to tell Cait your decision?"

"We both shall, my friend. I'm as anxious to see what the Lord and Lady have planned for your young ward as you are."

Now he allowed himself to smile at Fallon in understanding and anticipation. That smile turned to an amused chuckle as Fallon slid to sit on the floor next to the bed. Obviously, he had accepted his role as Cait's protector long ago and was in no hurry to relinquish it.

As he settled back to wait for Cait to awaken, Kirris let his mind flow back to when Berral had asked the girl to undress. For a moment, undisguised panic had filled the girl's eyes. Kirris had seen it and recognized it for what it was. Just as he recognized how she fought that fear down. In that moment he glimpsed briefly the inner strength she had to possess in order to have survived all Giaros had done to her. That strength had saved her life. Now, hopefully, it would help her start a new one, one where she could live and be whatever she wanted.

But what had really shaken him had been the scars marking Cait. They had not been confined to her back as he first assumed. Her legs, back, shoulders and chest showed all the signs of having been injured time and time again. Some of the scars looked like they had been caused by whips or the like. Others looked like blades of different shapes and sizes had been used. Each bore the signs of having been dealt so they would cause the most pain without seriously injuring her. Someone with a definite sadistic bent had tortured her. The questions remained as to who. Why? When?

And now they would have no answers. At least not for a while. That went against the grain with Kirris. He wanted to know who they should look for to make pay for such cruelty.

But, deprived at that target, he determined to do whatever was necessary to help Cait settle in and start her new life. And the first step to do that was to let her know what his decision was.

He did not have long to wait. A few minutes later, Cait moaned softly and shifted positions in bed. As her eyes flickered open, Kirris leaned forward, motioning for Fallon to join him. Then he smiled at the girl in reassurance, not wanting her to worry any more than she had already. Not that it kept the quick leap of fear out of her eyes as she pushed herself into a sitting position, clutching the sheet about her. Then, as if she could feel all the reassuring thoughts Kirris left unsaid, she relaxed just a little.

"Sir? Fallon?" Her voice was little more than a whisper as she looked from one man to the other.

"Cait, let me welcome you to your new home." He waited, watching closely as his words sank in. The look of fear fled from Cait's face and her eyes suddenly glistened with unshed tears. When Fallon nodded to her, assuring her that she had heard right, Kirris almost laughed as excitement brought a light flush to her cheeks. It was quickly replaced with a look of expectation and Kirris understood she still waited to hear the rest of it. "Child, you have two days to prepare yourself to stand as a Candidate to the Order. Fallon will be here to assist you, teaching you what you need to know and what you should expect of the Trials."

"Is truth?"

"It is, Cait," Fallon assured her, grinning proudly. "If you pass, you will begin your formal training in three days."

"I can't believe it. I simply can't believe it."

"Do," Kirris said simply. "Now, I shall leave you to Fallon's careful instruction. We will meet again in two days for the Trials."

As soon as the door closed behind the Knight-Commandant, Cait turned her attention to Fallon. When she did, the last of her tension and fear flowed away. She could feel his pride and relief as they all but radiated from him. Them he grinned and reached over to give her hand a quick squeeze.

"What now?"

"You need to get dressed. Wear something comfortable. We'll begin your preparation once you have," he told her.

With a nod, she tossed back the sheet and got to her feet. As she did, Fallon moved to the door. He paused and smiled to see her rummaging through her belongings for a pair of loose trousers and a tunic. Then, feeling his eyes on her, she turned and smiled, excitement pumping through her.

"Cait, there is one more thing you need to know," he began, suddenly serious.

Worried something might be wrong, something they had not told her, she clutched her clothes in front of her and waited. Her heart thudded so loudly in her chest she knew Fallon could hear it. Then she drew in a deep breath, striving for calm.

"Berral tried to restore your memory but could not. However, she did say that she's sure one day something will happen that will trigger it and you will remember everything. She seemed quite certain about it."

Bitter disappointment filled her and she closed her eyes against her tears. She had not dared hope, at least not out loud, that the Adept would be able to restore her memory but knew it had been a possibility. She had been so sure she would remember once she got to the Citadel. Now she might never know who she was and that tore through her, ripping her heart in two. Somehow, she had to get past the disappointment but how?

By remembering that you have a new life to live, one to build, she told herself firmly. The first step was to get dressed and let Fallon teach her what she needed to know for the Trials.

"It's all right, Fallon," she said and smiled slightly, seeing how he hurt for her. "When I next see the Adept, I'll thank her for trying."

"Good girl," he said in approval. "Now get dressed. I'll wait for you outside," he added and left the room, closing the door behind him.

Once alone, Cait exhaled heavily and then smiled. She might not be any closer to knowing who she was but she was one step closer to knowing who she was going to be. For that she could be thankful. She had a new life with new friends to be made and so much to learn.

And she had to do everything she could to thank him and prove to him that he had been right to risk so much to bring her to the Citadel.

With no time to waste, she tossed the clothes onto the bed and quickly set about getting dressed.

CHAPTER THIRTEEN

THE NEXT TWO DAYS WERE FILLED WITH ACTIVITY AND WONDER AS Cait prepared to stand as a Candidate. Each morning, Fallon arrived just after dawn only to find Cait already dressed and waiting for him. They started the day with an hour of meditation before going to breakfast. That was followed by workouts and then the afternoons were spent with the Knight doing all he could to explain exactly what Cait would face and the best approaches to deal with the Trials.

Cait listened closely, doing her best to soak in everything he said. Excitement warred with trepidation that built with the passing of each hour. For the first time that she could remember, she wanted something so badly she ached for it. The thought that she might not pass the Trials sent her into fits of depression she was hard put to defeat.

Even as the worst of her doubts plagued her, she felt a light, loving touch in the back of her mind. It was as if someone -- or something -- was trying to assure her everything would be all right. She clung to that feeling. It did not matter if it was simply her own subconscious trying to reassure her or if it was something else. All that mattered was that she remember that feeling and not give in to the doubts and fears that plagued her.

Finally, and yet all too soon, the morning dawned when she would take the field to stand as a Candidate. As the sun crept over the window sill, Cait tossed back the sheet and slowly climbed to her feet. No matter how hard she had tried, sleep had been elusive during the night. Even so, excitement overrode fear and nerves, giving her a feeling of readiness to face the day. She would pay for the lack of sleep later but, as long as it held off until after the Trials, she did not care.

Her morning ablutions took even less time than usual as she raced through them. Once dressed in the soft white trousers and tunic marking her as a Candidate, she assumed a comfortable meditation pose in the center of her bed. Even had Fallon not suggested it the night before, she knew she needed to clear her mind and still her thoughts before beginning the Trials.

Almost as soon as she closed her eyes, Cait's mind flowed free. She focused inward, searching out all the doubt and fear and visualizing them disappearing behind a door that locked them away. The moment she *heard* the snick of the lock, a deep-seated feeling of peace and confidence filled her. A warmth, like sun-heated water, flowed through and over her as if in answer to her prayer for the strength and courage to do whatever was asked of her that day. Then, a touch so gentle and loving she wanted to cry settled on her and she felt whole. More than that, she felt confident that there was nothing the Knight-Commandant or the Adept could ask of her that she was not prepared to accomplish.

When she opened her eyes a short time later, Cait smiled slightly. Fallon had been right. Meditation had helped. She felt better than she had in, well, she did not know when. Whether it had been the Lord and Lady, or simply her own common sense, she no longer feared the outcome of the Trials. That was in Their hands. Through Their grace, her future would be shaped.

She spent the next few minutes working to loosen her muscles. Stretching gently and then with more determination, she focused on warming up muscles still stiff from hours in bed. Fallon had told her much of the Trials would revolve around physical tests. What kind, he would not, or could not, tell her. But he had said to be prepared for a good workout. That meant she could no more ignore the physical preparation than she would the mental.

When a soft knock sounded at her door a few minutes later, Cait ran her hands down her tunic, settling it over her hips. Once satisfied with its lay, she crossed to the door, expecting to find Fallon waiting for her as he had the previous mornings since their arrival at the Citadel. She wasn't disappointed.

Standing before the door, hands clasped behind his back, Fallon grinned in anticipation. He wore the dark trousers and tunic that marked his rank as a Knight. Cait looked at them in surprise, immediately recognizing that they were not the soft leather or homespun he had worn since first coming into her life. Instead, they were made of a fine, soft weave. His heavy gold medallion with the crest of St. Arelion hung about his neck. Then, before she could do more than nod in greeting, he reached for her arm and drew her into the corridor, closing the door behind her.

"Ready?" he asked as a gong sounded from beyond the walls. She knew it was the signal for everyone to gather for the Trials.

"I think so."

Once more, fear and excitement filled her. Unconsciously, she chewed her lower lip until a sharp little pain alerted her to what she was doing. Without slowing her step, she closed her eyes for one short moment and sought the feeling of confidence that had filled her earlier. That warmth, so comforting and loving, gently enveloped her in a loving embrace and all her fear flowed away.

"Nervous?"

"A little." That was certainly the truth. "But not as much as I was earlier. I meditated and you were right. It helped. Truth to tell, it's almost as if most of my fears were eased by my prayers." Even though it was not a question, she pitched her voice so it invited a comment from him. Maybe he could explain the feeling to her.

"That is a very good sign, Cait." Relief filled his voice and she realized he was as nervous as was she.

"Fallon speaks true, Cait," Kirris commented as he and Berral joined them as they stepped outside. They both wore their dress uniforms -- or, in Berral's case, dress robes. "It means the Lord and Lady were listening and graced you with Their blessing."

All she could do was smile slightly at his comment. No matter what she wanted to say, she could not find the words. Besides, she needed to remain focused on what lay ahead. There would be plenty of time later to think about, and talk about, what happened during her meditation.

As they rounded the corner and approached the courtyard, Cait slowed and looked around in wonder. The night before, Fallon told her she would be only one of several standing as Candidate. That meant families and friends would be in attendance. Beyond that, because the presentation of Candidates was almost as important a day as that of Confirmation, many of those living near the Citadel would be in attendance. So would as many members of the Order as could be there without shirking their duties.

Even knowing all that, Cait could not hold back her gasp of surprise as they neared the courtyard. Just the day before, it had been an open expanse of green. Now it was ringed with tiers of bleachers filled with people. A large platform rested in the center of the clearing. Journeymen moved through the crowd, making sure everyone had a place to sit, answering questions about what was about to happen. Crowd noise, the rumble of voices and the sounds of movement, assaulted her ears and her mouth went dry.

What had she gotten herself into?

Before she could give in to the urge to turn and run, Fallon took her elbow and led her toward the platform. On the grass several yards from the edge of the platform rested six large cushions. Three young men and two young women, all near Cait's age, knelt on five of them. Fallon escorted her to the sixth. As she dropped to her knees, he took up his place at her right shoulder. Now all she could do was wait.

A few minutes later, Kirris and Berral climbed the steps to the top of the platform. As they did, the crowd fell silent. An air of excitement, of expectation filled the courtyard. Cait felt it almost as a living being. It circled and caressed, its touch soft and electric. Then, as an undercurrent, she sensed the nervousness and fear of the young man at her side. Casting a look out of the corner of her eyes, she saw the perspiration dotting his upper lip. At least she was not the only one scared just then.

"May the Lord bless all who gather here," Kirris began, his voice carrying to every corner of the courtyard even though he did not appear to be shouting. Cait wondered at his control and then turned her attention to Berral as the Adept stepped forward.

"And may the Lady grace us with Her presence and wisdom," the woman continued.

"And may St. Arelion give us the strength and wisdom to serve the Lord and Lady and spread Their word!" Kirris paused as the crowd echoed his prayer. "Welcome, friends and honored guests. We are here to witness the presentation of Candidates. There are six who would try their hands at the Trials this day. Do the members of the Order and our honored guess accept them to the Testing?"

"We do!" the crowd responded wholeheartedly.

"Then I present the Candidates to you and for the Lord and Lady's approval." He quickly named all six Candidates and their sponsors, leaving Cait and Fallon until the last. Then, once done, he instructed the Candidates to ascend to the platform.

Cait slowly got to her feet and nodded in appreciation as Fallon gave her a few last words of encouragement. The quick squeeze of her shoulder did almost as much to reassure her as did his words. Then she joined the other Candidates and climbed the steps. Keeping her eyes focused straight ahead, her breathing slow and steady, she moved to her place at the end of the line and waited, wondering what to expect.

Slowly, stopping before each Candidate in turn, Kirris and Berral began the Trials. First, they asked if the Candidate stood ready to pledge his or her life and service to the Lord and Lady and St. Arelion. Cait listened as her fellow Candidates answered in the affirmative with voices ranging from soft and fearful to too loud in an attempt to hide nerves. Her voice, much to her surprise, rang with firm conviction and her cheeks heated as Berral winked in approval.

Then, Kirris moved away, leaving Berral standing before her. Not knowing what to expect, Cait let the Adept carefully position her so both their faces could be seen by those gathered. Then, softly, she instructed Cait to kneel. Catching her lower lip between her teeth, Cait quickly did as instructed. Then, realizing what she was doing, Cait forced herself to quit chewing on her lip, focusing instead on the Adept's face. As she did, she breathed deeply and then exhaled, trying to blow out her sudden nerves as the Trial of Endurance began.

Berral reached out and gently placed her hands on either side of Cait's face, much as she had that first day when she probed the mindblock. Trying to remember the woman would do nothing to harm her, Cait closed her eyes. She slowed her breathing, striving for calm. Soon the Trial would begin and she had absolutely no idea what to expect. And, as she had learned rather painfully on more than one occasion, the unexpected could hurt you.

At first, she felt nothing different. Then, the tips of Berral's fingers grew warm, that warmth penetrating her temples. A cloud of uneasiness descended upon her. With it, all sounds and sensations of the crowd around her withdrew. No longer was she kneeling on the platform in the center of the courtyard. She was cold and wet. It was dark. The darkness was alive with sounds she could not identify but that she knew meant her no good.

Heart pounding, she felt the weight of slave bands around throat, wrists, ankles. *No!* she screamed silently. Not again. She couldn't live through that again. It wasn't real. Just images put there by Berral. She had to keep control. It wasn't real.

Abruptly, the sensation changed. No longer did she feel the slave bands. But the terror was still there. She was surrounded by men dressed in black. Swords cleared scabbards. Arrows filled the air. All around her, people fell, screaming in fear and pain even as death descended upon them. But she could flee. They hadn't seen her yet. If she moved carefully, she could get away and they would never know.

But she couldn't. The others needed her. She couldn't leave them to these bandits to be raped, killed, or worse. No, she had to find a weapon. Any weapon. If she died, it would be in a good cause. There, a sword. Movement behind her. Turning, she struggled to raise the sword but she couldn't. It weighed too much. She could do nothing to stop the blade coming down at her head. She was going to die now, without having done a thing to save these poor people.

No!

Breath coming in ragged gasps, fear threatening to erupt at any moment, she refused to give in. She would not fail. This was just an image put in her mind by the Adept. Just like the slave bands. It was only a test to see how strong she was, to put her determination and faith to a test. She would not give in.

It -- is -- not -- real!

Suddenly, it was over just as quickly as it had begun. Panting, sweat streaming off her face and soaking the soft material of her tunic, Cait opened her eyes and sagged back so she rested on her heels. Swallowing hard, she looked down at her hands, fear still roiling through her. As she did, she half-way expected to see the slave bands once more in place and Giaros standing before her. But no. Her wrists might bear the scars but they no longer wore the bands. Licking her lips, she looked up, surprised to see Berral standing before her, looking as tired and drained as she felt. Then, as she turned her head slightly, Cait let out her breath in a whoosh to see that she was the only Candidate still on the platform.

"Cait," Kirris began, just a hint of pride - or maybe surprise. She couldn't tell which. -- in his voice as he stood before her. "You have passed this first Trial with the blessing of the Lord and Lady. Return now to your sponsor. He will escort you to the training area where the next phase of the Trials will occur."

Reaching down with her right hand, she pushed herself to her feet. As she did, she could not believe how drained she felt. It was as if she had spent an entire day in the training ring working out against Lady Sharra. And there was still more to do? She prayed she had at least a few minutes to recover before having to continue.

The moment she stumbled off the last step, Fallon appeared at her side. He pressed a waterskin into her hands and urged her to drink her fill. Then, with his arm about her waist, supporting and guiding her, she did as he said. The water, so cool and refreshing, quenched her thirst. Unfortunately it did not ease her exhaustion.

But at least she had passed the first Trial.

All too soon, Cait answered the call to join the other Candidates in the training arena. She had used the few minutes of respite granted her to calm her emotions and slow her breathing. But she had not been able to put most of her exhaustion behind her. Now, as more than a dozen journeymen lined up opposite the Candidates, she swallowed hard. The physical portion of the Trials was about to begin and she was unsure she had the strength to see it through.

"Candidates, you know what lies before you," Kirris said as he and Berral stepped into the arena. "You either disarm or fight your opponents to a draw. Good luck and may the blessing of the Lord and Lady be with each of you."

With that, they stepped back. When Kirris gave a nod, a gong sounded, announcing the commencement of this phase of the Trials. Cait stood her ground even as she noted with one part of her mind that several of the other Candidates rushed their opponents. She knew better. She needed the extra time to recover just as she wanted it to see what she could learn about the young man who moved slowly toward her.

Suddenly, he moved in her direction, quickly closing the distance between them. Her eyes flicked to his hands and one corner of her mouth quirked up in a slight smile. Unarmed, he should not present much of a challenge. Especially not when he was foolish enough to rush her without at least feinting once to test her reactions.

As he came almost within arm's reach, Cait simply stepped to one side. Her right foot snaked out, tripping him as he rushed by, unable to stop his charge. As he went sprawling onto the hard packed dirt, Cait fell on him. Knee in the small of his back, her right hand closed about his right wrist and pulled it behind him. At the same time, her left arm wrapped about his neck and pulled, forcing him to arch into her. For one brief moment, he struggled in vain before Berral called a halt to the match.

Instantly, Cait released the young man and flowed to her feet. As she did, she caught movement out of the corner of her eye. Turning, she watched as Kala approached. Unlike her predecessor, she did not rush forward. Instead, she moved methodically, carefully. Her light colored eyes took in every movement Cait made. In her hands she held a length of thick rope. One heavily knotted end swung back and forth from her right hand, its length increasing with each swing.

Holding her ground, Cait nodded in acknowledgment of the challenge. Inwardly, she thanked Sharra and Bentallo for the training they had given her. Part of that training had included working against similarly armed opponents. Confidence growing, she closed her mind to everything but the blonde and waited for Kala's first move.

It came so quickly, so unexpectedly, Cait was almost caught off-guard. Kala feinted to the left. At the same time, the rope flew through the air to her right. Twisting to avoid the blow, Cait stepped to her right. As she did, Kala stepped forward, closing the distance between them. Suddenly, Cait dropped to the ground, rolling. Her legs scissored as she came out of the roll almost at Kala's side. Before the blonde could react, Cait's legs closed, one high, one low and Kala went down.

Dodging the elbow aimed at her head, Cait dove forward. The battle was short but intense. Her knuckles jammed as she drove them into the blonde's jaw. Stars exploded as Kala connected with a palm heel to her chin and she tasted blood.

Clamping down on the tears and pain, Cait shot a spear hand into the blonde's diaphragm. Kala's breath exploded in a whoosh and her grip loosened. Cait kicked out and, rolling to her knees, closed her hand around the rope. Shaking off the cobwebs, she rocked to her feet and quickly moved out of range of Kala's long legs.

Taking several steps away from the rest of the journeymen to give herself a few extra moments of reaction time, Cait gasped for breath. Her jaw hurt so badly that, for a moment, she feared it was broken. Then, wiggling it, seeing stars again, she knew it wasn't. But that did not make it hurt any less. All she knew for certain was she could not allow herself to dwell on the pain. Not yet. She still had at least one more opponent to face before this phase of her Trials was over.

As if that was his cue, Stefan stepped forward. Cait groaned softly as he did. Why couldn't he come at her with something easy like a knife or sword? Instead, he held a long stave in his hands. Its heavy ends were thickly padded. At least she could thank the gods for small favors.

And she had the rope. That meant she would not have to get in close and risk the stave right away. Even so, she had a very bad feeling that this part of the Trial was not going to be as easy as the others had been.

Not that Kala had been easy, she reminded herself as her jaw sent another shock of pain arcing through her head.

She quickly learned her concerns had been valid. When Stefan finally moved in for the attack, she barely had time to avoid his blow. For what seemed like an eternity, they fought. Neither could gain the advantage. Pain radiated hotly from where the buffeted stave had struck her ribs and Cait knew she had to find an opening before Stefan managed to land another blow.

Dancing back, breath coming in painful, ragged jags, Cait

played for time. Time to think, time to recover. Surely if she managed to keep him at bay a little longer, Kirris or Berral would call an end to the match. All she had to do was hang on. Just a little while longer.

Then, just as she came to the realization that the fight would not end that easily, she saw the opening she had been waiting for, praying for. Without warning, she dropped to the ground and tucked into a ball. She quickly executed a roll across the packed dirt of the area to Stefan's left. Committed to a lunge to his right, the young man could not move quickly enough to counter her move. With a wry smile, Cait rolled to her feet, ignoring the pain tearing through her chest and ribs, and tossed the rope at the stave. It wrapped around the end of the weapon and she dove again, this time in the opposite direction. The rope went taut and she gave it a yank, jerking the stave from Stefan's hands.

The fight was over.

Finally.

Thankfully.

Gasping for breath, tears stinging her eyes as her ribs reminded her just how badly they hurt, she slowly climbed to her feet. As she did, she dropped the rope to the ground. A glance across the arena showed that none of the other Candidates had yet to finish their Trials. At least she could rest for awhile until Kirris decided what else to put them through.

"Here, drink this, Cait," Stefan said as he pressed a waterskin into her hands.

Without a word, she held the skin to her lips and drank deeply. The desert in her mouth receded and the ache in her throat eased. Tilting back her head, she let the water flow over her face and down her neck, washing some of the dirt and sweat from her skin. Then, with a smile of thanks, she handed the skin back to Stefan and slowly limped across the arena floor in the direction of the one small patch of shade where she could sit and relax until the others finished.

"You did very well, Cait, very well indeed," Fallon said proudly as he joined her a few moments later. "It's been a long time since anyone but one of the knights has bested Stefan or Kala and never as easily as you just did."

Easily? Had he lost his mind? Or maybe he had not watched the same combats she had taken part in. There could be no other explanation for it.

"I'd like you to teach me that tuck and roll you used to disarm me," Stefan said as he dropped to the ground at her side. "It took me completely unaware."

"After my ribs heal. You struck a clean blow early into the match," she replied and was stunned by their looks of surprise. It seemed neither of them had realized she was hurt.

"You are to see a Healer just as soon as the ceremony is over," Fallon said firmly.

Before Cait could respond, the gong sounded once again. Instantly, the journeymen in the arena stepped back, that phase of the Trials over. As they moved out of the arena, Kirris and Berral stepped forward, summoning the Candidates to them.

Exhaustion pulling at her, pain making it hard to move, Cait levered herself to her feet. At least the others looked as tired and hurt as she felt. But it was over. All that was left was the waiting. She could do that. If nothing else, her time with Giaros had taught her patience. A few more moments would not hurt her.

But she did not have to like it. She smiled slightly as her own impatience flared despite all her good intentions.

One by one, the Candidates were once more presented to the crowd. This time, as they were, Kirris announced their acceptance as yeomen of the Order. For the first phase of their training they would return to compounds near their homes. Sporadic cheers greeted each announcement. With each new assignment, sponsors promised to oversee the yeoman's training. Then, one by one, the newest members of the Order were led off until only Cait remained.

Heart pounding, breathing shallow, Cait waited. As Kirris moved to stand before her, she swallowed nervously. Before, as she listened to the others receiving their postings, it suddenly dawned on her that she could be sent somewhere away from the Citadel as well. After all, Fallon had told her just the night before that it was not that uncommon a practice. But she didn't want that. She hadn't worked so hard to survive Giaros, to help Fallon defeat the bandits just to be told she had to leave.

"Brothers and Sisters, we have one last Candidate to consider this day," Kirris began and Cait closed her eyes, praying for the strength to accept whatever his decision might be. "Cait comes to us through Sir Fallon's sponsorship. She brings with her glowing recommendations from Knight-Commander Bentallo and Lady Sharra. We have all seen her performance this day. It is with great pleasure that I announce to all gathered that she has been accepted into the Order of Arelion by the grace of the Lord and Lady."

"But," Berral continued for the man before Cait could do more than breathe a deep sigh of relief. "That is not the end of it. For those of you who do not know, Cait comes to us from the duchy of Lineaus where she was discovered by Sir Fallon. She has no memory of her life before her arrival there. However, it is obvious from her performance today, as well as her performance at the Deneram Grove Compound, that she has trained long and hard with someone dedicated to our Order.

"Moreover, she has been favored by the Lady and that has been demonstrated today. Cait did more than simply survive the Trial of Endurance. She withstood more, much more than any other Candidate in recent history.

"She has also received the blessings of the Lord and St. Arelion. Lady Sharra wrote to Knight-Commandant Kirris, telling him how Cait fought her to a draw with the sword, something few of us can do, while tired from several hours in the training arena. Later, when rested, Cait defeated that good Lady. It is safe to say, Cait is no ordinary Candidate."

"Adept Berral speaks for us both," Kirris took up. "As Knight-Commandant of the Order of Arelion, I accept Cait's petition for Candidacy and ask if she is ready to take her vows and pledge her oath as a journeywoman of the Order."

Journeywoman? Cait shook her head, sure she had misheard. She had not been standing for journeywoman. No. All she had done was petition to become a yeoman, to learn the ways of the Order. There had to be some kind of a mistake. She couldn't be a journeywoman. She didn't know enough.

"Before you respond, Cait, listen to all we have to say," Berral said gently, smiling at her in reassurance just as if she could see the terror racing through her at the thought of being thrust into a life she did not feel ready to undertake. "Because of the special circumstances of your case, as well as the ambiguity of your Trials, you will not be assigned to a single discipline as a yeoman is when raised to journeyman status. Instead, you will train in both disciplines until your Calling is fully revealed."

"Please, I don't understand."

"Cait, the Trials almost always show us where a Candidate's calling lies. When they don't, the Confirmation ceremony raising a yeoman to journeyman will. Those who do well at the Trial of Endurance have the mental strength and discipline necessary to become a cleric or even an adept in the religious discipline. Those who excel at the combat trials are best suited for the knightly discipline. You did better in both those Trials than anyone has in a very long while. Because of that, we need more time to understand exactly what role the Lord and Lady wish for you."

"And that means more work and longer hours for you until that determination is made." Berral again. Did they practice that give and take or did it come naturally? "Do you accept these conditions and the responsibilities they involve?"

"I do." She answered without thought or hesitation, lifting her voice so all could hear. Even as she did, disbelief filled her. It was more, so much more than she had dared hope for. Her life inside the Citadel would begin as a journeywoman! She offered a silent prayer of thanks to the Lord and Lady as she waited for what was to come next.

"Then, Cait, do you swear to spend your life in the service of the Lord and Lady, upholding Their laws and spreading Their word wherever They shall send you?" Berral asked, voice and expression grave as she asked the question asked of all in her discipline.

"I do."

"And do you pledge your arm and your life to the service of the Lord and Lady? Are you willing to give your life for the protection of others as our patron, St. Arelion, did? Are you willing to do whatever is necessary to bring the blessings of the Lady's peace to the world even if it means giving up your life?" Kirris wanted to know.

"I do."

"Then, journeywoman, we welcome you to our disciplines and wish you health and wisdom on this journey you are about to undertake." As he spoke, Kirris slid the gold chain and medallion that formally marked her as a member of the Order over her head.

"Now, let us join our newest members in celebration!" Berral called, releasing everyone to the main courtyard where the festivities would be held.

"Cait, let one of the healers have a look at your ribs before joining the celebration," Kirris said with a smile as Fallon and Stefan joined them. "Report to me before the morning meal and I will explain your schedule and introduce you to your instructors."

"I understand, sir."

"Stefan, Kala, see that she does as the Knight-Commandant instructed. I'm not sure she's taken it all in yet," Berral added with a chuckle as the blonde joined them. "I'll have your belongings moved into the dormitory, Cait. Is the room next to yours still vacant, Kala?"

"It is, Adept."

"Good. Your things should be moved by the time you finish with the healers, Cait. I leave it to you, Kala, to see her settled in tonight."

"Of course." She gave Cait a wide, friendly smile as she draped an arm about her shoulders. "Come on. Let's get you treated and then we can join the celebration."

Too numb to argue and hoping her new friends might be willing to answer some of her questions, Cait let them lead her away from the arena. She had wanted a new life and it certainly looked like she was getting her wish.

But would she be able to live up to all the hope everyone seemed to have in her?

CHAPTER FOURTEEN

HER HEAD HURT. NO, IT DID MORE THAN HURT. IT FELT AS IF IT would fall off her shoulders if she moved. Groaning, she kept her eyes closed, one hand snaking out from under the covers to feel for injuries. Waking hurt and hurting was nothing new but this felt different somehow. The pounding in her head seemed to be internal. Her fingers as they probed oh so gently found no sign of external injury. So what happened? Why did she hurt so badly?

Because you're a damned fool. That's why.

That thought brought memory, vague to be sure. Memories of celebrating with Fallon, Kala and Stefan the day before. Then, that night, continuing the celebration with Kala and Stefan. She remembered eating and drinking more than ever before. A faint echo of Kala warning her to slow down or she'd be the worse for wear followed by Stefan saying to leave her alone only caused her head to pound more. And now she had to find a way to get out of bed and get dressed so she could meet the Knight-Commandant without dying -- or at least wanting to.

Slowly, carefully, she pushed into a sitting position. Once the room quit spinning, she opened her eyes. As she did, she realized she remembered nothing about her room from the night before. Exhausted, weaving from drink, she had simply stumbled across the room and fallen face down in bed. Now, looking down and seeing that she still wore her tunic and realizing someone had removed her trousers and boots, she prayed it had been Kala. Mortified at the thought it might have been Stefan, she groaned again.

Never again would she drink that much, no matter how much anyone else urged her on.

As she climbed to her feet, a soft knock sounded at her door. Groaning, she looked around for her trousers. When the knock sounded again, she muttered in ill-temper. Then she spotted the discarded trousers and stumbled toward them. Before she could pull them on, the door opened just enough for Kala to stick her head inside.

"I thought you'd be awake by now, Cait, and figured you might want this."

"This" was a mug of steaming tea and a white powder of some sort. Hoping, praying it was something to ease the pain in her head and the sudden roiling in her stomach, Cait motioned her inside. She all but grabbed the mug from the blonde and, cradling it in both hands, took a long drink.

"You look as bad as I felt when I woke," Kala said with an understanding smile as Cait dumped the powder into the tea and stirred it with her finger. The blonde winced slightly as Cait downed the rest of the brew without regard for its temperature.

"I am never drinking again," Cait moaned as she dropped onto the edge of her bed. "Please tell me you put me to bed." She turned pleading, bloodshot eyes to the young woman.

"I did. Of the three of us, I was in the best shape. In fact, after pouring you into bed, I did the same for Stefan."

"At least I wasn't the only one then."

Knowing the young man had been as bad shape as she had seemed to help. Or, perhaps, it was the powder. Whatever it was, the pounding in her head settled down to an almost tolerable level and Cait smiled her appreciation to her new friend. She might just live after all.

Now that her brain was finally starting to work, she took a moment to look around her new room. All she could remember with any clarity was that it was located on one corner of the second floor of the dormitory. She also vaguely remembered Kala explaining that, because they needed privacy for their studies and meditation, each senior journeyman had his or her own room. Juniors and yeomen shared rooms located on the upper floors of the dormitory.

As she looked around, Cait shook her head in disbelief. The room was much larger than she first thought. The bed sat against the far wall, a large trunk resting at its foot. A large braided rug covered most of the wooden floor. On a stand a few feet away sat a water pitcher and basin. A large window was cut into the eastern wall. Beneath it rested a table and several chairs. Cait guessed that if she opened the trunk she would find her clothes and the few personal belongings she had brought with her from Deneram Grove. Her sword and shield rested against the wall near a small fireplace. Above the fireplace, secured to the wall, hung the Order's crest. The only thing she did not see was her armor even though a stand for it rested in one corner. Then, before she could ask, another vague memory returned, one of Stefan telling her it had been taken to the quartermaster for repair and cleaning.

"Are you going to feel up to meeting with the Commandant this morning?" Kala asked in concern.

"Aye." She smiled gratefully once more at her new friend, glad Kala had taken pity on her and brought the tea and powder. "I think I'll be all right once I move around some."

"You will," the blonde confirmed. "Now, if you're like me, you're feeling a bit of the fool for drinking so much you really would like your head to fall off. It wouldn't hurt so much if it did." Here Kala gave her a wide, understanding grin and Cait had the grace to nod, very carefully, in acknowledgment.

"I've never done anything like that before."

At least not that I remember.

"Well, don't feel like you're the only one. We all do it and the instructors expect it. Classes today will be overviews and introduction of students only. They'll get down to business tomorrow."

"Thanks." At least that was one worry off her mind. "Now, I'd better get dressed. I'm supposed to report to the Commandant first thing," she added as a gong sounded from somewhere outside.

"I have kitchen duty during the noon meal but will you join me for dinner? I'll introduce you to some of the other journeymen."

There was a hopeful note to Kala's voice that called to Cait. She smiled and reached over to lightly touch the blonde's arm, a little surprised by her boldness as she did.

"I'd like that."

Apparently satisfied, Kala collected the empty mug and took it with her. Once alone, a soft sigh escaped Cait's lips. She really did have to hurry. So she gathered her clothes and bathing supplies and left the room in search of the bathing room. All of a sudden, a bath sounded almost as good as another cup of strong tea.

Half an hour later, Cait hurried out of her room. The warning bell for the morning meal had rung a few minutes earlier. That meant she didn't have any time to waste unless she wanted to be late and that was absolutely the last thing she wanted. What sort of impression would that give the Commandant and Adept if she was late meeting with them her very first day as an official member of the Order, or as official as any journeywoman was?

Walking rapidly, all but running, Cait hurried across the courtyard toward the administration building. As she stepped inside, she groaned softly to see Kirris and Berral approaching from the opposite direction. Surely they hadn't been coming to find her. She wasn't late - yet. Then, before the panic just beginning to bubble deep in her stomach could take root, the Adept smiled and lifted a hand in greeting. Relief rushed over Cait at the sight. So far, so good.

"Have a seat, Cait," Kirris said as they entered his office. He paused at the door long enough to instruct someone to see to it that their breakfasts were sent in. Then he turned, closing the door behind him. "I realize you probably wanted to eat with your new friends this morning but Berral and I need to have a few words with you before you begin your studies."

"I understand, sir." She gratefully accepted a mug of tea from the Adept without taking her eyes from the Knight-Commandant. As she did, she bit her lower lip, once more fighting the panic deep in her belly. Surely she hadn't done something already.

"Cait," Berral said as she took a seat next to her. She sounded so gentle, so loving that Cait closed her eyes for a moment, fighting the tears that pricked at her eyes. Then, feeling the woman's hand lightly grasping hers, she looked up and gave her a slight smile. "Cait, you have to trust us. We're your friends and your family now. Always remember that."

"I'll try."

"Good girl." Berral gave her hand a pat. "Now, you surprised us by how well you performed in both phases of the Trials yesterday. What we said afterwards was the truth. You performed better than any Candidate has in a very long while. But what really surprised us was the fact that you excelled in both phases of the Trials. That has us in a quandary. We're going to have to adjust our training techniques to accommodate your special needs and abilities."

"Please, I don't want to cause any trouble." She paused at

the sound of a knock. A moment later the door opened and a yeoman appeared with their meals. They waited for her to serve them and leave the office. "I want nothing more than to learn all I can so I can serve the Lord and Lady."

"And I assure you that is exactly what you'll do," Kirris said with a smile of approval. "The only trouble will be yours, child. Because you will be studying both disciplines, you will carry a heavier course load than your fellow journeymen. That is especially true because there will also be some classes you'll need to take that they already have. That means you will have very little spare time."

"That's all right." Spare time? Until Fallon came into her life, she didn't even know there was such a thing. Now she felt uncomfortable with it, still feeling like she ought to be doing something, anything besides just relaxing. "I wouldn't know what to do with any spare time."

"You'll figure that out soon enough," Berral assured her with a grin. "Now, Kirris and I will be your mentors while Fallon's away from here. We want you to feel free to come to either of us with any questions or problems you might have. It's our duty to do whatever we can to ease the path for those studying the ways of the Order. The only thing we won't do is intercede with your instructors without good cause. However, we will help with your studies if you need it. But, most important in your case, we want to know if you have any memories or feelings of familiarity about anything."

"I understand." But understanding and actually doing so were two different things. How could she take up the time of the two most important members of the Order?

"Good." Kirris nodded emphatically. "Now, your mornings will be spent training with the other journeymen. You will study tactics, weaponry, self-defense and equitation. The afternoons will be spent studying the priestly disciplines --

meditation, healing and ethics. You will meet with the judicar three evenings a week for history, government and the Codes. We want you to work with Stefan and Kala as much as possible. They'll help with your studies and in adjusting to your life here."

"All right."

"One word of caution, Cait. There may be a few of the juniors and yeomen who resent you because you skipped over them. Don't fall for their tricks or allow yourself to be drawn into a fight. They will soon enough realize how much harder you have to work than do they," Berral put in.

"I understand, Adept, but I don't understand why I was promoted over them."

"All either of us can say is that it is very obvious that you were trained long and well by someone in the Order," Berral replied with an understanding smile. "I no more understand why we had no prior knowledge of you nor why there was no hue and cry raised when you disappeared than you do. But the training you received is why you were raised to your current level. The rest is known only to the Lord and Lady. They will make everything clear when They are ready."

"One final word since you aren't familiar with our ways, child." Kirris again. "As a journeywoman, you have full access to everything within the Citadel except the armory. You may associate with anyone you wish. We encourage you to build friendships. They will help you settle in more than anything else."

"Yes, sir." She smiled slightly, wondering if she would be able to do as he said. She hoped there was the beginning of a friendship starting to develop between her and Kala and Stefan. At least she hoped so. She had never had a friend before, at least not one she remembered. Could she let her defenses down enough to allow herself to trust so the relationship could grow?

Gods, I hope so.

"Excellent. As soon As we've finished eating, I'll escort you to the training arena and introduce you to Knight-Commander Jerrod. Over the next several days, he will set your standard. Once he has, he will put you in the appropriate weapons classes."

"After the noon meal, join me in my office. I'll introduce you to your other instructors," Berral put in.

Feeling suddenly overwhelmed, Cait bent her head and reached for her mug of tea. Her life had changed so much in such a short time. She still wondered when she would wake up and find herself back in that hellhole with Giaros just waiting to hurt her again.

Cait entered the dining room the next morning and paused, unsure where to go. So many people, loud and noisy, already crowded around tables running the length of the room. Yeomen and journeymen with kitchen duty moved between the tables serving or clearing away. For a moment, memories of other times, times back at the tavern returned and she saw herself moving among the tables, serving those who for months ignored what was happening right under their noses.

Anger flared and she shook it off. It was nerves and lack of sleep and uncertainty about what she should do or where she could go. That was all. All she had to do was remember how different that morning was from all those she had endured in Lineaus. This was her new life and she had best adjust to it quickly, before the members of the Order decided they had made a mistake in admitting her to their numbers.

"Cait, over here!" Stefan called from a table to her right. "We saved you a place."

She pushed back her doubts and smiled a little shyly as she lifted her hand and returned Stefan's smile. Then she hurried to the table where he waited. With him were Kala, the young man she had defeated in the hand-to-hand portion of her Trials, and another she had not yet met. Then, as she neared, both Stefan and Kala hurried to greet her while the stranger poured her a mug of tea.

"Cait, I don't think you've actually met Damon even though you dealt with him quite effectively the other morning," Stefan said as he slid onto the bench at her side. Then he grinned as Damon glowered at him.

"And this other fellow is Ricard d'Aumale," Kala put in as she speared a slab of meat with the tip of her dagger from the platter in the center of the table. "He doesn't say much but, when he does, it usually makes sense."

"Pleased to meet you both," she said and smiled slightly. As she did, she remembered what Kirris had said about making friends.

"It is our pleasure, Cait," Ricard told her after giving Kala a long, piercing look. Seeing how the blonde blushed under his gaze, she guessed they had already paired off.

"Is what the Adept and Knight-Commandant said after the Trials true?" Damon wanted to know. He appeared to be the youngest of the group and, she guessed, the least worldly. Otherwise, he would never have questioned the leaders of the Order.

"It is." She reached out to spear a slab of meat. As she did, she remembered the Adept telling her to eat a good breakfast because the Weaponsmaster planned to put her through an intense workout that morning in order to set her standard.

"I'm sorry but it is difficult to believe you were actually enslaved in Lineaus."

"Why, Damon? Because you hale from there?" Stefan's

voice turned hard, condemning. Cait skewed around on the bench to look at him, surprised at what she saw. Why was he so willing to stand up for her, a stranger, against a friend? "Cait is one of us now. She wouldn't lie, especially not about something this important. If that isn't enough to convince you, I suggest you remember that the Adept tested her before allowing her to stand for the Trials. That should be more than enough to convince you Cait speaks true. If not, remember that Sir Fallon found her and freed her. He's certainly not to going be mistaken about anything so serious."

"But --"

"No, Stefan." Cait placed a gentling hand on his arm. As she did, she smiled slightly. She hadn't expected anyone to come to her defense any more than she had expected anyone to challenge her so soon after joining the Order. "If he comes from Lineaus, it must be difficult to accept what happened to me. But it is the truth, Damon, and I will forever carry the scars to prove it." Anger roughened her voice. How could this *boy* doubt her, much less doubt the Adept or Fallon?

"Sir Fallon could have been mistaken," Damon protested feebly.

"Was he mistaken about the bands that caused these?" She thrust her hands out before her, shooting her sleeves up to reveal the scars at both wrists. "Or this?" She pulled the collar of her tunic away from her neck to reveal the scars there. "You need to grow up, Damon, and realize there is evil in this world and it exists everywhere, even in your homeland. If you don't, you may well end up someone's slave or worse."

Furious with him for doubting the truth of what happened and with herself for losing control, Cait shoved to her feet. She had lived too long in a situation where she couldn't do anything to get away from those who didn't want to see what was happening under their very noses. She was damned if she was going to sit with someone like that now.

"Cait, don't. Please." Kala quickly climbed to her feet and reached out to stop Cait before she could leave. "I think we all agree you have every right to be upset. Damon isn't known for his ability to think before he speaks." The look she turned on the young man spoke volumes about her own anger with him.

"I'm sorry, Kala, but I have lost my appetite."

"No, please. I'll leave," Damon said softly as he stood. "But I'll apologize first. You were right. It is hard to admit such evil could exist in my homeland. But that doesn't excuse my behavior."

"Sit," she all but growled. She didn't want to drive a wedge between these friends. Hopefully, Damon had learned a lesson he wouldn't soon forget. "I apologize for losing my temper, but you have to understand that I spent close to a year in your homeland with no one acknowledging what was right before their eyes. To have you question it was too much like that time."

"Sorry," he muttered and they fell into an uncomfortable silence.

"What is your schedule today, Cait?" Kala asked, finally breaking the silence and effectively turning their attention to safer topics.

"I'm supposed to report to Knight-Commander Jerrod right after breakfast. Then I meet with Knight-Commander Alicia for tactics and finish the morning with an equitation class. This afternoon, I meet with the Adept. This evening I have a history lesson with the Judicar."

"Then they really were serious about training you in both disciplines," Stefan commented with a low whistle.

"Aye. Both the Adept and the Knight-Commandant explained they feel it best. It gives them the opportunity to determine where my Calling lies as well as letting me catch up in the classes you have already studied." She paused and took a long drink of tea. "And, if yesterday is any indication, they're going to work me every bit as hard as they said."

"Rough?" Ricard asked sympathetically.

"Just long. I met with each of my instructors as well as twice with both the Adept and the Knight-Commandant. We didn't finish until well after the evening meal. Today promises to be much the same."

"Then let us help any way we can," Stefan said with a smile of encouragement. She found herself smiling in response and that was a definite improvement over how she felt just a few minutes earlier.

"I will, I promise."

Less than fifteen minutes later, Cait hurried across the compound toward the main training arena. As she did, she lifted her head, gauging the time. The last thing she wanted was to be late for her session with the Weaponsmaster. Kirris had warned her the day before that Knight-Commander Jerrod was a stickler about punctuality and the Weaponsmaster himself had told her the same thing. Because of that, she wasn't about to risk being late and making a bad impression.

As she neared the training arena, Cait slowed and smiled slightly. None of the other students had arrived yet. Taking advantage of the opportunity, she moved into the arena. As she walked across the packed dirt, she nodded thoughtfully. The flat, even surface, so much like the training arena at the Deneram Grove compound, was ideal for hand-to-hand combat as well as for swordplay.

Head down, eyes focused on the surface of the arena, she walked its outer edges. As she did, she began swinging her arms back and forth to loosen her muscles. Then, she paced carefully across the width of the arena, noting as she did that the equipment shed effectively blocked the morning sun if she positioned herself just right. That might be something to keep in mind as the lesson progressed.

Finally, satisfied she knew the arena the best she could, she turned. Her eyes went wide and the color rose in her cheeks to find herself face-to-face with the Weaponsmaster.

"Knight-Commander." She nodded in greeting and then relaxed slightly to see the look of approval reflected in his green eyes.

"I hope this is an indication of what's to come, Journeywoman," the tall, slender man said in response. "You are here early and you are conscientious enough to check the area where you will be training so it will present no surprises."

"It only makes sense to be as prepared as you can, sir." What else could she say?

"Good." He smiled slightly, apparently satisfied by her answer. "Come. We'll get you outfitted for the class. The others should be here by the time we return."

With a nod and a shy, excited smile, she followed the man to the equipment shed. Once inside, the Weaponsmaster beckoned Cait forward. He spent several moments studying her before motioning for her to hold out her arms. The moment she did, he began piling on practice sword and dagger, padded vest and wooden shield. As he handed over each item, he explained that all but the most advanced students used the practice blades and vests. That precaution helped avoid serious injury.

With that, he led her back to the training area. As they neared, she saw that the other students had arrived. While she quickly pulled on the padded vest, Jerrod set the others to work. Then he turned his attention back to the new journeywoman.

"Cait, that's enough for now!" he called two hours later as she disarmed one of the best students in the class. "Class, that is how I want the rest of you to perform. She did that disarm without any hesitation or trouble. Now finish your exercises and report to your next class," he added to the others.

"What do you want me to do now, Commander?"

Cait wiped her brow with the back of her hand. As she did, she realized that she was literally drenched with sweat. It ran down her face and soaked her tunic. Her trousers were dusty and scuffed from where she had worked on the ground during the hand-to-hand portion of the class. Best not to think about how tired she was or how badly she had to smell.

"I realize you are supposed to meet with the Tacticsmaster this hour but I want you to come with me to see the Knight-Commandant first. I will let Lady Alicia know why you are late," he said, his expression suddenly closed.

Cait quickly stripped off the padded vest and returned it and her practice weapons and wooden shield to the equipment shed. As she did, she tried to think of anything she might have done that would have upset the Weaponsmaster. Why else would he want to take her to see Kirris? Swallowing hard, knowing she could do nothing save what he said, she left the weapons shed. The moment she returned, Jerrod motioned for her to come with him. Without a word, they made their way across the compound toward the administration building.

What would she do if the Weaponsmaster refused to train her?

"Yes, Jerrod. What is it?" Kirris asked as they were shown into his office a few minutes later. "Cait, there's a problem already, is there?" His voice quickened with concern.

"No, sir, not that I'm aware of." She wished the Weaponsmaster had said something, anything that might explain why they were there.

"Kirris, I assure you there is no problem where Cait's concerned," Jerrod said as he was seated before the Knight-

Commandant's desk. Cait stayed where she was, just inside the door to the office, not sure why she was there or if she wanted to remain.

"But?" Kirris prompted.

"Truth?" Jerrod waited until Kirris nodded. Then he turned and motioned for Cait to come sit next to him. "Cait here is much more advanced than any of us expected. In everything but hand-to-hand, I have no doubt she will be able to defeat our best knights once she's back into fighting trim and gains some confidence. The hand-to-hand will come quickly enough, especially since it appears that she has a natural talent for it."

"Jerrod, are you saying you can't teach her?" Kirris asked and Cait looked from one to the other in surprise. Surely the Weaponsmaster wasn't going to refuse to teach her. If he did, what would she do?

"I'm saying that with a little time and work, she could probably teach me a thing or two," the man answered and gave her a lopsided grin of approval that rocked her. He wasn't going to turn her away. He even seemed proud of her. "I'm also saying she will be wasted in the juniors' class."

"All right. Place her in the classes you feel will serve her best. You might consider putting her in with some of the knights at least once a week. From what you've said, it sounds as though the seniors' class might not be enough challenge for her either." Kirris paused and looked at Cait so long she fought the urge to squirm on her chair. "As soon as you've decided where to put her, let Alicia know. She'll agree with the changes, especially if it means she'll have more time with Cait. I'll leave it to you to speak with the Quartermaster to make sure Cait has the equipment she needs."

"Understood," the Weaponsmaster said.

"Now, child, this isn't a surprise," Kirris continued, turning a reassuring look on her. "Fallon, Sharra and Bentallo were very clear about their opinions of your abilities. I also anticipate there will be certain studies that will give you some trouble. All I ask is that you be honest with your instructors so we can properly place your standard."

"I will," she promised, relieved no one seemed upset with her.

"I know you will." Even though he smiled in reassurance, she found herself wondering what he really thought. "Now, run along. Lady Alicia will be waiting for you. Tell her that I need to speak with her after you're done."

"Yes, sir."

"And, Cait," he began before she could leave his office.

"Sir?" She turned to face him, wondering what was on his mind now.

"Try to find some time to relax tonight. Find Stefan and Kala and ask them to take you to the inn for a tankard of ale. You won't have many such opportunities for a while."

After promising to do as he said, she left the office, closing the door behind her. As soon as she was outside, she broke into a run. This meeting had made her very late for her next class and, despite the men's reassurances, she didn't want to do anything else to give the Tacticsmaster reason to be upset with her.

As she entered Kirris' office, Berral paused for a brief moment and nodded slightly. Because she was running late, the other had already arrived. As far as she was concerned, that was all for the best because it meant they could get right to business. The sooner the better because she was more than ready to find her bed after almost a week away from the Citadel.

"I was beginning to worry you wouldn't be able to join us," Kirris said softly as he moved to her side.

She smiled gratefully as he pressed a mug of mulled wine into her hands. "So was I," she admitted with a weary sigh. "The state of the temple in Westhover is a disgrace. The villagers have done nothing to maintain it. In fact, it looks as though some of them have been housing their livestock inside."

"No!" Alicia looked scandalized as she leaned forward in her chair.

"Aye," she confirmed. "I put some of our craftsmen to work setting it right and I plan to send several clerics there to find out why the temple was allowed to get in such a state."

"I'll ride out myself next week to speak with the lord mayor about the village's duty concerning the temple," Kirris said. "In the meantime, I'll assign several knights to go with your clerics." He waited as she dropped onto a chair and sighed wearily. "Now, I believe you each know why I asked for this meeting. So, shall we begin?"

"Has everyone had a chance to meet with Cait?" Berral asked. She sat up slightly, her exhaustion slipping away. She was more than a little anxious to hear what the others had to say about their newest journeywoman.

"Would you mind answering a few questions before we continue, Berral?" Daffyd, the Order's senior judicar, inquired. "You may be able to ease some of my concerns about this journeywoman."

"Of course."

"I understand you examined Cait when she first arrived. What exactly did you find?"

"Let's start with the physical first. Cait bears a number of scars, most of which are on her back and shoulders. They appear to be no more than two to three years old. She's been whipped numerous times. Some of those can be accounted for as coming from her time in Lineaus. The others appear to be from something similar to a multi-tongued lash. These are older and more numerous.

"She also has scarring at ankles and wrists. My guess is that the scarring is originally from when she was manacled and shackled and caused when she tried to escape her bonds or torturers. These scars were then made worse by the time she was forced to wear the slave bands."

"Do you have any idea who is responsible for doing this to her?" Alicia asked, voice strained with barely contained anger.

"I have no specific knowledge but my guess is that she was in the hands of those who look to Balaar. We all know that his followers are getting bolder. Besides, that makes more sense than what happened to her being political in nature. Surely we would have heard of one of the royals going missing."

"True," Jerrod agreed, a thoughtful expression on his face. "What about the mind-probe?"

"I verified all she and Fallon told us about the time after she woke in the slaver's tent. I will admit that I was more than a little surprised to find the mental block in place. None of the techniques I used could penetrate it. All I can tell you is what I told Kirris at the time. I believe with every fiber of my being that the block was put in place by the gods to protect her. Something happened to her during that time that she's not strong enough to remember -- not yet at any rate. One day something will trigger the block's destruction. When that happens, she will remember her past. Until then, she won't. It's as simple as that."

"But you're sure she's untainted?" Daffyd pressed and she pushed back her irritation. As the most conservative member of their council, his concern wasn't unexpected. But, tired as she was, she really did not want to have to deal with it.

"I am. The feel of the block is one I'm well familiar with," she assured him. Should she tell them more? She really wasn't sure because it was something she rarely spoke about, even with Kirris. But Cait's future might depend upon the outcome of this meeting so maybe it was time she finally explained.

"There is a part of my role as Adept that most of you are unaware of," she began, hoping she was doing the right thing. "As the Adept, I do more than lead the religious aspect of our Order and train our students. I have, on several occasions been blessed by the presence of the Lord and Lady. They have visited me directly with either warnings and visions that have helped prepare our people for their roles in our fight against the dark forces. Their touch has a very definite and distinct feel. The block I found in Cait has that same feel. That is why I'm so positive that her place is with us."

"I had wondered," Alicia commented with a slight smile. "What else?"

"I will admit that I had worried about Cait's emotional adjustment when she first arrived. To have been subjected to all that brute in Lineaus did to her and then to find herself suddenly ripped away is not something any of us could move past easily. Add to that the fact that she doesn't remember anything from before waking in the slaver's camp and there is the potential for some severe adaptation problems."

"You aren't worried now?" Kirris asked.

"No." She smiled slightly. "The morning before I left for Westhover, I stopped by the dining room. What I saw eased most of my concerns. Apparently young Damon let his mouth get ahead of his brain again and protested the truth of her slavery. She lost her temper, but not her control. Instead, she showed him the scars at her wrists and neck. Then she tried to leave. That is when Kala stopped her and asked her to stay, and she did. It proved to me she isn't afraid to show her emotions and that she is reacting as any of us would in such a situation.

Most of all, she is definitely forming a bond with Kala and trying to with Stefan. That may take longer because most of the abuse she suffered came at the hands of men."

"Does that ease your concerns, Daffyd?" Kirris asked and waited until the man nodded in response. "Then let us decide just what her placement is. Jerrod?"

"You know my thoughts. Cait is not only a natural but my guess is that she trained long and hard with a master before falling into the slaver's hands. Her sword-work will be as good, if not better, than mine once she's had some time to return to form. I won't even begin to guess what she will be like once she's had a steady practice routine.

"With the bow, she's adequate. She shows promise there just as she does in personal combat. With the first, she simply needs training. Conditioning is all that holds her back with the second. She's wasted in the journeyman sections in all but archery."

"Let's not raise her too far above her classmates, Jerrod. Put her in the Senior section in all but archery and arrange for her to work against the rest of us in her free time," Kirris instructed him.

"All right, but I don't think that will be enough."

"We will reevaluate when you feel it's necessary," the Knight-Commandant said. "Alicia?"

"The girl has an excellent grasp of tactics. I agree with Jerrod that she trained with a master, probably a member of the Order. Her instincts are superb. She just has to learn to trust them and herself."

"How does she rank with regard to the other journeymen?"

"I see no reason why she can't hold her own in Avrim's class, especially if Kala and Stefan continue to work with her."

"Then see to it," Kirris instructed.

"It appears to be my turn now," Daffyd commented. "In my

classes, she works hard and learns everything the first time. She's got an ear for languages and is quickly picking up her history and political lessons. Geography, however, isn't one of her strengths. Even so, she does whatever is required to learn the material. I wish all my students tried as hard as she does."

"That could go along with her memory loss. Weapons and tactics are natural skills. Books are not. Her body remembers things her mind doesn't," Berral commented softly, thoughtfully. "It is the same with me. She learns quickly, as though our ways are not unknown to her. I wish to the heavens we knew where she was from and who trained her."

"I think it fair to say that we all do." Kirris sighed and ran a hand through his thick hair. "All right. I recommend we place Cait in the Seniors' classes in all but your section, Daffyd. She takes the Juniors' there."

"I'll give her the new schedule tonight," Berral volunteered and they each nodded in agreement.

"Good. Now we each have duties to get back to." Kirris climbed to his feet. "We shall meet again in two days for our regular session."

The others, all but Berral, followed suit and left the office. She remained where she was until the door closed. Then she smiled and held a hand out to the Knight-Commandant.

"Tell me how our children are and then I'm off to find my bed for an hour or so," she said with a smile.

"Gladly. . . ."

Cait sat at her desk, doing her best to make sense out of a political treatise Daffyd had assigned her that afternoon when a knock sounded at her door. Shoving the treatise to one side with a sigh of relief, she stood. A moment later, she opened the door and found herself staring at the Adept in surprise. The last she had heard, Berral was still away from the Citadel. That she was back and standing there not only surprised Cait but reignited that thrice-damned sense of fear that always seemed so ready to strike.

"Don't look so worried, child," the Adept said with a reassuring smile as she stepped inside. As she did, she motioned for Cait to close the door and join her at the table.

"I apologize, Adept. I didn't know you had returned."

"Berral, please," the woman corrected and Cait's eyes widened in disbelief. She was supposed to call the woman by her name? That just wasn't done. Was it? "Cait, I am your mentor and, I hope, your friend."

"Berral," she repeated, still not quite believing it.

"Good girl." Berral waited until Cait took her seat. "Now, Kirris, Alicia, Daffyd, Jerrod and I met this afternoon to determine exactly what sections you should be in."

"And?" Cait all but held her breath as she waited for the woman to continue.

"With the exception of the Judicar's classes and Jerrod's archery, you'll be in the Senior sections. In Daffyd's classes, you'll take the Junior courses until you get caught up. I strongly recommend you continue working with Kala and Stefan as much as you can. As for your weapons training, you'll train with the Seniors as well as with the Knights on a regular basis."

For a long moment, Cait could only stare at the woman in disbelief. She had fully expected to be placed in the beginning sections of each of her classes. To be told that she would be in the same sections as Kala and Stefan thrilled her. It also frightened her. What if she couldn't do the work? Would they place her in the lower section or what?

"Don't look so worried, child," Berral laughed. "You'll do fine. Besides, we will be evaluating your progress on a regular basis."

"Anything else?" Her voice sounded far away and she wondered at it. Then, seeing Berral's smile of encouragement, she relaxed a little and allowed herself a smile in return.

"There is. You will also be working with me and, in your spare time, you'll be putting in additional workouts with Jerrod and some of our senior knights and clerics on the field."

Spare time? What spare time? The way it sounds, I'll be lucky to find time to sleep.

"I understand," she answered with a sinking heart. She already spent most of each evening studying. At least she hadn't been assigned a work section yet or had she? She'd better find out. "Ad-Berral, what about a work section? I know the other journeymen have been assigned to one."

"That's true. They have. You haven't been because of the extra classes you must take right now. But that doesn't mean you won't be given one later, once you catch up," she answered with an approving nod. "Now, do you have any questions or need help with anything?"

"Truth?"

"Truth."

"The Judicar assigned a treatise I can't seem to make any sense of."

"Let's see it. Perhaps I can help." That was all the encouragement Cait needed. She quickly retrieved the treatise from her desk and returned to the small table where Berral waited. "The Treatise of Treiste," the woman murmured and shook her head. "I can't believe Daffyd assigned this one so soon. The language is so difficult that most never get to the body of the text. So, let's see what we can do with it together."

Glad to have the woman's help, Cait hooked a chair with her foot and moved it to Berral's side. A moment later, they began, both determined to do all they could to prove to Daffyd that Cait was up to the challenge he had set.

Chapter Fifteen

"Well?" Kala dropped onto the chair at Cait's side with a heavy sigh. Hearing it, Cait smiled slightly in understanding. "What do you think old Avrim has in store for us today?"

"You can bet he's going to do his best to put us in our proper places," Stefan said from Cait's right. "I don't know why, but he certainly doesn't like us."

"I'm not sure he likes any of his students," Cait said seriously. This was an old conversation, one they had often revisited. "The only time he ever seems to relax is when he's on the field. Why he's an instructor is beyond me. He's certainly not too old to hold a post somewhere."

"Preferably one far from here," Stefan added with feeling.

"Too true," Kala agreed softly as the door at the back of the room swung open.

The room fell instantly silent. In the past year, the journeymen had learned very quickly that Avrim, one of their tactics instructors, demanded their full attention from the moment he entered the room. Those foolish enough to continue talking or concentrating on anything but him were quickly treated to such a vicious verbal attack that they were unlikely to ever repeat their mistake.

Now, seeing the man carrying an armload of books, Cait groaned softly. She had no doubt they were about to be treated to another grinding session where the knight did his best to prove just how ignorant each of them were about the realities of warfare. Then she saw the smoldering anger in his pale eyes and knew it to be a bad sign. Something had put his back up and that would make the class more unbearable than usual. Worse, he made no attempt to hide his anger which meant at least one of them would soon feel the sharp edge of his tongue.

"Today we shall be discussing the Battle of Kharsel Talum," the small but surprisingly broad man began as he placed the books on his desk at the front of the room. "I trust each of you have read and studied the assigned materials and are ready to begin."

For the next hour, he droned on and on about what he identified as the key points of the battle. Most of the journeymen kept their heads down, doing their best to at least look as if they were taking notes. No one dared make eye contact with the man or raise a hand in question. The routine was well-known. Stay silent, be invisible and never, ever question his wisdom.

Frowning at what seemed a particularly obtuse comment, Cait looked up from her notes. As she did, she bit back a curse to find Avrim standing in front of her. His upper lip curled back in a sneer and he reached down and snatched her notes from her.

Damn her luck!

"Well, well, well, journeywoman, you must believe you already know all there is to know about this great battle," he said, his voice openly derisive as he picked up her almost blank page and displayed it for all to see. "You have made hardly a single note since the class began. So, why don't you grace us with your wisdom and insight and finish the lecture?"

Cait stared at the man in shock and not a little fear. In that moment, he reminded her of Giaros and that churned up all the old memories. Biting her lip, she put a firm clamp on her emotions and her memories. She would not let him do that to her. He could yell at her. He could even throw her out of the class but he would not make her fear him as she had with the tavernmaster.

A sharp elbow to her ribs brought her back to the classroom and the knowledge that she couldn't just sit there. That would only serve to increase the knight's anger.

"Sir Avrim, it is not that I feel I know all there is about the battle," she began as she climbed to her feet. She prayed her voice didn't betray just how nervous she was. She refused to think about how her knees threatened to buckle under her. "It is just that during my studies to prepare for today's lecture, and then during what you've said, some questions came to me that I would like answered."

As she spoke, she could almost hear the silent gasps from her classmates. Beside her, Kala buried her head in her hands. Avrim simply stared at her in disbelief. From his expression, it looked as if he thought she had sprouted a second head and he didn't know what to do about it. Waiting for the upcoming explosion, Cait prayed he understood she only spoke the truth. That way he couldn't accuse her of shirking her duties to the class. Or could he? After all, one simply didn't ask questions, at least not of Sir Avrim.

"Very well, journeywoman, what sort of questions do you have?" he all but sneered.

For a moment, she said nothing, doing her best to find just the right words to begin. Then, seeing anger rising in the man's eyes, she licked her lips nervously. Her time was up. She had opened her mouth. Now she had to take the consequences.

"Sir Avrim, why was there no centralized command structure during the battle? It would have made coordination between the different armies much easier and more efficient. As it was, they were often at cross-purposes. An example of that is what happened when the Order attempted a mounted assault on the enemy encampment and the archers from

Fuercon opened fire, hitting the riders and their mounts."

"That was an accident!" Avrim roared, startling everyone. "Those archers were supposed to have attacked prior to the charge."

"I realize that, sir, and that is why I wondered if a centralized command structure might not have helped prevent such a tragedy."

"You young, impertinent little bitch. Who are you, nothing but a slave and a whore, to question what happened that day?" he snarled. "Nothing could have prevented that terrible accident. Besides, it didn't matter, did it? We won."

"All right, Selwyn. Make sure the other instructors know I wish to see them immediately following today's council session," Alicia commented as she and her aide paused outside one of the classrooms. "Then send word to Jerrod that I'd like a good workout, on horseback, this evening if he can set something up for me."

"Of course," the young man replied and frowned slightly as he committed her instructions to memory.

"Thank you. I'm going to look in on the yeoman class before the council meets. You can have the afternoon to yourself once you deliver those messages."

With a nod, he hurried off in the opposite direction. As he did, Alicia smiled slightly. Selwyn was one of the best aides she had ever had. Because of that, and much as she hated to deprive herself of his services, she was going to recommend he be transferred to one of the Order's compounds so he could continue to hone his administrative skills. He had all the makings of a good commander, if they gave him the chance to gain some experience.

Suddenly, the sounds of a man's voice raised in anger

caught the Tacticsmaster's attention. Concerned, she moved quickly and all but silently down the corridor in the direction of the voice. As she neared its source, she frowned in concern. Something was wrong, very wrong and she had no choice but to deal with it then and there.

"So, is there anything about the battle you think was done correctly, *journeywoman*?" Avrim demanded. As he did, Alicia paused and silently eased open the classroom door.

"All I asked was why the troops didn't adapt to the new forms of attack presented by the raiders," Cait said, mouth tight. From where she stood, Alicia could see how the young woman fought to control her rising temper. "By continuing to use battle techniques known to the enemy, techniques and tactics they were effectively countering, casualties were increased and the battle prolonged."

"Just because that fool Fallon couldn't wait to get into your pants, that doesn't give you the right to question how battle-experienced warriors fought that day." He moved so he towered almost threateningly over the young woman.

"That is enough!" Alicia snapped as she stepped into the room. She moved quickly to put herself between the two. Never had she been so angry with any other member of the Order. If she had her way, she would deal with Avrim then and there. But she couldn't, not yet at any rate. "You go too far, Avrim," she rasped. "Now step back and keep your mouth shut unless you want me to shut it for you."

For a moment, it looked as if he would argue. Then he turned on his heel and returned to the front of the room. If he knew what was good for him, he would stay there and stay silent until she specifically spoke to him.

Fearing what she would find, she turned her attention to Cait. In the year since her arrival at the Citadel, the young woman had thrived. Her instructors praised her hard work and dedication. As her confidence grew, she began making friends and, of late, Alicia had noticed how she had begun to mentor some of the younger students. But she also knew just how fragile Cait's ego still was. That thrice-damned tavernmaster had done more damage than they knew and the fact that she still had not recovered her memories from before waking in the slaver's camp still ate at her. Now Avrim, damn him, had very possibly undone all the good the past year had been for her.

Cait stood there, face pale, jaw set. Tears glistened in eyes that burned with anger and pain. The fact she refused to let the man see her cry spoke of the strength she was drawing on. But the damage had been done and, by all that was holy, Alicia would see Avrim pay for it. No one, and especially not a confirmed member of the Order, should treat another as he had their student.

Now she had to find a way to begin repairing the damage. But how, without doing further damage to Cait?

"Kala." She saw the cold fury in the blonde's eyes as she looked to where Avrim slouched against the far wall. "What happened just before I entered the room?"

"Lady Alicia, we were studying the Battle of Kharsel Talum. Sir Avrim wanted to know why Cait had not been making many notes and she said she had some questions about the way the battle was fought. She asked them and, well, you heard his response."

"Who is she to question the way her betters conducted the battle?" Avrim demanded as he started in their direction.

"Don't." Alicia didn't move except to place a reassuring hand on Cait's shoulder. But the command in her voice was as clear as was the warning. "If you value your place here, *Sir* Avrim, you will keep your mouth shut until I get to you.

"While you wait, consider this. Perhaps the freshness of youth and an eye that hasn't been blinded by loyalty sees things you might have overlooked," she continued. "Think on that for a bit."

"What did she ask? Stefan?" She looked to the young man, not at all surprised to see an anger that matched Kala's reflected on his expression.

"She wanted to know why there had not been a centralized command structure, noting that it might have helped prevent the mistakes that led to the Pelaquanese archers firing on our own cavalry."

For a moment, Alicia looked at Cait, her expression thoughtful. "Class, that is a very interesting and important question and one with a number of implications for us to consider." She hoped she had managed to diffuse what she knew was a very volatile situation. Not only did she have to figure out how best to deal with Avrim before he did any lasting damage to Cait or any other of their students but she also had to figure out how to turn this around into a teaching moment for the journeymen so they never repeated the knight's actions or behavior. "Cait, it is obvious you've given this a great deal of thought. What exactly do you want to know?"

"Several things, Lady Alicia," she replied, her voice soft. "First, why wasn't there a centralized command structure? Second, why weren't the *talents* of the knights and clerics fully utilized?"

"Give an example please."

"The ability to mindspeak could have been used to relay messages between troops immediately instead of having to wait for runners to carry the messages from command to the front line and back. Foresight could have helped plan the battles."

"Very good, Cait. Go on."

"Why weren't our tactics changed to meet the challenges of

the new weaponry fielded by the outlanders? And why weren't specialists used to harass their lines and attempt to assassinate their leaders?"

For one long moment, Alicia stared at the girl in surprise. She had known Cait possessed a talent for tactics but her questions went beyond a simple talent. She had just asked the same questions Alicia had over the years. Beyond that, she had managed to put aside her fear and worry about what Avrim might do to voice her concerns. Somehow, she had to find a way to help Cait past the damage Avrim's attack on her had done.

"Class, Cait has made some very good points. Your assignment for the morrow is to apply her questions and suggestions to the battle you are currently studying. Point out the advantages, as well as the disadvantages. Your results will be due at the beginning of the class. Until then, you are dismissed." She watched as the journeymen quickly prepared to leave, their relief was almost palpable. That alone convinced the woman she had arrived none too soon.

"Avrim, Cait, the two of you are to come with me," she continued just loudly enough for them to hear. When she did, Cait's face fell and she cursed herself for not phrasing it better. After all that had just happened, she knew what Cait had to be thinking. She must feel she was trading one angry instructor for two. Well, she would quickly put that fear to rest.

"Ma'am, I'm supposed to report to the Weaponsmaster now," Cait said softly as she gathered up her books and notes.

"He's to be at the council session and that's exactly where we're going, child."

She smiled at Cait in reassurance, once more impressed. No matter how scared she was, the journeywoman still remembered her obligations to Jerrod. Not many in her place would. The fact that Cait had, spoke volumes to Alicia.

As soon as Cait joined her, Alicia draped an arm about the girl's shoulders, hoping that the simple gesture would reassure her. It was also a tacit warning to Avrim not to do or say anything else to upset the journeywoman and, feeling Cait's fear at the thought of appearing before the Order's council, Alicia's resolve intensified. No one should fear appearing before the council for simply voicing a well thought out opinion or for asking pertinent questions.

So what had Avrim been doing in this class and how many others had he terrorized along the way?

"Avrim, go ahead and wait for us. We shall be along shortly," she said and then turned her attention back to Cait, pointedly ignoring the man as he stalked out of the room.

The moment the man had disappeared from sight, Cait seemed to almost collapse in relief. Alicia closed her eyes and prayed for patience and for the wisdom needed to deal with the young woman without causing further harm. She had no doubt harm had been caused. Cait had been openly challenged and humiliated by the man and, as far as the journeywoman knew, there was nothing to prevent it from happening again.

"Cait," Alicia began, voice as gentle and reassuring as she could make it. "All I want is for you to tell the council exactly what you asked in class. I've been trying to get them to reconsider how we act in battle for a number of years now. The fact that you, a journeywoman without any real battle experience, have asked the same questions I have is just too much of a coincidence to ignore. Will you do that for me?"

"Yes, ma'am," she replied and Alicia heard the doubt in her voice. Dear gods, Avrim had caused so much damage, too much. "But what about Sir Avrim?"

"You are going to have to tell the council what he said. Don't worry. I'll be telling them what I overheard. I promise, after today you won't have to worry about him. I give you my word."

Keeping her arm around Cait's shoulders, she guided the young woman out of the classroom. The sooner they got this over with, the sooner she could get to work repairing whatever damage Avrim had done not only to Cait but to the rest of the class as well.

"Alicia, is something wrong?" Berral asked, her voice sharp with concern, as they entered the council room a few minutes later. The Adept's eyes darted between an openly hostile Avrim and the Tacticsmaster and journeywoman.

"Unfortunately there is, Berral." She did not try to hide her anger as she guided Cait to one of the vacant chairs at the long table. She waited as the young woman was seated. Then she took her place behind her, her hands resting lightly on Cait's shoulders. "Something happened today in the senior tactics class that each of you need to hear about."

"You have the authority to deal with anything that happens in your section, Alicia," Daffyd reminded her.

"And I shall, Judicar." Gods, sometimes she wanted to shake the man and his grasp of the obvious. "However, some of what happens falls directly under the authority of the council as a whole."

"All right," Kirris said even though he was clearly as puzzled by this sudden turn of events as were the others.

"Avrim?" Alicia prompted and couldn't keep the condemnation or censure from her voice. Not that she wanted to. She wanted the others to know that she found the man's actions reprehensible.

"I was teaching the final battle of Kharsel Talum when this *journeywoman* began questioning the tactics involved," he replied with a sneer that spoke volumes about his thoughts regarding not only Cait's questions but Cait herself.

Alicia squeezed Cait's shoulders in reassurance. Then,

when Avrim fell into a brooding silence, she took up the story.

"I was coming down the hallway when I heard Avrim raise his voice. As I neared, it was clear that this *knight* was verbally humiliating and ridiculing Journeywoman Cait. When I entered the classroom, his body language was clearly threatening and it was apparent that he knew it," Alicia said.

Berral, her expression hard, leaned forward, elbows on the table. "What did you hear?"

"Do you want to tell them or shall I?" Alicia turned a cold expression on the tactics instructor. When he said nothing, she nodded once. So be it. "He called her a slave and a whore and then said that just because Fallon couldn't wait to get in her pants, it didn't mean she had the right to question what was done during the battle of Kharsel Talum."

For a moment no one said anything. Looking down at Cait, Alicia's anger flared once again. The young woman had bowed her head. Misery radiated off of her. Not wanting her to think she had done anything wrong, Alicia angled the chair to their right so she could sit on its arm and look Cait in the eyes.

"This is not your fault," she said softly. "Believe me and trust me. It will be over soon."

"Avrim?" Anger roughened Kirris' voice and his clenched his fists on the tabletop. Before he could say anything else, Berral reached out and laid a hand on his arm, silencing him.

"You're sure, Alicia?" the Adept asked softly.

"I am." She did not look away from Cait. She wanted – no, she needed – the young woman to know that what happened would not go unchallenged. "I heard it and the others in the class confirmed it."

"Cait." The Adept's voice was gentle now. "Did Avrim say what is alleged?"

"Yes," she answered without looking away from Alicia's face. Alicia nodded slightly and smiled in encouragement.

"Has he said such things before?"

"Never quite so bad." Cait spoke softly and Alicia's heart broke to hear the pain in her voice.

"She lies!"

"Does she?" Alicia countered before any of the others could speak. "Shall I call in each member of the class? Shall we ask them how many times you have verbally abused them?" So angry she shook, she fought for control. "I knew there were problems in your classes but I never expected this. You are a member of the Order. You swore to protect those weaker than you and to uphold the laws of the Lord and Lady. Yet you take pleasure in beating down those who have no recourse against you."

"Enough, Alicia," Kirris said. "Avrim, you are an embarrassment to the Order and have proven you aren't fit for your current duty. Return to your quarters and stay there. We shall send for you later to determine what should be done."

"But—"

"Go!" the Knight-Commandant snapped. He waited until the door slammed shut behind the man. Then he leaned forward and poured a glass of wine. Without a word, he stood and carried the glass to Cait. "Drink this, child. I am so sorry this happened to you."

"We all are," Berral said. "I take it there is more, Alicia," she added as Cait held the wineglass in both hands and raised it to her lips to drink.

"There is." Knowing the best thing she could do for Cait just then was to finish the tale, she drew a deep breath. She needed to get her anger under control before continuing. "As I said, Cait asked questions about how the Battle of Kharsel Talum was conducted."

"And that is when Avrim crossed the line?" Kirris asked. Alicia nodded once. "Cait, Avrim has never been one to abide by anyone questioning the way battles are fought. But that doesn't excuse what he said and I promise he will be dealt with."

"Thank you."

"I'm sure he has told all of you that any battle is fought well that is eventually won."

Alicia waited, holding her breath. If Cait responded to the Knight-Commandant's unasked question, they had a chance. Lord and Lady, don't let that fool have ruined her.

Finally, she looked up and locked eyes with Kirris. "He has but that's not a valid premise, sir. You have to look at the casualties and other losses as well as the ultimate outcome."

"Too true," he agreed. "Now, what questions impressed Alicia here so much while at the same time angering Avrim so?"

"It's all right. You can tell him," Alicia said softly when Cait did not answer right away.

The young woman drew a deep breath, as if steeling herself for what might happen next. "To begin with, the outlanders were employing new attack methods, mainly the use of the ballista and mongorel to bombard our lines with stones and fired javelins. Yet, nothing was done to protect the front line troops. New troops were simply sent in to reinforce those who fell until the machines could be taken. No counter-measures were even tried.

"Another point is the lack of coordination between the armies. Everyone seemed to operate according to their own agenda, often causing injury to allied forces. This could have been prevented by using a centralized command structure and by assigning knights or clerics who are gifted with mindspeech to each army.

"Another thing that bothered me was the fact that specialists weren't used. Their talents for sabotage and assassination could have helped end the war so much sooner.

"Then there's the use of the monarch's banner. That's just foolish. It pinpoints for the enemy the location of the monarch and the senior officers on the field. It's like painting a target on them and yelling 'Here I am. Come get me!'" She paused, looking as though she was scared she had said too much.

"Alicia, if I didn't know you better, I'd swear you had coached her on what to say," Kirris commented with a sigh. "But you wouldn't do that and she wouldn't be a party to such a thing. So, what do you want of this council?"

"Two things, Kirris," she was quick to say. After all, she might as well strike while the iron was hot.

"First, we have to deal with Avrim and in such a way those who look to us for training and leadership know we do not condone his actions. We knew there were problems but today has shown he cannot be trusted in the classroom any longer. I - - we -- can't risk him ruining someone as promising as Cait."

"Agreed. What else?"

"I want the council to consider the questions Cait raised and I mean really consider them. We have lost too many of our number these last few years because we haven't adjusted our tactics to the changes our enemy has made."

"She is right, Kirris. If one of our journeymen can come to that conclusion, perhaps it is time to reconsider our stance," Jerrod commented. As he did, he gave Cait a reassuring wink. Alicia smiled in appreciation, pleased he recognized the need to rebuild the young woman's confidence after the disaster of the morning's class.

"Very well," Kirris agreed. Alicia knew he hated change almost as much as Avrim but at least he didn't let it stagnate him. "Is there anything else you think we should consider, Cait?"

"There is one more thing, sir," she replied a little hesitantly and Alicia looked at her in question. Had she missed something?

"And what would that be?"

Cait did not answer right away. Instead, she once more studied her hands where they rested on the tabletop. Alicia could sense her uncertainty and wanted to help. But she had no idea what else the young woman had to say.

"Are we not to look at the records and ask questions? How are we to learn, and how are we to make sure past mistakes aren't repeated, if we don't?"

"An excellent question, Cait," Kirris said with a smile. "I can see why your instructors are so pleased with your work. It is as though your fresh eyes are exactly what we've needed for a long while. Now, to answer your question, we want you to do exactly that. I am sorry none of us realized just how entrenched Avrim had become. Now run along to your next class and don't worry about what happened. You did well today."

"Thank you, sir." She gave him a tentative little smile as she pushed back her chair and got to her feet.

"When you reach the training area, tell Janis that I want your class working out against one another on their hand-to-hand techniques, Cait," Jerrod added.

Alicia watched, a smile of pride on her lips, as the journeywoman quickly saluted the council before leaving the room. Then, as the door quietly closed, she turned her attention back to the others. This was most definitely not going to be an enjoyable council session.

"How bad was it, Alicia?" Berral asked, her concern for Cait clear.

"Very." She took the seat Cait had vacated and ran a hand over her face. She had never expected to hear a member of the Order speak to another the way Avrim had to the young woman.

"I suggest we all take a day to calm down before we deal with Avrim," Kirris said. "It will do him no harm to spend some time thinking about his actions."

"I don't want him near the students, any of them, ever again, Kirris."

"Nor do any of us, Alicia," the Knight-Commandant said. "But we need to consider what punishment, if any, he should face. I think it will be best if our tempers have cooled a bit."

She nodded, not happy but admitting he was probably correct.

"All I can say is he is very lucky Fallon isn't here," Jerrod commented and Alicia nodded.

There would have been no need for the council to meet had Fallon been in residence. He would have dealt with Avrim then and there, not that Alicia would have blamed him. After all she had been hard pressed not to do so herself.

"I think it best if we not take any action against Avrim for a few days," Daffyd said and held up his hand to keep any of them from speaking. "I'm not saying we don't act. But we have to realize that what he said in class today will quickly make the rounds of the dormitories. While Cait has many friends, she also has her detractors. There are those who feel that she has been receiving special treatment and they resent her.

"Avrim also has his own supporters, not only among the students but among our own numbers. If we are to make an example of him, we had best have more supporting our action than just his comments to one journeywoman."

Alicia ground her teeth in frustration. She wanted to object but Daffyd was right. "What are you proposing?"

"A full investigation. I, and a few of my people, will talk to all of his students, not only those currently in his class but those still at the Citadel who have had him in the past. We will also talk with the townspeople and we will question him. We do this following our own rules and make our case tight enough that no one can doubt the veracity of the charges against him."

"Very well." Kirris leaned back, a thoughtful look on his face. "Alicia, you are due to ride out shortly, are you not?"

"I am." Now she looked at the Knight-Commandant in question, not sure what he was getting at. "I was going to take a squad out to patrol the western sector. We've had a few reports of bandits operating in that area."

"Jerrod, would you say Cait is ready to ride such a patrol?"

For a moment, the Weaponsmaster didn't reply. Then he nodded. "I would."

"Berral?" Kirris looked at her in question.

"Agreed." She turned her attention to Alicia. "I think it best Cait be away from here for a few days. She needs not to be in the center of the speculation we all know will be swirling around here until we deal with Avrim. Do you think she could be of assistance on your patrol?"

Now it was Alicia's turn to take a moment to think. It wasn't unheard of for journeymen to ride patrol with confirmed members of the Order. However, they had usually been at the Citadel longer than Cait had. Then again, exceptions were made when needs arose and the need had most certainly arisen in this case. Besides, it would give her the chance to work more closely with Cait than she had of late. After what she had seen that day, it was more important than ever that she see just where Cait's standard was currently set.

"I do. With your permission, I would like Kala to accompany us. Cait will be less likely to think we are trying to separate her from her fellow students if we include Kala."

"Should you take Stefan or one of the others as well?"

Alicia shook her head. "No. When we take journeymen on

patrol, it is never more than one or two. To change that now will signal something is different and I don't think any of us want that."

"When can you leave?"

"We'll leave come morning. I'll meet with Cait and Kala after their last class to tell them about the assignment and give them instructions about what they need to do to prepare." She was already thinking about all that had to be done before the squad rode out. "I'll take my leave now. There is a lot to do to make sure everything is ready."

"I'll stop by your rooms later," Jerrod said and she nodded, knowing he would make sure she knew everything the council discussed after her departure.

CHAPTER SIXTEEN

THE LARGE WOLF STOOD OUTSIDE THE RING OF LIGHT CAST BY THE campfire, a very human looking smile on its muzzle. After so long, it looked as if the gods had finally smiled on him. Not only was one target within reach but so were several others. They might be enough to finally put him back into Balaar's good graces.

But he could not do it on his own. There were too many of the thrice-damned knights. He would need help, the type of help only his kind could give. A direct assault would be expected. But an attack by wolves would be something else, perhaps even enough to deal with all of them.

For a moment, he sat there, savoring the mental image of presenting Balaar the hearts of each of those lounging around the fire. He could see himself finally assuming his rightful place as Balaar's enforcer, perhaps even his heir. No more running and hiding, fearing Balaar's vengeance for his failure so long ago. That was the life he deserved, not this.

Backing further into the shadows, he took one last look at the campsite. It was tempting to sneak closer and try for his target. Only a heathy fear of swords and arrows prevented it. He had watched the group long enough to know she did not leave the safety of the light unless someone else was with her. Not that he expected any different. A year of watching, waiting and growing not only impatient but worried that he would never be able to get to her had taught him she rarely took chances.

Damn her and those with her.

At least it did not appear they would be returning to their compound soon. That gave him time to find others like himself. He would use them to accomplish his goal and then they would either bow down to him or they would die. They would make perfect sacrifices for those who would come after the pack that had dared attack members of the Order.

Satisfied, he melted into the shadows. There was much to do and, for the first time in a long while, the thrill of the hunt coursed through him.

Cait reined to a halt and looked around. Nothing appeared to be out of the ordinary. A cool breeze blew from the north, typical of most early spring mornings. A hint of dew clung to grass and stone. Here and there, a touch of color foretold the wildflowers soon to blossom. It was all so peaceful and welcoming after the winter and yet not as innocent as it seemed.

Something was out of place. Or, to be more accurate, something was missing. She had not seen, much less heard, any of the usual stirring of birds or animals she had come to expect the last week on the trail. With that realization came the memory of that night on the trail with Fallon when they had been attacked.

Frowning, she lifted her right fist, signaling her companions to halt. A moment later, Alicia joined her, the Tacticsmaster's dark stallion moving to stand shoulder to shoulder with Cait's gelding. When Alicia looked at her, Cait knew she had to explain. But something told her to be careful. If they were being watched, she didn't want to let the watchers know she was aware of them.

"Cait?"

"Listen."

Alicia looked at her for one long moment and then nodded. Cait marveled at how the woman managed to scan their surroundings without actually appearing to do so. Unless someone knew the Tacticsmaster very well, they would not see the tension in her body or recognize the concern lurking deep in her eyes. Then, when she looked once more at Cait, she nodded once.

"You keep on point, Cait," she said as she signaled the rest of the squad forward. "Aislin, you bring up the rear," she added as the knight drew close. At the same time, she used the hand signals she had drilled into Cait and Kala since leaving the Citadel to warn everyone to be on alert. "We'll set up camp as planned."

Cait nodded, touched her heels to her mount and urged the gelding into an easy trot. As she did, she shifted slightly in the saddle. Her sword, secured to her saddle by her right leg, was within easy reach. Like the others, she wore a dagger at her waist. Unlike them, however, she also had daggers in quick release sheaths on each forearm. A slight smile touched her lips at the memory of Alicia's reaction their first night on the trail. The Tacticsmaster had looked at the sheaths in surprise as Cait stripped off the padded leather jacket she had been wearing. Before Cait could explain, she had asked if the daggers had been the Weaponsmaster's idea. Cait said they were and that was the last they had spoken of it.

Alicia rode next to her. Cait glanced at her and nodded slightly. She had a feeling if she looked over her shoulder, she would see another of the knights riding at Kala's side. Even though they had been treated as equals for most of the scouting mission, Alicia had made sure everyone understood that, should they run into trouble, the journeywomen were to be protected. Part of her had railed at the special treatment but another part understood. She and Kala were not as well trained as the others and, because they were not yet Confirmed members of the Order, they would be easy prey for Balaar's followers should they be captured.

And prey she would never again be if she had anything to say about it.

Later, Cait and Kala tended the mounts while the others saw about setting up camp. As she made sure the picket was securely set up, Cait looked around. If possible, this site was even more defensible than their previous campsites had been. A slight smile touched her lips as she wondered how long before Alicia came and started quizzing them, not only about their current location but about what they had seen and heard on the day's patrol. She and Kala had learned quickly their first night away from the Citadel that the Tacticsmaster meant to make this a learning situation for them. Not that she minded. She had a feeling she would learn much more this way than she would in months of classroom study.

"Cait, what's going on?" Kala asked softly as they moved toward the center of camp.

For a moment, she didn't answer. Frowning, she wondered how much she should say. After all, she didn't know for sure anything was wrong. All she knew for sure was that she had had a bad feeling since morning. That wasn't exactly all. The fact Alicia seemed to be taking her concerns to heart also worried her.

"I'm not sure anything is," she answered just as softly and quickly explained her concerns about the morning ride.

Kala frowned slightly. Cait waited, watching as her friend thought about all she had seen and heard on the ride. Then, when Kala nodded once, she relaxed. At least her friend wasn't dismissing her concerns out of hand, not that Kala would. She had never done that as far as Cait knew.

"Come eat," Alicia called from the fire. "And we will continue our lessons from last evening."

Taking one last look around the campsite, doing her best to make sure she missed no detail of their surroundings, Cait did as the Tacticsmaster said. As she did, her stomach growled, reminding her it had been a long time since the midday meal.

The wolves took up their positions around the camp. For two days they had tracked the humans. For two days they had wanted to attack but had been held back, just as they had been held back from feeding. Now, hunger and the thrill of the hunt brought them closer to their animal side than ever before. What human was left in them was a distant memory, just as their leader had planned. He needed them angry and desperate, willing to do whatever was necessary to bring down their prey. Nothing else mattered.

Well outside the light cast by the dancing flames of the campfire, he stood. For more than an hour, he had studied the knights, waiting for them to finally retire. Until they had, he did not dare order the attack. Even with seven wolves at his command, it wouldn't be enough if they did not manage to catch the others off-guard. So he waited, still in his two-legged form.

His gaze followed the young woman he had failed to kill once before. She moved with a confidence now that she had lacked that earlier time. Was it because of the training the Order had given her or was it because she was not alone? Not that it mattered. Soon enough he would have her at his mercy, his jaws at her throat. Then she would remember what it was like to be his master's toy.

A smile of anticipation touched his lips at the thought. Once before he had had her at his mercy. She might not remember it but he most certainly did. Blood dripping from his jaws, he had tracked her as she tried to flee. She hadn't had a chance. Within minutes, he had her under his paws, his jaws closing around her exposed neck. Only his master's order to hold had stopped him. He had been denied his prize. But not this time. This time Balaar had given him the girl and he planned to make sure she paid dearly for the trouble she had caused him.

It would take her a long time to die.

One by one, the six members of the squad began to turn in for the evening. Finally, only his target and the older woman he had come to identify as the squad leader remained awake. They sat close to the fire, softly talking. He frowned, wishing he could hear what they were saying. But in his human form, his hearing was not as acute as when he was shifted. Soon, very soon, that would not be an issue. He would give them a few more minutes and then he would signal the attack. Even if the two women were still awake, they would be no match for his wolves, much less for him.

Moonless nights were the best nights for hunting, at least when you were the hunter.

"You have first watch, Cait," Alicia said as she stood. She stretched and looked around. A moment later, she looked at where Cait sat before the fire and gave her a slow wink.

Cait nodded, her pulse quickening. Even though there had been no sign close to camp of any trouble lurking in the shadows, she knew it was there. She could feel the eyes watching her, watching and waiting for the right moment to strike. Now she had to play her role and hope whoever it was that had been tracking them took the bait. If not, they would repeat the process for as many nights as it took.

Carefully feeding the fire, she thought about what they had found on the patrol since leaving the Citadel. The first two days had been unexceptional, even boring. Not that she had expected anything else. That close to the Citadel, it would have surprised her to find bandits or others acting against the law of the land. That had changed as they moved further away. Farmers talked of their stores being raided and merchants told of their shipments being hijacked on the way to market.

The day before, they had come across their first evidence of bandits. Two travelers had been attacked on the trade road and left for dead. By the time the patrol came across them, it was too late to save them. But they had not died without leaving clues as to who their attackers had been. One had drawn symbols in his own blood, symbols the Tacticsmaster had recognized. Cait had watched in growing concern as Alicia's expression darkened as she studied the two symbols. Then, without explanation, she had ordered the bodies buried and any personal belongings that might have been left gathered to be returned to their families.

Since then, they had all been more watchful. What one missed, another saw. Or so it seemed. Alicia had impressed on both Cait and Kala the need to pass on anything they felt or saw that seemed out of the ordinary. She did not care how improbable it seemed. She wanted to know about it. That was the only reason Cait had said anything that morning. Now, feeling eyes at her back, as well as from the sides and front, she wished she had been wrong.

Finally, his wait, his exile, was about to come to an end. An almost feral smile touched his lips as his fingers caressed the fur safely tucked away in the pouch that hung from his neck. A slight breeze chilled his skin but not for long. Soon he would once again run on four legs instead of two. Fur, thick and the color of the darkest night, would protect him. More important than all that, he would soon hunt and his prey had no idea her life was about to end.

One of the wolves crept close. Its ears lay flat against its head. It whined once and instantly fell silent as he turned to glare at it. He knew it wanted him to shift and call for the hunt. But it needed to learn its place just as its human form did. Not that he planned for it, or any of the others, to live out the night. Balaar demanded he make sure no one connect what was about to happen with him and he would not fail his master a second time.

"Soon," he said softly.

One by one, the fools in the clearing fell asleep. Before long, only his ultimate prey remained awake. It was time. She had to be tired after a day in the saddle. That made her easy prey, especially since his wolves would make quick work of her companions. He motioned for the wolf that had approached to return to its position. As it slunk off, he frowned. Any doubts he had were gone. The wolf had to die before it had a chance to return to its human form. Perhaps it might serve one last role. His death could show the woman what lay ahead for her. He liked that. Her fear might make up for some of what he had suffered for failing to insure her death before she left Lineaus. Holding the piece of fur between thumb and forefinger, he focused on his wolf. He had been many different animals over the years, but this wolf was his favorite. Strong and fast, it was the thing of nightmares. Now the time had come once again to prove just how fearsome he could be.

A rustling, so faint she almost missed it, came from her right. A trickle of sweat ran down her spine. Instinct almost made her look in the direction of the sound but she stopped herself. She could do nothing to let those who had been tracking them know she was aware of their presence. The success of Alicia's plan rested on the element of surprise.

Cait hoped the surprise didn't wind up being on them.

She stretched and then rolled her shoulders to ease the tension that tightened them. The fire crackled, a spark jumping high in the air. As it did, she glanced down. The fire had been very carefully built and tended that evening. All she had to do was reach out and she could grab one of four flaming branches. They could make excellent weapons if the need arose. Not that she had any intention of letting things get that far.

More rustling and the hair on the back of her neck stood on end as she realized it came from multiple sources. They had anticipated that but it didn't make the waiting any easier. Her left hand began creeping toward the hilt of her sword where it rested on the ground in front of her. To stop herself from grabbing the blade, she reached up and scratched her nose. All she needed to do was wait a little longer. Then the trap would be sprung and, hopefully, it wouldn't backfire on them.

This was so very different from the training exercises they had done back at the Citadel. There, the knowledge that no one would be hurt, much less die, if mistakes were made had always been in the back of her mind. Now she knew lives, even her own, rested on how she performed and it started with convincing those watching them that she had no clue they were out there.

Lord and Lady, help me.

Another rustling, this time to her right. Whoever, whatever was coming closer. Soon they would be close enough to see. For not the first time, Cait wished she possessed foresight. Before, she had wished for it so she could anticipate what her instructors might want. Now, she wanted desperately to know not only how many were approaching their camp but what they wanted as well.

"Down!" Alicia ordered as she rolled to her feet, bow in hand, as a howl shattered the silence of the night.

Cait dropped to her belly, rolling away from the fire. Her left hand closed around the hilt of her sword. All around her, she heard her companions tossing aside their blankets and leaping to their feet, weapons in hand. An arrow cut through the air, so close Cait could feel it, followed quickly by another. Almost instantly, a whine of pain from behind her sounded.

"Wolves," Alicia said as Cait rolled to her feet. "Form up!"

Instantly, the knights moved into a defensive formation. Backs to one another, facing outward, they formed a circle with Kala and Cait in the center. With them stood Alicia, her determination clear as she notched another arrow, her eyes already seeking her next target.

Heart pounding, Cait waited. Of all the scenarios she had imagined, this was not one. Why would wolves have tracked them for hours, maybe even days? It made no sense.

He threw his head back and howled in frustration. No! It could not be. How had those thrice-damned fools known they were there?

One of his wolves whined in pain as an arrow sliced through the air and embedded in its shoulder. Another arrow followed close after the first. The wolf went down. The scent of blood filled the air. Too much blood. The wolf would be dead soon. That was no loss. The wolf would have had to die anyway. But it was inconvenient. It would have been better if the wolf lived long enough to have taken out at least one of the knights.

Growling, he moved forward, nipping at the flanks of

another of his wolves as this one hesitated. They needed to press forward. They were wolves. The knights were no match for them. But if they continued to lurk in the shadows like scared cubs, that damned woman with her bow would pick them off one by one.

Once again, he threw back his head and howled. Almost instantly, his remaining wolves howled in response. They might not like what he ordered but they would obey. He was their master, just as Balaar was his. Like Balaar, he would reward failure with death and they knew it.

Another nip of the flank and he watched as the wolves surged forward. Satisfaction filled him as the five raced toward the camp. They would confuse and then overwhelm the humans. Then the girl would be his. He looked forward to dealing with her once and for all. He was tired of running, fearing his master would catch up with him and kill him at any moment.

Five wolves, snarling and snapping, circled the squad. Occasionally one would surge forward, teeth and claws seeking flesh and bone. The scent of blood, some human and some wolf, filled the air. Blade met flesh, hacking and stabbing, and no one gained the advantage.

Something was not right. Cait frowned, pulling Justus back as he cried out in pain. Blood poured from a wicked looking wound at his thigh. Mouth tight, Cait swallowed against the bile rising in her throat. She could not get sick any more than she could take her attention from the wolves. That was the mistake Justus had made and he had paid the price.

The horses!

Why were the wolves not attacking the horses? They were the logical targets. Tethered, they would be unable to flee. That made them easy prey. So why attack humans who would fight back?

Four wolves paced restlessly around the squad. All bled from various wounds. One dragged a rear leg behind it, one of Alicia's arrows buried deep in that flank. It would not be long before it collapsed. Another lay motionless a few feet away. That reassured Cait but she dared not relax. Not yet. None of them could until this was over.

Another howl filled the air. Almost instantly, the wolves pressed forward, slower this time but with a determination that worried Cait. There was something about them, an intelligence of sorts, that surprised her. They seemed to almost work in unison as they probed here, feinted there before trying to attack one or two of the knights holding the outer line.

"There!" Kala pointed toward the edge of the clearing. "Another wolf."

Cait nodded. She had seen the fifth wolf just after the last howl sounded. This one looked bigger than the others. Unlike them, it stayed back, almost as if it were watching what happened and waiting for the right moment to come forward. But that made no sense. If that were the case, it would imply an intelligence to the creature that neared human. That couldn't be possible.

Could it?

Then, out of the corner of her eye, she saw Alicia notch another arrow. How many did the Tacticsmaster have with her? She had been firing steadily, carefully picking her targets so no shot was wasted. Now she once more picked her target, this time the lone wolf.

"Watch our flank, Cait," Alicia said softly.

As if that were the signal to attack, one of the remaining wolves leapt. Cait ducked, staying clear not only of Alicia's line of sight but of the arrow as well. Once on the other side of the

Tacticsmaster, she straightened, sword in her left hand and dagger in her right. Her left hand swung in a wide arc, crossing in front of her. The edge of the blade caught the wolf in its far side. A whine of pain tore from its throat. Then it twisted in the air, its jaws snapping.

Cait's left foot slid back and to her right. As she pivoted, she drove her dagger into the wolf's neck. Determined not to lose her grip on the blade, she held on as if her life depended on it. She followed the wolf down, trapping it against the ground with her body. Twisting the dagger right and then left, driving it to the hilt into the heavily muscled neck, she ignored the pain along her left side as claws dug in. One of them would not survive this and she had no intention of dying, at least not for a very long time.

And not when she still had so many questions without answers.

"Get up!" Alicia ordered.

At the same time, a hand closed over Cait's arm and hauled her to her feet. Panting, she looked down. Blood, too much blood, covered her. Most of it was the wolf's. At least she hoped it was. Not that it mattered. Until the fight was over, she would be unable to check her wounds, much less treat them.

"You all right?" the Tactic's Master demanded.

"Aye." No need to tell her any differently. They were all injured. Worse, they were tiring. If they did not end this soon, they might fall.

Alicia nodded and notched her last arrow. Her expression was grim as she scanned the area. Then, spotting her target, she bared her teeth in an expression that was more frightening than anything Cait had seen on the wolves. The Tacticsmaster looked like a woman who knew their lives depended on her next shot. Miss and they were dead. Hit and it would all be over.

Lord and Lady, guide her shot.

Alicia notched the arrow and searched the shadows for the wolf. There was something different about it, something much more dangerous than the others. It was as if it watched the fight from afar, occasionally telling the attacking wolves what to do. Each time the larger wolf howled, the others pressed the attack. They seemed to almost work together. If she did not know better, she would think they had been trained to do this. But that was impossible. Wolves were wild animals and she knew of no one who could train them in such a way.

There!

Lurking at the edge of the clearing, the large wolf almost faded into the shadows. The yellow eyes, glowing with what looked suspiciously like anticipation, reflected the campfire. Then, as if sensing her gaze, its head swung and their eyes locked. She sighted down the shaft of her arrow and drew the bowstring back until the knuckles of her index and middle finger were locked in place along her jaw.

Inhale.

Exhale.

Wait . . . Wait.

Now!

She released and the arrow shot through the air, sailing toward its target. She watched as everything slowed and the world narrowed to the arrow as it winged toward the wolf. Too late, the creature realized it had gotten overconfident. Its howl of pain echoed through the trees as the arrow stuck its chest, driving the shaft deep through muscle and bone. Howls turned to whimpers as the wolf collapsed.

The other wolves broke off the attack at the sound of the larger wolf's howl. Instantly, the knights acted. Swords slashed and hacked. Cries of pain filled the air as blood poured onto the ground. The fight was over as quickly as it had begun. Five wolves lay dead or dying in the right of light cast by the campfire. Without doing more than quickly glancing at them, Alicia motioned for two of the squad to dispatch the wolves that still lived. As she did, she handed Kala her bow and, drawing her sword, strode across the clearing to where the larger wolf had fallen. It did not surprise her to find Cait following on her heels.

"Lord and Lady!"

She stared at the naked man weakly dragging himself away from the clearing. Her arrow had pierced the upper left side of his chest. Blood pooled around the shaft and covered that side. Seeing them, he stopped, his right hand reaching for the small pouch hanging around his neck. A bit of fur showed at the opening of the pouch.

Fear and revulsion filled her, as did determination. She had no time to waste. Her right foot flashed forward, her heavy boot catching him in the side, lifting and rolling him. He cried out and his right hand lost its grip on the pouch. Before he could grab for it again, she bent, her hand closing over the pouch. With a tug, she pulled it from his neck before she quickly stepped out of reach.

"Make sure those wolves are dead!" she called back to the others.

Lord and Lady, now it made sense. She blew out a shaky breath and fought the impulse to order the squad out of the area. As enticing as that might be, she had to find out if her suspicions were correct. If they were. . . .

"Alicia?"

Concern filled Cait's voice and, for the first time since leaving the Citadel, she cursed the fact she had two journeywomen with her. At least they had handled themselves well and she would be getting them back to the Citadel in one piece, albeit a bit battered.

Or she would as long as nothing else happened.

"Cait, I want you and the others to check those wolves. Look for pouches like this." She let the pouch she had taken from the man lying a few feet away dangle from her fingers. "But, unless you are completely sure the wolves are dead, do not touch them."

For a moment, Cait looked at her, her confusion obvious. Then the young woman nodded and hurried to where the other members of the squad checked the wolves. Swallowing hard, fighting down the revulsion she felt, Alicia turned back to her prisoner.

"You're dying, wolf. Tell me who sent you and what you were after."

"N-no."

She had to strain to hear him.

"Don't be a fool. Answer my questions and I swear we will ease your pain."

"T-this is nothing compared to what my master will do to you."

Alicia's expression hardened as the implications of what he said dawned on her.

"Then tell your master that his next messenger had best be better prepared than were you." She drew her dagger. Then she stopped. She would give him one more chance before she ended his life. "Tell me this, wolf. Why did you attack us?"

For a moment, he said nothing. He simply looked at her, his face a mask of pain. Then, as if without conscious thought, he glanced past her. She followed his gaze and felt her blood run cold. Cait knelt next to one of the fallen wolves, her back to them. The rest of the squad was to the left, out of the man's line of sight.

"Your master should have chosen someone better than you if you wanted to get to her," she snarled as she tightened her grip on the dagger. "She is one of ours." With that, she grabbed him by the hair, pulling his head back. As she slit his throat, she said a prayer for forgiveness. She never liked taking a life, not even in battle, but this was one life she gladly ended if it meant keeping Cait and the others safe.

"M'lady?" Cait's voice was soft, uncertain, as she once more joined Alicia.

"What did you find?"

"Each of them carried pouches like the one he did." The young woman nodded to the man's body. "M'lady – Alicia – what was he?"

"A skinwalker." She closed her eyes for a moment and breathed deeply as she strove for calm. "Listen up." She raised her voice enough so everyone could hear her. "We're breaking camp just as soon as we deal with the bodies. Drag the wolves together and burn their carcasses. Make sure nothing remains. Keep the pouches you found. Kirris and Berral will want to examine them."

"What about him?" Justus asked, pointing to the dead man.

"Him too." Then, feeling someone reaching for her weapons, she shook herself. She had to focus. Cait smiled at her and said she would clean the blades. Nodding, she let the young woman take them. She could have done it herself but it gave her another moment or two in which to collect her thoughts. "Everyone needs to be on their guard. Those were no ordinary wolves. They were skinwalkers. We will cleanse the area and see to our injuries and then we ride to the Citadel. The leadership needs to know about this."

CHAPTER SEVENTEEN

THE CITADEL ROSE BEFORE THEM, CLIMBING OUT OF THE EARLY morning fog that cloaked the area. Almost too tired to care, Cait blew out a relieved breath. Alicia had driven them hard since the attack. They had stopped only long enough to allow their mounts to rest. For the first time, Cait had actually slept while in the saddle. At least she thought she had. There were stretches of the ride she could not recall. Whether from sleep or simply shutting down for a bit, it did not matter. All that did was that they were finally there.

When Alicia held up her right fist, signaling for the squad to halt, Cait had a feeling she was not the only one to wonder what might be on the Tacticsmaster's mind. With the Citadel still too far away for Cait's liking, she slowly led her gelding to where Alicia waited. Once they were all close enough to hear without the Tacticsmaster having to raise her voice, she inclined her head in the direction of home.

"As soon as we are through the gates, I want them closed and secured. No one goes in or out without my permission until I've had a chance to brief the Knight-Commandant and the Adept. Kala, Justus, you are to locate them and tell them I need to see them immediately. Say nothing else to them or to anyone else you might come into contact with. If either the Knight-Commandant or the Adept demand an explanation, you are to say one word: Morrigu. Understand?"

The four nodded, their expressions grim.

"Cait, you are with me. I'm trusting you to watch my back

just as I will watch yours."

Cait swallowed hard. "Ma'am, are you expecting trouble inside?"

Gods above and below, if even the Citadel was no longer safe, what were they to do?

"No, but I haven't lived as long as I have without being cautious." She gave all of them a reassuring smile. "I know I have said it before but I am proud of all of you. You handled yourselves well in circumstances none of us expected. Hopefully, this will soon be over but, until we are sure, do not let your guards down."

With that, she nudged her mount forward. Cait fell into place to her right and slightly behind while the others took up their positions in the formation they had fallen into on the ride back. As they neared the main gates, Cait checked the ease with which she could draw her sword and dagger. As she did, she was aware of her companions doing the same. They were taking Alicia's warnings to heart.

Lord and Lady help them if there was trouble within the walls.

The heavy gates swung open as soon as Alicia answered the challenge from the watch on the wall. She guided her squad inside and then stopped, signaling for them to do the same. Almost instantly, a yeoman ran forward to hold the reins of her horse. She studied him, her expression set, before lifting her leg over the back of her horse and dismounting.

"Close the gate!" she ordered. "Squad, take up your positions. No one in or out without permission. You know your assignments."

"Lady Alicia," one of the journeymen on duty started. One look from her had him closing his mouth with a snap. Cait didn't blame him one bit for swallowing hard. Just then, Alicia looked like she would happily snap his head off if he dared open his mouth again. When the Tacticsmaster jerked her head to her right, indicating he was to return to his post, he turned and ran.

"Kala, Justus, off you go. Find the Knight-Commandant and the Adept. Cait and I are going to locate the Weaponsmaster."

Before she could continue, the sounds of several people running in their direction filled the air. Alicia quickly signaled for the squad to dismount. Tense, her left hand resting on the hilt of her sword, Cait waited. She tried telling herself that they were safe but she couldn't quite believe it. Not after what had happened just two days earlier. She had already known the evil one man could do to another. But she had never believed, not in her wildest dreams, that a man could turn into an animal and back. What else was there she did not know? More important, why had these people she trusted with her life not warned her?

A few moments later, Jerrod, followed closely by Stefan, slid to a halt in front of them. The Weaponsmaster took one quick look at the squad and his eyes narrowed. Cait had a feeling he saw every wound they bore and every line of exhaustion etched in their faces. She also knew without asking that he would support Alicia in whatever she said. Good. They needed that just then. She could trust the man just as she trusted the Tacticsmaster.

"Alicia?" A thousand questions echoed in that single word.

"I will explain once we are joined by Berral and Kirris," she promised, her expression grimmer than Cait had ever seen. When Jerrod continued to watch her, she sighed and said one word. "Morrigu."

The Weaponsmaster hissed in a breath. His eyes flashed and his hands fisted at his sides. Whoever or whatever this Morrigu was, the name alone was enough to stop all questions and, apparently, all doubts.

"Stefan, find Ricard, Saoirse and Gadiel. The three of you are to stand guard outside the armory until relieved. No one passes without authorization from either myself, Lady Alicia, the Adept or the Knight-Commandant. Now go."

For a moment, Stefan hesitated. He glanced at Cait and she knew he had as many questions as did she. Unfortunately, she had no answers to give him. So, with a shrug, she jerked her head in the direction of the armory. Hopefully there would be time later to discuss what happened and what it all meant.

"We had best waste no more time. Kirris and Berral need to hear your report," Jerrod said as Stefan raced off.

Alicia nodded. With Jerrod at her side, she hurried in the direction of Kirris' office. Everyone at the Citadel knew the morning schedule of the Order's highest ranking members. They began almost every day in the Knight-Commandant's office. Sometimes they were joined by the other Masters. There were even occasions when some of the more advanced students were asked to join them and share their insights into what was happening in their classes and with their training.

A moment later, Alicia turned and glanced back to where Cait stood. Seeing the Tacticsmaster looking at her, Cait swallowed hard, wondering what the woman had in mind now.

"You're with me, Cait," the blonde said and started off again, leaving Cait to hurry after her.

Five minutes later, they were shown into the Knight-Commandant's office. Kirris took one look at the three and instantly sent the young yeoman who had shown them in off to find both Alicia's and Jerrod's assistants. Then he closed the door, sliding the bar into place, insuring they would not be interrupted.

"Sit," Berral said as she stoked the fire across from Kirris' desk.

Cait watched as Jerrod and Alicia complied, taking two of the four seats in front of the fire. Once they had, Cait moved to stand behind Alicia's chair. She might not know what was going on, nor did she understand why the Tacticsmaster had insisted she be present, but she knew her place. She would stand prepared to meet any challenge, not that she expected one, until she was dismissed.

"Tell us," Kirris said simply as he took his seat next to Berral.

For the next half hour Alicia detailed everything that happened during their patrol. The others let her describe everything once and then they had her start over. This time, they peppered her with questions. By the time she finished, not a single detail, no matter how minor, had been omitted. Cait knew she should have been reassured by it all. Clearly they were not going to dismiss Alicia's concerns out of hand. But, seeing how worried the others now looked, she had a feeling things were a lot worse than she first thought. Gods above and below, she wished she knew what was going on.

Kirris leaned back and stared into the flames of the fire, his expression thoughtful. Then, in a burst of energy, he stood. They watched as he crossed to the door and unbarred it. The moment he opened it, one of those he had sent for, stepped forward. The Knight-Commandant spoke softly but there was no mistaking the seriousness of his tone or the surprise that flickered across the faces of those in the anteroom. Just as quickly as he had opened the door, he closed it, barring it once again.

"I have sent reinforcements to the armory and front gate." He held up a hand to stop the protests Cait saw Alicia about to make. "Don't worry. I sent only those Berral or I have worked closely with over the last few days."

The Tacticsmaster nodded and relief washed over Cait.

Whatever was going on, she knew she could take her cue from the blonde. If Alicia was satisfied with the actions Kirris had taken, she would be as well. Still, it would be nice if someone explained just what was going on and why they were all so worried.

"Alicia, tell me again about that last wolf," Berral said.

Cait looked at the Adept and frowned. In the past year, she had come to know the woman very well and there could be no mistaking both her concern and her anger. That anger was something new, something she had not seen from Berral except during the incident with Avrim.

Avrim. Could all this be related?

Cait shook her head. She saw no way what happened on the trail could relate back to what happened that day in the classroom. Even so, with the events coming so close together, she dared not dismiss the possibility out of hand. Could that be what the Adept was wondering as well?

"As I said, it was larger than the others and hung back from the fighting. It was as though it was trying to direct them in when and how to attack. There was an intelligence to it, moreso than with the others. I felt if we managed to take it out of the equation, the others would either scatter or panic or both. So I waited for my shot and took it."

Cait shuddered slightly, remembering that moment. She had known then how much rested on the blonde hitting her target. Had she known the rest of it – well, best not to think about that just then.

"And you are sure the man you found was also the wolf?" Kirris asked.

"Aye."

Cait didn't need to see the Tacticsmaster's face to know she looked troubled. Her worry radiated off of her.

"He may have been human but he had my arrow in his

chest." She paused and sipped the tea Berral had poured out for her earlier. "Besides, what normal human runs around the countryside in the nude, especially when a battle wages nearby?" There was a bite to her voice now. "Kirris, if you don't believe me, ask Cait. She saw as well."

Cait swallowed, remembering that moment.

"I did, sir." The Knight-Commandant might not have asked, but she owed it to Alicia to confirm what the blonde said. "The Tacticsmaster's arrows are unique. We all have come to recognize them, not only for the glyphs on the shafts but for the unique feathering she uses. So I knew the arrow the moment I saw it. I also happened to be standing with her when she loosed that last arrow. I saw where it hit. It may have been a wolf when she targeted it but it was a man when we got to it."

"A man with this around his neck." Alicia produced the small bag on the leather cord she had removed from the man's neck. She handed it to Jerrod who looked at it for a moment before placing it carefully on the table they four sat around.

For a moment no one said anything. Berral reached out, the fingers of her right hand not quite touching the bag or the small piece of fur sticking out of its opening. Cait watched as the Adept paled. Then, before anyone could protest, Berral's fingers closed about the bag and she tossed it onto the fire. As she did, she offered up a soft prayer for protection that they all echoed.

"Skinwalker," she hissed as the fire crackled and smoke billowed up the chimney. "Open a window and air the room."

Cait quickly moved across the office to do as the Adept instructed.

"Aye," Alicia confirmed. "We found similar tokens on all of the wolves but that was the only one to shift back to human."

"He was the alpha then." Kirris leaned forward, elbows on his knees. Then, as if realizing Cait was still there, he motioned her back from the window. As he did, he stood and pulled up a chair for her. "Cait, sit."

Not sure she really wanted to because she felt the attention would now be on her, but also knowing she had no other choice, she did as he said.

"Now, Alicia said you were the first to realize something was amiss. Tell us what you felt." The Knight-Commandant's voice was soft, almost gentle, and she relaxed a little.

"Sir, you know how it is out on the trail. You get used to the sounds around you until they almost disappear. Still, some part of you is aware of them so, when those sounds are no longer present, you realize it." She paused and was relieved to see all three of them nod in agreement. "That is what happened. I suddenly realized I hadn't heard any of the usual birdsong or the like for a while. It bothered me, especially when I had seen nor heard anything to cause the silence. So I told Lady Alicia and she put us on our guard."

Now she thought about those long hours in the saddle as they continued to ride their patrol. How difficult it had been to carry on as if nothing was the matter when every instinct screamed danger was close, just waiting to ambush them. But all of them had carried out their orders and had acted as if nothing was amiss.

"Alicia?" Berral looked at the woman, her expression thoughtful.

"I will freely admit something had been bothering me that morning but I had not yet identified it. Once Cait told me of her concerns, I knew she was right." She smiled in encouragement at Cait from across the table.

"And you are sure the man you and Lady Alicia found after the fight was the same as the wolf you had seen?"

"Aye, sir. I have no doubt about it." She had so many questions about what happened. "Please, you seem to know what the man was, if man he truly was. But I don't. What is a skinwalker and why would he attack us?"

For a moment, no one spoke. Then Berral stood. Cait watched as the Adept moved around the table to where she sat. Berral's hands were gentle as they reached for hers.

"Cait, we owe you an apology."

An apology?

"You have done so well since your arrival here, not only with your studies but with how you have truly become one of our own. Because of that, we made a grave mistake, one that could have cost you and the Order dearly. We forgot that you have no memory of most of your life. We forgot that you don't know all the tales we grew up with, tales that have their basis in fact. That is something I promise you now we won't forget again."

"Adept, I don't understand."

And she didn't. What did her lack of memory have to do with what happened?

"Cait, skinwalkers are men and women who have the ability to change their forms. There are rituals involved and the skinwalker must have at least a bit of the skin or hide of the creature he wants to change into on his person," Kirris said.

"Is that why you told us to make sure the wolves were dead before touching them?" she asked the Tacticsmaster.

"It is. The most powerful skinwalkers can take on the form of other people, but they have to touch to do so."

"A-are there skinwalkers in the Order?" She was unsure how she felt about that.

"We have a few who can shift or become an animal of one kind or another. But it is a very rare gift and they are not skinwalkers. They do not need to have the pelt of the animal on them. Their *talent* comes from the Lord and Lady and not from ritual or blood magic." The Adept knelt, her hands still holding

Cait's, her expression serious. "Cait, skinwalkers are not all evil but because many of them turn to blood magic to make it easier to change forms, they are often found among Balaar's followers."

"And this Morrigu Lady Alicia spoke of?"

For a moment no one spoke. Then Berral sat back on her heels, a frown tugging at the corners of her mouth. "Morrigu is one of the dark gods, Cait. The irony is, one of your lessons for next week was to be on her and her followers. She comes in two forms. One an enticing woman, capturing followers through wile and deception. The other is a silver wolf with blue eyes, the eyes of a human. The wolf can go where the human cannot and vice versa. Her followers may be warriors or scavengers. They care not as long as the money is good and the goal is to do harm."

Cait nodded, her expression grim. Even though she knew she had never heard of Morrigu or her followers before, something about the story felt familiar. Just as it had been with other things over the past year, some faint wisp of memory teased her, giving her a glimpse of what might have been without ever letting her reach out and grab it. This time, however, instead of feeling frustrated, she felt reassured. She still had questions, too many questions, but they would have to wait.

"How do we fight them if they can change not only appearances but shapes as well?"

"I told you she thought like a warrior," Alicia said with an approving grin. "Before we answer your question, Cait, tell us what you felt and sensed when we came upon the injured man."

For a moment, she said nothing. Instead, she closed her eyes and thought back to the moment. There had been surprise and disbelief. Those were the easiest to remember because they had been the strongest emotions at the time. There had even been relief that the fight was finally over and they had all survived. But, now that she thought about it, there had been something else as well. But what?

"I'm not sure how to explain it," she said, her eyes still closed. "Now that I think about it, there was something as I neared him. It was as though the air had become thick, oily. There was an underlying stench, like rotting flesh."

She shuddered at the memory. In the heat of the battle and the emotions of the aftermath, she had not realized what her subconscious registered as she followed Alicia. The sight of the naked man where she expected to find a wounded wolf had overridden everything else. Now she had to remember those feelings and make sure she never made the mistake of missing them again.

"I'm impressed, Cait. Most don't sense that much about a skinwalker and certainly not the first time they encounter one." Kirris looked at her thoughtfully and then, as if recognizing her frustration with herself, he smiled in reassurance. "Remember that. It may save you or others later."

She nodded and did her best to commit it to memory.

"Is there anything else you think we should know?" Berral asked.

Cait shook her head.

"Listen closely then. Lady Alicia did the right thing by sealing the front gate. Until we are sure no one has infiltrated here, we have to take care. Unfortunately, people are going to want to know what is going on and why. When you leave here, people are going to ask you about what happened while you were on patrol and why Alicia acted as she did. They are going to know that you have been in here with us and will expect you to have answers to their questions. Do not tell them anything. I want to believe we have no spies among those within the compound walls but we have to be sure. Simply tell them that you are not privy to what is going on and you are sure the Adept and I will explain soon," Kirris said.

'I understand and will do as you say." Not that she would have said anything anyway.

"Get yourself to the Healer now, Cait. After your injuries have been treated, change clothes and return here," Berral said. Then she paused, her expression thoughtful. "I would prefer you go straight to the Healer but we need you to perform one duty for us first."

"Of course, Adept."

"Find the other Masters and tell them they are needed here. It wouldn't surprise me if you find most of them waiting nearby but you may need to look for one or two of them. Once you've delivered my message, then go to the Healer. Only after she has treated you is she to join us."

"I understand." Cait stood, suddenly ready to leave what she had a feeling was soon to become a war council.

"Go, and return as soon as you can," Kirris told her.

Without a word, she stood and, after bowing to the four, left. She needed time. Time to think about what she had heard and time to think about what she had learned. Unfortunately, she had a feeling time was the one luxury that would be in short supply.

Two hours later, Alicia leaned back and blew out a breath. After briefing the other Masters, Kirris had excused all but Berral, Jerrod, Daffyd and Alicia herself. She had gone over her report once more for the Judicar, answering his questions and additional ones from the others.

What had surprised her was Daffyd's reaction upon learning Berral had burned the skinwalker's pouch. From the way Berral's eyes narrowed, she wasn't the only taken aback by the man's comments. Before either of them could comment, Jerrod had spoken.

"Why, Daffyd?" His face was a stone mask, not that Alicia could blame him. "Do you not trust Alicia's report? Or is it that you think you know more about those she and the others encountered than our Adept?'

The Judicar shook his head, his expression betraying his surprise at being questioned so. "Of course not! But it was evidence of what happened and should have been examined."

Alicia ground her teeth. She and Daffyd had never been close, certainly not the way she and Jerrod were. The Judicar was too hidebound, too tied to what he could see and feel. There were times, like now, when she wondered how he had managed to be confirmed in the Order. Oh, she knew the Lord and Lady sometimes chose those without special *talents*. Perhaps his need to have proof of everything was exactly why he had been confirmed. Perhaps his role in the Order was to not take things on faith and, in doing so, make sure the rest of them were not led astray simply because they did take something on faith. But, at the moment, she would rather he be a little more flexible.

"Evidence or no, the Adept and Knight-Commandant saw and agreed with my conclusions." Alicia made no attempt to hide her frustration.

"Peace, Alicia." Daffyd held his hands up before him. "I meant no disrespect to anyone."

She ran a hand over her face and then looked back at him. "I know."

"I hear a *but* in there, Alicia," Kirris said.

"Not really. However, there is one thing we haven't discussed and that is the skinwalker's target."

"You mean those godsforsaken bastards were after more

than just attacking your squad."

She nodded. This was the one thing she had held back in her earlier reports. She had not wanted to discuss it with all the Masters, knowing it would have begun a lengthy debate about what it meant and how they should respond. But now was time for her to share what she had seen and what she suspected.

"Aye, Jerrod. Before I dispatched the skinwalker, I asked why he had attacked the squad. We were alone. I had sent Cait off to make sure the rest of the squad searched the other wolves for the pouches like I had taken off of the skinwalker. He didn't answer but he looked past me. Only one member of the squad was in his line of sight – Cait. They were after her."

"You're sure?" Kirris asked, his expression troubled.

"I have no doubt about it. I don't know if the man, if you can call such a creature man, had been watching Cait since we left here or if it was sheer dumb luck that had him crossing our path. It doesn't matter which. But it does tell us that someone hunts her and I have to wonder if it has to do with how she wound up in the hands of the slaver to begin with. It also means we have to make sure she stays safe. Once we have done that, we have to find out what happened to her and why. Most of all, we need to find out who was behind it all."

"Agreed," Kirris said. "But our first step is to make sure there are no traitors to our cause within the Citadel's walls."

Alicia nodded, glad he was not going to waste any time. In reality, the Citadel was a small city. Not only did it house the training facilities for future members of the Order but it was home for those members not assigned elsewhere. There were merchants and tradesmen who, along with their families, made their homes within the walls of the complex. Then there were those who traveled there on a regular basis to trade with the Order. Because of that, they had no way of insuring the loyalty of all who might be there at any given moment and, as the Order had learned on more than one occasion, anyone could be corrupted given the right trigger.

Fortunately for Alicia's peace of mind, the others agreed. Perhaps the trouble with Avrim had made them realize they needed to keep a closer watch on their people. Maybe it was something else, something she did not yet know about. Whatever the reason, just then she didn't care. It was more important that they did whatever it took to insure there were no traitors in their midst than worry about the reasons why the others agreed.

"And Cait?" she asked. "What about her?"

For a moment, no one answered. As one, they looked at Berral. They knew the Adept had fostered the closest relationship with the young woman of them all. More importantly, at least from Alicia's point of view, she knew Berral understood how important it was to protect Cait without having her chafe against any restrictions they might put on her. Going hand-in-hand with whatever action they took, they needed to make it clear to everyone – student and confirmed alike – that Cait was not being punished. She had proven herself time and again to be not only all they could hope for as a candidate and student but as a person who was already a valued member of the Order. Perhaps it was time to make sure she and everyone else knew it.

Cait looked out the window and sighed softly. More than an hour had passed since she had returned to the Knight-Commandant's office. In that time, she had been offered food and drink, as well as an apology from the yeoman who was trying valiantly not to look too anxious or too curious about what was going on. Not that Cait blamed him. In the year she had been at the Citadel, she had never experienced anything like the events of the last few hours.

It was so strange to look out over the courtyard and see none of the usual activity. Instead, only a few confirmed members of the Order were visible. She knew without asking they were Masters or their assistants. No one else, to her knowledge, had been cleared to leave their quarters. For the moment at least, the Citadel appeared to be all but deserted to the unknowing eye.

Finally, after what seemed an eternity but could not have been more than an hour or so, the door to the inner office opened. Cait turned in time to see the Adept appear. Berral glanced around and then, seeing Cait, she smiled and motioned her forward. Knowing better than to delay, Cait quickly crossed the room in the Adept's direction.

"Have a seat, Cait," Kirris said as Berral closed the door behind her. "Have you had anything to eat?"

She shook her head. Even though it was now well past the noon hour, food had been the last thing on her mind. As if understanding, Alicia poured her a mug of water. Then she pushed a platter of meats and vegetables in her direction, telling her to help herself. They had just finished their meal and she needed to eat. Before Cait could respond, Jerrod simply dished her up a healthy serving and then jabbed a finger at the plate, leaving no doubt what he meant for her to do.

"First, Cait, our apologies for keeping you waiting," Kirris said. "As I am sure you understand, we needed to meet with the other Masters about what happened and then we had to form a plan of action to respond to those events."

She nodded, her mouth full.

"While what happened is unusual, it is not unheard of. It does, however, point out some of the dangers we face as members of the Order. More than that, it reminds us that we have to take care, even here in the Citadel. The very fact that followers of Morrigu and her kind were operating this deep inside the Imperium means we are all in danger. So our first act has to be insure that the Citadel and all who seek refuge here are safe."

Another nod.

"Our first step will be to limit the comings and goings here at the Citadel until we have had a chance to check every person, no matter what their age or their position. It won't matter if that person has been confirmed into the Order or not. It is obvious there is deeper trouble in the Imperium than we thought. Civil war still threatens to the east and the trouble with the Wastelanders continues to grow. So the last thing we need is to have the Order or our allies undermined by the followers of Balaar."

"Sir, I understand that. What I don't understand is why I am here."

She could not keep the fear from her voice. Did they doubt her loyalty, her commitment to the Lord and Lady?

"Cait, we will be starting with the senior members of the Order and then work our way through the confirmed members, the students and then everyone else. As our people are cleared, they will be set to either assisting in the search for infiltrators or they will be sent out to our compounds with messages from Kirris and myself about what has happened and what action they are to take in response. For now, however, you are one of the few I know to be loyal to the Lord and Lady. So you shall be working with the five of us as we do our best to make sure there is no danger here in the heart of the Order."

Cait sat back, her fork midway between plate and her mouth, and she looked at the Adept in disbelief. Relieved though she might be to know they did not suspect her, this was almost more than she could take in. Then another thought came to her and she knew she had to say something.

"I will do whatever is necessary to protect the Citadel and enforce the will of the Lord and Lady," she said softly, doing her best to figure out how to phrase what came next. "I have but one thing to ask. What about Sir Avrim? Could his actions be an indication that he has lost faith in the Order?"

Or could it be an indication of something much worse?

"An excellent question and one we will answer," Berral assured her. From the grimness of her expression, Cait felt sure the Adept had been wondering the same thing.

"Berral and I will address everyone before the evening meal. In the meantime, we have a great deal to do. I want to make sure we have enough people cleared and in place to man the gates and other strategic locations within our gates before nightfall. Cait, you will accompany Alicia and Jerrod. Watch and listen. If you see or sense anything you think they should know, do not hesitate to say so."

"Aye, sir."

"We will meet back here an hour before the evening meal. In the meantime, good hunting and watch your back."

Each of them stood and, with bowed heads, accepted the prayer of guidance and protection Berral offered up. Then Cait hurried after Alicia and Jerrod as they left the office, wondering as she did what the next few hours would hold.

CHAPTER EIGHTEEN

THE MOMENT THEY STEPPED OUTSIDE, THE TWO MASTERS MOVED in the direction of the armory. Her head still reeling to have been included in what needed to be done, Cait followed. As they neared, she frowned slightly. In the time since the patrol arrived back at the Citadel and Jerrod had set Stefan and the others to guard the armory, her friends had been relieved. Now the Assistant Weaponsmaster stood guard with two others, a knight and a cleric Cait recognized but did not know well. They stood a bit straighter as Jerrod and Alicia neared.

"We sent the others back to their dormitory with instructions to remain there until they are sent for," the Assistant Weaponsmaster reported.

"Very good. Has anyone tried to approach the armory?"

"A few before word circulated that everyone was to report to their homes or places of business. None tried to gain entry. They were simply trying to find out what is happening."

A few minutes later Cait found herself standing in the middle of a room just inside the main entrance. Lining the walls were various stands. Some held quilted gambesons and others maille hauberks. Jerrod circled her once before he moved to one and then another of the stands. It wasn't long before he and Alicia had helped her into gambeson and hauberk. Then they watched as she strapped on leather greaves and pulled on her own well-worn leather gloves. Jerrod once again circled her, checking the fit of her gear.

"It will do." He nodded and started pulling on his own

gear. "I would prefer each of us to be in our own gear," he said a few minutes later. "But your gear, as well as Alicia's, needs to be cleaned and checked after your patrol and we don't have time for that. Find yourself a sword and dagger, Cait. I don't think we will find trouble but we will be prepared for it if it finds us."

"You can count on me." Even if she did not know exactly what she was supposed to do.

"Cait, we are trusting you to watch our backs. But we need you to do something else, something more important," Alicia said. "You are to listen and to feel. You know what that skinwalker felt like. We need to know if you feel anything out of the ordinary as we work. Anything that seems out of the ordinary, anything you have a question about, speak up."

"I understand."

"Good. Then let us begin."

The sun had long since disappeared below the horizon by the time the two Masters called an end to their work. In that time, they had questioned half a dozen knights and clerics. Much to Cait's relief, each had been cleared. Still, she did not know whether to be amazed or terrified at what she had been part of. She knew what the Adept could do. She had experienced a small example of it firsthand when she stood as a Candidate upon her arrival at the Citadel. But she had not expected the two Masters to be able to interrogate other members of the Order in such a way that there could be no doubt about their veracity. She had so many questions about what they did but this was not the time to ask.

Truth be told, she wasn't sure she would ever want to ask because that sort of power frightened her.

"You did very well, Cait," Alicia said as she draped a companionable arm around the younger woman's shoulders. "I know you must have a number of questions and I promise we will do our best to answer them."

"Thank you." Before she could say anything else, her stomach growled and she ducked her head in embarrassment.

"Come, you'll be bunking with us tonight," Jerrod said, leading them in the direction of the small cottage he shared with the Tacticsmaster. "In fact, until we have cleared your fellow students, you will be staying with either the two of us or with Berral and Kirris."

"But—"

"Cait, we are tasked with not only making sure there are no traitors among us but also with keeping you safe," Alicia said seriously. "Just as you are tasked with helping keep us safe. That is easier done if we stay together."

Even though she had a feeling there was more to it, Cait nodded. She would agree – for the moment. But the time would come when she would ask her questions and she hoped the Masters would be ready to answer them then.

"Don't look so surprised, Cait," Alicia laughed as Jerrod disappeared into the rear of the cottage after saying he would see to dinner. "He is the better cook. Be honest, after sampling my cooking while on patrol, do you really want to eat more of it?"

She couldn't help it. Cait grinned and shook her head. The Tacticsmaster might be many things but a good cook she was not.

"Jerrod learned early on that if he wanted a good meal with me, he had to prepare it himself. In the five years we've been together, it is an arrangement that has worked well for us."

"Is there anything I can do to help?" she asked as she followed Alicia into the sleeping chamber.

"No. Besides, I have a feeling there are questions you would like answered." Alicia rifled through the drawers of a bureau and produced a pair of loosely woven trousers and a matching tunic. Cait caught them mid-air and began stripping out of her armor.

"I do have a few." She sat and toed off her boots. "I did not sense anything arcane in how you and Sir Jerrod questioned the others and yet you could tell when they were not being entirely truthful. Did I miss something?"

Alicia finished removing her own armor and pulled a soft tunic over her head. Then she smiled at Cait and shook her head. "No, you didn't miss anything. There was nothing arcane about what we did. We had the advantage today of knowing those we spoke with almost as well as we know ourselves. So we knew what tells to look for."

"Tells?" she asked as they returned to the main room.

"Tells," Jerrod confirmed. He, too, had removed his armor. His soft leather trousers and loosely woven shirt were much like what Cait had often seen him working out in when he was not on duty or teaching a class.

"Cait, we all have things we do, little things that give us away when we are lying or trying to give ourselves time to think about how to answer a question. Take Lady Janis. When she is stressed, she plays with her hair. When she needs time to think, she chews the right side of her lower lip. If she reaches up to play with her hair and then stops herself, dropping her hand to her side and fisting it, she is lying. That is her tell."

"D-do I have a tell?"

"When you are nervous, you look to your right and catch your lower lip between your teeth." Alicia grinned as Cait caught herself about to do just that.

"That isn't to say we can't be lied to. If a person is aware of their own tells, they can try to hide them. That is why having two, or even three, sets of eye on them helps. What one of us misses, the other might catch," Jerrod added.

"Remind me never to gamble with either of you. I have a feeling I would leave the game with a much lighter purse."

"I guarantee you would," Alicia said with a grin. "Now, just because there will be no formal classes for several days, that doesn't mean you don't have lessons to learn. While Jerrod finishes preparing dinner, let's you and I go over the fight and see what could have been done differently."

"You have half an hour," Jerrod told them. "After dinner, we will plan our approach for the morning. Then I recommend the two of you make it an early night. The next few days will be long and tiring."

The messenger cowered before him, his fear so strong it was almost alive. That would normally amuse him but not now. Not when faced with yet another failure from those he had entrusted with what should have been a very simple mission. Wolf had been a fool. Worse, he had been a prideful one. That alone was why he and those he had called to him lay dead so far from their homes. They had deserved to die. The only thing he regretted was that their deaths had come at the hands of the fools from the Order. He would have made them beg for mercy before he finally killed them. They would have become a message to all those like them. Fail Balaar and die in agony.

Well, those fools had families. They would become the message now. Any others who thought they could fail the masters would learn that not only would they pay the price but so would those they cared for.

His lips pulled back and he bared his teeth as his anger flared once again. All he knew for certain was that Wolf and the others were dead. By the time his messenger found them, their bodies had been burned and the area cleansed. That meant the fool had been unable to get close enough to examine what little remained of the bodies. So he knew not if Wolf and the others had died in battle or if they had been captured and executed. That meant he had to assume the fools had revealed not only why they had been following the Order's patrol but also his plans for the girl.

Gods below, could that fool have told them of his ultimate plan? For years he had moved in the shadows, building his forces and preparing for the war that would finally put him in power and that would topple the Imperium. He had been careful not to tip his hand and reveal too much. Bribes and blackmail, kidnappings and murder had been his tools. Balaar had favored him and everything had been going according to plan.

Until Wolf failed him. First he failed where the girl was concerned by not killing her when he had the chance. Then he failed by not telling him where the girl was, leaving her to be rescued by the Order. At least they knew not who she was. That would be all they needed to figure out what was going on and who was behind it. Not that he planned to leave that one mistake uncorrected for long. The girl would die and sooner rather than later. He simply had to choose a better agent to carry out his orders than he had with Wolf.

But that still left the Order. Its members might suspect what was coming but no one else did. His eyes and ears in the Imperium told him how none of the High King's advisors felt there was anything to worry about. All he had to do was continue being careful and make sure none of the future forays into the Imperium could be tied back to him.

But that all could be in danger if Wolf had talked before he died. If he had, then everything had changed. The Order would tie Wolf and the others back to him and that could bring disaster to all his carefully laid plans.

Furious, he surged to his feet. Without warning, his gloved fist caught the messenger across the face in a savage backhand. The man fell, sprawling on the stone floor at his feet. A heavy boot connected with the man's ribs and the sound of them breaking filled the room. He strode out, soothed a little by the death rattle of the messenger. He had been unable to kill the ones who failed him, so the messenger had to pay the price. No loss there and it would be a warning to the others who served him.

Whether he wanted to or not, it was time to push forward with his plans. Of necessity, there would be a few changes, something to throw those fools with the Order off his scent, at least for a while. Besides, while the Imperium had always been his ultimate target, there was one other, one that had been in his sights for so long. He should have dealt with it when he first had the chance. Now he had best move on it before anything else happened.

Cait stared out the window, her mind going back over the events of the day. A knock sounded, startling her out of her reverie. Without turning, she called for the newcomer to enter. A moment later, the door swung almost silently open. She knew without turning that it was the Adept. There was a feeling of security that always seemed to fill any room the woman might be in. That feeling was just as real, just as alive as what she had felt from the skinwalker. It was also stronger and something Cait welcomed after the last few days.

"Alicia said I'd find you here."

Here was the library on the second floor of the administration building. It had been reopened just that morning even though only a few had been cleared to use it. Because she was not needed just then – and she knew it wasn't that she wasn't needed. She had no doubts Alicia and Jerrod had decided it would be best if she did not take part in the questioning of her fellow students – she had come there to study. Only studying had not occurred. She had spent the time thinking about what she had seen and heard for the past week.

"I needed some time to think."

"Understandable." The Adept crossed the room to stand next to her. "And have you found any of the answers you seek?"

"No." She knew better than to lie. She respected Berral too much to even hedge. Then, remembering her manners, she turned and indicated they should sit at the nearest table.

"Come, walk with me," Berral said. "I think we need to talk."

Hoping this meant the woman would be willing to answer at least some of her questions, Cait nodded. A few minutes later, they made their way across the courtyard toward the Adept's cottage. At least today the Citadel seemed to finally be coming back to life. People, mostly knights and clerics but a few tradesmen hurried to and fro. Hopefully it would not be much longer before everything returned to normal.

If that were possible after what had happened.

"Before we start, have you been taking care of your wounds?" Berral asked as she closed the door behind them.

"Lady Alicia has made sure of it."

The Tacticsmaster had actually done more than that. Each morning and evening for the past two days, the blonde had personally cleaned and rebandaged each of Cait's wounds. When Cait had asked about it, Alicia had shrugged and said it was always easier to treat someone else's wounds than your own. That was true. Still, Cait wondered if there might not be more to it than that.

"Don't look so worried, Cait. Alicia can be a bit of a mother hen at times." Berral smiled in reassurance. "I won't lie. There is always concern when dealing with skinwalkers and the wounds they inflict on their victims." When Cait opened her mouth to interrupt, Berral held up a hand to stop her. "Not that there is a fear you might turn. They don't have that sort of power. But they are corrupted beings and that means infections are possible. That is why Alicia has been so careful about your wounds."

"I had wondered."

"So, for the future, should you ever come across a victim of a skinwalker, you have to make sure their wounds are cleaned thoroughly. The first few days after the attack are always the most critical. If you can stave off infection that long, then you have won the battle. Now, here are the signs you look for to identify wounds caused by a skinwalker and what to look for to identify and treat an infected wound. . . ."

As she spoke, the Adept helped Cait out of her tunic and trousers. Before she really knew what was happening, Cait found her wounds being carefully checked. Berral's hands were gentle as she cleansed each wound and then rebandaged them after applying more of the healing salve. By the time she finished, Cait knew there was nothing to worry about.

"Come help me prepare some dinner for us. You can ask your questions while we work."

"Berral," she began as she carefully peeled one of the potatoes the Adept had handed her. "I am not sure what to ask first."

"The beginning is usually a good place to start."

Cait rolled her eyes. "All right," she chuckled. "After we returned from patrol and reported what we found, you said there was much you had simply forgotten I might not know. How do we make sure that doesn't happen again?"

"We talk. I, and the others, will tell you the tales of our

childhood. You will be given full access to the library, not just the student sections. Make use of it and ask any questions you might have." She glanced across the small kitchen and smiled. "Cait, this was our failure and not yours. We were all fortunate it did not have more serious consequences than it did. I swear we will do all we can to make sure such a mistake doesn't happen again."

"May I ask another question?" She rinsed the potatoes and began dicing them for the stew. When Berral nodded, she drew a bracing breath. "Why have you and the Knight-Commandant had me working so closely with Lady Alicia and Sir Jerrod these last few days?" Now it was her turn to make sure the Adept did not interrupt. "I'm no fool. I know they haven't needed me with them and I am certainly not qualified to determine if confirmed members of the Order might have been tainted by Balaar."

For a moment, the Adept said nothing. Then, after dropping the potatoes Cait had prepared as well as the rest of the vegetables into the post, she motioned for them to move into the next room. Suddenly wishing she had not asked her question, all Cait could do was follow.

"First of all, you were needed and, from what Alicia and Jerrod have said, you did very well assisting them," Berral said as they were seated. "You were the extra eyes and ears they needed. They were able to focus on those they had to question and not worry about anything else.

"You also learned by watching them. You saw how they questioned the others, not leaving anything for chance even with people they have known and trusted with their lives for years. They taught you about looking for tells, about listening to the inflection of people's voices and watching how they react. Those are two very good reasons to have had you working with them, reasons why you will be with them again tomorrow."

"But—"

"But you still think there is something else, something you haven't been told."

Cait nodded.

Berral blew out a breath and Cait knew she was right. There was more going on than she had been told.

"Cait, before Alicia dealt with the skinwalker, she asked why he and his kind had attacked the patrol. He didn't respond but he did react to her question. He looked past her. The only member of the patrol visible to him, besides Alicia, was you."

"M-me?"

The Adept nodded. "Cait, it could mean nothing. The skinwalker was dying and he could have been looking past you to something Alicia did not and could not see. But we aren't going to take any risks." She motioned for Cait to finish dressing. "As you said, you aren't stupid. Far from it, in fact. So you know even though we have never discussed it in any real detail with you that we have been trying to discover not only how you managed to fall into the slaver's hands but also where you come from and who you really are. That is one of the main reasons Fallon has been gone so much since he brought you here. But he isn't the only one we have looking into it."

"I don't understand." She pulled her tunic over her head and looked at the Adept in question. "You have all said that if I came from an important or influential family, the Order would have been contacted when I went missing. So it is obvious that can't be the case. So why would the skinwalker be interested in me?"

"We don't know." From the tone of the woman's voice, she was as frustrated by the not knowing as was Cait. "And I don't want you obsessing on it because we don't know for certain that you were the target. But we will not dismiss it as a possibility either. So we will do whatever we can to not only protect you but to train you to identify danger from the likes of the skinwalkers and others who look to Balaar and the other dark gods." She waited, closely watching Cait as the young woman considered what she had said.

"Berral, could it be as simple as Fallon rescued me from Giaros and brought me here? Could the skinwalker, or whoever he answered to, have considered they were simply retrieving their property?"

Now it was Berral's turn to consider what Cait said. "You may be right. It would not be the first time slavers went after those who had escaped their grasp."

"If that's the case, could we use it to try to track them down and stop them once and for all?" Cait couldn't swallowed hard, not quite believing what she had just said. She was offering herself up as bait in order to track and capture those who had enslaved her. The danger of such a mission wasn't lost on her but she would not let herself think about it, at least not yet.

"No." Berral shook her head. "We will continue our search but we will not offer you up as the sacrificial lamb."

"But if it helps end—"

"Cait, no. Not unless that is the only way we can proceed and, right now, it is far from it." She moved across the room, whether to put distance between them or to give herself a moment to think, Cait could not tell. "We don't know for sure you were the target but we are not going to risk that you weren't. So you will have to bear with us as we add even more to your training."

She did not groan, at least not too loudly. She already carried more class and training time than any other journeyman. It sounded like she would be adding even more. If it kept her and those around her safe, she would do so gladly.

"And that, my dear, is part of why you are with me

tonight." The look Berral turned to her was nothing if not beatific. Not that it fooled Cait one bit. "Tonight we start trying to determine just what talents the Lord and Lady have blessed you with."

"What?" She stepped back, shaking her head. "I thought we always waited until Confirmation for that."

"Usually but not always." Berral bent and reached for one of Cait's boots before handing it to her. "And this is something all the Masters agree on. After talking with Alicia and hearing what she had to tell us about how you performed on the patrol, and hearing your version of it, we all feel it is clear the Lord and Lady have already blessed you with at least one *talent*. Now it is up to us to see that you are trained to use it to your advantage."

Cait's brow furrowed. What was the Adept talking about?

"Cait, think. How did you know something was amiss before Alicia, a seasoned knight with a strong gift of battlesight and foresight to a lesser extent? She did not sense anything wrong until you brought it to her attention. And that wasn't the first time you have shown such an ability. That night on the trail with Fallon. You woke knowing there was danger. Because you did, you both survived that encounter. Whether foresight or another of the godsgiven *talents*, we don't know yet. Hopefully, we can find out and start strengthening your use of it."

For a moment, Cait said nothing. It was almost more than she could take in. All she could do was nod and turn her attention to pulling on her boots. She had a feeling this would be the last chance she had to relax for a long while. Before she allowed herself to, however, there was one last question she knew she had to ask.

"Berral – Adept, if what you say about the skinwalker targeting me is correct, then should I remain here? My presence here or anywhere else where the Order has an interest puts our people in danger. I can't risk something happening to anyone else because of me."

"And that is what I told Kirris you would say." She waited until Cait had pulled on her boots and then motioned for her to come with her. When they entered the sitting room, she led the young woman to a chair and then turned to pour them each a glass of wine. As she did, Cait sighed. She had a feeling the Adept was much more prepared for this conversation than was she, not that that wasn't usually the case.

"I appreciate the fact that you are worried about your fellow members of the Order and, before you protest, you are a member even though you have not yet been Confirmed. All of those accepted as yeoman or higher are. You know that." She paused, her gaze never wavering until Cait nodded. "You also know that our duties more often than not put us in danger, especially when we are away from the Citadel or whatever compound we are assigned to." Another pause until there was another nod. "And, even though we are considering the potential that you were the target of the attack on your patrol, we do not know for sure. So there is no reason for you to leave. We will simply continue to be vigilant, just as we should always be. Agreed?"

Cait didn't respond. Instead she considered everything the Adept had said. No matter what she thought, Berral had been right about one thing. They had no proof, one way or the other, about why the skinwalkers had attacked the patrol. So, for the moment at least, she would do as the woman said and not obsess about it – at least not too much. She would redouble her efforts to learn everything she could and, most of all, she would trust in the Lord and Lady to guide her.

But she was damned if she would sit still and let others be harmed because of her. The moment she suspected that might happen, she would take action, whether the Adept approved or not.

CHAPTER NINETEEN

"CAIT." STEFAN MOVED TO WHERE SHE STOOD AT THE EDGE OF THE packed dirt training arena. "Are you all right?"

Four days had passed since her conversation with the Adept. Finally, the Citadel had been declared safe and life was slowly starting to return to normal. One example was the notice all the yeomen and journeymen had waiting for them when they woke. Classes were to resume that morning. As she read the note, part of Cait had been relieved. She had missed her classes and her friends. Another part, however, dreaded the return to normal because she knew the others would be asking about what had happened on the patrol and why it had forced Kirris and Berral to lock down the Citadel. Her friends would leave off their questioning when she asked, at least she hoped they would. But there would be others who would not be so easily dissuaded.

And that was not something she looked forward to.

"Aye," she said just as softly. "Glad classes have started again."

"That makes one of you," Kala said with a grin as she joined them. "Cait, can you tell us what was behind what has been going on?"

She sighed. The last thing she wanted was to lie to her friend. Well, not the last thing. The last thing she wanted was to discuss what happened. She still was not sure how she felt, not only about the action taken to insure the safety of everyone within the Citadel but about all she and the Adept had discussed the last few days.

"Kala."

"Cait, we won't push but you were the only unconfirmed member of the group talking with everyone. We figure something happened on your patrol and that was why."

"I can't go into it but this much I can say. Yes, something happened on the patrol that worried our leadership enough that they felt the action they took was necessary. As for me, they had me working with Sir Jerrod and Lady Alicia in the hope I might learn something from them."

Not exactly a lie and it had the added benefit of being, in its own way, the truth. She could live with that. She had to.

Before she could say anything else, Lady Lyara Pahlke, the Assistant Weaponsmaster, approached. She looked around, her eyes taking in each of the journeymen who waited for the class to begin. She was still something of an unknown to them, which was one reason Jerrod had her working with them. Only two months back at the Citadel after a year's assignment at one of the more remote compounds, she had learned new techniques from the locals as well as having honed her own skills against mountain raiders and those who would see the local leadership overthrown.

It did not take long for her to set the class to work. For the first half hour, she led them in a series of exercises, first individually and then in groups of twos and threes. There were a few grumbles when it became clear Lady Lyara was not going to take it easy on them. Finally, after one of them, a second year journeyman complained just a bit too loudly, the Assistant Weaponsmaster stopped the class and moved to the center of the training arena.

"Cait, front and center," the tall, athletic redhead said.

Cait stepped forward, silently cursing each one of her fellow classmates who had been grumbling. They might not have been working out this past week but she had. Jerrod, Alicia and even Lyara had had turns training with her. The last thing she wanted or needed was having the redhead use her to make a point. She was sore enough as it was. Unfortunately, she did not have a say in it. Resigned to what was about to happen, she assumed the ready position and waited as Lyara followed suit.

For the next ten minutes, the two fought, neither able to find an opening to deliver what would have been a death blow were they using real blades. Even using her weak-side hand, Cait was able to hold her own against the redhead. So, instead of seeing their classmates quickly *killed*, the journeymen were given an exhibition of what was expected of each of them.

"Enough!" Lyara said, finally signaling an end of the match.

Cait stepped back and sank to her knees, panting heavily. Both she and Lyara were covered with sweat. This might have only been a practice match but Cait felt as if she had been in real fight. Wiping her face with the back of her left hand, she looked up to where Lyara sagged wearily against the three bar fence.

"I want to hear no more complaints from any of you. Remember this, you will not always get to choose when and where you are forced to fight. You have to be prepared to do so to the very best of your ability when sick or tired or injured. Lives of others may rest on how well you handle yourself." Lyara's voice was harsh as she moved to stand in front of the two who had been the most vocal in their complaints.

"You are here to serve the Lord and Lady. If that means laying down your lives to do so, you will. That is often part of our duties as members of the Order. It is my duty to give you the tools to prevent that from happening one moment sooner than necessary. Now, how many of you even tried to work out, much less practice, during the past week?"

She pinned each of them with a steady look. Of the dozen journeymen in the class, only four raised their hands. Looking around, Cait fought the urge to shake her head. Her hand was up as were Stafan's, Ricard's and Kala's. Everyone else suddenly seemed to be focused on anything except the Assistant Weaponsmaster.

"Cait just demonstrated one of the lessons the Weaponsmaster wants each of you to master. While her sword work with her right hand isn't as strong or as fast as it is with her left, it is strong enough to keep her alive in battle. You must never forget that the day may come -- in fact, it most likely will come -- when your lives will depend on your ability to fight well from both sides.

"Now, I want you to split into pairs and continue with the exercise. Cait, catch your breath while I run to the armory. I want to make sure everything is ready for the next class."

As Lyara hurried off, the others quickly broke into pairs and began working. Cait wearily moved to the edge of the arena and leaned against the fence. So far, the morning had been exhausting, both mentally and physically. It was good to have a few minutes to collect her thoughts and catch her breath.

That moment of peace didn't last long, however. Just a few minutes after Lyara departed, Cait heard a soft footfall behind her. A long shadow fell over her as a feeling of dread filled her. Drawing a deep breath, knowing what she would find, she looked over her shoulder.

Avrim stood a few feet away. The knight wore leather trousers, padded gambeson, maille hauberk and leather greaves. His swordbelt was fastened about his waist. Heavy leather gloves protected his hands. The look in his eyes warned Cait she was in more than a little trouble. He looked so much like Giaros had when she tried to escape. Doing her best not to let him see just how scared she was, she slowly stood and turned to face him.

"Sir Avrim." At least her voice was steady.

Avrim was in high temper as he made his way toward the weapons area. He needed a workout badly. Ever since that thrice-damned Alicia had interrupted his class, his movements had been restricted. Despite his years of dedicated service, of all the sacrifices he had made, he had been treated no better than a common criminal. And why? Because he dared demand respect not only for himself but for the Order.

It just wasn't fair!

Each day for the last fortnight, he had expected Kirris or Berral to come tell him what his punishment would be for doing nothing more than his duty. It wasn't his fault that their protégé was unable to grasp the lessons he set for her. Perhaps he should have kicked her out of the class. He had certainly wanted to but no. It had been his job to teach her and now he would pay the price for trying to do just that.

Even now, he did not know why the leadership had not handed down his punishment. It was as though they had forgotten him. Then, without explanation, the Citadel had been locked down. Just as suddenly, and even more unexpectedly, he had been told he could leave his rooms but he was to make no attempt to leave the compound nor was he to attempt to approach that little bitch. Well, that was just fine with him. He had no more desire to see her than he assumed she did him.

Not that the gods seemed to agree.

Standing at the edge of the training arena, practice blade close to hand, was the one person he did not want to see. For a moment, he considered turning around and returning to his room. Then he decided not to. Why did he have to retreat, especially after having been confined for so long? Determined not only to show that he would not be intimidated by her presence but that he was still her better, he continued on his way, a plan starting to form in the back of his mind.

Still, he dared not continue if any of her champions were close by. Pausing in the shade of the one of the outbuildings, he looked around. In the training area beyond the one where the journeywomen stood watching others of her class working out was the yeomen's class practicing their hand-to-hand. Nowhere to be seen was that bastard Jerrod or any of his assistants.

Perhaps he would get in a better workout than he first thought. He would at least be able to teach the little bitch something about manners and respect before anyone interfered. Then, seeing the still healing cuts and bruises marking her face and arms, he grinned and the thrill of the hunt filled him. If the gods were fair, he would soon be adding to them.

"Tell me, journeywoman, why aren't you practicing with the rest of your class?" he asked as he stepped up behind her. As he spoke, he rested his right hand on the hilt of his sword.

Cait swallowed hard and did her best not to let her expression betray her thoughts. Of everything that could have gone wrong that day, this had to be the worst. Berral, and then Jerrod, had warned her that the man was going to be given limited freedom to move around the Citadel. It was not something the two of them or Alicia had wanted but the other members of the Knights Council had overruled them. They thought the delay in dealing with the charges Alicia had brought against him warranted the move. She had not liked the idea when she first heard it and she certainly did not like it now.

"Assistant Weaponsmaster Lyara instructed me to wait for her return from the armory."

She prayed he did not realize how his presence unsettled her. It helped that her voice did not betray the nerves that suddenly knotted her stomach.

"There's no sense in your sitting idle, girl, while your classmates work. I came for some exercise. We shall work against one another. Collect your blade," he said coldly.

Wishing she had a valid reason for disobeying the man but knowing she did not, Cait obeyed. As she did, she tried to figure out some way to back out. The bad blood between the two of them was reason enough but he was armored and carried a real blade while she was in her practice gear and armed only with a blunt wooden blade.

A hiss sounded to her left and she quickly glanced in that direction. It did not surprise her to see the others slowing their pace as they watched what was about to happen. She did not know whether to be relieved or not when Stefan and Kala slowed almost to a stop. Concern was mirrored on their expressions and she gave a quick nod. Hopefully, if things went bad, one of them would go find help.

Lord and Lady, guide me.

The moment Cait's hand closed about the hilt of her practice sword, the knight attacked. Backpedaling frantically to get out of range, she hissed in pain at the man's blade left a long, bleeding gash down her left arm. That hand went numb and she could no longer feel the blade in her fist. Cursing, she quickly switched the blade to her other hand, fighting down her fear. She had to keep her focus or he would hurt her even worse.

"Stefan!" Kala gasped.

Cait staggered back, shifting to the right, her left foot sliding to the rear as she attempted to protect her injured arm. Blood flowed freely from the wound and dripped to the dirt at her feet. Even though she had to be in pain, her expression did not show it. Instead, she wore a mask of concentration as she blocked yet another attack from the knight.

"Sir Avrim, hold!"

Stefan raced forward. As he did, Cait worked frantically to block the blows that continued to rain down on her. As she did, Kala watched wood fly from the practice sword. Good as she was, Cait did not stand a chance against Avrim as long as she was armed with only a practice blade. His sword was cutting away at it and Kala could see how he was trying to embed the blade into it in such a way that he could disarm Cait.

Frowning, Kala realized something else and she hissed out a breath in disbelief. Despite everything Avrim had done, everything he was trying to do, Cait did not appear to be mounting any sort of offense. She was defending herself and nothing more.

"Go get Berral or Kirris or someone, Kala!" Stefan yelled when Avrim refused to break off his attack. "I'll find Lyara."

Scared for their friend, the blonde vaulted the three bar fence and raced toward the administration building. As she did, she could hear Stefan pelting off in the direction of the armory, calling for the Assistant Weaponsmaster. Hopefully, one of them would find help before it was too late.

"All right. Does anyone have anything else we need to

discuss?" Kirris asked. He hoped not. After the last week, he wanted to have one afternoon, just one, where he could relax with Berral and their children and forget about his obligations as Knight-Commandant.

"Just one and I think we all know what it is." Berral looked as serious as she sounded. "We have put off dealing with Avrim long enough."

"Under normal circumstances, I would agree," Daffyd said from his place down the table. "But I have not yet concluded my investigation."

Alicia leaned forward, her expression stormy. Only Jerrod's hand on her arm kept her from saying anything.

"What have you been doing then, Judicar?" The Weaponsmaster all but spat out the man's title. "You have had the time Cait was away with the patrol and then the days when those you needed to speak with were confined to their dormitories. Why have you not concluded your investigation?"

"I was doing the same thing you were," Daffyd said, his voice cold.

"He raises a good point, especially since it was at your recommendation we agreed to give Avrim limited freedom of the Citadel," Alicia put in.

Kirris spoke before the Judicar could respond. "Daffyd, have you spoken with the others in Cait's class?"

"Yes." He ground out the word, leaving no doubt that he did not appreciate being second-guessed.

"And did they confirm what Cait and Alicia reported?"

"They did."

He pushed back his chair and climbed to his feet. When Berral opened her mouth to say something, Kirris shook his head. It was easy to see the man was troubled. As he watched the Judicar pace the length of the office and back again, Kirris thought he knew why. Daffyd and Avrim had been journeymen together. They had remained close friends over the years. Perhaps they should have asked someone else to investigate the charges against the man but Kirris had not wanted to give the impression that they did not trust the Order's judicar.

"Daffyd, let me ask you this. If anyone else were involved, would you be prepared to move forward with the case?"

He blew out a breath and nodded. "My apologies, all of you. I have let my personal feelings interfere with the performance of my duties." He returned to his chair and drained his cup of tea. "I have known Avrim since I first arrived at the Citadel to stand as a Candidate. He was not always the bitter man he has been of late. I am also ashamed to admit that my own concerns about Cait have colored my actions in this matter."

For several long moments, no one spoke. Kirris did not need to look at the others to know how they felt about the Judicar's confession. From the beginning, he had been the one to express concerns about the journeywoman Berral, Alicia and Jerrod had taken under their wing. For much of the past year, Kirris had seen nothing wrong with the man's caution. After all, they did not know anything about Cait's past. Besides, he had always been the one to err on the side of caution. But, with each month that passed, it became more and more obvious that there was something special about Cait. Now he had no doubts she belonged at the Citadel. In fact, were he to be honest about it, he saw her doing great things for the Order – assuming she did not die in the process, something all too many of the best of them had done since the martyrdom of Saint Arelion himself.

"While I would like time to talk with others who have served with Avrim and who are not currently at the Citadel, you are right. It is time for us to deal with this matter."

Kirris nodded, knowing how much it hurt the man to say

so. "How long do you need to be ready to present everything to the entire council?"

"I could do it tomorrow but would prefer an extra day."

"Very well. Unless there are any objections, we will convene again in two days to determine what action, if any, we should take concerning Avrim and his current assignment."

Before anything else could be said, the doors at the far end of the room flew open. Kala stumbled inside. Kirris surged to his feet, alarm written on his expression, as the blonde lurched across the floor toward the council table. There was no mistaking her concern or her anger as she came to a halt at the opposite end of the table from where the Knight-Commandant stood. He waited, wondering what could have happened to have caused the young woman to violate protocol by entering the room without so much as knocking to announce herself. As he did, he felt the others watching them, all just as worried as was he by Kala's unexpected arrival.

"What is it, Kala? What's wrong?" Berral asked as she stood and moved to stand next to Kirris.

"My apologies, Adept, but there is bad trouble in the training arena."

"Has someone been hurt?" Jerrod was on his feet, poised to leave the moment if that were the case.

"It's Cait, sir." She bent at her waist, hands on thighs, gasping for breath.

"Well spit it out, Kala. What's happened?"

"Sir Avrim showed up at the training area after Lady Lyara left to make sure everything was ready for her next class. Before she left, she had given Cait leave to rest for a few minutes because the two of them had just finished sparring. Sir Avrim found Cait alone and insisted she work against him. Adept, Knight-Commandant, Cait only has her practice blade and he's using a real blade. He's not holding back and I think he is trying to hurt her." Her words all but ran together as her fear forced them out in a rush.

Before Kirris could say anything, Jerrod rushed out of the room, Berral and Alicia on his heels. Kirris cursed softly. Damn Avrim. Had the man gone mad or was there something even worse at work?

"Kala, catch your breath. Once you have, return to the training area. We will need to speak with you as soon as we have the situation in hand."

"Aye, sir," she panted.

With that, Kirris hurried after the others. He was aware of those he passed as he raced across the courtyard looking after him in concern. One or two called out questions, asking what was wrong and if he needed help. He didn't answer. He had no answers to give. All he had were his prayers that he made it to the training area before serious harm came to their journeywoman.

The sounds of fighting reached him before he saw the combatants. That was worrisome enough. More worrisome were the calls he heard from not only Lyara but the other journeymen as well, calls demanding, some pleading, for Avrim to stand down.

"Avrim, hold!" Kirris yelled the moment he was close enough to the arena to see what was happening.

In the center of the arena, Avrim continued to press his attack. There was a look of madness to him as he did. Cait, sweat running down her face, expression tense with pain and barely repressed anger, did her best to evade or counter each of his strikes. Her tunic and trousers were slashed in several places, blood visible at each.

Why wasn't she doing more than countering his attacks?

Somehow they had to stop Avrim before he did serious damage to the girl. Kirris cursed as the man's blade kissed

Cait's left cheek, trailing blood behind it. Pain flashed in the young woman's eyes. Kirris would have drawn his own blade had he been wearing one. Avrim had gone too far and the emotional damage he was inflicting was on Cait would be as devastating for her as the physical damage.

As if realizing the same thing, Jerrod acted. Without warning, he launched himself into the battle. As he moved between Cait and her attacker, he shoved her to one side. Then, with Avrim off-balance by the sudden change in opponents, the Weaponsmaster knocked the blade from his hand. He followed it up with a sharp upper cut that sent the older man sprawling to the ground.

"May you be damned to the Triple Hells of Ortisano!" Jerrod rasped angrily as Lyara and several others pelted up to take the fallen knight into custody. "Well?" His voice was ice-cold as he turned to face both Kirris and Berral.

"Hold him," Kirris said. He heard his anger and did not care. Let everyone within earshot know he would not stand by and let anyone, no matter who they were, abuse another the way Avrim just had.

CHAPTER TWENTY

CAIT HISSED IN PAIN AS AVRIM'S BLADE LEFT A LONG, SHALLOW CUT down her off-arm. Anger welled up with the pain as did a sense of betrayal. Why was he doing this? Even as the question formed, she pushed it back. The *why* didn't matter, not when she needed to concentrate on keeping out of the reach of his blade.

A large part of her wanted to press him, to take the fight to him. She knew better. Armed with only a practice blade, it would be difficult to continue countering his sword. Sooner or later, he would manage to get enough of a purchase on it to strip it out of her hand. Then she would be disarmed, without even a shield to protect her.

Worse, he had done nothing but taunt her once the fight began. He refused to back off, even when Lyara, followed closely by Stefan, returned. Lyara had tried to stop the fight only to find herself on the receiving end of Avrim's backhand that had sent her staggering back. Now she was telling the other students to stay back even as she sent Stefan to the weapons shed for her own weapons.

Suddenly the sound of the Knight-Commandant calling for the fight to end filled the air. Without dropping her guard or looking away from Avrim, Cait stepped back. When Avrim took a step after her, she stiffened, ready for a new attack at any moment. Then the knight snarled that it wasn't yet over before complying.

"What is going on here?" Kirris demanded.

"I am just giving this journeywoman a lesson," Avrim began, his blade flicking forward suddenly and leaving a long, bleeding gash down Cait's cheek. She hissed in pain and stepped back, cursing herself for dropping her guard.

"Not another move, Avrim!" There could be no mistaking the Knight-Commandant's anger. "Lady Lyara?"

"I left the journeywoman to rest after the two of us finished our workout while I went to make sure all was in readiness for the next class. Stefan came for me, telling me that Avrim had demanded Cait work against him. The only problem was that he was fully armed and armored and the journeywoman was not, nor was she given a chance to remedy that."

Avrim shifted and Cait stepped back once again. Before she knew what was happening, Jerrod moved past her, shoving her to one side. Then, with Avrim off-balance by the sudden change in potential targets, the Weaponsmaster knocked the blade from his hand. He followed it up with a sharp upper cut that sent the older man sprawling to the ground.

"May you be damned to the Triple Hells of Ortisano!" Jerrod rasped angrily as Lyara and several others pelted up to take the fallen knight into custody. "Well?" His voice was ice-cold as he turned to face both Kirris and Berral.

"Hold him," Kirris said.

Not quite sure she dared relax her guard, or believe the danger was over, Cait waited. She held her practice blade before her, ready to react to an attack from any quarter. For the first time since arriving at the Citadel, she no longer felt safe. She questioned her faith in people she had trusted not only to teach her but to help protect her. All that faith and trust had been destroyed in a matter of minutes.

Damn Avrim!

Pain from her cheek and the other wounds inflicted by Avrim simply reinforced her anger and doubts. Not ready to trust anyone but herself, she shifted slightly to her right. Now she could watch almost everyone and the sun was no longer in her eyes. Now all she had to do was figure out what to do next.

"Cait?" The Adept stepped close, her expression concerned.

"Berral?"

The Adept's eyes burned with an anger unlike anything Cait had seen from her before. She had a feeling it would not take much to push the Adept into taking direct action against Avrim. Perhaps it was time those who did not work closely with her learned that Berral truly was the one to be feared of the two of them.

"Cait?" She spoke softly, her worry clear in her voice and on her expression. "It's over. He won't hurt you again. I promise."

"Damn him, Berral!" Her eyes flashed and she stepped back, putting distance between her and the woman she had considered her mentor. As she did, her lips pulled back and she bared her teeth. Her fingers tightened around the hilt of her practice blade, her knuckles white. When she glanced across the arena to where Jerrod and several others held Avrim, she felt a touch of relief to see they looked as angry as she felt. "You told me, all of you, to trust that you would deal with him." She jabbed her practice blade in Avrim's direction. "But you didn't. Why? Is this how you protect those who come to you looking for help?"

Kirris stepped forward only to be stopped by the Judicar. Daffyd shook his head, his expression grim. Cait watched, her anger building. She had no doubt he was at least part of the reason why the Knights Council had not yet dealt with Avrim. From the beginning, she had known Daffyd had doubts about her. Had he let those doubts override the evidence?

"Do not blame the rest of the Knights Council, Cait," he

said as he stopped a pace or two from where she stood. "The lack of action was my fault. I allowed my feelings for Avrim to interfere with my duties as judicar. The others kept asking when I would be prepared to present the case against him and I delayed. All I can say is that the man he has become is not the man I knew, the man I called friend." He shook his head, his misery clear.

"Cait." Kirris moved to stand next to Berral. "You have my apologies as well. I should have pushed Daffyd harder but I will admit I let the need to secure the Citadel distract me and that is my fault. All I can say is that we had just named the time to hear the case against Avrim when Kala came for us." He paused, watching as she considered what he said.

"And now?" Her voice was so cold, she almost didn't recognize it.

"Let me ask you this. Why did you not fight back?"

"That is what I'd like to know, youngster," Jerrod said as he joined them. "You could have easily bested that fool, even armed with only a practice blade. Yet you did not fight to win. You fought only to protect yourself. I thought I trained you better than that."

She opened her mouth to respond and then closed it with a snap. It was a valid question and one that deserved an honest answer. "You did but I knew it would serve no purpose save to make him more determined. I couldn't kill him and that's what it would have come to." Now it was her turn to fall silent for a moment. "Had I killed him, you would have had no choice but to expel me from the Order and that was not something I was willing to risk. You needed to know, to understand what sort of snake is in our midst."

She waited, wondering how they would respond. To keep from looking at Berral, or even Kirris, and risking seeing something she did not want to see, she kept her attention on

Avrim. Lyara and several others held him where he stood. The anger reflected on the Assistant Weaponsmaster's face almost reassured her. Lyara, at least, was as upset about what happened as was she. Maybe she had overreacted and Avrim was the exception and not the rule.

"Jerrod, you have trained and sparred against both Cait and Avrim. Could she have bested him had she wanted to?" Kirris asked.

Cait looked at the Knight-Commandant, not sure she heard right. Then she looked at Jerrod and saw the wicked glint that shone in his eyes as he nodded.

"I have no doubts she could have easily bested him."

"Cait, if we were to give you leave to fight without restraint against Avrim, are you willing to do so?" He held up a hand before she could answer. "And are you physically able to? I can see how you have been wounded and I won't let you hurt yourself further in the process."

"I won't kill him." If that was what he wanted, he would have to find someone else to do it.

"And I won't ask you to. However, if you feel you are up to it, I think it will do you a great deal of good to meet him on equal footing."

Cait waited, wondering if he had anything else to say. If she were honest with herself, she would have to admit that part of her wanted nothing more than to meet Avrim on the field and show him exactly what she could do when she wasn't holding back. She wanted him to know fear the way she had. But she could not give in to that kind of thinking. She would not let herself turn into the sort of person he had become.

Still, it was tempting, so very tempting.

"Cait, we may be human but we don't allow anyone to act as Avrim has this day. He will be punished. You have my word on that. That said, I agree with the Knight-Commandant. If you are able, you deserve the right to stand against Avrim on equal terms," Berral commented.

She said nothing. Instead, she nodded, her expression grim. Kirris nodded in response and then turned to where Jerrod and Alicia stood. "Leave Lyara and the others to guard Avrim. I want the two of you to help Cait prepare. She is to be armored as he is and she can choose her own weapons. I will not limit her to the same blade as the *knight*." He spat out the word.

"No! You can't!" Avrim struggled against the hands that held him.

"I can and I have," Kirris said. "Cait, if you need to see the Healer first—"

"No. Best to get this over with."

Before anything else could be said, Alicia and Jerrod took up positions on either side of her. As they escorted her to the weapons shed, she finally relaxed her guard. She could trust these two. She had to trust them. Just as she had to trust the Adept and Knight-Commandant. If she didn't, Avrim had already won.

"Sit." Alicia pointed to the wooden table against the wall just inside the door. "Damn it, Cait, sit down and let me see to your wounds."

Surprised by the force in the Tacticsmaster's command, Cait did as instructed. Alicia took a moment to gather what she needed to cleanse the worse of Cait's injuries and then bind them up. As she did, Jerrod collected the gear the young woman would need. They worked in silence, not that Cait needed them to say anything to know they were furious. The anger radiated off of them and she was glad not to be the target for their ire.

"Now, young woman," Jerrod said as he laid out her gear. "If I ever hear of you refusing to do whatever was necessary to end a fight that could otherwise end in you being seriously injured – or worse – I will teach you a lesson you won't soon forget."

Or maybe some of that anger was aimed at her.

"I couldn't." She hissed in pain as Alicia treated her injured arm. "I knew I could hold out long enough for someone to get there to stop the fight. But the two of you have drilled the Codes as well as the Order's own rules in me. I knew if I seriously hurt or killed him, I would be expelled from the Order. I couldn't risk that."

The Citadel had become home. All she hoped now was that Avrim had not ruined it for her.

"Are you sure you are up to this?" Alicia asked a few minutes later as she and Jerrod helped Cait into her gear.

"I have to be." Hopefully, she could keep the pain at bay long enough to do what she needed to.

"What weaponry?" Jerrod asked.

What weaponry indeed? She was more comfortable with a single blade and shield but Avrim knew that. Worse, his attack on her had given him the opportunity to gauge her reactions and responses. He knew, or at least should know, how she would react now. The problem was that her injuries would hamper her. The wound to her left arm would prevent her from wielding a broadsword the way she would need to in order to defeat the man. While she could use her off-arm to wield a lighter sword, she was worried about using her left for shield work.

"Two blades," she said.

Jerrod nodded and disappeared into the back room where he and the other weapons instructors kept some of their personal equipment. By the time he returned, Alicia had finished securing Cait's greaves in place. The young woman stood and took a moment to settle her equipment in place.

Then she turned and her eyes went wide as she saw what the Weaponsmaster held in his hands.

"I wish we had time to get your own blades, Cait, but the longer we delay, the more time Avrim has to recover and plan his attack." He carefully settled the leather belt around her waist and fastened it. "You have worked with these though and should be comfortable with them."

She nodded, watching as he slid the sword into place at her side. Then he handed her the curved blade he had trained her with the last few months. Similar to the sickles farmers used to clear their fields, the curved blade could chop or slide depending on the angle of the strike. She knew Jerrod kept the spine of the blade sharpened as well, making it even more dangerous. Between it and the sword, she should be more than a match for Avrim.

"Are you ready? Kirris asked a few minutes later as the three returned to the arena.

"I am."

Amazed that her voice was so strong and steady, Cait moved to stand before the Knight-Commandant. She bowed respectfully to him. Then she crossed to the Adept. Without a word, she sank to one knee in front of the woman. Her head bowed, she waited, hoping Berral understood what she wanted and needed.

"May the blessing of the Lord and Lady be with you, Cait, and may the strength and courage of Saint Arelion guide your hand." The Adept's voice was soft, her concern clear. "Cait, watch him. He feints to the left when he starts to panic," she added so softly no one else would hear. At the same time, she ran a light hand over Cait's head.

Feeling better, Cait climbed to her feet. As she moved to the center of the arena, she kept her eyes on Avrim. Lyara and the others still held him firm. Then, at a nod from Kirris, they released him. But the Assistant Weaponsmaster did not return his sword. Instead, she followed him as he took up his position opposite Cait. At Kirris' nod, she handed over Avrim's sword. Cait waited as Lyara cleared the arena.

Lord and Lady, give me strength.

"We had better be right about this," Alicia said softly as she and Jerrod joined the Adept. At the same time, Cait and Avrim took their places in the center of the arena.

Berral said nothing. How could she? The last thing she wanted was for Cait to have to square off against another of the Order. The fact she was doing so under these circumstances was almost more than she could accept. Never before had she thought one of their own would stoop so low as to attack a journeyman. That Avrim had, and without any provocation, worried her. How had Avrim managed to live amongst them for so long without any of them seeing what he had become? Had they become so overconfident that there could be even more danger for their people inside the Citadel?

No, she knew that wasn't the case. Any others who felt as Avrim did would have been discovered over the last few weeks. This was an anomaly. That was all. She had to remember that, believe in that. Then she would have to do whatever it took to heal any damage, mental or physical, he had caused Cait.

"We have to be right," she said just as softly. "I wish there was another way but I feel Cait has to do this to prove to herself that she is strong enough to stand up to Avrim and any like him."

As if that was his cue, Kirris stepped forward. "Hear me! The Knights Council gives leave to Journeywoman Cait to stand against Avrim, knight of the Order. Sir Avrim violated his oath when he attacked her earlier, forcing her to defend herself with only a practice blade. Now he will face her in fair combat." He turned his attention to Avrim. "The fight will commence upon my command and will end on my command. Failure to comply will result in the Weaponsmaster taking the offending party into custody. Is that understood?"

"Aye," the two combatants replied.

"Very well. Take your positions." He moved to the edge of the arena where the rest of the Knights Council stood. Behind them had gathered many of the students and other members of the Order.

"I want all those present to think on this. While we of the Order are only human, we cannot allow our petty jealousies and resentments to rule us. That, unfortunately, is something Avrim forgot," Berral said. "Avrim has preyed upon one he saw as weaker, both in the arena and in the classroom. Cait came to us for training and for protection and nurturing, as do all who want to join the Order. Avrim used his position to force her to make a choice between defending herself and facing expulsion not only from the Citadel but from the Order as well or risking being injured or worse. That cannot and will not be allowed to go unanswered.

"Cait, you are not to hold back. Do you understand?"

"I do, Adept."

"Very well," Kirris said. "Weaponsmaster, you may begin the fight."

With a nod, Jerrod stepped forward. As he came to a halt between Cait and Avrim, he motioned for them to step back. They did and he studied them. Berral suspected he was giving Cait one last moment to prepare. Then he stepped back and gave the signal. The fight was on.

A collective gasp rose from those gathered as Avrim leapt forward, blade slashing downward in an attempt to end the fight quickly. He attacked like a man possessed. He slashed

and hacked in an attempt to get through Cait's defense. Instead of retreating, the young woman held her ground, her blades blocking every attack. Unlike earlier, however, it was obvious that she was no longer simply playing for time, hoping someone would come along to stop the fight. Instead, she feinted right and left, testing his reactions. More often than not, her strikes slid past his guard.

A cheer went up from the crowd as Cait drew first blood. Seeing it, Berral breathed a sigh of relief. She saw the concentration on Cait's face, the determination to win. Hopefully, it would be enough.

"She fights well," Kirris said softly as Cait trapped Avrim's blade between her two and deftly flicked it out of his grasp.

A moment later, she left a carefully controlled cut down his right cheek, a near mate to the cut he had given her. As he staggered back, he hissed in pain and blood welled up before flowing down that cheek. Instead of pressing her advantage, Cait stepped back, never taking her eyes from her opponent.

"Retrieve your blade and resume the fight, Avrim," Jerrod ordered.

Keeping a close watch on Cait, the man did as he was told. This time he did not attack right away. Instead, he danced around, feinting left and then right, testing Cait's reactions. For her part, she let him. A slight smile touched her lips as she kept just out of reach, forcing him to come to her. Berral watched and realized what the young woman was doing. She was forcing Avrim to expend more energy in the chase, wearing him down even quicker.

Good girl.

For the next few minutes, they watched as the pattern was repeated again and again. Within moments of pressing his attack, Avrim would be disarmed, another cut left to remind him just how badly outmatched he happened to be. Then

Jerrod would step in, telling the man that the fight was not over. When Avrim failed to retrieve his blade, Jerrod would do it for him. Then he would call for the fight to resume.

A look of desperation on his face, Avrim once again changed tactics, this time going on the defensive. When he did, Cait simply moved forward, forcing him back until they circled the edge of the arena. There was a sense of expectation to the onlookers as Cait continued to press him. They watched as her sword flashed in the sunlight as it thrust and parried, opening Avrim's guard time and again. Then, as the man's anger once more got the best of him, she simply stepped back and waited, flicking his sword away yet again when he charged her.

"Quit playing with him," Berral heard Alicia say softly. Frowning, she glanced at the Tacticsmaster and wondered if, while they were helping Cait prepare for the fight, Alicia and Jerrod had planned out her tactics.

At the same time, Cait's attitude seemed to change. No longer did she appear to be merely toying with Avrim. Instead, she pressed the attack. This time, instead of disarming him, she simply slipped inside his guard. Her blades flashed, forcing him back toward the center of the arena in a frantic attempt to avoid blow after cutting blow.

Avrim sobbed in fear as he struggled to avoid Cait's blades. His boots scuffed along the packed dirt surface of the arena. When his feet became tangled, the crowd gasped. Berral watched as time seemed to slow. Avrim's arms flailed the air, windmilling in an attempt to keep his balance. His sword arced through the air, sun glinting off of it. He fell in a sprawling heap. Before he could roll to his feet, Cait stepped forward. Her booted foot caught his shoulder and he fell back. His eyes went wide and he drew a quick breath as the tip of her sword found the soft spot of his exposed throat.

"I yield!" Tears of fear and frustration rolled down his

cheeks, pooling darkly on the dirt beneath his head. "Kirris, by all that is holy, please call her off."

"What say you now, Avrim?" the Knight-Commander asked.

"I was a fool. I admit it. I was a vain fool who deserves whatever punishment you and the Knights Council sees fit." He swallowed and Berral knew he was doing his best to become one with the ground, anything to avoid the point of Cait's blade.

"Let him up, Cait."

She nodded and stepped back, never taking her eyes from her target. The moment her blade had been removed from his throat, Avrim scooted back just as fast as he could. By the time he gained his feet, Cait had moved across the arena, putting more than enough room between them to insure nothing else happened.

"Y-you could have easily killed me, journeywoman," he said softly as Jerrod stepped forward to retrieve the blade Avrim had dropped. "Even with a practice blade you could have bested me easily. Yet you did not. Why?"

Berral bit her lower lip, wondering how Cait would answer. Avrim had heard her earlier explanation, as had everyone else. What Cait said now would seal her place within the Order, the start of a reputation she would never be able to leave behind her. Gods above and below, she hoped the journeywoman spoke wisely.

"What good would have come from it?" Cait asked in return. "Your anger, foolish though it was, would have only increased. Fighting you, causing you injury would have cost me the one thing that matters to me – the Order. I couldn't let that happen." She paused and Berral held her breath, wondering what the young woman was about to say. "Besides, I could not understand how you, a Confirmed member of the Order, saw me as such a threat that you felt it necessary to attack me."

"Foolishness and ego." Avrim shook his head, his expression miserable.

"Enough," Berral said. It was time to end this but not while everyone looked on. Besides, Cait did not fool her. The younger woman was hurting badly and several of her wounds had reopened during the fight. "Lady Lyara, Sir Bertram, escort Sir Avrim to his quarters and hold him there. I will see to it that a healer is sent to treat his injuries. He is not to leave his quarters until the Knights Council sends for him."

"Come," Lyara said and motioned for Avrim to lead the way.

Berral watched as they left the arena. Then she turned her attention to Cait. "As for you, Cait, you did very well. I know I speak for all the Knights Council when I say that we are proud of you. Jerrod, Alicia, make sure she finds her way to the healers. Once her injuries have been treated, the three of you report back to the Knight-Commandant's office. It is time to deal with this matter once and for all."

"Adept?"

Hearing the concern in Cait's voice, Berral smiled slightly. "Child, you are in no trouble. In fact, you conducted yourself better than I am sure I would have in your position. Now go let the healers look at you. We will talk more once they have. I promise."

CHAPTER TWENTY ONE

"WHAT DID THE HEALER SAY?" BERRAL ASKED AS ALICIA AND Jerrod finally joined the rest of the Knight's Council.

The Adept did not try to keep the worry from her voice. More than an hour had passed since Kirris had called an end to the fight between Cait and Avrim. Since then, she had listened as Daffyd again explained to Kirris and the other members of the council why he had delayed bringing the evidence against Avrim to them. She had no doubt the Judicar would have been offering to step down had the Weaponsmaster and Tacticsmaster had not arrived.

"She needs a day or two without strenuous activity," Alicia said. "The worst is the cut on her face. She turned away from it and that saved her eye and most of the cheek. But Avrim's blade cut close to the bone along her jaw. The Healer isn't sure she can prevent it from scarring."

Berral's mouth grew tight and she forced herself to relax. Vanity did not play much of a role in Cait's life but to have a scar on her face would be almost as bad as the scars she bore at wrists, ankles and around her neck. Damn Avrim!

"And Cait?"

"She is angry and hurt and confused." Jerrod poured wine for first Alicia and then himself. "She doesn't understand why Avrim acted as he did. Worse, she doesn't understand why this council failed her. She is trying very hard not to let this push her back into the fear she knew with the tavernmaster back in Lineaus but you can see that it is difficult for her. Trust is not something that comes easy for her and she trusted us. We betrayed that trust and I pray we haven't lost her as a result."

"Where is she?"

"In the outer room. You said you wanted to meet with her after her wounds were treated." Alicia's tone left no doubts that she expected Kirris and the others to do whatever was necessary not only to reassure Cait but make it up to her for letting her be placed in danger.

"Make sure she gets something to eat. We need to discuss what happened and then we will meet with her," Kirris said.

The Tacticsmaster nodded and quickly left the office, closing the door behind her. When she returned a few moments later, she looked a little less like she wanted to rip off the heads of those waiting for her. She returned to her place at the table and nodded in response to Berral's unasked question.

"Let us not waste any more time," Kirris said even as he motioned for everyone to eat. "Daffyd, is there any doubt that Avrim had been abusing his position as instructor?"

The Judicar looked at his plate and shook his head. As he did, Berral could almost feel sorry for him. She, probably better than most of them, knew how close he had been to Avrim over the years. Because he remembered the dedicated young man he once knew, Daffyd had found it difficult to accept that his friend had turned into a bitter, vindictive man.

"No. He browbeat them, refused to listen when they asked valid questions, tried to intimidate them into compliance. What Alicia heard that day appears to be fairly representative of what happened on a regular basis in his classes." His fingers played with his cup. "I had been ready to recommend he be assigned to something other than teaching before this afternoon's events."

"Jerrod, what did Lyara have to say about what happened?" Berral asked.

"Not much more than what she said at the time." He went on to describe how his assistant had used her workout with Cait to demonstrate to the class their latest lesson. Then she had left Cait to rest while the others worked and she made sure everything was ready for the next class. She had not known anything was amiss until Stefan had come for her.

"What is your recommendation now, Daffyd, after what Avrim did in the arena?"

"Part of me wants mercy for the man I once knew but another part believes we should make an example of him." The misery in his voice a few moments earlier had been replaced with resignation. "There is no question that he must be removed as an instructor. If we were to follow the Codes to the letter, he should be removed from the Order and imprisoned for his actions."

"But?" Kirris prompted.

"There are no buts." He shook his head to forestall any other interruptions. "Avrim clearly stepped far over the line and must pay for what he did. As must I. My failure in bringing the initial charges before this council has to be discussed."

"Should we hear from Cait before we decide what to do about Avrim?" Kirris asked.

"Not yet." Berral shook her head when he started to speak. "We broke faith with her by not acting. We failed her, and the other students as well, when we did not realize what Avrim was doing in his classes. We failed her when we did not act quickly to discipline Avrim. We failed her again when we failed to protect her from his need for vengeance. We have to be able to tell her that we are taking action to insure he never again hurts anyone else."

"Berral's right," Alicia said. "And not just for Cait but for everyone who looks to the Order for guidance and protection. If we can't protect our own, how can they rely on us to protect them? If we let our members assault those who have come to us for training, how can those outside of the Order trust us?"

"Very well. I want to hear what each of you recommend." Kirris sat back and looked at Berral. "Your thoughts?"

"First you, Daffyd. It serves no purpose right now to continue to flail yourself for what you did or did not do." She pinned the man with a firm glance. "Did you err? I think we all will agree that you did. But we, too, erred in not pressing the matter when you did not. Yes, we were distracted by what Alicia and her patrol found. Not that it excuses us. So tell me, Judicar, should we all step down for failing to do what we should have or do we learn from it and make sure nothing like it ever happens again?"

For a moment, the man said nothing. Then he hung his head. No one spoke and Berral found herself holding her breath. If they could not get past this, what hope did they have of properly dealing with Avrim and the damage he caused to all the Order?

"No, Adept." He glanced up, his expression troubled. "I badly erred but, as you said, flailing about it will not solve the problem now."

"Good." She frowned as she sipped her now cold tea. "As for Avrim, we have to make an example out of him so that everyone understands that such actions will not be tolerated. My recommendation is that he be stripped of all rank and sent to one of the remote compounds in the north. There he is to be closely watched and instructed. His days are to be spent in meditation and penance. Should he violate our Codes again, then he will be returned here in irons to face the full justice of the Codes for all his offenses."

"It's not enough," Alicia said. "Not after what he did today."

"What would you have us do?" Kirris asked.

"He should be removed from the Order and made to stand before the Imperial Council to answer the charges against him." As she spoke, Jerrod nodded in agreement.

"Would you have us give the enemy a weapon to use against us?" Daffyd asked. "If it becomes common knowledge that one of our own could sink so low as to abuse his students and then physically attack one of us, the confidence of those who look to us for guidance and protection will falter. With what we have learned and what we suspect, dare we risk that?"

"Dare we not?" Jerrod countered. "How far would he have gone had we not arrived at the training arena when we did? He refused to heed Lyara when she told him to stop the attack. When she attempted to intercede, he turned on her. Can we continue to allow him to be one of us?"

Berral sat and listened. For more than an hour, the debate raged. Only one thing was clear. None of them wanted to sentence Avrim to death, something they very well could after his actions that day. But they also could not come to an agreement about what to do. Finally, just when she was about to suggest they break for a few minutes, Kirris rapped his knuckles on the table, calling for silence.

"I think it is time for us to hear from Cait. She is the one he injured and I think we all agree it went beyond the physical injuries. She has seen the worst of us. Now she needs to see the best of us and she needs to know we will take her concerns and wishes into consideration in dealing with this matter."

At his nod, Berral stood. When she entered the anteroom a moment later, she found Cait standing before the window overlooking the courtyard below. Then she noticed how the young woman's left arm rested in a sling. When Cait turned toward the door, the Adept's heart clenched to see the swelling to her face and the bandage covering the cut that ran along the line of her jaw.

Without a word, she crossed to where Cait stood. With gentle hands, she tilted the young woman's head to one side, letting her look not only at the wounds not currently covered by bandages but also letting her look into Cait's eyes. The pain and anger reflected in them worried the Adept. Would Cait ever be able to get past them so she could trust again?

Even so, she knew the anger was a good sign. It meant her protégé was not letting what happened in the training arena thrust her back to the hell that had been her life with Giaros. As long as Cait continued to fight, to refuse to become anyone's victim, they had a chance.

At least she prayed they did.

"I'm sorry you had to wait so long," she said. "Will you meet with the council now?"

For a moment, Cait looked at her. From the young woman's expression, the question had caught her off-guard. "Adept, I will if you want but it is not necessary. I have decided what I must do."

Berral swallowed hard. Never before had she heard such coldness in Cait's voice. Gods above and below, had they lost her because of Avrim?

"Cait, I won't lie. We failed you horribly and I understand if you cannot find it in yourself to forgive any of us. All I can ask is that you give us a chance to prove it will never happen again." She paused, wondering if the young woman would agree and knowing she might not were their roles reversed. "We want to hear your thoughts on what should happen to Avrim."

"All right."

Relieved that she had agreed to that much at least, Berral nodded and motioned for her to lead the way.

"Well, I feel like we have each been well and truly schooled," Kirris said with a rueful smile as soon as the door closed behind Cait. Berral had to agree. While she might have started out hesitant, by the time she finished, Cait had left no doubts in any of their minds concerning what she felt about what happened and how they had handled – and mishandled – the situation.

"If I didn't know better, I would think you had coached her, Berral," the Knight-Commandant added. "She sounded so much like you did at her age."

"No, I was never that pragmatic and especially not after I'd been the focus of someone's unprovoked attack." Not that she had ever suffered anything close to what Cait had at Avrim's hands.

"She continues to surprise me." Alicia shook her head. "And she made good points. The question now is what are we going to do?"

Silence fell around the table. Berral sat back and looked at her companions. As she did, she fought the urge to smile. Instead of resuming the argument about what course of action they should take where Avrim was concerned, they at least gave the appearance of considering what Cait had said. Now the Adept hoped they took the young woman's words to heart. If not, she felt sure they would find Cait gone from their midst before too much time passed.

And that was something she wanted to prevent if at all possible. After today, she was more convinced than ever that Cait would be an important member of the Order – assuming they did not manage to drive her off in the process.

"I say we do as the journeywoman recommended. Avrim has proven he is not worthy to call himself a member of the Order. His possessions, all that he has amassed since joining the Order, are to be forfeit," Daffyd said. "I would add one more thing to her recommendation. We hold Avrim in the cells until the High King, or his representative, can attend. That will serve two purposes. First, it will give more weight to our actions. Second, it gives us more time to question him. As much as I hate to admit it, it is obvious that he has an issue with the journeywoman. So we have to ask if, even by mistake, he revealed to anyone that she was going on patrol with Alicia and the others."

"I agree with Daffyd," Berral said, relieved the Judicar had finally managed to put aside his personal feelings for Avrim.

The vote was quick and decisive. After so much arguing earlier, they were all in agreement. At least that much had been accomplished. Now they had to find a way to repair the damage done by Avrim, not only where Cait was concerned but with the entire Order and all who looked to it.

While Kirris stepped into the anteroom to order Avrim removed from his quarters to the cells below the temple, Berral sent for more food and drink. She had a feeling it was going to be a very long night. If any of them saw their beds before morning, she would be surprised.

"Now, I believe we need to discuss a certain journeywoman," Kirris said as he returned to his place at the table.

"She certainly surprised me the way she handled herself on the field." Daffyd leaned forward and poured wine for first Alicia and then himself. "She fought like someone with years of training under her belt, not a student who has been here less than a year and a half."

"Jerrod?" Kirris prompted.

"I told you her first week here that she is not only a natural with a blade but that she had been taught long and well by someone, most likely a member of the Order." His pride in the young woman shone on his expression. "She knows techniques most of us could only wish for. I would like to know who trained her and why we had not heard of her."

"I agree," Alicia said from his side. "Her grasp of tactics borders on inspired. We saw that with her questions that first brought the problems with Avrim to our attention. Watching her today, I saw something else, something I had wondered about when we first arrived on the scene."

"What's that?" Berral wanted to know.

"Ask yourselves this. How did she manage to avoid serious injury or worse without a shield and only armed with a practice blade? It's true that Avrim is not the master swordsman Jerrod is. He isn't even as good as most of us at this table. But he is erratic and that makes him a very dangerous opponent. Yet Cait managed to hold her own without mounting any sort of offense." She paused, giving them time to think about what she said.

"Now consider her actions on the field after she was allowed to arm and armor herself. Yes, Jerrod and I gave her a few instructions but nothing that would account for how easily she kept disarming Avrim. It was as if she knew his moves before he committed to them. Add to that the way she knew there was trouble on the trail both on her way here with Fallon and then on patrol with me and, well, I think it time we consider the possibility that the Lord and Lady are already blessing her with Their gifts."

"She is right, you know," Jerrod said. "I have seen it during our training sessions."

"Could it not just be part of the training she has had?" Sanaa, the Healer, asked.

"No, I don't think so." The Weaponsmaster shook his head, his expression thoughtful. "There is something else as well. She has become a mentor of sorts to some of the younger students. Her classmates look to her as a leader. We saw the loyalty they feel for her today. Stefan dared enter the ring in an attempt to stop Avrim. He only left when he failed and he realized he needed someone of rank to get through to the man."

"What are you recommending?" Kirris asked.

"I want someone else to see her and judge her training. While I am more than convinced she trained long and well with someone from the Order, there are times when I see something else as well. My guess is that, wherever she is from, before she fell into the slaver's hands, she trained not only with one of our own but with someone who spent time with one of the better mercenary companies."

"Why do you say that?" Berral looked at him in surprise. In all their previous discussions about Cait, he had never mentioned the possibility that she had trained with a merc.

"Your protégé has a real affinity for short swords and knives. We don't tend to give much focus to them. But some of the better merc companies do, recognizing that there are times and places where stealth and smaller blades are much more efficient than a sword or bow."

"That's why you suggested she wear those arm sheaths," Alicia said.

"It is. It didn't take long for me to realize she had more than a passing skill with knives. Since I have a fondness for them myself, I knew she might adapt quickly to the quick release sheaths. If they help save her life down the road, all the better."

"So what are you asking?" Kirris wanted to know. "I assume there is a request in there somewhere."

"There is." Now Jerrod grinned that cat and bird grin Berral long ago learned meant he had something up his sleeve. "I'd like to invite a merc we are all well-acquainted with, and who we have worked with on occasion, to come and have a look at Cait. It could be that he will see something about her that will help us finally discover where she hails from and how she fell into the slaver's hands."

For a moment, Berral simply stared at the man. No wonder he looked so pleased with himself. He had very carefully maneuvered them into the position where they were almost forced to do as he suggested. The fact that she had a good idea of who he wanted to invite had her smiling almost as broadly as he. If she was right, they were about to turn the more tradition-bound members of the Order on their ear – again.

"Jerrod, who?"

"Connal Firehawk."

Berral waited, wondering how the others would react. She knew from long experience that Kirris would prefer almost anyone other than the mercenary captain. Even after all their time together, she did not know whether the Knight-Commandant disapproved of her brother because he had chosen to become a mercenary or because he had chosen not to complete his training to join the Order.

Still, Kirris had proven pragmatic where her younger brother was concerned on other occasions. During the last major outbreak of hostilities with the raiders from the south, he had hired Connal's company to supplement the troops the Order sent to secure the border. But working with them to quell rebellion, or worse, was a far cry from welcoming him to the Citadel and asking his advice on what to do about one of their own.

"I have concerns," Kirris said, his expression grim. "We are trying to not only reassure Cait that she has nothing more to fear here but also those outside the Order. How will they view us bringing in a known mercenary? Are you willing to admit he might know something we don't?"

"Since when have any of us ever suggested we know

everything?" Alicia countered. "Kirris, do not let your prejudices blind you the way loyalty did Daffyd."

"I am doing no such thing!"

"Yes, you are and you know it." Berral spoke firmly and waited until he turned to look at her. "You have never forgiven Connal for not completing his training here. There have been others who began training to join us but have, for various reasons, decided their calling lay elsewhere. You have never held it against them and yet you continue to do so where Connal is concerned. Is it not time to let go of your anger and disappointment in him and admit that he chose the right path for him?"

Kirris opened his mouth and then closed it with a snap. "All right, but will you finally tell him that his chosen surname is ridiculous?"

Berral threw her head back and laughed. She couldn't help it. Like many in his profession, Connal had adopted a new surname when he joined his first mercenary company. Some did so in order to protect their families against reprisals. Others did it because they did not want their families to find them. Some did it because they had been raised bereft of a real family. For his part, Connal had done it because he had not wanted any to think he would trade on who and what his sister was. He had chosen the name Firehawk because, at that time, he had used a hawk in battle and, when it was framed against the early morning sky, it looked like it was on fire.

Now, almost ten years after leaving the Citadel to strike out on his own, he commanded his own mercenary company. It was not one of the largest companies in the Imperium but it was one of the most well-respected. As a result, the High King often had Firehawk's Irregulars under contract to help defend the Imperium against attack.

"Are you sure this is the best course of action?" Sanaa

asked.

"I am," Jerrod said.

"And I agree," Alicia put in.

"I assume you have no qualms about sending for him." Kirris looked at Berral, an expression of resignation on his face.

"You assume correctly."

"Then send word asking him to come meet with us. Do not tell him why. Just say it is important."

Berral nodded, understanding his caution. Messages could go astray and she did not want to advertise the fact they were actively attempting to discover who Cait was and where she hailed from.

"What else?" Kirris asked.

"I want to discuss Cait's current assignment," Alicia said.

"Very well."

Cait rolled over and opened her eyes. She felt as if she had not slept. Every time she closed her eyes, she found herself back in the arena, Avrim standing before her. This time, however, he was armed and she was not. He had her at his mercy and, like Giaros before him, he was going to teach her that she was nothing, less than nothing.

Tossing back the sheet, she sat up. Judging from the faint light coming through the window, dawn was not that far off. Without lighting a candle, she gathered up a pair of loose trousers and a tunic. Maybe if she got out of there for a while, she would be able to clear her mind enough to sleep.

Once outside, she moved quickly, almost silently across the courtyard. As she did, she breathed deeply. The crisp, clean morning air filled her lungs. A few lights flickered in windows of the buildings surrounding the courtyard. Other than that, she could have been alone in the Citadel.

A soft step behind her brought her up short. Her breath caught and her pulse quickened. Nerves on edge after the events of the previous day, she spun, her hands moving into position so she could counter any attack. Then, seeing Berral standing before her, she straightened. As she did, she schooled her features. The last thing she wanted just then was for the Adept to realize how conflicted she still was.

"Cait, are you all right?"

The concern in Berral's voice did her in. Gone was all the anger. Even most of the hurt fled, leaving only the confusion about why Avrim had acted as he had. Before she knew what she was doing, she stepped forward. Berral's arms drew her close, holding her as the tears finally came.

"Shh, Cait, shh," the Adept soothed. "It's all right. Everything is all right."

"Sorry." Running her hand under her nose, she sniffled and tried a smile.

"No apologies needed. Shall we go inside now?"

"I guess." She stepped back and looked at Berral, her head cocked to one side. "What are you doing out so early?"

"I was coming to check on you."

She started to reach out to drape an arm across Cait's shoulders and then hesitated. Cait saw and blew out a breath. She knew the Adept was trying to make amends. Part of her wanted to put what happened behind her. But it was hard, so very hard. For the first time since her arrival there that she had been thrust back into the emotional hell she had known in Lineaus. Still, it had been through the actions of just one man. Berral had stood for her just as she always had.

Could she put it behind her and go back to how things had been?

"Avrim?" She hated asking because so much rested on the

answer.

"We decided to do as you suggested but with one change. He is being held in the cells under the temple until the High King or his representative can get here. It is important that everyone knows we will not stand for what Avrim did." She reached out again, this time resting her hand very lightly on Cait's injured arm. "Is that satisfactory?"

She nodded, not trusting herself to speak. She had prayed they would do the right thing but, after the events of the morning, had not dared hope. Now, knowing they were doing as she asked, everything seemed much better. She was not ready to forgive, not completely at any rate, but at least she did not feel the need to flee the Citadel before something else happened.

Which was good since she had a strong suspicion the gods would not approve. They did not tend to reward cowards.

"I know it is early, but will you come with me?" Berral asked.

Cait nodded. She expected the Adept to lead her back to the Knight-Commandant's office, or perhaps to her own. Instead, Berral started off in the opposite direction. It did not take long to make their way to the cottage she and Kirris shared. Wondering what was going on, Cait followed her inside only to come to a halt to see not only Kirris but Jerrod and Alicia there as well.

"Sit, child."

Berral put action to words and pressed her down onto one of the chairs before the fireplace. Then she was gone. Judging by the sounds that followed, the Adept had made her way to the small kitchen. When she appeared a few moments later, she carried two mugs of steaming tea. She handed one to Cait before taking the seat next to her.

"I take it Berral told you what the Knights Council decided

about Avrim," Kirris said.

"Yes, sir."

"Are you satisfied?"

"Yes, sir. Thank you."

"Cait, earlier today, you said that you had made a decision about what you needed to do. Would you mind sharing that decision with us?" Berral asked.

Cait cursed her foolishness in not holding her tongue. She had not realized the Adept had heard her. After staring into her mug for a moment, she looked up. There was nothing to do but tell the truth.

"If I tell you my decision has been rendered moot, would that satisfy you?" she asked in return.

"Cait, had you decided to leave us if we had not taken action against Avrim?" Alicia asked.

She nodded, worried they would not understand.

"Can't say as I blame you," Jerrod said. "But you've changed your mind."

"I have." She wanted to pace but dared not for fear they might think she was trying to leave. Despite what happened that day, she owed them so much. She wanted them to understand what she felt and why she felt the way she had. "I'm not proud of how I felt but I did not see how I could remain here if Avrim was not dealt with. It isn't just because of what he did to me although it would be a lie to say that didn't have a lot to do with it. But I had to wonder if he was willing to treat me as he did, what would he do to the next yeoman or journeyman he did not approve of? I could not, in good conscience, remain in that situation."

"Will you accept our apology for not seeing what was happening sooner and for allowing what happened today?" Kirris looked tired. They all did. But there was a weight of responsibility, of guilt, to him she had never before seen.

"Sir, one thing the Lord and Lady teach us is that we choose our own paths. That is what Avrim did. I don't hold the Knights Council responsible for his actions. It is true that I had wondered why you had not acted before now. Those questions and doubts were answered when you met with me earlier."

Not that it would be as easy to forgive Daffyd as it was the others. He alone, as far as she was concerned, had delayed things and that, in turn, had led to the morning's events. But, after seeing his regret, she had a feeling he would do whatever he could to make sure he was never again swayed by personal feelings when it came to his role as Judicar. Perhaps the Lord and Lady had used the events of the day as an object lesson for them all.

"And what do you see as your path now, Cait?" Berral asked.

She gave the Adept a slight smile. "You never did ask the easy questions, Adept." Easy it might not be but it was a valid one. "My place, as long as you allow it, is here. I want to finish my studies and stand for Confirmation into the Order. Then I shall go wherever the Lord and Lady send me."

"Very good, Cait, and we agree with you." Berral smiled in approval. "And that is why we wanted to see you."

"Cait, you present us with a quandary," Kirris took up. Now he smiled and she looked at him in open question. "We've spoken with each of your instructors. Each of them tell us the same thing. You do everything they ask and then some. There are some, like Jerrod and Alicia here, who say there is little more they can teach you, that experience is all you need now."

She waited. He was obviously building up to something but what?

"What Kirris is trying to say is that the Knights Council has decided to reward your hard work," Berral said with a smile. "Now, you might not think it is much of a reward because you will be working as hard, if not harder, than you have since your arrival here. But we think it is the best thing for both you and for the Order."

"And?" Cait's eyes narrowed as she looked at the Adept. Something was up and she was damned if she could figure out what it might be.

"What would you say to becoming my assistant, Cait?" Alicia lifted her hand, warding off anything Cait might have said. "You know the position will be vacant after the next holy day. You also know me well enough to understand that I would not be offering you the position if you were not more than qualified for it. You proved yourself on patrol and then again today."

"But—"

"That's not all, Cait," Jerrod said, grinning. "I want you to assist Lyara until she moves on to her next assignment. Then you will become my assistant as well."

"And you and I will continue our classes. Your encounter with the skinwalker showed a deficiency in your education that we must fill," Berral added.

Cait stared at them, convinced she had misheard. That was the only explanation that made sense. There was no way she, a mere journeywoman, could fill the positions they mentioned. If this was their way of trying to make up to her for their failure where Avrim was concerned. . . .

"Before you answer, there is something else you need to know, Cait," Kirris said. "We would have been having this discussion with you soon in any case. Today's events simply gave us the chance to discuss it with the Knights Council instead of waiting for our next meeting after the Holy Day. So do not make the mistake of thinking this is simply a way for us to assuage our consciences."

She set her mug to one side and looked from one to the

other. The four said nothing. She had no doubt they knew what was going through her mind. Part of her wanted to leap at the chance to work more closely with the two masters and the Adept. But the other part, the part that wasn't quite ready to let go her suspicion and doubt made her hesitate. It just seemed so coincidental and she did not believe in coincidences.

"I am honored." And she was. "But I can't. The assistants to both the Weaponsmaster and the Tacticsmaster are positions held by Confirmed members of the Order. I am only a first year journeywoman." One with at least another year of instruction ahead of her.

"You were right again, Berral." Kirris shook his head, a smile playing at his lips. "The Adept said you would raise just that concern."

"And I will tell you what I told him I would," the Adept said. "You are not a mere first year journeywoman. Think about the classes you have been taking. Are they first year courses?"

"Some are," she hedged.

"No, even your class with Daffyd has progressed so you are caught up with the second and even some third years." Now Berral moved to sit on her heels in front of her. "Cait, you have far surpassed anything any of us expected of you when you first arrived. I thought you knew how proud we are of you and of all you've accomplished."

"I – thank you." What else could she say?

"As for your concerns about not having the status or rank to be Alicia's or Jerrod's assistant, we thought about that as well." She glanced over her shoulder to the others.

"Cait, the Knights Council did talk about one other matter today besides Avrim," Kirris said. "In a little more than a fortnight, we shall be celebrating the Feast of the Ten Blessings. During the celebration we will be announcing new postings for certain members of the Order. There will also be some of the yeomen standing for promotion to journeyman status and you shall be standing for Confirmation."

There were no words, absolutely no words. Surely she had hear wrong. The Knight-Commandant could not have said she would be standing for Confirmation. She hadn't been there long enough and there was still so much she did not know. Yet there was no doubting the way the four watched her, waiting for her to say something.

"I'm not sure she believes you, Kirris," Jerrod said and chuckled softly.

"Sir, thank you but that wouldn't be fair to those who have been here longer than I have." Panic bubbled just below the surface and she prayed none of the others realized just how much she wanted what they offered or that she knew she wasn't ready.

"Cait, you know better than that." There was just a hint of reprimand in Berral's voice. "Readiness to stand for Confirmation isn't the amount of time they have been here but how much they have learned and how they have proven themselves. You have done both of those above and beyond what we have asked and expected. It is time for you to stand for Confirmation."

"This isn't a dream?" She grinned, still not sure she dared believe it was real. These four were offering her everything she had been working so hard for.

"It is no dream," Berral said. "Will you accept what we're offering?"

"One question first?" She waited until the Adept nodded. "Is there any possibility Fallon can be here? I owe him so much and I would like him to see that I have done everything he wanted for me."

"I have already sent word," Kirris assured her.

"I promised each of you, just as I promised Fallon when he brought me here, that I would do my best to be a strong asset to the Order. My goal has always been to stand for Confirmation. I never thought it would happen this soon. Thank you and I will do my best to make each of you proud and to bring honor and glory to the Lord and Lady."

"You already have," Berral said. "Now, we haven't pushed before but when you stand for Confirmation, we would like to introduce you with the name of your choice. If you wish to be known only as Cait, that is how it shall be. However, if you wish to be known by another name or if you wish to claim a surname, you may do so now."

A surname. She could give herself a real name, an identity beyond the former slave. It would not bring back the life she did not remember. But it would help make her feel whole in a way she had not since waking in the slaver's tent. But what surname should she choose? She glanced down and, as she did, she shifted slightly in her chair. This was not something to decide without some thought.

A slight smile pulled at the corners of her mouth. She had known almost from her first memory that, no matter what someone else called her, she would call herself Cait. No other name had come to her and, at the moment, none seemed right. Hoping Berral, as well as the others, would understand, she knew what she had to say.

"May I have some time to think about it, maybe even talk with each of you about it?"

"Of course." Berral gave her hand a squeeze. "This is not something that must be answered right now. You don't have to choose anything if you don't wish."

"I know." All of this, everything that had happened that day, was almost more than she could take in.

"And you are feeling more than a little overwhelmed right

now," Alicia said. Cait nodded, glad someone understood. "I don't know about the rest of you, but I would like to find my bed for an hour or so before the day begins." She stood but stopped when Kirris motioned for her to stay.

"We should all try to get some rest," he agreed. "But, before you go, there is one more thing. I would like all of you to meet in my office ten minutes before the morning meal. We will announce to the yeomen and journeymen what steps are being taken with regard to Avrim. You too, Cait."

"We'll meet you there," Jerrod said as he stood and slid an arm around Alicia's waist. "Cait, I know the Healer has you on limited activity for the next few days. Since I have no desire to face his wrath, no classes until he clears you."

"But—"

"Don't worry. You will have more than enough to keep you busy." Berral smiled, excitement lighting her expression. "Meet with both Jerrod and Alicia and find out what they have in mind for you. I'll be meeting with you as well to help you prepare for your confirmation and to start filling in some of those holes we discovered in your knowledge."

"Thank you."

"Why don't you stay the night, or what is left of it, here, Cait?" Kirris suggested.

"A grand idea," Berral said in approval. "Come, I'll help you prepare for bed. Sanaa will have all our heads if he discovers you have not slept come morning."

CHAPTER TWENTY TWO

THE BELL RANG THREE TIMES, ITS BRIGHT, JOYOUS NOTES CALLING for silence. Those gathered quickly found their places. A hush fell over the crowd as Kirris and Berral stepped forward, motioning for those taking to the field that day to assume their places. Licking her suddenly dry lips, Cait drew a deep breath and took a step forward. Even as she did, she found it hard to believe she actually stood there. She might be the only one standing for Confirmation but there were others on the field with her. Kala, Stefan and others she had trained with were there to prove they were ready to promote to their final year of training. Those whose Calling was the knightly discipline wore dark blue leather trousers, soft white tunics and vests that matched their trousers. Those in the priestly discipline wore the same uniform save for the color – that of the deepest, clearest lake under a bright morning sun.

Only Cait's uniform was different. Because she had not yet received her Calling, she wore black leather with a white tunic. It wasn't that different and yet it marked her as something apart from the others. Until that morning, when she saw how she would stand out from the others she had spent so much time with over the last year and a half, she had not realized just how different her status at the Citadel had been. Until then, she had convinced herself that the powers-that-be had been cross-training her because she had not had the earlier training of her classmates. Now she knew better. She had to accept the fact that she was different from them and that sent her nerves ratcheting up even higher.

Without preamble, Kirris greeted those gathered and instructed everyone there to stand as Candidates to report to the main training arena. That day, unlike when Cait had stood as a Candidate, they would start with the physical Trials. There was a nervous murmur from those taking to the field before Lady Lyara signaled for them to follow her.

"Those testing for promotion and standing for Confirmation, step forward." Kirris' voice rang out and the world seemed to narrow.

On legs that shook, Cait made her way to where Berral stood at the base of the platform that had been constructed over the last few days in the center of the courtyard. As she did, Kala, Stefan and the others who had been Called to the knightly discipline moved to where Kirris stood. She would join them soon enough – she hoped.

For more than two hours, Cait found herself put through a series of Tests challenging her knowledge of level of mastery of herbs and healing as well as her religious education. It culminated when she once again took her place in front of Berral. Dropping to her knees, she did her best not to think about the first time she had knelt before the Adept. She had not known what to expect then. Now she did and it would be very easy to let her fears and nerves take hold.

"Relax, Cait," the woman said so softly Cait knew no one else would hear. "Now open your mind."

Cait closed her eyes and said a quick prayer as she felt the tips of Berral's fingers on either side of her face. The air suddenly seemed alive. It licked at her skin and electrified her hair. As the atmosphere became heavy, almost repressive, Cait turned her focus inward. Centered and anchored, she let her consciousness flow outward. In her mind's eye, she saw the area immediately around her in a swirl of reds and blues. The energy seemed to originate from the Adept. As understanding dawned, Cait smiled slightly. This was not a test of endurance but one of recognition.

Moving her hands away from her body, her palms up, Cait focused on the swirling energy. Her palms tingled as she reached forward, visualizing the swirls slowing and anchoring onto her upraised hands. Her lips parted and she exhaled slowly, as if cooling a cup of hot tea. The swirls slowed some more, turning from brilliant reds and blues to soft golds and greens. Then, suddenly, she closed her hands and thrust her arms over her head, opening her fists and releasing the energy into the air above her.

As she did, she slowly became aware of her surroundings. She opened her eyes and grinned. Gold and green sparks soared over her before falling gently to the ground. One quick look at Berral showed the woman was just as pleased with her performance as was she. Hopefully, that was a good sign.

Cait hoped so because she felt the draining that was always present when she had to collect and redirect energy without preparation. The energy it took had to come from somewhere and, when she could not raise it from an outside source, it had to come from her. As a result, she felt as if she had just run several miles in the noonday sun with a full pack on her back.

"Well, Cait, I have to say you aren't being subtle about it," Berral chuckled in approval.

"I-I didn't do it," she said softly, her eyes following the last of the sparks as they slowly drifted to the ground. "All I did was gather the energy and then expel it. The fireworks weren't planned."

"Not by you, at any rate." Berral smiled and gave her shoulder a quick pat. "Rest for a bit now, Cait. You have a few minutes before you must report to Kirris to begin the next phase of your Testing."

With a nod, she carefully climbed to her feet. As she made her way across the courtyard to where Kirris and the others waited, she did her best not to stumble. After that rather showy display, she did not want to follow up with a pratfall. So she concentrated on putting one boot in front of the others, her eyes focused on the ground ahead. Then, much to her relief, a yeoman was there to help her to a place in the shade where she could rest while another yeoman brought cool water and a damp cloth to wipe her face with.

For those few brief minutes, Cait allowed herself the luxury of complete relaxation. She wiped the sweat from her face and neck before drinking deeply. For a few minutes, she could forget that how she did after that would determine what she would do with the rest of her life.

A shadow fell across her. She looked up and nodded to find Alicia standing before her. The Tacticsmaster wore the soft leather clothes and padded vest she often donned when they worked out against one another. Her well-worn gloves were tucked beneath her belt. With a smile and a nod, Alicia extended a hand. Cait reached up, grateful for the assistance, and climbed to her feet. It was time for the next phase of her Testing to begin.

"You know what to expect?" Alicia asked softly as they walked.

"In a way. The Knight-Commandant told me I will have as many as six battles, all to first blood or submission. All against knights. Other than that, I haven't got a clue."

"That is about it. Your sword has been brought for you as have your daggers and shield. It is a no rules match. Anything can be used as a weapon, just like real life."

"Understood."

"Good." Alicia fell silent and Cait wondered what was on her mind. "Cait, I meant what I said. It is a fight without rules.

Anything can be used as a weapon."

With that, the Tacticsmaster peeled off and moved to join the other knights taking part in the Testing. Puzzled by what she had said, Cait hurried to take her place. She knew Alicia had been trying to tell her something. But what?

"Journeywoman, are you ready to begin this last phase of your Testing for Confirmation?" Kirris asked.

"I am." It amazed her that she sounded so firm and strong. None of her exhaustion or nerves showed.

"Then step forward and prepare yourself."

Cait nodded. Then she realized he no longer wore his ceremonial uniform. Instead, he was dressed much like Alicia and the others. There could be only one explanation. He planned to be among those knights taking part in her Testing. She had not expected that and, judging from the sound of surprise coming from the onlookers as he joined Alicia, no one else had either.

"You will face at least six matches. Winner is the one to draw first blood or force a submission. Once a match ends, the next will immediately begin. There is no time limit. Do you understand?"

"I do."

"Then gather your weapons and choose your spot. The Test begins as soon as you do."

Breathing deeply, Cait accepted the twin daggers in their quick release sheaths a yeoman handed her. The youngster waited, ready to help, as Cait fastened them into place on her forearms. Once satisfied, she accepted her sword and shield. Not taking any chances, she checked each item. Then she stepped forward. The sooner the Trial started, the sooner it would be over and she would finally know what the Lord and Lady had in store for her.

A moment later, Alicia took up her position opposite Cait.

With a flick of her wrist, the Tacticsmaster saluted, her blade slashing through the air. Cait returned the salute and then settled into a fighting stance. It was time for patience. As much as she wanted to press the attack, she would not. She would wait for the Tacticsmaster to make the first move.

For what seemed like an eternity, Alicia simply stood there, her sword moving slowly in an arc before her. Her eyes locked with Cait's and a slight smile lifted one corner of her mouth. As it did, her left shoulder dipped. That was what Cait had been waiting for. She had seen that particular feint many times when they sparred with one another.

Right foot moving forward, her left to the side, Cait sidestepped the woman. Alicia twisted, bringing her blade into a backhanded swing to block Cait's strike. Leaning away, Cait kept her eyes locked on her opponent. Hopefully, Alicia would not change her normal tactics. If she stayed true to form, this might not be too long of a fight.

Not long but very physical. Alicia seemed determined to push Cait as much as she could. Where she would normally use a hit and run method of attack, the smaller woman worked in close, her shorter sword a definite advantage. More than once, Cait found herself twisting painfully, awkwardly away from a blow before Alicia could draw first blood. Then, as the Tacticsmaster danced in close once more, Cait knew what she had to do. After all, hadn't Alicia said everything was legal?

With a smile, Cait feinted with her sword. Alicia reacted exactly as she hoped. The woman took a step to the right, her blade arcing upward to counter. Her shield dipped. The moment it did, Cait acted. Instead of slashing with her sword, she dropped her shield to the ground. That fist flashed upward. Alicia grunted in a mixture of pain and surprise as Cait's fist connected with the point of her chin. She staggered back, a trickle of blood flowing from her lower lip where she had bitten it.

Shaking her head, a look of amusement on her face, Alicia swiped at the blood. "Very good. Now let's see how you do next."

Cait quickly scanned the area, looking for her next opponent. As she did, she carefully shifted so her back was to the sun. She wanted every advantage she could get. Then, seeing Jerrod strolling toward her, she knew she needed that advantage and more. The Weaponsmaster would be an even more difficult opponent than had the Tacticsmaster.

And, unlike Alicia, he did not wait to attack. He walked purposefully up to Cait and, without warning, his short sword swung up from where he held it next to his leg. At the same time, he used his dagger to try to score a quick win. Cait backpedaled, out of his reach as she released the shield she had reclaimed only moments before. If Jerrod wanted to use two blades, then she would as well.

Ducking and dodging, calling upon every instinct she had, Cait countered his every move. His attacks came in lightning-fast flurries that often had her withdrawing to regroup. Then, as he pushed her back for at least the fourth or fifth time, she cursed softly. He wasn't protecting himself. He was simply using speed and intimidation to force her into making a mistake. Which she had absolutely no intention of doing.

Time to turn the tables.

Grinning, Cait attacked. With sword and dagger moving in intricate patterns, she forced her advantage. Taken by surprise by her sudden change in tactics, the Weaponsmaster stepped back to avoid her attack. She continued to press him, pushing him further back. Then, without warning, she dropped, rolling and coming to her feet next to him. Her dagger flashed out and nicked the skin just above the wide leather band protecting his left wrist. He nodded in approval and saluted before stepping back.

Panting, sweat running down her face, Cait moved back to where she had started. As she did, she dared one quick glance around the arena. Then, knowing she could not let her attention wander, she blew out a breath and focused. Two fighters down, at least four more to go.

Half an hour later, Cait fought to stay on her feet. Three more opponents had stepped forward and been defeated. Every breath hurt and she could drink a lake dry. All she wanted was to sink to the ground and rest. But she couldn't, not yet. She had at least one more opponent left to fight.

"Let us see what you can do, Journeywoman," Kirris said as he stepped forward.

A flash of resentment ran through her. If the Knight-Commandant had wanted to fight her, couldn't he have done it when she was at least a little less exhausted? Even as the thought formed, she shook her head. That wasn't the purpose of the Trials. She had to prove she could take care of herself and, by extension, others. The enemy would not wait to give her time to refresh herself between battles. So why should he?

She bowed her head and assumed the ready position. Even as she did, instinct had her closely watching the man. She had a feeling this was not going to be the straightforward fight the others had been. No, Kirris had something up his sleeve. She would just have to wait to see what and hope she could counter it.

The fight was on. An excellent swordsman in his own right, Kirris pushed Cait, taking advantage of her exhaustion. Even so, she managed to block his attacks before he could mark her. Just when Cait thought the fight might last for a while, Kirris stepped back. She looked on in surprise as he lowered his sword and switched it to his left hand. Then he raised his right hand, almost as if he were reaching out to her.

Cait frowned as she felt a subtle change in the air. The hair on her arms stood on end, much like it would during a lightning storm. She knew that feeling and watched, frowning to see the Knight-Commandant's fingertips beginning to glow.

Damn!

She lowered her blade. When Alicia told her to expect anything, she had not thought the Tacticsmaster meant something like this. Kirris was gathering energy around him and, unless she missed her gues, he was about to send it flying in her direction. She had been on the receiving end of a similar attack from him once before and did not relish the thought of finding herself tumbling end over end before losing consciousness. She would rather be kicked by a mule. So she had to counter.

But how?

Instantly, instinctively, she sent energy to her personal shields. As they firmed up, it felt like a comforting presence around her. Then she felt the itching in her left palm as energy pooled in it. Instinct or the Lord and Lady, she did not know and did not care. All that matter was that somehow she knew what needed to be done.

"No!"

Kirris thrust his hand toward her. As he did, she stepped forward, leaning toward him. Her left arm extended and that fist opened, as if she were releasing something. The air shimmered between the two combatants. Cait drew her left hand back toward her, passing over to her right before once more flinging it out toward Kirris. He grunted in surprise, his eyes widening, as her nearly visible energy ball flew in his direction. His hands blurred as he dropped his sword and then tried to counter her. She smiled grimly before pressing her sudden advantage.

Suddenly, Kirris stepped back and called an end to the

match. Not quite believing it, Cait dropped to her knees. It took all her energy not to lean forward so her head could rest on the ground. Never before had she been so exhausted. Every muscle ached and her body would soon be screaming for fuel after the demands she had put on it.

"Very good," Kirris said. "You have five minutes to rest. A yeoman will bring you something to drink. Then join us at the platform."

"Drink this," the yeoman who had helped her earlier said as she pressed a waterskin into her hands. A moment later, she wiped Cait's face with a cool, damp cloth.

"Thank you." She drank her fill and then handed the waterskin back to the girl.

A few minutes later, she stood. Feet dragging as if she was shuffling them purposefully in the grass, Cait made her way toward the platform. As she did, she glanced skyward. The sun was well past its midpoint. It was no wonder she was exhausted. Hopefully, she would soon be allowed to find her bed.

"This has been a most wondrous holy day," Kirris began from the center of the platform. "I welcome everyone who has come to observe the Feast of the Ten Blessings this day. We remember the sacrifices made for us, not only by Saint Arelion but also by those who have served the Lord and Lady over the years. We have been privileged today to welcome a new class of yeomen into the Order and to see a number of our journeymen promote to their next level. Most of all, we have seen a journeywoman stand through one of the most rigorous testings in memory in her attempt to be Confirmed into the Order." He paused and motioned for Cait to join him and Berral on the platform.

"You never fail to impress us, Cait," Berral said softly as the young woman knelt before them.

"Cait, you have passed your Trials for both the priestly and knightly disciplines," Kirris took up. "Did you feel any particular Calling during them?"

She shook her head, wondering what it meant. Would having no Calling prevent her from being Confirmed? Surely she had not gone through all this for nothing.

"You have been an enigma from your first day here. It is no surprise that you continue to be one," Berral said with a smile. "Do not look so worried. There is nothing to be afraid of. It is clear the Lord and Lady do not wish you to be placed into a single role, at least not yet."

Cait blew out a relieved breath.

"So, Cait Hawkener, are you prepared to pledge your life to the service of the Lord and Lady?" the Knight-Commandant asked, lifting his voice so all those gathered could hear.

"I am," she said.

As she did, she felt a thrill at hearing the surname she had chosen for herself. Alicia had told her how some members of the Order used hawks to scout ahead. She had seen firsthand how Lyara used her hawk as a weapon. The bird's talons were tipped with metal and Cait knew it would attack on command. The beauty and strength of the hawk, its ability to hunt and survive, had called to Cait when she thought about it. So, after discussing it with Berral just the night before, she had chosen Hawkener as her surname.

"Then let us welcome you into the Order of Arelion, Lady Cait." Berral draped the heavy gold chain with its medallion marking Cait as a Confirmed member of the Order over the young woman's head.

For a moment, Cait kept her head bowed as she silently offered up a prayer of thanks. As she did, a loving warmth enveloped her. As it did, all her concerns and fears flowed away. She felt refreshed and alive as she had not in memory.

This was what she had trained so hard for. This was what she wanted to do with her life. It did not matter if she had no memory before waking in the slaver's tent. All that mattered was that she now belonged to the Order. She would willingly do whatever was necessary in the service of the Lord and Lady.

Then, as if that simple thought was the key, the warmth seemed to spread. It filled her, letting her know this was her proper place. Then it seemed to focus on her left forearm and then the right before slowly leaving her.

Not quite daring to breath, she reached for her left sleeve and slowly pushed it above her elbow. As she did, she heard Berral's gasp of surprise a split second before she echoed it. There, running from wrist to elbow, was the image of a hawk, its wings just beginning to unfurl, its head raised and mouth opening as if it were giving a hunting cry. Vivid colors seemed to bring it to life. Swallowing hard, she looked up at Kirris and Berral in question.

What did it mean?

"I think we have our answer," Berral said softly, her eyes never leaving Cait's arm.

"Aye." Kirris looked and sounded as shaken as Cait felt. Then, as if realizing the others could not see what they did, he visibly shook himself and helped Cait to her feet.

"This is a great day for the Order, my friends, an historic day. Today we have seen a journeywoman test in both disciplines and pass with little trouble. She has proven herself worthy not only by our worldly standards but also by those of the Lord and Lady. It is my privilege and my honor to present to you, Knight-Cleric Cait Hawkener."

Knight-Cleric? Cait mouthed silently before turning to face those gathered. What did that mean for her? For the Order?

"Join us in my office as soon as you've freshened up, Cait. I have a feeling we need to discuss what this means before we join the celebration," Berral said softly.

Cait nodded. Then she glanced at the Adept, a look of speculation on her face. Of the three of them, only Berral did not seem completely surprised by what had just happened. In fact, she appeared to be amazingly calm. What could that mean?

"All right."

Hopefully by then, all of this would make sense.

The cheering of the crowd grated against his control. How could everything have gone so wrong? He should have known better than to risk having others deal with the problem. They had each failed him and this was his reward. This – this Knight-Cleric should have died long ago. She had been in his grasp. It would have been so easy to snuff out her life but he had not. He had wanted to make sure it happened far from where anyone might connect it with him. That had been his first mistake. His second was in selecting as his agents those foolish enough to fail him.

At least one thing still worked in his favor. She had yet to remember who she was. Nor had she remembered what happened to her. That meant he had time to complete the plan he had put into motion so long ago. But that would not happen should she glance his way and remember.

"Come," he rasped out as he turned and started to push his way through those trying to get closer to the platform to see the newest Confirmed member of the Order.

"But, sir, aren't you going to stay?" his companion protested, struggling to keep up. "You are expected at the evening meal."

"I don't have time for this foolishness, Markus. You can send word back to the Knight-Commandant with my regrets –

after we are away from here."

"Sir—"

He spun in the older man's direction, his eyes flashing with barely contained anger. "Do you dare lecture me on duty?"

"N-no, sir." Markus backed up a step, his hands waving his denial.

"Find our mounts then. I want to be away from here at once."

Away from there and free to plan what his next move would be. He would deal with the girl but there were other matters needing his attention as well. All he had to do was play his cards right and everything would fall into place. Soon these fools, as well as those at the Imperial capital, would realize they had nurtured the biggest, most dangerous snake possible in their midst. By then it would be too late and he would have cut off the heads of all his enemies, literally and figuratively.

"Berral, can you tell me what in the Nine Hells just happened?" Kirris demanded the moment they were alone in her office.

She turned to face him, smiling gently. She knew he had wanted to ask just that throughout the twenty minutes it had taken them to work their way to her office. He had fairly vibrated with impatience, not that she blamed him. To say the events of the day had been unusual was putting it mildly. These Trials had been unlike any she had ever witnessed.

"I have no more answers than do you," she said as she poured them each a glass of wine. "Perhaps Cait will have some explanation when she arrives."

It was possible but Berral doubted it. She had seen Cait's disbelief at the unexpected turn of events. Not that she blamed her.

As if that had been a signal, a soft knock sounded at the door. A moment later, it swung open and Cait stepped inside. She had obviously taken time to bathe and change clothes. Her dark hair was still damp and she had pulled it back into a braid, a leather thong woven in to help hold it in place. She now wore a pair of soft, black leather trousers and a matching jerkin that laced up one side. Wide wristbands made from three intricately woven pieces of leather were in place as well.

The Adept noted all that in passing. What caught and held her attention was the sight of the young woman's bare forearms. She had expected to see the hawk but she felt her breath explode out of her lungs at the sight of Cait's right arm. There could be no mistaking the Lady's avatar. With a hand that shook, Berral reached out and lightly traced a finger over the beautiful dolphin rising out of the sea foam.

"Do you have any other surprises for us?" she asked softly as she looked into Cait's eyes, eyes that were still wide with shock.

"Lord and Lady, I hope not," the young woman said fervently. "Isn't this enough?"

"I take it you had no more warning than we did," Kirris said almost drolly.

"Absolutely not." She looked down as she held her arms out before her. "All I can tell you is that while you were Confirming me, my left arm and then the right felt warm. Then there was a feeling of love and approval washing over me. That's when I looked and we all saw this." She nodded to her left arm. "I never thought to check the right."

"I think we need to sit and relax," Berral said firmly. She had a feeling that her companions would remain standing there, trying to figure out what happened until morning if she let them. Without waiting to see if they complied, she turned to pour Cait a glass of wine. "Now, Cait, tell us what you can."

"There's nothing to tell." Her frustration was clear from the strain in her voice to the way she drank most of her wine in a single gulp. "I was so tired after finishing that all I was worrying about was not falling on my face. The physical was bad enough but then having to resort to the arcane against you, sir." She shrugged.

"Cait, when you were working against Kirris, how did you know he was about to use an arcane attack against you?"

"The same way I knew what you were doing at the beginning of my tests. I *felt* it, felt the change in the air around me. Believe me, I remember all too well the other time he did that to me. I ended up flat on my back and unconscious for half an hour. I didn't want to end my Test like that."

"You *felt* it?" Kirris leaned forward, his expression intense.

Berral understood. This was something new where Cait was concerned. To the best of the Adept's knowledge, her protégé had never before sensed the gathering of energies necessary for an offensive or defensive move before. Could this be yet another gift from the Lord and Lady, a new Talent for Cait to add to her arsenal?

"I did." Cait caught her lower lip between her teeth and Berral recognized what it meant. The young woman was thinking hard about something and it was not difficult to guess what. "When you were first testing me, Berral, I could see the energy patterns. That is what made it so easy to counter them. It was as though all I had to do was reach out and take the energies and redirect them."

"Well, that answers one question." Kirris leaned back in his chair with a sigh. Then he smiled and reached over to pat Cait's knee. "It would seem the Lord and Lady have given you another Talent, a very useful one on a number of different levels. Of course, you might not appreciate that as we train you on how to use it."

"And these?" Once more Cait shoved her arms out in front of her. "And by all that is holy, what is a Knight-Cleric?"

Berral looked to Kirris. When he announced Cait's rank, she had been surprised. This was nothing they had discussed ahead of time even though they had talked about the possibility Cait might not show a particular Calling. Beyond that, the rank Kirris had raised Cait to had never before existed in the Order. So where in the hierarchy of things would she fall? And, more importantly, how would the more conservative members of the Order react to a new rank? There was so much involved in what happened, so many implications and potential consequences, that the Adept's head swam.

"You are," Kirris said simply, a smile playing at the corners of his mouth. Berral chuckled softly and relaxed a little. He was regaining his sense of humor and that was good.

"Knight-Commandant!" Cait protested. Her humor had yet to return, not that Berral blamed her. After all, she would probably be slumped in a corner, mumbling incoherently if she had suddenly found the avatars of the Lord and Lady adorning her arms.

"Kirris," he corrected almost gently. "And, as for your question, all I can tell you is that it is right. Not only did you far surpass what we expected of you, you excelled at both disciplines. You managed to perform to the standard I require of my Knight-Commanders and, from what I could tell, you did all Berral requires of those she assigns as clerics or soothsayers."

"He's right, Cait," Berra confirmed. "And, if you weren't so stubborn as to show no particular Calling, you would have been named to one of those ranks. It is unusual but not completely unheard of."

"So a new rank, one designating your unusual talents, has been created," Kirris said. "Now the question becomes what is your place in the Order's hierarchy?"

"I don't want a place!" Something close to panic filled her voice only to vanish when Berral chuckled.

"You may not want it, Cait Hawkener, but you have it. None of us can deny it." She motioned to Cait's arms and their very visible reminders of just who and what the young woman was. "In fact, the point that you never wanted power or position may very well be why the Lord and Lady have blessed you as They have."

That bore some consideration but it could wait until later.

"Gods above and below, what am I supposed to do?"

"For now, exactly what you have been doing. You will continue to act as assistant to Jerrod and Alicia. You will train with both Kirris and myself as you learn how to use your Talents. I have a feeling this is just the beginning for you, my friend." Berral smiled at her in encouragement. "As for where you fall in the hierarchy that, too, has been decided for us. The Lord and Lady have made it clear you are second only to the two of us. So I propose you become our third. We will train you in the administration of both branches of the Order along with everything else."

"Berral is right. I have a feeling you are the first of a new breed for the Order. If what we fear is coming, we are going to need you and those like you. But you are still young and you need seasoning. We will help with that."

"I can't say I like this but what else is there to do?" She shook her head, almost as if by doing so she would awaken from whatever dream held her. "Duties?"

"Just what we've said." Kirris paused and looked at Berral in question.

"I want you to help with my introductory classes as well." The Adept wondered if the young woman would realize that would be as much of a learning experience for her as would time spent in lectures or the library.

"Uniform?"

For a moment, no one spoke. That was another valid question. Cait was neither knight nor cleric and yet she was also both. The idea of combining their uniforms did not feel right nor did asking her to choose one over the other.

"For the moment, until we think of something better, I think a variation of what you are wearing now will do," Berral said. Relief filled her to see Kirris nod in agreement. "You will need to think of something for when the weather cools and then there is the issue of formal uniforms but, for now, what you are wearing works very well."

"I agree. It will keep your markings visible, reminding everyone just who you are and what you represent."

"Now, before we join the celebration, let's find you new quarters. Would the cottage next to ours be satisfactory?" Berral asked.

"Cottage?" Cait shook herself. "Keeping an eye on me?" She chuckled softly and Berral relaxed to hear it. Hopefully that meant Cait was returning to normal, or as normal as any of them would ever be after the events of the day.

"No," she assured the young woman. "It just happens to be free and it will reflect your position in the chain of command. Besides, it will keep you close in case you need anything over the next few weeks."

"If that is taken care of, we do have a celebration to get to." Kirris stood and extended a hand to Berral. "Let's go introduce the rest of the Order to our newest member. Then I suggest we each get good and drunk. We can worry about everything else come morning."

Berral couldn't help offering up a prayer for protection. Trouble was brewing. If she had any doubt, the events of the day convinced her. The only times the Lord and Lady made

Their will known in as public and impressive ways as They had that day was when something near cataclysmic was about to happen. She prayed they had enough time to give Cait the training she would need. Otherwise, she feared life as they knew it would come crashing down around them.

Lord and Lady, protect us and give me the strength and wisdom needed to help guide Cait as she does your bidding.

AUTHOR'S NOTE

Sword of Arelion is one of those books I never thought I'd write. Well, that's not quite correct. It is one of those projects most writers have that seem to haunt us, teasing us with glimpses of a plot but never quite coming together. Until, of course, it is the last thing we want to write.

That's what happened with this book. I had just finished writing *Duty from Ashes* and was preparing to begin *Nocturnal Challenge*. I had *Challenge* plotted out. I had the first chapter started and **WHAM!** this book was suddenly alive in my head, drowning out all others. What it didn't tell me until I was nearing the end was that it wasn't the end, not really. This is just the first of several books.

What surprised me most was how much fun I had writing *Sword*. I hope you have as much fun reading it. Cait is the sort of main character I enjoy. She is flawed and scarred but she doesn't let herself be a victim. She is also headstrong and more than a bit impulsive. That gets her in trouble from time to time but what are you to do? She isn't perfect – thank goodness.

The second book in the series, *Dagger of Elanna,* should be out around the first of the year. Of course, that assumes my muse cooperates and doesn't hit me over the head with something else that demands it be written *NOW!*

IF YOU ENJOYED *SWORD OF ARELION*, CHECK OUT THESE TITLES BY THE AUTHOR:

NOCTURNAL ORIGINS (*Nocturnal Lives*, Book 1)

Some things can never be forgotten, no matter how hard you try.

Detective Sergeant Mackenzie Santos knows that bitter lesson all too well. The day she died changed her life and her perception of the world forever. It doesn't matter that everyone, even her doctors, believe a miracle occurred when she awoke in the hospital morgue. Mac knows better. It hadn't been a miracle, at least not a holy one. As far as she's concerned, that's the day the dogs of Hell came for her.

Investigating one of the most horrendous murders in recent Dallas history, Mac also has to break in a new partner and deal with nosy reporters who follow her every move and who publish confidential details of the investigation without a qualm.

Complicating matters even more, Mac learns the truth about her family and herself, a truth that forces her to deal with the monster within, as well as those on the outside. But none of this matters as much as discovering the identity of the murderer before he can kill again.

NOCTURNAL SERENADE (*Nocturnal Lives*, Books 2)

Lt. Mackenzie Santos of the Dallas Police Department learns there are worst things than finding out you come from a long line of shapeshifters. At least that's what she keeps telling herself. It's not that she resents suddenly discovering she can turn into a jaguar. Nor is it really the fact that no one warned her what might happen to her one day. Although, come to think of it, her mother does have a lot of explaining to do when – and if – Mac ever talks to her again. No, the real problem is how to keep the existence of shapeshifters hidden from the normals, especially when just one piece of forensic evidence in the hands of the wrong technician could lead to their discovery.

Add in blackmail, a long overdue talk with her grandmother about their heritage and an attack on her mother and Mac's life is about to get a lot more complicated. What she wouldn't give for a run-of-the-mill murder to investigate. THAT would be a nice change of pace.

NOCTURNAL INTERLUDE (*Nocturnal Lives*, Book 3)

Lt. Mackenzie Santos swears she will never take another vacation again as long as she lives. The moment she returns home, two federal agents are there to take her into custody. Then she finds out her partner, Sgt. Patricia Collins, as well as several others are missing. Several of the missing have connections to law enforcement. All are connected to Mac through one important and very secret fact -- they are all shapeshifters. Has someone finally discovered that the myths and bad Hollywood movies are actually based on fact or is there something else, something more insidious at work?

Mac finds herself in a race against time not only to save her partner and the others but to discover who was behind their disappearances. As she does, she finds herself dealing with Internal Affairs, dirty cops, the Feds and a possible conspiracy within the shapeshifter community that could not only bring their existence to light but cause a civil war between shifters.

NOCTURNAL HAUNTS (novella)
(Part of the *Nocturnal Lives* series)

Mackenzie Santos has seen just about everything in more than ten years as a cop. The last few months have certainly shown her more than she'd ever expected. When she's called out to a crime scene and has to face the possibility that there are even more monsters walking the Earth than she knew, she finds herself longing for the days before she started turning furry with the full moon.

Check out these titles written as Ellie Ferguson:

HUNTED

When Meg Finley's parents died, the authorities classified it as a double suicide. Alone, hurting and suddenly the object of the clan's alpha's desire, her life was a nightmare. He didn't care that she was grieving any more than he cared that she was only fifteen. So she'd run and she'd been running ever since. But now, years later, her luck's run out. The alpha's trackers have found her and they're under orders to bring her back, no matter what. Without warning, Meg finds herself in a game of cat and mouse with the trackers in a downtown Dallas parking garage. She's learned a lot over the years but, without help, it might not be enough to escape a fate she knows will be worse than death. What she didn't expect was that help would come from the local clan leader. But would he turn out to be her savior or something else, something much more dangerous?

HUNTER'S DUTY

Maggie Thrasher is looking for a man, not to love but to kill. Duty to her pride and loyalty to her family demands it. Joshua Volk has betrayed pride, pack and clan. All he cares about is destroying the old ways and killing anyone, normal or shape-changer, who gets in his way. Jim Kincade is dedicated to two things: upholding the law and protecting the pride from discovery. When Jim is called to the scene of a possible murder, the last thing he expects is to discover the alleged killer is a tracker from another pride. Now he's faced with a woman who is most definitely more than she appears. Complicating matters even more, there's something about her that calls to him and his leopard is determined to claim her for his own. Joshua Volk is looking for revenge. Maggie killed one of his own. His vengeance will bring Maggie's worst nightmares to life. Is the passion between Maggie and Jim enough to defeat Volk's plans or will Maggie's determination to fulfill her duty to her pride be the death of them both?

HUNTER'S HOME

They say you can never go home. That's something CJ Reamer has long believed. So, when her father suddenly appears on her doorstep, demanding she return home to Montana to "do her duty", she has other plans. Montana hasn't been home for a long time, almost as long as Benjamin Franklin Reamer quit being her father. Dallas is now her home and it's where her heart is. The only problem is her father doesn't like taking "no" for an answer.

When her lover and mate is shot and she learns those responsible come from her birth pride and clan, CJ has no choice but to return to the home she left so long ago. At least she won't be going alone. Clan alphas Matt and Finn Kincade aren't about to take any risks where their friend is concerned. Nor is her mate, Rafe Walkinghorse, going to let her go without him.

Going home means digging up painful memories and family secrets. But will it also mean death – or worse – for CJ and her friends?

WEDDING BELL BLUES

Weddings always bring out the worst in people. Or at least that's the way it seems to Jessica Jones as her younger sister's wedding day approaches. It is bad enough Jessie has to wear a bridesmaid dress that looks like it was designed by a color blind Harlequin. Then there's the best man who is all hands and no manners. Now add in a murder and Jessie's former lover – former because she caught him doing the horizontal tango on their kitchen table with her also-former best friend. It really is almost more than a girl should be expected to handle. . . .

Written as Sam Schall:

VENGEANCE FROM ASHES
(Book 1 of *Honor and Duty*)

First, they took away her command. Then they took away her freedom. But they couldn't take away her duty and honor. Now they want her back.

Captain Ashlyn Shaw has survived two years in a brutal

military prison. Now those who betrayed her are offering the chance for freedom. All she has to do is trust them not to betray her and her people again. If she can do that, and if she can survive the war that looms on the horizon, she can reclaim her life and get the vengeance she's dreamed of for so long.

But only if she can forget the betrayal and do her duty.

DUTY FROM ASHES
(Book 2 of *Honor and Duty*)

Duty calls. Honor demands action.

Major Ashlyn Shaw has survived false accusations and a brutal military prison. Now free, she finds her homeworld once again at war with an enemy that will stop at nothing to destroy everything she holds dear. Duty has Ashlyn once again answering the call to serve. She has seen what the enemy is capable of and will do everything she can to prevent it from happening to the home she loves and the people she took an oath to protect.

But something has changed. It goes beyond the fact that the enemy has changed tactics they never wavered from during the previous war. It even goes beyond the fact that there is still a nagging doubt in the back of Ashlyn's mind that those who betrayed her once before might do so again. No, there is more to the resumption of hostilities, something that seems to point at a new player in the game. But who and what are they playing at?

Will Ashlyn be able to unmask the real enemy before it is too late?

www.ingramcontent.com/pod-product-compliance
Lightning Source LLC
Chambersburg PA
CBHW020238200626
46816CB00001BA/22